T0359850

MADELINE MARTIN

Schooling London Ladies

Two classic historical stories

Published by
Quills
An imprint of Harlequin Enterprises (Australia) Pty Limited
(ABN 47 001 180 918), a subsidiary of HarperCollins
Publishers Australia Pty Limited (ABN 36 009 913 517)
Level 19, 201 Elizabeth Street
SYDNEY NSW 2000
AUSTRALIA

MIX
Paper | Supporting
responsible forestry
FSC® C001695
www.fsc.org

CONTENTS

Madeline Martin is a *USA TODAY* bestselling author of historical romance novels filled with twists and turns, steamy romance, empowered heroines and the men who are strong enough to love them. She lives a glitter-filled life in Jacksonville, Florida, with her two daughters (known collectively as the minions) and a man so wonderful he's been dubbed Mr. Awesome. Find out more about Madeline at her website, madelinemartin.com.

HOW TO TEMPT A DUKE

Author Note

Thank you so much for reading *How to Tempt a Duke*. I wanted to briefly reflect on the strange marriage portrayed at Gretna Green. I've always been a fan of truth being stranger than fiction—this is one of those cases. When I researched who officiated weddings at Gretna Green in 1814, when *How to Tempt a Duke* is set, I discovered it to be Joseph Paisley. He died in 1814 and allegedly performed ceremonies while very drunk, and toward the end of his life, he even performed them from his bed. Given the time period I was writing, I had to write this into my story. I hope you enjoy this slice of strange historical fact as much as I did.

To Tracy: thank you for your guidance,
your encouragement and your friendship—
you helped make this incredible dream
come true for me.

Prologue

As reported in the *Lady Observer*, from the evening of April the fifth, 1814, the below *on-dits*—following a very detailed account of lobster patties, chilled oysters and a decadent lemon syllabub.

What is a sumptuous affair without a bit of scandal?

It all began when a certain Belle of the Season danced not only a second set with a blue-eyed earl with whom we are all acquainted, but a third. As if that were not enough for the rapacious attendees to feast upon, the Earl then took the lady's face in his hands and kissed her.

Mercy me!

Following this salacious display of affection came their official announcement of engagement, which produced a collective look of relief from the attendees. And disappointment from some, I'd wager, as there are always those who love a taste of scandal to season their tongues.

Suffice it to say the entire scene was quite riveting. Some might even say romantic.

And perhaps this Lady Observer *might agree, were it not for the other person in this tale who warrants consideration. After all, before the Belle of the Season emerged in mid-March and blossomed with the enviable beauty of a summer bloom, there was another who caught the cerulean gaze of the Earl.*

There was no mention of an engagement, this is true, but all believed there would be in time. Including the lady, no doubt.

While one cannot blame the Belle of the Season, to whom the burgeoning relationship was unknown, neither can one blame love, which strikes fast and without warning.

Regardless of where the blame lies, the tale has not ended happily for a lady who masks it so well she's earned the unfortunate moniker of Ice Queen.

She has watched the entire heartbreaking scene unfold before her dry eyes with a composure tightly reined, as if she were bored. While this only perpetuates rumors of her cold nature, one cannot help but wonder at her ability to maintain such stoicism after everything she's been through in recent years.

If her heart is truly ice, as some claim, it stands to reason that it would shatter more easily when broken...

In other observations, Lady Norrick's gown was quite the thing. So many beads adorned her dress she had to keep sitting to alleviate its pressing weight...

And on went the article, further educating those who had been unable to attend on how very fine Lady Norrick's gown was...

Chapter One

April 1814

There it was—between a cataloged detail of the lobster patties and a thorough description of Lady Norrick's ball gown lay the entire tale of Lady Eleanor Murray's most humiliating moment.

And a perpetual reminder of that blasted moniker.

Ice Queen, indeed.

Inside she was anything but ice, with untethered emotion lashing and writhing until an aching knot settled in the back of her throat.

But ladies were not to show emotion—and she was, after all, a Murray. Murrays were strong. They did not show fear. And they certainly did not concede to hurt, no matter how it twisted within one's soul.

She stared down at the crinkled page in her hands. The corners of the paper fluttered and called to attention the way she trembled.

She wanted to read the story again and wished for the usual: a detailed account of dinner, as always very thorough, told through the eyes of the *Lady Observer*, and trifling little *on-dits* that did not include her. Simple, ineffectual tales—like pointing out someone who had had two glasses of champagne instead of one, or whose reticule might have been left behind after the guests departed, followed by speculation as to why it had been left with such haste.

But the words of the story had not changed. Lady Alice had swept late into the Season, bright and beautiful and devoid of the desperation clawing at Eleanor. Every man had been drawn to her—including Hugh.

Eleanor's heart gave an ugly twinge.

Not Hugh. Lord Ledsey. She no longer held the right to address him or even think of him so informally. That right belonged to Lady Alice now. To make matters worse, Lady Alice was such a kind soul, and so lovely a person, it rendered her impossible to dislike. How very vexing.

The life Eleanor had envisioned with Hugh—summers at Ledsey Manor, the Season spent at Ledsey Place, freedom from having to plod along in the dreaded search for a suitable husband—all of it now belonged to Alice.

Eleanor's throat went tight. Dash it—she was about to cry.

A delicate knock sounded at her closed door.

She quickly shoved the paper under the pillow of her bed, blinked her eyes clear and grabbed up a book. "Enter."

The Countess of Westix swept into the room, followed by a footman carrying a large boxed parcel. Eleanor's mother indicated the dressing table with a wave of her hand and then addressed her daughter. "I'd like a word with you."

The footman obediently placed the parcel on the seat before Eleanor's dressing table and left the room, closing the door behind him.

Eleanor eyed the curious package first, and then her mother. The Countess wore a lavender evening gown sparkling with beadwork over a net of black lace. She was lovely, despite the silver in her golden hair, which had been coiffured to its usual state of perfection. There was not a wrinkle of worry or anger on her smooth face, but still Eleanor's stomach gave a familiar wrench—as it did any time her mother entered her room.

A lecture was forthcoming.

But what of the curious gift?

Her mother regarded the book Eleanor held. "What are you reading?"

"The Festival of St. Jago," Eleanor replied slowly.

Surely her mother had not come into her room to discuss her selection of literature?

The Countess tilted her head dramatically to the side. "Upside down?"

Eleanor focused on the page for the first time. It stared up at her from its flipped position. Exactly upside down.

Drat.

"Perhaps you were reading something else?"

The Countess of Westix lifted her brow in the way she always did when it was obvious she'd spotted a lie. That look had plagued Eleanor through the course of her very rigid childhood. Or at least after Evander had been sent to school, following the incident with their father, since when life had become impossibly strict.

Eleanor set the book aside with careful measure. The *Lady Observer* gave an incriminating crackle from beneath her pillow.

The Countess sat on the bed beside her daughter. "I read it, too. And I've heard the rumors—what they say about you."

Eleanor pressed a fingernail into the pad of her thumb until it hurt more than her mortification. It was a trick she'd used as a girl, when emotion threatened to overwhelm her, as though she could pinch the feeling out of herself with the sharp sensation.

She did not want to be having this abysmal conversation with her mother, having to relive the awful moment *ad nauseam*. Hadn't the experience itself been torment enough?

"I'm proud of you, daughter. You've maintained your composure."

The Countess settled her hand on Eleanor's arm. The touch was as awkward as it was foreign. Her mother immediately drew away her cold, dry fingers and tucked the offending appendage against her waist.

"It is I who is ashamed."

The shock of those words left Eleanor speechless. Her mother was without even a modicum of impropriety.

"I did not have a good marriage with your father, God rest his soul." The Countess regarded Eleanor with a cool look. "He came from a strong clan before his family was elevated to the English nobility. It was his belief that all emotion was weakness, indicative of one who was base-born, and his family had worked too hard to climb high to be considered common. Murrays are strong. They do not show fear."

Eleanor bit back a bitter smile. She knew those words well and had spent a lifetime listening to them being recited. After all, she knew the story well enough. Her father had not allowed any of the *ton* to look down on them for being Scottish, for not having been members of the nobility since the dawn of time.

"I gave up a piece of myself when I married your father," said her mother. "I didn't realize..." Her eyes became glossy. She pursed her lips and gave a long, slow blink before resuming. "I didn't realize I would be making my children give a piece of themselves away as well."

This show of such emotion left Eleanor wanting to squirm on the bed with discomfort. This was immediately followed by a shade of guilt. After all, her mother was voluntarily peeling back a layer of herself to offer a rare peek within, and Eleanor could think of nothing but her own uncertainty on how to handle this foreign and precarious moment.

Her mother rose abruptly, alleviating the uncomfortable tension between them. "I aided in the suppressing of your feelings until you were rendered emotionless...cold. I did not see that until this incident." She sighed and the rigid set to her shoulders sagged slightly. "I'm sorry, daughter. And I will right that wrong tonight." She strode to the box and pulled off the cover.

Eleanor slid off the bed and peered into the opened parcel. Nestled within was a length of folded black silk.

"It's a domino and mask." The Countess gracefully scooped a black silk mask from the box. "There's a wig as well. To protect your identity."

To cover her hair. Of course. Anyone seeing the garish splash of red would immediately know Eleanor's identity. The color had come from her father and it certainly had not offered Eleanor any favors. Not like her mother's green eyes, which Eleanor was grateful to have inherited.

Eleanor stared down at the pile of black silk and her

heartbeat gave a little trip. "Where am I to go that I should need a disguise?"

"I've paid a courtesan to teach you what I cannot."

Eleanor jerked her gaze to her mother in absolute horror.

"Oh, she wasn't always a courtesan," the Countess replied. "She'd once been a sweet vicar's daughter, which is how she is known to me. Difficult times do harsh things to women who have no other options." She pressed her lips together in a reverent pause. "The woman is discreet, and she will teach you to be more genuine, more receptive. Less like me. I don't want you to have a cold marriage or an austere life, in which every detail is perpetually calculated." The mask trembled in her mother's loose hold. "It's been so long since I've allowed myself to soften I fear I would be a poor tutor."

She pushed the mask into Eleanor's hands.

Her fingers closed around the silk without thought. "A courtesan?" she gasped. "I'll be ruined. *You'll* be ruined."

Her mother leveled her with a look. "Your father is dead, your brother is missing, I am getting old, and you are already two and twenty. The Season is halfway over and your one prospect has found another woman. You do know that if Evander is gone three more years he'll be declared dead and your cousin will inherit everything?"

Eleanor's thoughts flinched from the mention of her brother. It ached too much to think of his absence. He had left four years ago, to seek the adventure his father, the previous Earl of Westix, had once relished. In a world of turmoil and war, his prolonged absence gave them all cause for concern. Not that they had relinquished hope. Not yet, at least. But that did not mean they did not worry.

Her mother was correct in her harsh assessment. Eleanor's prospects were bleak.

The Countess was also correct regarding Eleanor's cousin, Leopold. He was a rapacious young popinjay, with an eye on Evander's title and any wealth he could squander on eccentric clothing and weighted gambling tables. Eleanor would get little from him before he managed to consume it all.

"Perhaps next Season will be better," Eleanor said. "I know I'm already nearly on the shelf, but—"

"There isn't money for another Season." Her mother pressed a hand to the flat of her stomach, just below her breasts, and drew in a staying breath. "Your father spent it traipsing around the world. Evander didn't leave to follow in his path—he left to repair it. To save us from financial ruin."

Eleanor maintained her composure—a near impossible feat when the world seemed to have tipped out from underneath her. "I didn't know…"

"I wouldn't have expected you to. It's not information I would have willingly shared. At least your father had the forethought to establish a trust in my name after we were wed. Which is why you've had the Seasons you've had so far."

The confident tilt of her mother's head lowered a fraction of an inch. Weariness etched lines on her face, and for the first time in Eleanor's life her mother appeared truly old.

Their situation was indeed dire.

Eleanor unfurled her fingers and regarded the mask crumpled against her damp palm.

"This may be your only chance, Eleanor," the Countess said. "Learn how to be less cold, how to appear more welcoming. Dispel the rumors and rise above the label they've placed upon you. Be in charge of your own destiny."

Her mother touched her face with icy fingertips. Eleanor did not pull away, but instead met the anxiety in her mother's stare.

The Countess's brow creased. "I want a better life for you."

Eleanor's heart pounded very fast. Surely her cheeks were red with the effort of it? "Do you trust her, Mother?"

The Countess of Westix nodded resolutely. "I do."

"Then so shall I." A tremor of fear threatened to clamber up Eleanor's spine, but she willed it away. "When do I start?"

The Countess turned to the window, where the sky beyond had grown dark. "Tonight."

Charles Pemberton was the new Duke of Somersville. The news was unwelcome, for it meant that in the six months it had taken him to return to London his father had died.

He stood by the desk in the library within the massive structure of Somersville House, his father's letter clutched limply between his fingertips.

It did not feel right to sit at the desk, when for so many decades it had been the previous Duke of Somersville who had resided behind the great expanse of polished mahogany. The entire room had been off-limits to Charles for the majority of his life, and it left everything within him feeling too hard, too desolately foreign, to offer any comfort.

Charles regarded the letter once more. Not the one which had taken months to reach him where he had been exploring in a remote location on the outskirts of Egypt. That one had informed him that he must return home immediately.

No, he held the letter which reminded him of a promise made—a promise woefully unfulfilled.

Rain pattered on the windowpanes outside, filling the room with an empty, bleak drumming. It was fitting, really, as it mirrored the torrent raging through him. His father had been the biggest part of his life—the reason Charles had sought to travel from the first. To witness the wonders of the world which had made his father so much larger than life in his eyes. To make his father proud of him for the first time in Charles's life.

And now the Duke was dead.

Ridiculous that the notion still had not thoroughly soaked into Charles's mind. Or perhaps it was his own guilt which prevented it. After all, he'd vowed when he'd left for his Grand Tour that he'd seek out the Coeur de Feu—the renowned ruby stolen from a French collector in the mid-sixteen-hundreds. It was said to be the size of a man's fist and to burn with a fire at its core—hence its name: the heart of fire.

It was the one artifact that had eluded his father, and therefore the one with which the previous Duke had become obsessed. It had been Charles's intention to seek out the stone, but he'd been so busy in the last years, experiencing new cultures, learning from the people there and their way of life. Time had seemed limitless and his father had seemed immortal.

Charles's legs were too heavy to keep him standing, and yet still he could not bring himself to rest in his father's cold chair. The grand home and all its fine furnishings might belong to Charles now, but he very much felt a stranger among his father's effects rather than their new owner. His new title fitted as uncomfortably as did the rest of his inheritance.

He looked down at the letter, which his father had left for Charles to read upon his return to London. It had been hastily written before the Duke's death and was crumpled from where it had been found, clutched in his fist. Even to look at it wrenched at Charles. He hadn't been there for the funeral. He hadn't been there to say goodbye.

The note was not filled with lamentations of time lost or proclamations of affection for Charles, who was his only living child. No, the letter contained only one scrawled line.

Find the journal and use the key to locate the Coeur de Feu.

Of course. The Coeur de Feu. Charles's greatest failure.

"The key" was a flat bit of metal the size of a book, with twenty-five small squares cut into it. The Adventure Club insignia had been stamped into the bottom right corner, indicating the key's proper direction for use. Its size matched perfectly with the various journals his father had had in his possession, all embossed with a gilt compass—the insignia of the Adventure Club.

The club had been started by his father and the Earl of Westix, and other members of the *ton*, several decades prior.

Charles had, of course, tried fitting the key into the journals. While the size of the metal piece matched perfectly with the books, it did not reveal anything more than garbled letters. Charles had tried to scramble the random offerings, rearrange them and put them together again. Yet none of his attempts created successful words—at least none that made any sense.

"Your Grace..." A voice sounded on the edges of Charles's thoughts.

Charles braced his fingertips over the desk atop one of

the books, lest he leave prints on the polished surface. His father had always hated fingerprints on things.

"Your Grace?" the voice said again.

Perhaps the journals the late Duke referred to in his note were not within this collection. Westix had a stash, after all. Charles had been present and had seen his father's objections on how the artifacts had been split after the final venture of the Adventure Club fifteen years before—specifically the ownership of important artifacts and documents.

"My Lord," the voice snapped.

Charles turned in response to the familiar form of address. His valet, Thomas, was at his side with a parchment extended.

"With all due respect, Your Grace, you *are* Your Grace now."

Thomas was ever the loyal companion. The man had traveled around the world with Charles, never once complaining, no matter how dismal the conditions. And they had indeed been dismal at times.

Regardless, Thomas always managed a smile and a pot of warm water for a proper shave. And so it was that Charles knew his valet was not being disrespectful in issuing the gentle reminder.

Charles nodded appreciatively. "Yes. Correct."

A roll of thunder rattled the windows. Thomas cast a disparaging look outside. "It would appear that Miss Charlotte is in town and she asks that you join her at her home immediately. Her servant also bade me give you this."

"Miss Charlotte? Lottie?" Charles asked with a note of surprise.

Thomas lifted a brow and handed the parchment to

Charles. "Yes, Your Grace. She is apparently most eager to speak with you."

Charles unfolded the parchment and glanced at the letter.

Don't say no, Charles.

He couldn't help but smile at that. How very like Lottie. She always had been bold with her requests, even when they were children. It seemed like a lifetime since he'd last seen little Charlotte Rossington, the vicar's daughter from his local church near Somersville Manor. They'd grown up together, and had held a platonic fondness for one another ever since.

She'd grown into a beautiful woman, with dark hair and flashing blue eyes, and was so similar in coloring to him that people sometimes confused them as brother and sister. They'd been close enough to be siblings.

He hadn't seen her since just before he'd left for his Grand Tour. There would be much to catch up on. By his estimation, and with his knowledge of her sweet, charming nature, she was most likely married with the brood of children she'd always wanted.

The night was abysmal, but even the storm was preferable to a dreary house filled with ghosts and failed promises.

Charles folded the note. "Have the carriage readied, Thomas."

He smirked to himself as his valet departed. It truly had been far too long since Charles had seen Lottie.

Chapter Two

It had indeed been a considerable amount of time since Charles had seen Lottie. He nearly did not recognize the sultry woman standing before him in the sumptuously decorated drawing room. It was too finely appointed for a vicar's daughter—as was her tightly fitted gown of deep red silk far too tawdry. Especially when compared to the modest high-necked gown he'd last seen her in.

Gone was the wide-eyed innocence of her smoky blue eyes, and in its place was a smoldering vixen with a length of midnight curls tumbling over one nearly naked shoulder. A courtesan.

Charles stared a moment longer than was polite while the five years stretched out in the silence between them. Her fingers twisted against one another at her waist—a childhood show of nerves even her new guise could not mask.

"I'm sorry about your father."

"I'm sorry about *you*," he replied.

Lottie winced and looked away. "I didn't have a choice,

Charles. There is no choice when your father dies and leaves you destitute."

Charles shifted his weight. The crisp new Hessians he wore pinched at his feet, and the slight discomfort was nearly unbearable when coupled with such agitation. "You could have wed."

Lottie's chest swelled and those damn fingers of hers started twisting again. "I could not."

"What *is* this prattle?" Charles paced over the thick carpet. "Lottie, you're lovely. You've always had the attention of men. How could you not find a husband?"

"I didn't say I couldn't find one."

"If you could find a husband why would you not—" Comprehension washed over him like cold rain.

Lottie scoffed at his apparent consternation. "*Now* you understand."

Oh, he understood.

Lottie had been compromised.

The little girl who had tagged along behind him until he had finally allowed her to join him at play. The girl he had regarded with the same undying affection one would a younger, more vulnerable sister. And some rake had ruined her.

"Who is the scoundrel?" he growled.

"No one I'll ever confess to you." She strode across the room, away from him. But not before he saw the hopeless misery in her eyes.

She still loved the man.

Charles followed her. "Why didn't you ask me for help?"

She drew a bottle of amber liquid from a shelf and pulled free the stopper. "Even if I could have found a way to contact you I have never been one for charity." She splashed a finger of liquor into a cut-crystal glass and pushed it into his hand.

He accepted the drink and took a long sip. Scotch. Very fine Scotch. "It wouldn't have been charity," he protested.

She regarded him with quiet bemusement. "Oh? And what, pray tell, would it have been?"

"Securing a future for you."

A sad smile plucked at the corners of her mouth. "I'm not your responsibility, Charles."

He settled his palm on her shoulder, the same way he'd done when she was a girl and had needed comfort: when her kitten had scaled a tree too high for her to climb, the time she'd skinned her knee and torn a new gown, the day her mother had died. He'd always been there for her.

Except, apparently, when she'd needed him most.

"You know I've always regarded you as a sister. I've always cared for you as if you were."

"But I'm not your sister." She waved him off. "You're going to make me cry with all that."

Indeed, her nose had gone rather red. She poured a second glass of Scotch and carried it over to a chaise, where she settled comfortably.

"I tried the opera first. I did well there, and…and offers began."

Charles took the seat opposite her and swallowed the rest of his Scotch at the word "offers."

Lottie pulled at a corner of the window coverings and peered into the darkness. "I resisted at first, of course," she continued. "But the expense of such a life was more than the income it generated. After a while, I couldn't refuse."

Charles stared into the bottom of his empty glass and savored the burn trailing down his insides, pushing past his heart and splashing into his gut.

"This is far grander than I've ever lived before." She indicated the room.

It was indeed fine. The dark wood furniture was polished to a shine, the walls were covered with a luxurious red silk, the floors layered with soft carpets.

"You intend to continue in this…this occupation for a while?" he asked.

She leaned toward the window and glanced out once more. "No. At least I have the hope not to. Which is part of the reason I've called you here."

"What the devil are you looking for out there?" He got to his feet and glanced out the window to the quiet street below.

"A new opportunity." She beamed up at him and traded his empty glass with her full one.

A warning prickled along the back of Charles's neck. "I don't know what scheme you're up to, but please presume I'll want no part of it."

Lottie crinkled her nose and laughed, reminding him all too well of the girl she'd been.

"Nothing like that. Oh, Charles, you do know how to make me laugh."

She shook her head and the length of midnight curls swished against the disconcerting swell of her nearly exposed bosom.

"I'm waiting for a countess's daughter to arrive. A young lady who has fallen on rather unfortunate times. I'm to instruct her in the art of flirtation."

Charles eyed Lottie skeptically.

She put her fingertips to the bottom of his glass and lifted it higher, toward his mouth. "I could use the help of a gentleman," she said. "It would do well for her to have someone to practice on."

The glass was to his lips now, but he resisted and pulled his face away. "There's something you're not telling me."

"Plying you with drink isn't going to work, I take it?"

She gave a little mock pout he'd never seen before. The type of expression made by a petulant mistress rather than a well-mannered vicar's daughter.

He didn't like it.

"I think you know me better than that."

"Very well." Lottie lowered her hands and freed his glass. "She's the daughter of the Earl of Westix."

Charles lifted the Scotch to his lips once more. Of his own volition. And drank.

The Earl of Westix.

The Adventure Club would never have disbanded had it not been for the Earl. Charles's father would still have all the journals and would have been able to find the Coeur de Feu on his own had it not been for the Earl. Charles would never have been such a disappointment in failing to fulfill that one final wish.

And Lottie knew all of this. She knew, and yet she still asked for Charles to aid one of Westix's whelps.

"Oh, dear," Lottie said with a frown. "You're turning quite red about the face."

"Why would you presume I would be willing to help any offspring of that devil?"

"The lady has had quite the time of it." Lottie lifted her forefinger. "First her father died, some years ago, then her brother vanished, and now the man who had been courting her has proposed to another."

She held out her three extended fingers, as if the physical demonstration might alter his wits. Her pinky came up, bringing the total count to four.

"And because every woman deserves a second chance."

The latter was expressed so solemnly Charles knew Lottie was not only referring to Westix's daughter but to herself. No doubt she was aware that the best way to win his acquiescence was through staggering guilt.

She knew him too damn well.

"Just imagine it, Charles." She sat upright. "If there is one countess willing to pay for her daughter's education—the kind that cannot be obtained at any reputable institution—there will be more. Every mother wants her daughter to be desirable and to wed. Who better to teach such subtle seductions than a courtesan? I could even educate married women on the pleasures to be had in the bedroom—"

"Enough," Charles ground out. "For the love of every sacred saint, please cease this talk of intimacy."

He set his glass down and paced about the room, all too aware of Lottie's anxious stare. Helping her would be a betrayal of his father's trust, and hadn't he already failed him enough?

Charles's head snapped up as an idea struck him. But if he aided this Westix chit, perhaps she might be so grateful for his assistance she would assist him in locating the lost journals.

From her watchful perch, Lottie straightened in anticipation.

"I'll assist you," Charles said at last. "However, I'll do so on one condition."

She tilted her head in silent inquiry.

"You put on a shawl."

She rolled her eyes playfully. "Very well." She peered out the window and beamed victoriously up at him. "And your timing is perfect. She's just arrived."

Eleanor awaited her fate alone. She had been divested of her domino, wig and mask—all taken by the footman. Without the shield of those items she was left feeling exposed in her precarious surroundings, and far too vulnerable.

The double doors of the drawing room were closed and oil lamps cast a flickering golden light. A harp sat in the corner, its shadow stretching over the thick Brussels weave carpet like a great beast stretching for her. Childish fear nipped at her and left her with the urgent desire to lift her feet from the floor, lest it make a grab at her.

A glass of sherry sat in open invitation on an elegantly carved table beside the chair. If it hadn't been for the bust of a woman with her breasts thrust out that was set behind it, Eleanor might have accepted the proffered indulgence.

But, while she appreciated the consideration, she was quite certain she could manage her nerves well enough on her own without the aid of alcohol. In fact, she knew she could. Murrays, after all, were strong.

The double doors parted and a woman with tumbling curls of dark hair appeared. A crimson gown hugged her trim figure and a black lace shawl lay over the swell of her generous bust, lending her a far more decent appearance than Eleanor had expected.

"I am Lottie."

Her voice was as smooth and sensual as her face—the kind which left other women with a disquieted sense of inadequacy. Was it any wonder men paid for her time?

Eleanor hid the discomfiting thought behind a tight nod

and had opened her mouth to speak when a tall man entered the room.

The low lamplight gleamed off his dark hair and shadowed his sharp jaw. His skin appeared golden beside the porcelain fairness of Lottie's, as if he'd spent much time in the sun. The brilliant blue of his eyes practically glowed against his gilded skin.

He was, by anyone's estimation, an extraordinarily handsome man.

Eleanor stiffened. "I was not told that a man would take part in my lessons."

Lottie smiled easily. "Darling, how would you learn to properly converse with a man if you hadn't anyone to practice on? Your mother knew it was a possibility and she trusts me." She regarded the man. "And I trust him."

He returned Eleanor's curious stare with a nonchalance so casual she felt foolish for voicing her fears.

"What is his name?" She spoke with equal indifference, as though she was entirely unfeeling. Except that she wasn't. Her insides trembled like set jelly and her bones ached from the rigidity of her muscles. "We haven't been introduced."

"I will allow my introduction when you permit yours."

The man's voice was deep and smooth. Eleanor lifted her chin a notch, uncertain if his response was meant in flirtation or insolence. Regardless, she wouldn't deign to reply. She had not come here to be mocked.

"This is a prime example of why I've employed his assistance."

Lottie threaded her hand through the crook of the man's elbow and drew him closer. He appeared to hesitate before Lottie gave him a firm tug.

"One can never anticipate what another will say." She

gazed up at him pointedly. "He'll add a level of spontaneity to our lessons. And, I assure you, flirting with *me* for practice will be nowhere near as exciting as with him."

"Ladies don't flirt."

Eleanor's gaze flicked to the man as he was led closer. He was tall, his chest broad and his waist and hips narrow where his breeches encased his strong thighs. Heat touched Eleanor's cheeks, and something deep inside bade her to stand and raise herself to her full height, to meet whatever challenge his presence had thrown at her feet.

"Oh, but they do," Lottie said in a softly chiding tone. "It's slight, mind you. A subtle play of words slipping between two people as if it were a language only they knew."

Lottie was right, of course. Both about flirtation and about the subtlety of it, like a carefully memorized dance. Eleanor had done it with Hugh. Twice. Both times had been immediately followed by a rush of heady excitement.

And wasn't she the fool for having permitted herself to be so audacious?

Her heart flinched, the way it always did when she considered those rare quiet moments with Hugh. Lord Ledsey.

"This will proceed more smoothly if you are honest with yourself and with me." Lottie kept her voice kind, taking the edge from the words. "There are things ladies are not supposed to do and yet still actually do—with finesse, mind you. I think we can both agree that flirtation falls within that category."

Eleanor's palms were sweating within the confines of her gloves. She wanted to run from the room, rip them from her hands and let the cold air wash over her hot skin. But she had been raised to be stronger than that.

"I'm amenable to that consideration."

"Excellent." Lottie's easy smile returned.

But it wasn't excellent. Not at all. The room was too dark, the walls too close, the expectation placed on Eleanor far too great. However, for all she did not wish to be at Lottie's town house, receiving this instruction, she was, at her core, a Murray—and Murrays did not show fear. Even when they tasted the metal of it in their mouths and were subjected to the tingling of it up their spines.

She would do this, attract a suitable husband, and then she would pretend as though it had never happened. She peeked at the man once more—a curious thing her eyes kept doing. Did he *have* to be so very handsome? And did he have to stare at her so unabashedly?

"The sherry is for you," Lottie pointed out. "If you'd like it for your nerves."

While tempted, Eleanor feared reaching for the glass might result in her brushing one of those marbled breasts gleaming in the lamplight. No, she would hold firm to her original resolve.

"Thank you, I'm fine."

Lottie clasped her naked hands together. "In that case, let us begin."

Chapter Three

Charles found the Westix chit prettier than he'd expected. Her hair was the same brilliant red as her father's, her eyes pale. Though whether they were green or blue or some color in between was imperceptible in the muted light. She was fair, her skin a lovely porcelain-white, and her back was so straight that looking at such rigidity made his shoulders ache.

It was evident she was attempting to appear brave, but he knew that all Murrays at their core were cowards. No matter how this woman tried to play it, she was exactly the same as her father.

"Let us start with introductions."

Lottie released Charles's arm and beckoned him. He stepped closer, the obedient dog in this ridiculous dance.

The delicate muscles of Lady Eleanor's neck stood out and a heavy awkwardness settled over the room.

"If he frightens you, I can send him away." Lottie spoke

in the same careful tone she'd used with the parishioners a lifetime ago.

Dear God, he wished Lady Eleanor would confess her fear and he could leave. He ground his teeth. Except there were the journals, of course—the reason he'd agreed to this damned fool of a scheme. He needed her to like him.

Lady Eleanor stood abruptly, reaching the impressive height of Charles's chin. She tilted her face upward and peered boldly up at him. Green. Her eyes were green. And wide and attentive with a feline intensity.

"I am not so easily discouraged."

Conviction laced her words, but the gentle flaring of her nostrils told a different tale. She was indeed scared. In truth, how could she not be put off by such a bizarre scenario as the one they all found themselves thrown into? At least the girl had sense.

She stood close enough that the tip of one satin slipper touched the shiny toe of his boot, and her soft breath whispered over his chin with every exhalation. The sweet scent of jasmine floated around him. It was delicate and feminine, and seemed almost too gentle for the woman in front of him.

In truth, they were improperly close—as if the scene was not already indecent enough, with a lady of her breeding meeting a woman of Lottie's—

He couldn't finish the thought.

Yes, Lottie was a courtesan, but he could not consider her as such. Not when to him she'd always been just sweet and gentle Lottie. A woman now forced to bow and scrape to this spoiled brat.

"You needn't be alarmed." Lottie carefully drew Lady Eleanor back to a more respectful distance. "We do not intend you harm or ruination. We want to help—which is why

I agreed to work with you. And…" Lottie indicated Charles. "It is why Lord Charles is here as well."

If Lady Eleanor hadn't been watching him so intently he would have given Lottie a curious look. She doubtless had her reasons for lying about his real title, and if her intention had been to set Lady Eleanor at ease, her effort proved successful. Lady Eleanor's shoulders lowered a notch and she nodded to Lottie.

"I should like to present Lady Eleanor," Lottie said grandly.

"I'm pleased to meet you."

Lady Eleanor's cool tone diffused the warmth of the greeting. Indeed, she appeared anything but pleased.

"I'd like to believe you mean that," Charles said, before he could stop himself.

Lottie shot him a hard look. Lady Eleanor met his gaze, brazen and without charm. "Perhaps that's why my mother has risked our reputations for my tutelage."

"He doesn't know the details of why you're here," Lottie said. "I should have explained it, but I—"

Lady Eleanor put up a hand to stop her.

"You must not have been long in London if you haven't yet read of the infamous Ice Queen." Lady Eleanor's brow quirked on an otherwise expressionless face. "A woman on the edge of spinsterhood, who lost her one chance at a proposal of marriage by the very coolness of her demeanor." Her eyes glinted like hard emeralds. "My mother has sent me here as she believes having Lottie teach me to flirt and project myself as being more genuine will dispel the rumors of my unaffected disposition."

"And what do *you* think?" Charles asked, his curiosity slightly piqued.

"I'm skeptical." Her reply came without hesitation.

Behind her, Lottie pursed her lips.

"Skeptical that you can be taught?" he prompted.

Lady Eleanor gave a tight smirk. "That it will have much impact. I must overcome preconceived notions sufficiently to entice a man to seek my hand in marriage. All in…" Her head tilted in apparent mental calculation. "All in the better part of two months."

Time was most certainly not in her favor. The woman was practical in her assessment.

"Does it matter who is on the other side of that proposal?" Charles studied her as he spoke, to see if she even bothered to flush at his statement. She did not.

"Women do not have the luxury of time and choice, as men do."

It was a simple reply, but it was the truth. Charles knew he had his own ducal obligations to tend to, but he did have time. Even if it took several years he could find the ruby, return to London and still acquire a wife within weeks of his arrival. Days, if necessary.

"Then we ought to get to work, oughtn't we?" Lottie stepped closer between them. "First, I'd like to observe how you comport yourself when introduced. Properly."

She regarded the Westix brat.

"Lady Eleanor, think of making eye contact and trying to look sincerely happy to meet Lord Charles."

Lady Eleanor shifted her weight from one foot to the other in reply. Clearly she was anything but happy to meet him. The feeling was mutual.

Lottie ignored the subtle display of sullen defiance. "Lady Eleanor, may I introduce Lord Charles?"

Lady Eleanor's gaze met his and raked into his soul.

There was something in the way she gazed into his eyes, unapologetic and resolute. Not at all like the demure ladies of the *ton* he'd grown used to when he'd last lived in London. No wonder she put people off.

Lady Eleanor extended her hand, which Charles accepted and bowed over, kissing the air just above the knuckles of her white kidskin gloves.

When he straightened, she offered a stiff nod and said, "I'm pleased to meet you."

Her speech and manners were immaculate. Everything was as expected in polite society, except perhaps her bold stare.

Lottie nodded to herself. "Good. Proper." She put her finger to her lower lip. "But without feeling."

"I assumed feelings were not necessary with strangers," Lady Eleanor countered.

"They are when you want to encourage strangers toward matrimony." Lottie indicated Charles. "Let your eyes linger on his, but try not to be too direct, and give a smile when you say it's a pleasure to meet him. Convince him. He should believe everything you say." Lottie swirled her finger in the air and said, in perfectly accented French, *"Allez, on recommence."*

Charles bit back a groan. They might very well be there until morning.

"We'll be doing this all night, I presume?" Lady Eleanor's tone was not enthusiastic. "Being introduced *ad nauseam* until one of us finally pleads for mercy?"

"It will be me," Charles volunteered with a wink. If he was going to win her over and get those journals, a sense of camaraderie might go a long way.

She shot him a bland look in response, before turning her

gaze to Lottie. "This is entirely ridiculous. I won't meet the same man over and over. It will not improve the poor image that most of the *ton* has of me, and nor will it change their minds. Call for my carriage." She closed her eyes, as if the act pained her. When she opened her eyes once more, her composure was fully restored. "Please."

"May I ask if there is something keeping you from this?" Lottie inquired. "Something you are afraid of?"

"I am afraid of nothing," Lady Eleanor stated firmly.

Lottie's brow pinched and she opened her mouth. But rather than offer a protest, she nodded and slipped from the room in a whisper of costly silk. A blanket of uncomfortable silence fell over the room and smothered any sense of companionship.

"You said you were skeptical." Charles lifted the glass of untouched sherry and drained it, needing the drink far more than she. Its sweetness followed the burn of alcohol and clung cloyingly on his tongue. "Perhaps you meant pessimistic?"

She eyed him warily and backed away, clearly aware of the inappropriateness of their being alone together. "Because I'm not playing along with this preposterous charade?" she asked.

"Because you're too afraid to even give it a chance." He didn't know if he was attempting to aid Lottie with this goading, or if he was doing it out of malice. Perhaps a bit of both.

Her gloved hands fingered the fabric of her skirt. "This is…abnormal."

While he agreed, he was not about to confess as much. He was, after all, there to aid Lottie. And if the chit left now he wouldn't have the opportunity to get the journals.

"I've learned that being unconventional often delivers stronger results than what is common," he said. "You came here because you want to prove everyone wrong. Why are you letting them be proved correct?"

The muscles along her slender throat tensed. "I came here because I have no choice."

Lottie entered the room with a man trailing behind her. "Your carriage is here. Ferdinand will see you out."

Lady Eleanor turned her attention from Charles and allowed the footman to help her don an absurd blonde wig, as well as a mask and black domino.

Lottie did not move from her path. "I do hope you'll reconsider."

Lady Eleanor gave Lottie a slow nod. Without another word, the Earl of Westix's daughter followed Ferdinand from the room.

Lottie's composure drained away and she sank onto the settee. "Well, that was an utter failure."

Charles watched the empty hallway where Lady Eleanor had disappeared. "I confess I fail to feel sympathy toward her—especially when she doesn't appear to find any fault with her current demeanor."

Lottie peeked at him through a curtain of dark hair. "You weren't exactly welcoming. What happened to the charming Charles I once knew?"

Her words made Charles wince. He hadn't meant his prejudice against Lady Eleanor to be so obvious. "Apparently we've all changed."

Lottie pressed her lips together rather than give him the cutting reply he deserved. "Will you try to speak with her?" She gazed up at him, her expression imploring. "I cannot, but surely you can. I know she walks in Hyde Park with her mother often."

It was on the tip of Charles's tongue to decline—to end this foolish charade. But once more the thought of the journals swam into his mind. Damn it. Not just the journals, but finding a way to assist Lottie.

He hated seeing her like this, catering to the rich with every part of herself. She didn't deserve this life.

"I'll consider it," he offered grudgingly.

Though in truth he'd already made up his mind. While he might hold contempt for Westix, and his whole blasted family, Lady Eleanor was the key to righting his great failure.

Nothing could ruin a lovely day in Hyde Park for Eleanor like unpleasant conversation. And truly there was no worse conversation than the general nagging of one's mother.

The Countess's face was hidden by an extraordinarily large white bonnet. Not that Eleanor needed to see her mother's face to know she was disappointed. The clipped tone of her voice provided all the evidence necessary.

"Will you not go again tonight?"

Eleanor wanted to cover her ears rather than endure her mother's tedious inquiry once more. She slid a glance behind them to her maid, Amelia, who knew well of the arrangement. After all, it was she who had aided Eleanor in her disguise the two days prior.

"The one lesson was enough, I assure you."

Eleanor kept to the left of the path to ensure her mother stayed in the shade. While the stroll did wonders for her mother's digestion, the late-afternoon sun wreaked havoc on her headaches.

The Countess made a sound of disagreement. Then she

turned the expanse of her bonnet toward Eleanor and regarded her daughter with careful scrutiny. "Tell me again why it was so awful?"

Eleanor waited for a woman in a butter-yellow dress to pass before answering. "It was…uncomfortable…and odd. She wanted me to pretend to be introduced to a man there several times."

Her mother's face did not offer any conveyance of sympathy, or even shock that a man had been involved. Eleanor suppressed a sigh. She would have no support from her mother.

"Then you are happy to resign yourself to the fate of being a spinster?" Her mother's face had flushed a brilliant red. She snapped open her fan and waved it in front of her face to diffuse the onset of heat she'd been suffering from of late. "And you're happy with being relegated to the position of poor relation once Leopold has what little remains of our fortune?"

Eleanor had practiced the art of emotionless disinterest for so long it came naturally. Even still, at the mention of Leopold's name she found herself having to concentrate to keep from letting her expression crumple in censure.

"And what of love?" her mother asked.

"Love." Eleanor said the word as flatly as she felt the emotion was. She had never, after all, truly believed in it. "You've always said love is for fools and fiction."

Her mother stopped fanning herself. "You should toss aside all I've ever taught you. It will bring you naught but misery." Her gaze slid to the path behind Eleanor. "Speaking of misery…"

Eleanor turned to find a couple walking toward them. The two were leaning close to one another, deep in conversation. She'd recognize the man's wavy brown hair and bold nose anywhere. Hugh and his blonde-haired, perfectly beautiful betrothed, Lady Alice.

Eleanor's heart gave a turbulent knock against her ribs. If love really was for fools and fiction, then surely Hugh and Lady Alice were the biggest fools of all. And as Eleanor felt a pang of envy at such closeness, what did that make her?

The sun shone at their backs and lit them in a halo of gold. It obviously wasn't bad enough that their faces were glowing—their bodies had to as well.

They neared, and the knock at her ribs turned into a steady banging. She prayed heartily that they might continue to walk by without notice. She did not want added humiliation on a day already gone awry.

The couple slowed as they neared Eleanor and her mother.

Please pass by.

But, unfortunately, they did not pass by.

No, they stopped, and Lady Alice turned the lovely force of her open smile on Eleanor and her mother. If nothing else, Eleanor hoped that perhaps there might be some snideness to Lady Alice's tone—some nasty upturn to her mouth or a disagreeable conversation which would sanction a justifiable dislike of her.

"Oh, Your Ladyship, Lady Eleanor—it's so good to see you," Lady Alice said with delicate and authentic pleasure. "Lady Eleanor, your bonnet suits you so very well. Isn't it the loveliest day you've ever seen?"

The expression on Lady Alice's face was sweet enough to bring to mind visions of angels. She even paused to offer a smile for Amelia.

Eleanor inwardly sighed. Of course she would not be

lucky enough to find fault with Lady Alice, who was, as she'd always been, agreeable, kind and absolutely perfect.

And she was right. It *was* a fine day. Even with Eleanor's stolen future standing so happily in front of her she could not deny the beauty of the day.

"It truly is lovely," she conceded.

"Good day, Lord Ledsey." The Countess of Westix's tone was cool in her address to Hugh.

Don't look at him.

If he replied to her mother Eleanor did not hear him. She intentionally gazed in the direction of the Serpentine River, where Lady Alice was looking with a wistful expression. The water glittered under the sun and reflected the wide stretch of the cloudless sky. A weak breeze swept from the river and brushed away some of the heat from Eleanor's blazing cheeks.

She would stare at the Serpentine for ages. Anything to avoid looking at Hugh. But, dash it, her traitorous eyes immediately disobeyed the direct order and slid over to the face which she'd one day anticipated being that of her husband. An ache began in the center of her chest, where her heart was still raw and wounded. She kept her smile small, for it felt brittle enough to crack if given too much effort.

Her mother had been so proud of Eleanor when Hugh had directed his affections toward her, and the pressure of the *ton* had eased from her shoulders. Lady Eleanor, with her garish red hair, had finally found a man who might be willing to wed her.

Except he had not been willing. And his newfound affection for Lady Alice had left her scalded with mortification.

Eleanor should have expected such fickleness after his

intentions toward her had come upon her so abruptly. At the time she had been too grateful to think on it.

She was not grateful any longer.

Hugh looked at Eleanor—a momentary flick of a glance, as if she were not worth his time. And when he had a woman such as Lady Alice on his arm surely she was not.

It was at times like this that Eleanor was thankful for her father's insistence that she never show emotion. Because at times like this Eleanor agreed that one must appear strong. She wore her indifference like a shield, staunchly guarding her wounds from prying eyes.

Hugh's hand came up suddenly and waved at a man several paces away. "Ah, here he is now."

Lady Alice gave an excited clap. "Oh, wonderful—he's made it after all."

The man stopped between Eleanor and Lady Alice. He was tall enough to block the sun from where it shone into Eleanor's eyes, but not so tall that she had to peer up at him foolishly. His hazel-green eyes crinkled nicely at the corners.

Hugh clapped the man on the back. "This chap went to school with me several years back. May I introduce the Marquess of Bastionbury?"

A part of Eleanor—a sad, pathetic part—perked up at the mention of his name. According to the *Lady Observer*, the Marquess was the most eligible man on the marriage mart. A man Eleanor had not yet had the opportunity to be introduced to.

The ladies all nodded their amenability. "By all means," said the Countess.

Hugh indicated Eleanor's mother first. "My Lord, may I present the Countess of Westix?"

Her mother offered a stiff curtsey and nodded.

Hugh's eyes met Eleanor's and her pulse gave a pitiful leap. "And the Countess's daughter, Lady Eleanor Murray."

Lottie's voice sounded in Eleanor's head, reminding her to meet the man's eyes. Eleanor nodded and held his handsome stare, but the smile trembled on her lips.

The Marquess nodded and then his attention slid away. To Lady Alice.

Hugh squeezed Lady Alice's slender arm with an embarrassing show of affection, which Lady Alice did not chide him for. "And now may I present Lady Alice Honeycutt, my betrothed?"

Lady Alice nodded and let her regard linger on the Marquess, much in the way a butterfly might over a choice bloom. A pretty blush colored her cheeks. "It is so very good to meet you, My Lord. I've heard such great tales."

Her smile was dainty and her eyes practically danced with the sincerity of her joy. She held out a hand to the Marquess, who readily took it and let a kiss whisper over her gloved knuckles.

The Marquess was genuinely engaged in Lady Alice's attention. Even her mother had a whisper of a grin teasing the corners of her stiff mouth. Lady Alice was warm and endearing, while still maintaining her cultured poise. An impeccable balance of breeding and manners and kindness.

And a glaring reminder of what Eleanor had been doing so very wrong.

In truth, Eleanor found Lady Alice's behavior bordering on inappropriate. Her father would have been appalled at such behavior, and no doubt would have been violent in his distaste for it. But he was not here now. He was dead, having left them with no fortune, Evander missing, and a wall of ice to melt.

Alice's open warmth was the line Lottie had mentioned in the lesson—the acceptable level of flirtation. Skirting propriety, subtle and delicately danced, therefore being socially acceptable.

Was this the kind of woman men wanted?

Eleanor didn't have to ask the question. She already knew. It was in the tinkling laugh Lady Alice did not suppress, in the measured, meaningful way her gaze met those she conversed with, and how men swarmed to her side, eager for any scrap of attention she was willing to offer.

Regret nipped at Eleanor with sharp teeth. Perhaps she ought to have let herself be introduced to Lord Charles several times more. She should have been more patient with the process.

"If you'll excuse us?" said the Countess. "We must be on our way."

Eleanor let her mother lead them in the direction of a group of the Countess's friends, where they clustered together in an array of colorful pastels, chatting under a tree by the river. Conversations blended around her, but her mind was unable to focus on any single one.

"Ah, there is Lady Stetton." Her mother nodded toward the shore of the Serpentine River.

Energy hummed through Eleanor's veins. She did not want to stop the steady rise and fall of her feet as she walked. To do so might give her mind cause to churn. And to think of all her failings—those she did not wish to ponder over.

"Do you mind if I go on a bit further with Amelia?"

Her mother eyed the path and gave an approving nod. "Join us once you've collected yourself."

Her mother swept off the trail and headed in the direction of Lady Stetton, leaving Eleanor and Amelia to continue onward. The absence of her mother's barrage of questions was a balm to Eleanor's racing brain, and she filled all her tumultuous thoughts with the rustling of trees and the twittering of birds.

"Forgive me," Amelia said in her gentle maternal voice. "But there is a man watching you."

Eleanor followed Amelia's stare to where a tall dark-haired man was indeed watching her, his eyes brighter than the clear sky overhead.

He smiled in invitation, his teeth impossibly white against his tanned skin. Her stomach sank. There would be no avoiding him, no matter how much she wished to.

She would have to speak to Lord Charles.

Chapter Four

Charles had anticipated that he might see Lady Eleanor. It had been his sole reason for a promenade through Hyde Park.

She was a beautiful sight, in a white gown with a pale green ribbon tied under her bosom and matching green ribbons on her bonnet. The color made her eyes stand out like emeralds beneath the brim of her bonnet. She had been pretty by candlelight, but by the light of day she was even comelier.

Her expression, however, mirrored that of a person being sent to the gallows. After the exchange of introductions Charles had overheard, it was quite evident that Lady Eleanor Murray was not having a good day.

It might have been kind to allow her to continue by and let her lick her wounds. If he were a sensitive man he might have allowed it. But he was not, and she had the journals he needed.

He stepped in front of Lady Eleanor and bowed. "Do you mind if I join you?"

Lady Eleanor hesitated long enough to suggest she did. Yet when her maid whispered inaudibly to her Eleanor subtly shook her head, and the brown-haired lady's maid stepped behind Lady Eleanor to make room for him.

"That would be lovely, Lord Charles."

Lady Eleanor's tone was flat and suggested it was anything but. Ever the charmer.

He ought to correct her, he knew—let her know he wasn't merely Lord Charles, but the new Duke of Somersville. Perhaps had she not been looking so crossly at him he would have been more inclined. But he owed this woman nothing.

Later. Perhaps...

He straightened and held out his arm to her, as was polite. She threaded her slender arm through his and rested her gloved hand atop the cuff of his jacket. Her light jasmine scent whispered at his senses. Although this time, in the afternoon's gilded light, with her dressed in delicate colors and gentle ribbons, the soft sweetness of her perfume seemed more fitting.

Lady Eleanor gave a little sigh. "I suppose you're here to convince me to return to Lottie's?"

"I thought I might give the idea a go," Charles replied.

Tree canopies spread over the path like an awning and blotted out the heat from the sun, leaving the air cool and fresh. Charles took a deep breath and let the quiet crunch of dirt under their feet fill the silence. Lady Eleanor's maid walked a few feet behind them, to grant privacy while still maintaining prudent proximity.

"Do you think you'll have any success in convincing me to return?" Lady Eleanor asked after a moment.

So much for any hope that she might make this easy. He

glanced back over his shoulder, to where the Earl of Ledsey and Lady Alice still conversed with the dark-haired Marquess.

"If I were a betting man, I'd wager on it."

Eleanor's arm stiffened against his. "You saw?"

"I overheard," he said. "On my honor, it was quite by accident."

"What a wild coincidence…" she said blandly.

Charles did not bother to apologize.

"May I be frank with you?" Lady Eleanor asked abruptly. "Or rather, ask you to be frank with me?"

He inclined his head. "I believe our history dictates a level of candor."

Lady Eleanor glanced around them. The path had gone empty and they were all but alone. At least for a few moments. Or as alone as one might be with a chaperon in tow.

She stopped and stared up at him with her catlike green eyes. Perfectly sculpted red curls framed her porcelain forehead. In fact, everything about her was so carefully refined it made him long to see something skewed out of place.

"What is so unappealing about me?" she asked.

She asked it bluntly, almost casually, the way one might ask what would be served at supper that evening.

He hadn't expected such a question and found himself quite without words. After all, she was Westix's daughter, and certainly that brought her a plethora of ill traits.

"I truly wish to know so that I might see how to improve," she said. "I am from excellent lineage, and my manners are impeccable. I move in all the right circles. I know I don't have the kind of beauty Lady Alice possesses, and that my hair is…awful. But what else is it about me, about my person, which is so heartily distasteful?"

She turned her head away before he could see any kind

of expression cross her smooth face or come to her eyes. She quickly began to walk once more, as if she regretted what she'd said. Her speech had been one of hurt, but her tone had been without feeling.

Perhaps there was more to his enemy's daughter than Charles had wagered.

He resumed his stroll beside her at the slow pace she'd set. But, for all her steady pace and dispassionate voice, her hand trembled when it returned to his arm.

"You want my honesty?" he surmised.

"Yes."

Charles hesitated. These words would be important, ultimately forming her decision to return to Lottie's and setting the foundation for a friendship which might allow him access to those damned journals.

"May I begin first by saying that while Lady Alice is indeed lovely, so too are you."

Lady Eleanor looked up at him sharply, her eyes wide and the fullness of her pink lips slightly parted. After all her careful hiding behind an emotionless mask, the shock on her face was a surprise.

"I do not find your hair 'awful,' as you say."

In truth, its color was vibrant and beautiful. Any distaste stemmed from the reminder of her relationship to a man whom Charles so bitterly detested.

Lady Eleanor turned her head away and regarded the path once more. Several more people had filled the area around them, and he kept his voice intentionally lowered to ensure their privacy.

"It is your demeanor which is unwelcome."

Lady Eleanor did not react.

"Are you sure you wish me to continue?" he asked.

She exhaled and nodded. "Yes. I believe I need you to."

And in truth she was right. She *did* need to hear what he had to say. For her own good, and to increase her desire to return to Lottie's for lessons.

He went on as bade. "You are cold, as they say. Polite? Yes. But you have no *joie de vivre*…your delivery is without feeling. You have no…*passion*."

"Passion is vulgar."

"Passion is necessary," he countered. "It's what colors our world, what provides change and excitement. A woman like you, so without passion, is like a painting without depth. You will go through life in an endless routine of changing gowns and attending luncheons and soirees until they all blur together. You will meet every encounter with bored uninterest, to the point of teetering on disdain, as if nothing will ever be enough to please you. And one day, when death comes knocking at your door, you will look back on the nothing of your existence and realize that you never once lived a day in your life."

It wasn't until the entire, ugly and honest truth was out that he realized the depth of the cut in his words.

Lady Eleanor had stopped. The shade of trees had thinned out and her bonnet was dappled with splashes of gold. She turned toward him, pulled her arm from his, and slowly lifted her face. Her eyes gleamed in the light, glowing like gemstones with the gloss of what appeared to be carefully restrained tears.

The realization struck Charles in the chest.

He had gone too far.

He opened his mouth to apologize, but Lady Eleanor spoke first.

"My mother and her friends are waiting for me."

She nodded to the women on the riverbank. The entire group looked their way—and immediately snapped their heads in the opposite direction once they realized they'd been caught.

Lady Eleanor gently cleared her throat. "Thank you for your candor. Good day, Lord Charles."

She ducked her head down, hiding her face with the rim of her bonnet, and slipped away. Her gait was stiff, her back ramrod-straight and her shoulders squared. The maid hurried along after her.

Charles watched Lady Eleanor walk away, feeling very much the cad. He'd assumed such a speech would render him victorious, and yet his joy had been marred by something rather unexpected—the stab of guilt.

Later that evening Charles sat among a collection of his father's greatest acquisitions. If Charles hadn't thought it possible to feel any lower than he had after his honest assessment of Lady Eleanor, he'd underestimated what coming home to Somersville House would do. Especially as he surveyed the unboxed treasures.

There was a sarcophagus containing an intact mummy, found in a sealed-off tomb in the Valley of the Kings. The paint stood vivid blue against un-flecked gold, as if it had been created only weeks ago rather than centuries before. Its discovery had earned his father a private audience with the King. Then there was a gold scarab encrusted with priceless jewels, of which the *ton* had talked for three months.

Charles hefted an ancient tome into his grasp. The pages within the leather binding were unevenly cut and yellow with age. They crackled when handled. But the drawings and words within were still dark with ink. The discovery of this particular book had left scholars in a state of frenzy.

Every item found by his father in a foreign world and brought to London had been met with praise and acclaim. And Charles had been witness to it all his life—first as a young boy, peering from the stairs, later from the corner where his governess had grudgingly allowed him to sit, and later by his father's side, as an honored son. That was, until the Duke had begun to suffer from gout and declared himself too old for travel.

Charles set the tome down gently on the desk and regarded the key, studying its flat, cool metal surface.

It had indeed been a sad day when the Duke of Somersville had had to put away the old floppy hat he'd worn during his Adventure Club days.

At the time of its dissolution, the club had still been obsessed with locating the Coeur de Feu. Each man had gone about his own adventure, following leads on its location and documenting his journey. It had been when they returned home that everything had dissolved around them, their trust ripped apart by perfidy and speculation.

The Duke and the Earl of Westix had been the wealthiest of the men in the club, but they had not been the brightest. Only one man, whose name was never mentioned, had been cleverer than the rest, and had put his findings in code. And, while the previous Duke of Somersville had somehow obtained the key, and had known of its purpose, he had not known which of the journals was needed.

Charles had already been through all the journals at Somersville House, of course. He'd found nothing but descriptions of places the members of the club had gone, and accounts of treasures acquired. Until his father's effects were returned from their country estate there was nothing more to look through.

Regardless, Charles was certain the one he needed lay in the Earl of Westix's home.

He let the key slip from his grip and the metal sheet fell silently against the thick Turkish carpet. There was a story behind that carpet as well, only he couldn't recall it at the moment.

Every item in the house had a story—had come from a different homeland, after a new adventure. He put his face in his hands and let the coolness of his fingers press into the heat of his skin. They all had far better stories than his own—the son who had watched with adoration the father whose magnificence he would never measure up to...the sole heir who had cast aside his promises in search of his own adventures.

His father had been larger than life, experiencing every day to the fullest. Charles couldn't believe he was gone, leaving him with no more chances to fulfill his promise and finally gain what he had always wanted—his father's respect and pride in his accomplishments rather than always standing in his father's shadow.

A knot formed stubbornly in Charles's throat.

"Your Grace?"

A man's voice nudged gently into Charles's awareness. He looked up and met the dark gaze of his valet.

"Your Grace, you asked to be reminded when it was near time for you to depart for Miss Lottie's."

Charles nodded. "Thank you, Thomas. I'll be down in a moment."

Thomas glanced at the treasures surrounding Charles.

"Several doors down there is another room filled with the items you discovered on your own travels."

The trouble with good valets was the way they oftentimes were far too perceptive.

"They aren't the same." Charles looked at a jade pendant of an elephant with gilt tusks.

"You are a good man, Your Grace. He would be proud of what you've accomplished in such a short period of time."

Charles nodded absently. His father wouldn't be proud. Not after his failing to locate the Coeur de Feu. No, his father would be disappointed.

The thought sliced into him as he recalled his father's last words, hastily scrawled with the desperation of a man with only moments left to live. And once again he felt the crushing weight of disappointment, because they'd been about the damned ruby.

Thomas bent in front of Charles and lifted the key from the floor. "When you're ready, Your Grace?" He carefully set it on the desk beside the massive tome and departed.

Charles sighed, but the weight in his heart did not lighten. He had committed many wrongs in his life, and all the treasures of the world wouldn't make it right. Getting those journals from Eleanor would be a start.

In truth, she had wormed her way into his thoughts several times since their discussion. Her forthright demand for what she might do to improve herself had taken him aback. And yet it had been refreshing. It was a rare thing indeed for a member of the *ton* to request an opportunity to better oneself. Not in dance or watercolor or singing, but in the general composition of their personality.

Charles got to his feet and strode out the door. He stopped at the top of the stairs and gazed down to the entrance hall below, where polished marble gleamed in the candlelight. He'd stood there so very many times before, watching his father prepare to leave for another trip.

When he was a boy he'd held onto the ornate railing, his small fingers curled around the cool wood, as if clutching it would keep his father from leaving again. When he was an adolescent he'd propped his elbow on its bannister and let his imagination carry him to the places his father would go, where Charles knew with the whole of his heart he would also venture someday.

And this was where Charles had seen his father for the last time...

The bustle of servants began to calm and Charles found himself alone in the foyer. His blood danced in his veins at the thought of the impending adventure awaiting him—the foreign lands, the excitement of experiencing everything he'd ever heard about from his father and had spent a lifetime dreaming of.

The back of his neck prickled with the awareness of being observed. He turned and looked up the curving stairs to where his father leaned heavily on a carved ivory cane just at the top.

They'd said their farewells already. Promises had been made to pursue the Coeur de Feu, *and wisdom and advice had been passed from father to son.*

The Duke did not make his way down to offer another goodbye. Instead he stood at the top of the stairs, leaning on the cane gone yellow with age, and nodded down at his son.

This time it was the Duke of Somersville who was seeing Charles off. And this time it was not just information which had been passed from father to son, but a role...

The memory wrenched at Charles's heart. Not because

he hadn't been there to offer his father a final farewell when the Duke had passed on, but because he had failed.

There would be no moving on with Charles's life until the gem was found. The dukedom could wait. It had been unattended for the previous six months, after all. Charles was young. He had time for life to wait as he finally fulfilled his promise.

The steel of determination set in his spine as he climbed into the waiting carriage. He would get those journals by any means necessary.

Chapter Five

Late evening was often the hour of illicit deeds. Eleanor's deed posed no exception. She slipped into the town house on Russell Square in Bloomsbury, utilizing the servants' entrance for discretion.

It wasn't until the footman had led her into the drawing room that she allowed him to take the domino from her shoulders, the wig from her head and the mask from her face.

While last time divesting herself of her disguise had left her trembling with vulnerability, now it rendered her lighter, freer. Perhaps now she saw the lessons for what she hadn't fully understood previously that they were: a second chance. Possibly her only chance.

Not just in acquiring a husband, but in living her life. Having passion, as Charles had said. Being a painting with depth.

The very idea of it prickled over her skin. She had restrained her emotions for so long, the very idea of letting them free was exhilarating.

Her mother had been equally eager to have her attend another lesson, especially after she had been seen in Hyde Park, speaking with a mysterious man. Eleanor had remained closed-lipped about Lord Charles, and her mother had been too pleased with the development to press for more information.

Eleanor watched the door with anticipation—waiting for it to open, for Lottie to saunter through it with her sensual confidence. And for Charles to follow behind her.

Perhaps Eleanor ought to have been offended by the bluntness of his words—certainly they had stung. But they had also thrown open the doors of her comprehension. What might have been the harshest criticism had also been the introduction to opportunity.

A glass of sherry, she noticed, was sitting once more on the small table beside the buxom bust. She leaned over the marble woman, considering... Her eagerness to change, however, did not extend far enough to allow her to reach between the pert nipples and claim the glass.

The doors swept open and Eleanor lurched around like a child caught doing something naughty. Lottie passed into the room like a queen. The length of her black curls cascaded down her right shoulder and the blue silk gown she wore made her skin gleam like the flawless surface of a pearl. Charles entered the room behind her and bowed low.

"Good evening, Lady Eleanor."

He rose and bestowed upon her a charming smile, which she ought to have ignored but which set her heart tapping at an odd rhythm.

"It's good to see you again."

There was a genuine note to his tone, indicating he was indeed happy to see her. Her cheeks went warm.

"So wonderful to have you back." Lottie clasped her hands together and pressed them over her chest.

"Forgive my previously disparaging attitude," Eleanor said. "I didn't understand how valuable a chance this was. If your generosity is still extended, I am eager to avail myself of and continue with the lessons."

Lottie waved at the air. "Oh, pish—there's nothing at all to forgive. And of course I'll continue with your lessons. I'd never have taken you on unless I truly wanted to instruct you." She touched the underside of Eleanor's chin, the way a mother might do a cherished child. "You are going to be magnificent, dear one. You need only to believe in yourself."

The touch and her proximity were startling, but the affection behind both was innocent. It served to endear Lottie to her all the more.

"Shall we start with introductions?" Eleanor asked gently.

Lottie gave an appreciative laugh. "By all means, let's." She cleared her throat and straightened, her demeanor taking on a regal bearing. "Do you remember what I told you?"

Eleanor nodded. "Make eye contact, smile, be sincere." The way Lord Charles had just been.

Suddenly the understanding of it all washed over her with even more clarity.

"Perfect." Lottie waved Lord Charles closer.

He obligingly stepped forward. The strength of his muscular thighs was visible beneath the light-colored fabric of his pantaloons.

Oh, dear.

A sudden thought occurred to Eleanor. Was Lord Charles

a client of Lottie's? They would cut a fine pair, with their dark hair and beautiful blue eyes.

Except he was smiling at Eleanor as if she were the only woman in all the world. How very devastating of him. And how very different from their last meeting.

What had changed? Her stomach twisted. Was it that he felt sorry for her? Did he find her so piteous that he had taken it upon himself to make up for it with flattery?

"Lady Eleanor, may I introduce Lord Charles?" Lottie indicated him.

Eleanor extended her hand and Lord Charles bowed over it. His fingers curled around hers and his mouth kissed the air above her gloves. Though his lips never touched the kid-skin, she swore she could sense the heat of his mouth over her knuckles, like a caress against her skin. The sensation was not unpleasant.

When he rose from his elegant bow she let her eyes meet his and linger. "It's a pleasure to meet you, Lord Charles." She infused the words with everything she could dredge up—gratitude at his temerity in being honest with her the prior day, the kind of charm he offered her, even her hope of becoming a better person than she might otherwise be.

His smile broadened. Was it truly possible for one's teeth to be so brilliantly white?

Lottie laughed somewhere a world away. A joyous sound that dragged Eleanor back to the sumptuous red silk detail of the drawing room, where that nude bust stared boldly at her behind the temptation of a sherry glass and a wide gilt-framed mirror reflected Eleanor's own flushed cheeks and sparkling eyes.

Was that truly her in the mirror?

She quickly looked away, to ensure she was not seen staring at her own reflection.

For a moment she had allowed herself to be drawn into the alluring pull of Charles's presence, sharing his confidence. For a moment, she had been someone else, open and sincere. The realization, however, brought back the sensation of being completely vulnerable. She had worn her expressionless mask for so long that without it she was naked.

"Oh, Lady Eleanor, that was so very marvelous."

Lottie nodded appreciatively at Charles, and the look between them was intimate, conveying so much more than a friend aiding another.

Immediately a wave of humiliation curdled the success Eleanor had mustered. What a fool she'd been, blushing at a courtesan's lover as if he might find her truly enchanting. Hadn't she already learned her lesson once before when it came to men who offered interest in her?

"Shall we try again?" Lottie asked.

Eleanor nodded, even though the shine of her newfound opportunity had greatly diminished. Not that she'd expected Lord Charles to find her truly interesting. But he'd said she was lovely.

Was she so desperate to be found attractive? Especially with a woman like Lottie in the vicinity?

"Lady Eleanor, may I introduce Lord Charles?" Lottie said in her silky voice.

Eleanor lifted her eyes, but found Charles's gaze harder to meet this time. "It's lovely to meet you." She heard the rigidity in her own voice and lifted her hand awkwardly.

Charles did his part with the same smoothness as before. Again and again and again he demonstrated his mastery over his part of the introduction. Again and again and again Eleanor found she could not with hers.

The flare of hope began to dim. She was lacking once more. Inadequate.

Lottie's question from the prior lesson surfaced in her mind once more—the way it had many times since the query had been issued: What was Eleanor afraid of?

Eleanor had the answer. Or rather the answers. For there were many. After living behind the shield of her apathy for so long, to lower it was frightening. To be sincere was to be vulnerable, and to open herself to what rejection might do to that fragile, exposed part of her.

She could not stomach such embarrassment again. She could not be a failure.

Charles was home late that evening from Lottie's. They'd worked with Lady Eleanor for longer than before. All to no avail. He was weary of introductions. Indeed, Eleanor's disappointment in herself had been evident in the flush of her cheeks, despite her otherwise cool demeanor. And, though she was Westix's daughter, he had not been able to help the swell of sympathy.

She had persisted, patiently facing each new introduction with a determined set to her brow. He'd wished he could give her the passion she so lacked, could encourage the flame of life in those green eyes.

Charles's butler, Grimms, took his coat, hat and gloves as he entered Somersville House. "Good evening, Your Grace." Grimms offered a formal bow. "I believe you'll be pleased to learn that your father's effects have arrived this evening. All have been placed within the library."

Charles's exhaustion fell away, to be immediately replaced by excitement. He hadn't anticipated the arrival of his father's items from the country estate for at least a few more days.

"Thank you, Grimms."

The butler inclined his head, showing the glossy skin atop his head where his snow-white hair no longer grew, and strode off.

Charles immediately made his way to the library, and found a mountain of wooden crates beside one of the curio cabinets laden with his father's treasures. At least twenty boxes, by his estimation. Going through the lot of them would take a considerable amount of time.

"Welcome home, Your Grace." Thomas entered the room and held up a metal hook with a grin. "I heard you were back and thought you might require some assistance."

"Your timing is impeccable as always, Thomas."

Charles stepped back from the pile to give his valet better access. Thomas pulled down the top box with a grunt and shoved the point of the hook into the narrow gap under the lid. He pushed, and the top lifted off with a splintering crack.

Inside were stacks of papers and journals. Enough to take the night to get through—if Charles was lucky.

Thomas regarded the contents within the box and lifted his brows. "Fancy a brandy?"

Charles ran a hand through his hair. "I think that might help."

His valet quit the room, leaving Charles alone with piles of correspondence and notations written in the Duke's neat, narrow writing.

The first few layers were accounts for the country estate—a detailed overview of funds spent and rents collected. Those were followed by letters from museums and from scholars, thanking the Duke for his contributions to their institutions.

Charles stopped and took the time to read those, awash in his father's greatness. Interesting how even when he had been alive Charles had always felt on the outside, looking in with awe.

Eventually he carefully set the correspondence in a stack to one side. Next he lifted a large journal from the box. The gilded compass on the front indicated that it had been part of the Adventure Club. Unfortunately, the pages were too large to fit the key.

Charles opened the cover, regardless. The spine creaked and crackled in protest at its disuse. Clearly the journal was older than the others he'd gone through previously. Indeed, the first page placed the previous Duke thirty years ago, somewhere off the Nile in Egypt. A careful perusal revealed only his father's handwriting.

Charles strode to the desk, hesitated, and then reverently sat upon the chair his father had occupied for so many decades. The leather was cold beneath him, and stiff to the point of providing little comfort. He would have Thomas find him a more accommodating one the following day.

For the time being Charles settled back rigidly and perused the aged book. He'd read all the Adventure Club's journals in his possession, and traveled their adventures vicariously. This was the oldest he'd seen, and the first written only by his father.

Thomas came in and placed the brandy before Charles. "Shall I open another box?"

Charles shook his head. "This will do for now. Thank you, Thomas."

The valet nodded and left Charles alone with the journal.

The brandy remained untouched while he delved into the words written by his father.

The pyramids rose before me, dotting the horizon with triangles, their tips pointing toward the sun. These wondrous fossils of an age long dead are rife with treasures beyond my wildest dreams, ready for presenting to England.

Thus far my findings have been well received, at least by the English. It would appear there are some within Egypt who begrudge my presence. People who declare the excavations pillaging and deem these sites sacred.

For those unable to apply reason, certain documents can be replicated to allow us the access we require.

It was a perfectly constructed plan from one of our members—a man who has proved himself a genius in his approach to dealing with these obstacles as well as finding treasure.

He shall surely be a worthy asset among us, especially in gaining access to the most guarded treasures.

Charles paused in momentary confusion. Surely his father didn't mean he'd bribed people and forged documentation? There had been many instances when Charles had heard descriptions of finding tombs and temples long-ago abandoned and left to fall in on themselves in the middle of nowhere.

Charles's father had been a good man, with a name honorably built on the findings of great pieces which he'd shared with England. He'd been a hero—one who would never have stooped to such low levels as deceit and theft.

Not his father.

Charles read through the rest of the journal, which described the findings within the tomb in considerable detail. No further suggestion or implication was made of any untoward acts.

The absence of such eased the twist in Charles's stomach. Surely his father's earlier words had been written merely as a precaution, in the event that he'd need to go beyond the rules a little in order to bring an item home. The Duke had been an honorable man whose efforts had always been morally sound.

Charles closed the book and lifted the glass of brandy. He drank half in one great swallow before settling back in the seat. His mind nudged from his father to the distraction of Lady Eleanor.

There was something strange about the way the lesson that evening had gone—how she'd seemed so fully connected one minute and then separated the next. Regardless, she had appeared to be positively affected by his more pleasant demeanor.

He would need to meet with her again and ensure she did not fall prey to discouragement. She had to continue her lessons with Lottie and her association with him.

He was surprised to find he rather looked forward to it.

Chapter Six

Eleanor didn't much care for a walk in the park two afternoons later—any more than she'd cared for the soiree she'd been forced to attend the prior evening. Not when all she could ruminate on was her utter failure.

And Lord Charles.

Blast it. Why had he regarded her with such appeal? And why had she reacted to it so?

She would be meeting with Lottie again that evening. Perhaps Lord Charles, too.

The very idea of it made her insides flutter and her palms grow damp. A sensation that was as pleasant as it was disconcerting.

She thought again of how he'd looked at her...when everything had faded to a dull focus and her world had seemed to right itself. A grin played over her lips.

Eleanor strode along the worn paths of Hyde Park with Amelia walking at her side. While her maid had been all too eager to join Eleanor that fine spring day, she seemed to sense her mistress's need for solitude and remained in pleasant silence.

"Lady Eleanor."

A familiar, warm voice interrupted Eleanor's musings. Her stomach churned with myriad emotions: trepidation, fear, and most of all excitement. They all swooped and tangled together into a nervous whirl.

"Lord Charles."

She turned in his direction and nodded politely as he bowed. There was just enough time for her to salvage her composure before he straightened.

"I hoped I might find you here," he said.

He wore a pair of fine buckskin breeches and they gave him a casual, comfortable appearance. It was altogether very attractive, that look...

"You were looking for me?" She lifted a brow in the manner her mother often affected, hoping her face mirrored skepticism and not hope. Hope would be foolish.

Amelia quietly shifted to walk behind Eleanor, allowing her a modicum of privacy with Charles.

"I feared you might be disappointed after the last lesson," Charles said.

"I wasn't pleased," she conceded. "I'm not doing as well as I'd hoped."

He held out his arm to her. "May I walk with you a moment?"

There was no hesitation on her part, as there had been previously. She slipped her arm through his. "Of course. Thank you."

As they began to walk together she could not help but notice the solidity of him beneath his sleeve. And he smelled of foreign spices—something pleasant and exotic she could not quite place.

"I'd like to be frank with you once more," Lord Charles began. "That is, if you are inclined to hear my opinion on the matter?"

"I am," she replied, despite the jangle of her nerves. "I wish to learn."

But, while she was being truthful in expressing her wish to learn, the idea of hearing more criticism of her person dragged her lower into herself.

"Why do you wish to learn?" he asked.

"To obtain a husband befitting my station," she replied readily. After all, it was what was expected of her—what was necessary.

"I think there's more to it than that."

His response took her aback, and the subsequent silence left her contemplation hanging between them. It would be easy to push the answer down inside her and bury it beside the rest of her emotions. But wasn't she trying to unearth them all? Wasn't she trying to be warmer? More approachable? Didn't she want to have depth?

"I don't want to live a life without passion," she said, in a quiet voice only he would be able to hear. "I enjoy reading so I can experience the emotions of the characters, to revel in their liberation to express them. But they are fictional and do not suffer the consequences we do. I have always been envious of the ability to express oneself so completely. I want to be free to *feel*."

Her heart raced at her confession. She had given merit to the truth and said it aloud for the first time in all her adult life.

Charles smiled warmly. "I think you are on the right path, Lady Eleanor."

"Why, then, is it so difficult?" she asked.

"You did well initially the last time," he answered. "But then you changed. I feel there was a reason for that, and I hope I might be able to help you identify what it might be."

Eleanor was glad to be walking beside him, with the brim of her bonnet covering her face, lest he see the heat blazing through her cheeks. After all, such things were impossible to mask, no matter how one schooled one's face.

She knew exactly what had been responsible for the change in her at their prior lesson. It had been her own foolishness. The way she'd so easily reacted to Lord Charles's kindness, the recollection of her mistakes, and the reminder of how painful it was to love.

"Have I overreached in my frankness?" he inquired.

Eleanor realized she'd been contemplative for too long. "No."

"How did you feel when you made the first introduction?" Charles asked.

Beautiful.

Desired.

"More genuine," she answered. "As though you were meeting me as a person and I you, rather than just performing the stiff formality of introduction."

"I thought as much." There was a note of delight to his tone. "I felt the connection as well."

Eleanor hated the little flip her stomach gave, and hated how difficult it was to force herself not to turn toward the allure of his handsome smile.

Lord Charles deftly guided her around an aging couple in front of them who walked at a much slower pace.

"And how did you feel after?" he prodded.

Foolish.

Embarrassed.

"Exposed…" she breathed, almost choking on the suffocating memory.

"Ah, yes."

This time she did glance up at him and found him nodding to himself.

"You do realize the appeal of such openness?" he asked.

"No," she said slowly.

"The stiffness of your formality is what you've conformed to. It's not who you are. The feeling of exposure is what comes when you let your shield slip and grant others the opportunity to see who you are."

His explanation served to heighten her sense of vulnerability.

"I don't think I like that." No, she *knew* she did not like that.

"Because it feels foreign?" He paused. "Lottie once asked what you were afraid of. Perhaps this is your answer."

"Perhaps." It was all she would allow. The full truth would stay locked within her.

A gentleman tilted his hat to Eleanor from a passing carriage, catching her eye. Only then did she realize it was Hugh, with Lady Alice. Clearly they had been in her line of sight for some time on the road ahead and she was seeing them only now.

Interesting…

So, too, was the lack of heady anxiety seeing the two of them typically produced in her.

"When the shield slips away," Charles was saying, "it lets a man glimpse the true woman beneath."

"And you saw me?" she queried.

"I did." He said it softly, as if he were considering something.

"What did you see in me?"

Her pulse ticked wildly. After their last conversation, did she truly want to hear this?

"You're bold...you meet challenges head-on rather than cowering back from them. And there *is* passion in you. It's simmering below the surface, but it's there and it's beautiful."

"Do you find *me* beautiful?" Eleanor immediately regretted the brashness of her question.

Lord Charles stopped walking. Improper though it might be for him to stop her rather than her stopping him, the offense fell away when she met the blue of his eyes and felt the way they seemed to swallow her whole.

"I do," he said earnestly.

But Lord Charles was not a man she ought to want. Not a man who should make her stomach flutter with such confusing emotion. Certainly not a man who stayed in the company of a beautiful courtesan.

"Do you think other men will find me so?" she asked.

A muscle worked in his smooth jaw and he stared down at her for so long she felt all the hope in her begin to wilt.

"Yes," he said at last. "Yes, I do."

She breathed a sigh of relief and gently nudged them both forward into a walk, to avoid attention after being gone too long. Already she knew her mother would have more questions about the mysterious man at Hyde Park.

"So I ought to allow myself to show flashes of vulnerability?" she surmised.

"Yes."

She was indeed fortunate to have a man like Lord Charles at her side in this process of social edification, someone insightful and honest. The entire process had begun to pry apart her instilled ideals. Where once politeness and emotional stoicism had dominated her world, now she began to find an appreciation for the candor of her conversations with Lord Charles, and even the instructional detail Lottie provided.

The idea of the two together nipped once more at Eleanor. A reminder, yes, but still a curiosity.

"I confess lowering my shield, as you put it, is difficult," she confided. "I was raised to keep my emotions reined in, that only the common show emotion."

"Most of us are raised to eschew passion and exuberance," Charles replied. "But not to the degree you were."

Eleanor considered his words before replying. "My father was Scottish, and worried he might be judged by the *ton* for it. But he was also a man used to controlling everything. Including his emotions."

"Including you?"

Eleanor flinched at the idea, and at the truth behind it. Everything had always had to be just so with her father. The servants, her mother, the preparations prior to his adventures, even the silly little club he'd been in with his friends and his need to dictate how everything went. She had never really considered the element of his control, and how far it had truly extended.

"Might I ask you something?" she inquired.

"Of course."

Charles's arm was warm under hers...strong. A deep, dormant part of her was tempted to stroke her fingers over his forearm. She shoved the thought aside and held her hand stiffly in place.

"It's not my place to know," she said. "I am merely curious."

"Ask your question, Lady Eleanor."

Very well. She drew in a deep breath and asked the question she couldn't get out of her head. "Are you one of Lottie's lovers?"

Charles's mouth twitched with the beginnings of a laugh. He and Lottie! Lovers!

Truly, the idea was preposterous to imagine. Lottie with her sharp tongue and how well she knew him. He would have all the trouble in the world with a woman like her. And not the kind he might enjoy.

He pressed his lips together to suppress his mirth but a choking chuckle emerged from his throat.

"Lord Charles?" Lady Eleanor peered up at him from beneath the rim of her bonnet. Her brows had pinched downward in an expression of apparent concern.

"Forgive me." He shook his head. "No, I am not one of Lottie's lovers, nor will I ever be."

Lady Eleanor pulled her head forward once more, shadowing her face with that damned bonnet. Her arm on his had gone stiff again.

"I see my mother ahead." Eleanor nodded to a group of women visible through the trees. "I should join them."

Charles found himself disinclined to leave Lady Eleanor's company—a surprising realization. After all, she *was* Westix's daughter.

"I didn't mean to laugh," he offered by way of quick apology. "Lottie and I grew up together as children. I've always viewed her as a sister. So you see I could never possess any romantic inclination toward her. In fact, the very idea… It was unexpected and I found it amusing. Please know I was not laughing at you."

Why was he working so damned hard to reassure her?

"I truly must go." She glanced toward the group of ladies once more. "But I want to tell you how I appreciate the honesty of our discussions. I've never had anyone I could speak so candidly with before. I find it…refreshing."

Her expression was soft—hopeful, even. Had she truly not had anyone she could be sincere with? If that were the case, she had gone her entire life hiding behind the severity of society. Was it any wonder she worried now at pulling down her mask? Especially being the daughter of the Earl of Westix.

Charles was glad he had accepted Lottie's offer to aid Eleanor. It appeared she was as much a victim of her father as they had all been.

"I enjoy our conversations as well." Once the words were out of Charles's mouth he realized he'd spoken with truth. He did appreciate them. Which was an idea that would have rendered his father truly disheartened. The daughter of the Earl of Westix was still a part of the terrible Earl.

She gave Charles a smile that hovered between pleasure and reticence. Her teeth sank into her full lower lip in a most becoming way. Most ladies did it purposely. Lady Eleanor, however, was not the type to attempt so silly a girlish gesture with intent, which made the action all the more alluring.

And, God, but didn't she have a sensual mouth? Full and shaped for kissing, with a slight cleft in her bottom lip. How had he not noticed before?

He watched as she headed in the direction of her mother.

Had it been his imagination, or had her cheeks been stained with a blush before she left him…?

Several hours later he found himself in Lottie's drawing room as they awaited Eleanor's arrival.

She was fascinating, this daughter of his enemy. Through their conversations he was beginning to obtain a comprehension of what had established her unbending fortitude. Her brazen questions had helped him glean a hint of the woman beneath. There was strength there, of course—an inner strength he did not often see in most people—but there was also a hidden hunger for life, something she was afraid to unleash.

"You're smiling," Lottie accused. She pointed at his face. "Did you find what you need for the Coeur de Feu?" She stood up a little taller with excitement. "Do you know where it is?"

Reality crashed into his ruminating. He was consorting with the enemy—*enjoying* it, no less—and was not a single step closer to obtaining the stone.

Charles ground his teeth in frustration and shook his head. "It still eludes me. Damn them for making this so difficult."

"If it isn't the stone…" She pursed her lips and captured him in the line of her scrutiny. Her mouth fell open. "Is it a lady?"

Charles smirked and turned away to fill a glass with liquid resilience, seeing the possibility of a Lottie-mandated inquisition. "I assure you, it is not."

"Oh, pish. You can't fool me." Lottie's voice drew closer as she did. "Everyone is susceptible to love. Even *you*." With the last word, she tapped the tip of his nose.

Love. The idea was laughable. Of all the people to

love, the offspring of the Earl of Westix was the last on Charles's list.

He splashed a bit of Scotch into his glass and slid a sideways glance in her direction. "I find your jaunty assessment reprehensible."

"It's all part of my charm." She propped a hand on her hip and grinned impishly up at him. "Aren't you supposed to wed now that you're a duke?"

"After I've found the stone," Charles muttered into his glass, and took a sip of his Scotch.

The butler appeared through the double doors. "Lady Eleanor has arrived."

Charles kept his face impassive, lest Lottie manage to notice any change in his features. While he did not hold affection for Lady Eleanor, he *was* anticipating seeing her with pleasure. After all, she was softening toward him through their discussions. It would take a few meetings more, but if things continued he would no doubt convince her to give him the journals.

It was only a matter of time.

Chapter Seven

Being open was extremely difficult for Eleanor at her next set of lessons, despite the allure of it. Her first bout of tedious introductions proved her absent genuine appeal, and the second didn't let the feigned enjoyment reach her eyes.

In truth, pleasantness was a trying feat to perform when one's stomach was knotted into a storm of anxiety.

Charles nodded encouragingly at her. "Perhaps think of a humorous thought or event."

"You know ladies are not to give in to the effects of mirth. It's common." She hated her father's words on her own tongue, and yet she could not fully cast them aside. "And it's impossible to think of anything comical with the two of you staring so expectantly at me. As if I'm…on display. It's most unsettling."

Lottie tapped a finger on her bottom lip in contemplation before jolting upright suddenly. "I have an idea. Do excuse me."

Charles met Eleanor's gaze in the empty room—too

beautifully blue, too familiar. The unease in her stomach tightened.

"Smile at me," he said. "I promise not to ravish you in the time Lottie is gone."

He winked at her, the rogue.

Eleanor stretched a smile over her lips once more. Her mouth trembled with the effort.

Lord Charles cocked an eyebrow in a debonair display of consideration. "You look like you're trying too hard to smile."

The man was insufferable.

"I *am* trying too hard to smile," she exclaimed.

"Well, it's coming across as a blend of grimace and snarl, as though you intend to tear out my throat."

A smile did come to her lips then, natural and easy. "And what if that was my intention?"

"I prefer nibbles to bites," he answered. "Just below my ear, if you should like to know."

Eleanor's tongue went thick in her mouth and stuck fast, paralyzing the prospect of saying anything witty or even vaguely intelligible. Her stare drifted to his neck, where strong muscle showed at his tanned throat. Was he serious? About nibbling his neck?

After all, how *did* one nibble against another's skin? Was it in dainty pinches between the front teeth, as when she ate at the edges of a delicious marzipan flower, too pretty to eat and too delicate to keep? Or perhaps an act akin to the nip of one's lip in a moment of consideration?

And how would it feel? To the one being nibbled and the one doing the nibbling?

Lottie reappeared suddenly with a basket carefully

propped against her hip. "I believe these ought to elicit some warmth."

She set the basket carefully on the ground. Eleanor leaned close and lifted the blanket on the top to reveal a lazy gray tabby nestled along the bottom. Half a dozen puffs of gray-and-white fur wriggled over her soft belly.

"I thought Silky had been getting fat on her complacent life here in London." Lottie stroked the mother cat's head, affectionately rubbing her ears. A contented purr vibrated in the air. "Turns out she was merely in a delicate way. Aren't they terribly precious?"

She scooped up one of the furry bundles with her cupped hand and cradled it to her chest. The mother watched vigilantly as her baby was taken. A squeaking cry came from the ball of fur, repetitive and desperate.

Lottie pressed a kiss to the tiny gray head and grinned at Eleanor. "Would you like to hold one?" She cradled her hands around the small bundle and its cries fell silent as it snuggled against her.

An eager excitement dashed through Eleanor. "The mother won't mind?"

"Silky is grateful for the reprieve, and I know you'll be gentle."

At Lottie's words, the gray tabby licked her paw and scrubbed at her face, confirming her mistress's claims. Eleanor did not wait for a second invitation. With the same care she'd seen Lottie utilize, Eleanor lifted up the wriggling warmth of a new kitten.

The pitching mewls of protest began immediately and a fat belly writhed against her palm. The kitten's claws dug into Eleanor's skin like miniature needles, but she was not so easily deterred. She cooed quietly to the baby and tucked it against her chest. The mewling ceased.

"Focus on how you're feeling right now," Lottie said in a low, soothing voice. "The kitten offers no judgment, no scrutinizing assessment. You are protection and you are comfort to her. Let yourself cast aside your fears and embrace the quiet delight of such a treasure. There is no need to ever be afraid of being who you are."

Eleanor set her attention to Lottie's words. The kitten's belly rose and fell with even breaths beneath a delicate set of ribs and its blue eyes blinked slowly closed. How very precious. And how true were the words of instruction.

There was nothing to be afraid of here, in the presence of people she trusted, while cradling a small cat who had fallen asleep cupped between her palm and her chest.

"Lady Eleanor..."

Lottie's smooth voice nudged into Eleanor's enjoyment of a kitten lying fast asleep just above her heart.

"I'd like to introduce you to Lord Charles."

Eleanor looked up and found Charles watching her with a smile quirking his full mouth. She beamed up at him. "It's lovely to meet you, Lord Charles." The kitten shifted at the sound of her voice and climbed higher on her gown with its needlelike claws. Eleanor couldn't help but giggle at its clumsy movements. "I'd curtsey, but I am otherwise detained. I do hope you'll forgive me?"

"If you swear to look at me like that again someday, I will forgive you any transgression."

There was a low softness to his tone and it pulled at something deep within her chest. He was watching her with a pensive expression that made the skin around his eyes tighten in a very alluring manner.

"Lady Eleanor, you are a beautiful young woman, but when you smile you are wholly and completely captivating."

Captivating?

Her?

She'd always been prim, proper and well-behaved. Perhaps beautiful, if she were inclined to believe his prior compliments. But captivating—never.

"Thank you." She said it in a clear voice, which was a wonder in and of itself when the rest of her had turned suddenly weak and trembling.

She turned her attention where it was the safest in application—to the slumbering ball of warmth nestled against her chest. Emotions held exceptional power. She'd spent her entire life fighting against them, squeezing, strapping and binding them into a solitary, biddable place. How could she simply let loose the stays? Would they not all explode in a riot of chaos?

There was perhaps only one way to find out: to cast her fate to the stars and allow Lottie to help pull free the ties.

Charles had grudgingly admitted that Eleanor was a pretty woman. Even her red hair, which some of the *ton* had described as gaudy, he found uniquely fascinating in the way it set off the creaminess of her skin. But when she smiled, truly smiled, it transformed her face into a beauty no one could deny.

Good God. If she greeted every man with such open affection, and if they all were granted the glint of those bewitching green eyes, Lady Eleanor would be in no danger of consigning herself to a spinster's life.

The kitten had settled itself contentedly against the elegant curve of her collarbone. Funny that Charles hadn't noticed before the lovely smoothness of her fair skin, the graceful arch of her long neck.

Lottie caught Charles's eye. She lifted her brows in a confident manner which radiated the unctuous touting of her victory.

For her part, Lady Eleanor had dropped her attention back to the furry body cuddled against her.

"Now that you've been properly introduced, perhaps we ought to progress to conversation," said Lottie, and carefully lifted the kitten from her lap and replaced it alongside its mother.

Lady Eleanor removed the kitten from her chest and laughed softly as the beast tried to crawl back up her arm. After a few moments she freed the creature and returned it to its mother. The smile hovered in her eyes and left a particularly lovely flush to her cheeks.

Lottie gently set aside the basket in a quiet corner of the room and pulled the blanket over it. Lady Eleanor elegantly rose to her feet and he saw the familiar stiffness take up residence in her shoulders. But then after a lifetime of wearing such rigidity it could not be cast aside with the ease of a cloak. It would take time…practice.

Except all the time it took to perfect was time Charles was without the journals.

He had been sitting on the floor beside the ladies, but now pushed himself to his feet without ceremony. After all, there was no proper protocol for the etiquette involving ladies on the ground playing with animals.

Now standing, he offered a courteous bow. "How are you this evening, Lady Eleanor?"

The transformation was immediate. The light in her eyes was shuttered, leaving stark politeness in its place.

"I'm well, thank you." Her words were devoid of the

friendliness they'd been brimming with only moments before. "And how are you?"

"Well, thank you. I wonder if I might be fortunate enough to claim you for a dance?" He grinned down at her in the hope that she might relax more. "Forgive me for being so bold, but I must say you look lovely this evening."

She gave a perfunctory smile. "Thank you. I'd be honored to dance with you."

A thick and uncomfortable silence thudded between them.

Lady Eleanor's brow puckered. "This is terribly awkward…"

"Perhaps I may offer some suggestions." Lottie appeared beside them. "You are a reader, from what I understand?"

Lady Eleanor's face lit up. "I am."

"And do you immerse yourself in the stories when you read them?"

"Oh, indeed," breathed Lady Eleanor.

Charles stared in wonder. Was Lady Eleanor truly being *wistful*?

"Close your eyes and imagine being a character in one of your favorite books during a romantic scene."

The expression on Lady Eleanor's face relaxed, and when she opened her eyes once more there was intimacy in her expression. Lottie nudged Charles and nodded at him.

He offered Lady Eleanor the lazy half smile women had always seemed to hold in high regard. "Good evening, Lady Eleanor. You look enchanting. I trust you are well?"

Lady Eleanor peered up at him through a veil of black lashes. "Quite, thank you. And yourself?"

Good God. "All the better now."

A tinge of color swept over her cheeks. A glint of something mischievous shone in her eyes. When she looked at him like that, as if she were teasing him with a secret, he could stare at her all day. It was suddenly too easy to imagine her laid out on a chaise longue, the top of her gown falling from a naked shoulder, that glorious red hair spilling over the swell of her breasts.

"Dance with me this evening." He hadn't said it as an invitation or an offer. It was a command, and one he wished he had the right to make.

She met his eyes and held his gaze. "With pleasure, My Lord."

He held out his hand and she took it, her kid leather gloves soft in his palm.

"Superb…" Lottie's voice stole into the private moment.

Charles eased back at once, granting room for her to approach. The interruption was exactly what he had needed.

Westix.

The reminder blared through his mind. She was the daughter of his enemy. He was here for the journals. What the devil was he doing, letting himself be swept away by a mere smile?

"Lady Eleanor, how simply marvelous." Lottie clapped aloud, as if it were an opera that played out before her instead of a conversation. "You let a piece of yourself free. I saw it on your face. One such look to a man will make him feel important. He will not be able to stop his thoughts from fixing on you, focused and wonderfully enraptured."

It appeared Lottie had a strong grasp of what made up the male mind. Charles did his best not to be affronted by her perfectly accurate assessment.

Eleanor inclined her head graciously, accepting the praise with humble pride. "Your instruction has been integral, Lottie." Those green eyes turned on Charles and her mouth opened in preparation to speak.

A knock sounded at the great double doors. The footman entered and announced that Eleanor's carriage had arrived.

"Has it been an hour already?" she exclaimed.

"It has, unfortunately," Lottie replied. "Shall we expect you tomorrow?"

Lady Eleanor settled the blonde wig on her head, albeit slightly askew. "Please do. Especially if I might see the kittens once more."

Lottie laughed, and Charles felt his own lips teased into a smile by her gleeful hope.

"You may certainly see the kittens once more." Lottie delicately straightened the wig, so all the bounty of that red hair lay hidden by the coiffure of pale tresses.

Once Eleanor had departed, Charles turned his attention to Lottie and found her watching him with a small smirk, her hand propped against her hip.

"You were in rare form tonight, Your Grace." She lowered her head and teased him with a coy expression. "I think you've changed your mind about Lady Eleanor."

Indeed, he had not. A lovely smile or no, the woman was still the offspring of the Earl of Westix. Even if he'd made her life as difficult as he'd made Charles's. And, while Lottie was aware of Charles's need to acquire the journals from Eleanor, she didn't know it was his primary reason for accepting the opportunity to aid her in this bizarre venture.

He brushed at a bit of kitten fur on his sleeve and didn't deign to reply.

"Hmmm…"

Lottie nodded slowly, her head tilted in purposeful observation, her gaze sharpening too perceptively for his taste. As though she knew something he did not. And he didn't like it one bit.

Chapter Eight

The following evening Charles took his time, deliberately not arriving early at Lottie's. He refused to feed her implication that he might harbor affection for Lady Eleanor. Indeed, he rejected the very idea. Why, his father would turn about in his grave at such a consideration.

"Any more discoveries in your search for the stone?" Lottie asked, once they were settled in the drawing room.

A servant entered and placed a glass of sherry on the small side table, the same as was done every night when Lady Eleanor came.

"She never drinks it." He nodded to the full glass.

"It's there if she wants it." Lottie shrugged and turned her attention back to him. "And that's a no on the stone, I assume?"

He had uncovered nothing of use in the pile of boxes from the country estate. Not that he'd expected his efforts to yield what he needed. After all, his father would have easily uncovered the ruby's location if the necessary information had been in his possession. No, Westix had to have it. Why else would the late Earl have refused to relinquish any of his items?

Charles tapped his finger impatiently on the mahogany tabletop holding various bottles of liquor. "If only I had *all* the journals."

If only he were close enough to Lady Eleanor to ask her for them. But he'd made far too much headway with her to risk losing all by asking too precipitously. Especially with Lottie's future at risk.

"Have you ever considered approaching the Countess of Westix for them?" Lottie asked.

He gave a grunt of dissatisfaction. "And have Lady Eleanor discover who I am?"

"She'll find out eventually. Do you truly think you can keep up this charade and fool her forever?"

"It was your decision to introduce me as Lord Charles."

Lottie threw her hair over her shoulder and gave him a saucy look. "I hadn't planned on you getting so close with her."

The doors opened, saving him from having to respond. The subject of their conversation entered in a whisper of silk, her cheeks pink from the chill of the night air.

"I have been invited to Lady Covington's masquerade ball this Tuesday. Do you think I might be ready in time?"

"I have no doubt you will," Lottie answered with great enthusiasm. "Being masked will make it all the more convenient. It will keep you from being overly formal, help you to be more yourself. You will be *wonderful*."

"Wonderful" was not a word in Charles's vocabulary at present. After all, a suitor would distract Lady Eleanor from

Charles and impede his opportunity to become well enough acquainted to beseech her for the journals.

"My mother is delighted with the change she claims she sees in me already," Lady Eleanor continued, oblivious to his lack of enthusiasm. "She is convinced I'll be an enormous success and has already secured a time for me to meet with a modiste tomorrow afternoon, to have a new costume fashioned." Lady Eleanor hesitated and bit her lip in a rare show of nervousness. "Are you quite sure I'll be ready? I've had more failures than successes, and I don't think I can carry a kitten with me in my reticule."

Lottie settled a comforting hand on Lady Eleanor's shoulder. "We have several more lessons before the night of the masquerade, and your mask will help embolden you. Mark my words, you'll be magnificent."

"Have you chosen your costume?" Charles asked, more boorishly than he'd intended.

Something rather unpleasant knotted in his stomach, and he didn't like it any more than he relished the opportunity slipping through his fingers.

Lady Eleanor had distinctly caught his note of disapproval, because her attention fell on him and her brows flinched. "An Ice Queen."

Lottie clapped in pleasure. Charles drowned a groan with some brandy. He could envision her all too well, sparkling in a wash of white, pale blue and glittering crystal, and giving the brilliant smile that transformed her prettiness into real beauty. Suitors would be crawling about her like ants on a dropped pastry.

Even in his fog of personal misery he couldn't ignore how clever the costume truly was. After all, what better way to make her entrance into the good graces of the *ton* than by throwing their own very moniker for her in their face?

"Pray tell, what do you envision for your gown?" Lottie asked, with excitement gleaming on her face.

Charles did not bother to listen to the reply—not when his mind was spinning around the discomfort of his own internalizations. He had several days before the ball. If he pressed his luck the odds might be in his favor. But if he pressed too hard he might ruin his chances.

There was always the option of the truth, of course. Lady Eleanor did not yet know who he was, nor what his identity might mean to her family. He was unsure how Westix's family regarded his father.

So, either he could tell Lady Eleanor the truth and ask her outright for the journals, while hoping for her compliance. Or...

Or he could have Thomas find out when Lady Eleanor would be at the modiste and he could go to Westix Place to meet with the Countess. Lady Eleanor need not ever be aware of their meeting.

Once he had what he required, and if the information necessary was indeed in the journals, he would be gone once more and the deception of Lord Charles would be inconsequential.

"Lord Charles, are you well?" Lady Eleanor's voice pulled him from his thoughts.

"Of course."

He set his unfinished brandy down. If he was going to call on the Countess of Westix the next day he had to begin preparations. After all, Thomas was good, but even he needed time.

"If you'll excuse me? I must take my leave."

Lottie's mouth fell open. "Now?"

"Yes. There are matters which require my attention. I am unsure if I can make it tomorrow evening. Or the night following that." Charles straightened the lapels of his jacket rather than allow himself to meet the shocked stares of the two ladies. "Forgive me."

"Please do stay, Lord Charles." Lady Eleanor approached him.

The sweet jasmine scent drew his attention. He met her imploring expression.

"I can't do this without you." Her smooth forehead furrowed. "I feel as though I'm finally beginning to comprehend what's expected of me. But I need *you*."

She needed him. Such a caress to his ego. But needing him in the flippant way she did would not grant him what he wanted.

"You have been ideal to practice with," she added. "And I've truly appreciated it."

Part of him wished they had more time, that there might be more of an opportunity to procure her trust and friendship. And yet her father Westix remained lodged in Charles's mind. Westix and the wrong done to Charles's own father.

This woman was not for him. Marriage was not for him. Not when the need to explore ran in his blood and the Coeur de Feu still needed to be found. He required those journals with urgency.

Utilizing that thought, Charles steeled himself for what he must do. "Forgive me, Lady Eleanor." He bowed low, more to break the hold of her gaze than for civility's sake. "You are in superb care with Lottie, and you will excel at flirtation at the ball. I am certain you will be the Diana of the matrimonial hunt."

Without another word, he straightened and strode from the room, set on seeing his promise fulfilled.

Eleanor had developed doubts about attending the modiste appointment that afternoon. Life had been so very different when she hadn't been aware of their dire financial circumstances. And so, when her mother had fallen prey to the crippling effects of another one of her headaches, Eleanor had been all too eager to cancel the appointment and remain at home with the ailing Countess.

That choice led to a fascinating series of events—beginning with Eleanor taking tea with her mother in the drawing room. Oftentimes taking tea soothed the rougher edges of the Countess's debilitation.

Their butler, Edmonds, entered the room, with a silver tray perched atop his fingertips. He stopped before the Countess, presenting the tray with his usual grace. Her mother lifted the card from it between the pinch of her fingers and her lips tucked down at the corners.

Eleanor sat higher in her seat, attempting with what she hoped was discretion to read over her mother's shoulder. Without success. The print on the card was too small from where she sat.

The Countess nodded at Edmonds. "Send him in and tell Bessie to bring in another setting for tea."

"As you wish, my lady."

"Someone will be joining us?" Eleanor inquired politely.

The Countess cast a dubious look her way and lifted a brow. "Don't think I didn't catch you craning your neck. I appreciate you taking to your new lessons with such sincerity, but please ensure your manners do not suffer."

Chastened, Eleanor regarded the bits of tea leaf floating about the bottom of her dainty porcelain cup.

"If you must know," her mother began, "our visitor is His Grace the Duke of Somersville."

Somersville… The name was familiar.

"He and your father were at university together. They had their…" her mother swept her hand through the air with a disdainful gesture "…their *club* together. Until they fought like children over some of the items they'd found and ruined the club along with their friendship."

She sighed and rattled off the details with the ennui of a person reciting a list of tedious daily tasks.

"The Duke died in his sleep several months past. I'd heard his son was out adventuring and has now returned to claim his title, his estate, and most likely the dusty relics from our study."

The slight roll of the Countess's eyes was all the explanation Eleanor needed to know what her mother thought of the Duke. She understood now why she recalled the name. Her father's face had turned purple every time the name Somersville had been mentioned. There had even been an incident when the Duke had paid a visit and shouting had been heard from the study.

Whoever the new Duke of Somersville was, he was not a friend of the family.

"Why did they quarrel?" Eleanor spoke in a quiet voice to keep their conversation from carrying down the hall, where the Duke might overhear.

Her mother took a careful sip of her tea. "Mummies' bones, fragments of old pottery and the like. The lot of it is a bunch of dreary rubbish, if you ask me. I gave the previous Duke nearly everything he asked for after your father died, having no purpose for it myself. It would appear his son is under the illusion that I have been inclined to retain some." She set her cup in the saucer. "The Somersvilles are nothing if not persistent. I know if I decline seeing him now there will be another card tomorrow and another the next day until I finally concede."

Unwelcome Duke or not, this would be the first person Eleanor had met since she'd begun her specialized edification with Lottie and Lord Charles in earnest. Her nerves disturbed the mirrored surface of her tea with a perceptible tremble. She set her cup down, lest it rattle in its saucer.

Should she use this Duke for practice? A test prior to her grand attempt at Lady Covington's masquerade ball?

Her father would be appalled if he were alive. And *that* was the final reason she needed to convince herself it was a good idea.

She ran through the instructions in her head. *Be kind, be genuine, make eye contact, smile. Pretend you have a kitten in your lap.*

She looked down at her empty lap. For the life of her she could not recall the feelings the kitten had evoked. But she could make out the perfect seedcake on her plate, and had the sudden urge to nibble a piece before the Duke arrived.

Was that the kind of nibbling Lord Charles had alluded to?

The thought popped in her head, unbidden and unexpected. A newly familiar heat rose in her cheeks. It was rather shameful, really, how often the memory of that conversation played itself in her mind, and the curiosity it aroused.

"Eleanor, have you heard a word I've said? What ails you, child?"

Her mother's admonishment sliced through the endless winding of Eleanor's wayward musing.

"And why in heaven's name do you keep staring at your lap?"

"I'm looking at the kitten."

The words slipped from Eleanor's mouth before she could stop them, and earned her a baffled, reproachful look from her mother. Fortunately it was at that exact moment that the dastardly Duke of Somersville entered their drawing room.

Lottie's most important words whispered in Eleanor's mind: *Believe in yourself.*

She looked up—but the warm smile gliding over her lips froze and swiftly faded.

For it wasn't the Duke of Somersville at all, standing before her.

The man who strode proudly into the room, with his fathomless blue eyes and immaculately tailored jacket, was none other than Lord Charles.

Chapter Nine

Damn. Charles had not expected to see Lady Eleanor beside her mother, the Countess of Westix. He was, in fact, so surprised he almost asked why she hadn't gone to the modiste as planned.

He bowed low to cover his shock. "Good afternoon, Your Ladyship."

Lady Eleanor's mother was a handsome woman, with a fine bone structure beneath a face almost untouched by age. Her green eyes were sharp with the scrutiny of assessment.

"Allow me to introduce my daughter—Lady Eleanor Murray."

Her words were hesitant, as if she hadn't wanted to say them. He might be a duke, but the Countess found him wanting.

Lady Eleanor offered a smile so hard and brittle it made the baring of her teeth in those earlier sessions appear friendly by comparison. "It's a pleasure to meet you, Your

Grace." And by "pleasure" she unmistakably meant not at all anything remotely pleasant.

Rather remarkably like when Charles had first met her.

"Do sit down." The Countess indicated the empty place setting for him.

Truth be told, he'd rather take tea in the company of vipers at this point than the ladies of Westix Place. The vipers would doubtless prove less dangerous. But he had arrived with a purpose, and he could not back down simply because events had not transpired as expected.

He gave his thanks and settled himself opposite the ladies on a dainty rose-colored chair. "You've added new wall coverings." He nodded to the spread of saffron-yellow silk along the walls, with painted birds flitting about its glossy expanse.

"Several years ago," the Countess stated dryly. "It's been some time since we've been graced with your company. Would you have some tea?"

Graced indeed. Charles nodded. "Yes, strong, if you please."

While the Countess's attentions were otherwise occupied, Charles chanced a glance in the direction of her daughter. Red stained Lady Eleanor's cheeks and her eyes glittered with a hidden emotion she would not permit her face to convey. Regardless of her hiding what she was feeling, he knew it was not good.

Forgive me, he mouthed.

She cut her gaze from him.

"Your Grace…" The Countess offered him a cup of black tea.

The Countess of Westix *did* pour a good cup of tea. So long as it wasn't laced with poison.

"Thank you. Your tea is always top-notch."

"You flatter me." She did not appear flattered. She appeared as though she wished to be anywhere but there. "I presume there is a reason for your visit?"

He ought to ask for the journals and be done with it. It was, after all, why he'd come. A quick glance at Lady Eleanor's tightly pressed mouth and her blatant attempt to keep from meeting his gaze were evidence enough of her anger at his ruse. Asking for the journals would surely leave her further incensed.

The Countess plucked a lump of sugar with the sugar tongs and lifted her brows with impatient expectation.

Damn it. There was only one thing he might do and possibly retain his budding relationship with Lady Eleanor and get the hell out of this mess.

Charles held his cup and blew at a curl of steam while he gathered his composure. "I intend to court your daughter and came to seek your approval."

The Countess's mouth fell open and the lump of sugar splashed into her tea with an indelicate plop. "Surely you jest?"

The skin along the back of his neck prickled with Charles's awareness of Lady Eleanor's observation. He glanced in her direction and found her staring at him not like a woman eager to be courted by a duke, but a woman wholly and completely bewildered.

Frustration tightened through him. Why the devil hadn't she gone to the modiste?

"I do not jest," he said levelly.

"I was not aware you had even been introduced." The Countess of Westix stirred her tea, seemingly quite recovered. "You are the son of the Duke of Somersville and a member of the Adventure Club. I have seen the accounts of what transpired within that club." Her lip curled with censure. "I am well aware that you have begun traveling, as your father once did, and I can assure you that you will never acquire leave to court my daughter."

Charles's heart thudded harder in his chest. The Countess of Westix had seen accounts of the club's adventures. The journals. She *did* have them.

Her face had gone an unpleasant shade of red and she had folded her lips on themselves in an obvious attempt to stop herself from saying more. "Is that all, Your Grace?" She drew out the last words, making the title seem less of an honor and more of an offense.

"Yes, I believe it is." Charles set his tea on the table, regrettably untouched, and got to his feet. "Thank you for your time, Your Ladyship." He let his gaze finally fall on Eleanor and found her staring up at him, her expression unreadable, her cheeks a bright red. He nodded in her direction. "Lady Eleanor."

He bowed to them both.

"Good afternoon, Your Grace." The Countess of Westix lifted her tea to her mouth, took a sip, and looked out through the window into the gardens with an air of clear dismissal.

Charles took his leave, stopping only to gather his hat and coat from the footman, and even those he was sorely tempted to abandon in an attempt to flee all the faster.

Having faced such utter failure in his alternative attempt to collect the journals from the Countess, he was now forced back to his initial idea—to win over Lady Eleanor and convince her to give it to him.

He only hoped he had not pushed her away with the unexpected shock of his offer to court her and with the greatness of his lie. But, more than that, he hated it that this new change in plan might somehow see her hurt.

After an hour of her mother's fuming, and far too many seedcakes, Eleanor made her way to her room. No longer was she in shock—she was angry.

How dared Lord Charles—*His Grace the Duke*—put her in such a position?

She'd had to lie, of course, building on his perfidy in order to protect Lottie, who had doubtless had no part in this. Eleanor could not abide the idea of that sweet woman receiving punishment from the Countess of Westix for Somersville's deceit. But why had he asked to court Eleanor?

Why not wait until the ball, allow himself to be properly introduced to her, and *then* ask to court her?

The idea of him doing exactly that swam in her mind. Him impossibly handsome in some roguish costume, her in a glittering gown made for an Ice Queen, taking a turn about the room, dancing, laughing, speaking at length.

It was a whimsical dream. Most likely a foolish one.

A nudge of something uncomfortable crawled into her mind. She'd mentioned she would be at the modiste. How terribly odd that he should arrive unexpectedly to offer courtship when he had known she would be out.

She recalled the look of choked surprise when he first saw her. He had not expected her to be there.

For all his bravado in speaking out to her mother, Eleanor knew one thing for certain: he had not visited in order to ask to court her. He'd been there for something else, and she would find out exactly what he was after.

Chapter Ten

Charles hadn't thought Lady Eleanor's back could possibly get any straighter. But then she hadn't known him to be so blatant a liar and a fraud before. His stomach swam with unease as he peered through the door crack to where Lady Eleanor was perched tightly on a chair in Lottie's drawing room.

This was not going to go smoothly.

Lottie nodded at him, and he knew it was time to make their wrongs right. She strode in first, with Charles following behind her, as they'd always done.

Lady Eleanor rose from the stiff-backed seat she hadn't truly needed and turned a blank face in his direction. Despite her implacability, her cheeks were flushed with a brilliant red, as they'd been during tea. She was not as unaffected as she would have liked herself to be perceived.

Charles stepped around Lottie. "Lady Eleanor, I can explain. If you'd give me—"

"I understand well enough." Her eyes flashed behind her

emotionless mask. "You thought I'd be at the modiste, and you presumed to impose upon my mother in my absence so your identity might remain a secret. My presence startled you into offering to court me rather than admit your true purpose."

Well. There wasn't much more to add to it than that. She'd surmised it quite succinctly. Surprisingly and rather unfortunately.

"You lied to me when I confided in you."

Her voice gave a delicate tremble. The slight break in her tightly reined composure cut into him more deeply than any slice she could make with her tongue.

"Why were you there?"

Charles remained mute, unable to tell her, unable even to open his mouth under the weight of the truth.

Lady Eleanor scoffed. "You can't even *tell* me? After you lied about why you were there? After you lied about your title? After you lied about finding me desirable enough to court?"

"It was me," Lottie said softly. "I didn't tell you he was a duke. I only meant to keep you from casting him out due to your fathers' association. I knew he would be ideal to assist you and I trust him implicitly."

Lady Eleanor regarded Lottie for a long moment. When she finally spoke, Charles knew the words were meant for him.

"Your trust is more steadfast than my own. But then he did not seek to avoid you as a means of taking advantage of your mother. He did not make a fool of you."

Lady Eleanor drew in a long, slow breath and carefully let it out, the inhalation and exhalation both very apparent in the silence of the room. "I need your help, Lottie, or I would leave posthaste. The Duke of Somersville, however, is no longer necessary, and I find his assistance bothersome. Will you be so kind as to ask him to leave?"

The request smacked Charles in the chest like a punch. This woman who had confided in him with their candid discussions, who had smiled at him with all the warmth of a summer sun, was now casting him out. But then, he truly deserved it. His deception had been deplorable and his cover attempt unforgivable.

Lottie pulled her head back, as if she too had been viscerally struck by so powerful a request. She turned to Charles, all pretense of poise and her newly adopted sensuality giving way to wide-eyed shock. Her mouth opened and closed without issuing either an order or a protest.

Charles would not be able to call himself a gentleman if he left Lottie in the awkward predicament of having to choose between her sole pupil and source of income and her lifelong friend.

He bowed first to Lady Eleanor, and his heart dragged into his stomach as though it had been affixed with a weight. "Forgive me my transgressions. I understand that they were egregious and hope you do not seek to exact your frustrations upon Lottie, as she truly wants nothing more than to help you succeed." Next he bowed to Lottie. "I shall take my leave."

Lottie nodded, her eyes luminous with regret and quiet gratitude.

He strode from the room with all the confidence a cad such as he could muster. His error had been egregious indeed, and the cost had been heavy. Aside from jeopardizing the opportunity to reclaim the journals, he had also compromised his ability to help Lottie in her new endeavor. There was also the loss of Lady Eleanor's hard-won trust.

The entire ordeal left his stomach knotted and a dull, aching sensation in his chest.

Rather than show him out, Lottie's butler escorted him to the library. "Miss Lottie will wish to speak with you once Lady Eleanor has gone."

Charles gave him an appreciative nod and sank into an oversized chair beside the hearth. He stared into the flames, watching them writhe and twist against one another as a similar inferno blazed within him.

At long last, the door to the library groaned open.

"She's gone," Lottie said in a somber tone. "And she's quite upset. I do not believe she trusts often...but I think— I think she did trust you."

Charles closed his eyes against the pain of Lottie's words. There was more truth to what she said than he wanted to admit. He knew Lady Eleanor had indeed spoken to him in confidence. Their conversation on the path flashed back to him, when she'd thanked him for his honesty and expressed her genuine appreciation for having an opportunity to speak frankly. She'd given him her confidence and he'd responded with betrayal.

He'd hurt her.

The thought made something in his heart wrench painfully.

Regaining his composure, he rose from the chair and faced Lottie. "I should have told her the truth about my title."

Her brow creased. "I never should have put you in that situation. I worried it would frighten her off."

"I never should have gone to her mother." Charles put into

words his deepest regrets. "Nor should I have attempted to hide my true purpose by asking to court her. Rather than flatter her, I have deeply offended her." He shook his head. "I do not know how to fix this, Lottie."

She sighed—a weary, defeated sound. "And you have not acquired what you need to find your lost stone."

Charles blinked. The journals. Yes. He had not even considered them in light of his misdeeds. *Damn.* But how the devil did Lottie know...?

"How did you know I needed information from her?" Charles asked.

Lottie gave him a sad smile. "Because I know you far too well, Charles. Your hatred for Westix is strong enough that there would need to be a motivation greater than myself to lure you into aiding me in this endeavor."

Charles truly was a cad. He ground his back teeth, but it did not quell the disgust tightening through him.

"But you still assisted me." Lottie patted his forearm. "I know if I'd come to you for help when I needed it all those years ago you would have been there."

"I would have been," Charles said resolutely. "I still would now."

Lottie's mouth tucked at the corner. "You needn't worry about me, but I *would* like you to make things right with Lady Eleanor."

Charles scoffed. "I doubt she will speak to me ever again."

"I disagree." Lottie tapped her lips in thought. "Go to the masquerade ball."

Charles wished he had a glass of liquor in his hand—something strong enough to burn away the ache in his chest. "She has no desire to see me."

"Nor talk to you, nor hear your explanation. But if you're at the ball with her…" Lottie smiled and gave a musing nod at her own plan. "She can't refuse a dance with you—unless she isn't planning to dance at all, which we know she won't do. It will be the perfect opportunity to explain yourself."

Truly, the idea was preposterous. His actions had only proved correct everything she'd grown up learning: it was best for him to stay behind an unaffected shield and to dim all emotion.

"I would suggest honesty this time." Lottie leveled her gaze at him. "What other choice do you have?"

A heavy sigh pressed from his lungs. "You're right." He owed it to his father to try again to get those journals. And he owed it to Lady Eleanor, whom he had never thought he would be beholden to, to explain the breach of her hard-won trust.

"Of course I am." Lottie gave a nonchalant shoulder-lift at her victory. "So you'll go?"

"As long as I can get an invitation on such short notice."

Lottie laughed at that. "You're the new Duke of Somersville, just arrived into London after a five-year absence during which you traveled the world in search of ancient treasure. You could show up in rags and they'd still welcome you."

No doubt his appearance would set all the tongues wagging. He cringed at the idea. "I'll go as a pirate," he said grudgingly.

Lottie's expression became serious. "I know you loathe balls, and other such social functions, but Lady Eleanor is going to be nervous. She could use a friendly face to settle her nerves." She tilted her head in consideration. "Or at least a familiar one. Someone to help ward off the legions of suitors who will seek her attention."

Charles narrowed his eyes. *Legions of suitors.* He nearly scoffed again. But then recalled his idea of her gown, of how she would appear as an Ice Queen with her fire-red hair. Lottie was correct.

"I've said I'll go," he said gruffly. Grumpily, really, if he was being honest. "So I can have another shot at getting my father's journals," he added for good measure.

"Of course. For the journals."

Lottie gave him a coy look he did not think he liked. But, while he didn't appreciate her implication, or the annoying way she tapped his nose after she said it, he was looking forward to another opportunity to claim the journals.

And, blast it, he was anticipating with pleasure seeing Lady Eleanor as well.

To make things right, of course.

Or so he told himself.

Eleanor's decision to be an Ice Queen for the masquerade ball had been the product of the mind of the woman she *wanted* to be, not necessarily the woman she truly was. In her mind, wearing the dazzling pale-blue-and-white gown would make her heedless of people's opinions. She'd thought she might sweep into the ball like a queen, make the wittiest of remarks and confidently meet the eye of every eligible peer in the room.

She could not have been more wrong.

Everything she'd recently learned cautioned her against giving in to the desire to frost over, while every innate defense within her demanded she curl up inside herself. What was left was a very miserable and socially confused Eleanor. Her mother's expectant stare did not help, and nor did the pressing watchfulness of the masked attendees.

Why, why, *why* had she insisted on trying to throw the *ton*'s words back at them? And why had her mother insisted on her having the costume made?

Now Eleanor was merely a fool draped in a costly gown and the burden of intense disappointment.

No one had approached her…no one had asked her to dance. No one had even bothered to acknowledge her or beg an introduction. The weight of failure crushed in on her. She tried to stave off such thoughts, and instead repeated the rules Lottie had given her.

Smile. Be sincere. Make eye contact. Believe in yourself.

Those last words made her want to give a choke of laughter. For how could she believe in herself when she didn't even feel comfortable behind a physical mask?

Even as she tried to relax, every muscle in her body locked up, followed by the stiffening of her limbs and the straightening of her back to an impossible level of rigidity. The shield was up, locked so tightly in place that it could not be brought down by all the kittens in London.

"Lady Eleanor."

The smooth, masculine voice was entirely too familiar. Her stomach twisted in anger and her heart gave a walloping thump against her ribs. She turned and met the brilliant ocean-blue eyes of the Duke of Somersville.

A fascinating thing happened then—for, despite the hostility of her ire, and in spite of the lies of omission and blatant betrayal offered by the Duke, Eleanor immediately felt herself soften.

"Your Grace." She offered a slight curtsey.

"You did dress as an Ice Queen after all."

His mouth quirked up. The arrogance in his expression scraped over her ragged nerves.

"Evidently," she replied.

"Ah…an unforgiving Ice Queen," he amended.

Eleanor glanced over the black fitted breeches, ruffled shirt and old-fashioned black jacket. The growth of hair on his jaw was unshaven, giving him a dangerous air. In fact, all of him appeared rather dangerous and far too alluring.

"And what are you? A rogue? *Lord Charles?*"

The Duke of Somersville swept into an elaborate bow and straightened. "I am a humble pirate."

"Shouldn't you possess at least a modicum of humility in order to refer to yourself as humble?"

He smirked. "Touché! You make me regret leaving my sword at home. I hadn't realized I'd be up against so sharp a wit."

Eleanor found her lips curling into a smile. She was flirting, she realized, and comfortably. What was more, she was enjoying herself immensely, even though she was furious with him. How could he make her do that when she was so irate still?

His expression turned serious—a rather becoming look with his whisker-darkened jaw. "Dance with me, my unforgiving Ice Queen."

She studied him for a long moment, the answer hovering on her tongue. "If I refuse…?"

"I daresay your mother might be glad of it. But you won't refuse me. To do so would be considered rude, and the Ice Queen, while unforgiving, is anything but rude." He held out his arm to her.

"Am I so predictable?" She slid her arm through his.

"No, actually." He grinned at her, his teeth all the more startling white against his whiskered jaw. "Not at all."

The quiet amusement in his tone created a slow, pleasant warmth in her stomach as he led her through the room toward the dance floor.

"It was inexcusable for me to lie to you." His voice was little more than a low hum beneath the chatter of surrounding conversations.

The quiet joy in her ebbed. "You made me a fool."

Heat scorched her cheeks and suddenly she regretted her decision to dance with him. She would take ill manners over yet another humiliation at the hands of this man.

"No." His eyes locked on hers. "I was the fool. I have enjoyed our friendship and now I've ruined it." His brow lifted and he turned his head slightly to the side. "Almost ruined it?" he asked hopefully.

She wanted to sigh in exasperation. How was she supposed to keep her wits about her when he looked at her so beseechingly?

She clenched her jaw. If he wanted to continue their friendship she would get what she wanted from this son of her father's enemy: *answers*.

"Why did you do it?" Before he could answer, she added, "And I warn you not to lie to me this time."

Several people stared at them as they passed, their eyes alight with interest…watching. But then they were always watching, were they not? How could she be genuine when she was so very much on display?

Eleanor's body began to stiffen once more.

The Duke of Somersville's arm tightened, drawing her closer to the strength of his body. "I vow to be completely truthful going forward. You have my word as a gentleman."

He came around to face her, preparing for the opening of the dance. Her heart fluttered. The waltz.

She had only practiced it before with her dance master. In fact, she had been sorely tempted to decline each time she practiced because of the dance's vulgarity.

Though the patronesses of Almack's had sanctioned it, and given their permission to the *ton* in doing so, Eleanor had never actually performed the steps at a ball. No doubt her father would have locked her in her room for all eternity for even considering doing so now. And with the Duke of Somersville, no less.

The Duke gave her an encouraging nod and she stepped toward him, placing her left hand on his jacket as his arm came around to lightly touch her shoulder blade. The brush of his gloves whispered over her back, where her skin was bare.

A shiver tickled through her. It was easy to understand why the waltz was considered so scandalous.

He gave her a half smile, boyish and lazy and altogether too charming. It set her heart pounding before the dance could even begin. How would she endure an entire set thus?

She found herself so near to him she could make out every single eyelash around his eyes…could see the beautiful blue was flecked with a subtle pale green she'd never noticed before. The exhalation of his breath teased against the length of her neck like a gentle breeze, tantalizing and intimate. Her stomach quivered and her nipples drew tight where they pressed into the security of her stays.

"Why did you lie to me?" she asked, determined not to let herself be swept away by his attractiveness, determined not to let his transgressions pass without accountability.

The opening notes of the waltz cut in, and the Duke lifted his arm to meet the fingertips of her raised right hand.

His expression became earnest. "I was afraid if you knew whose son I was you would hate me."

She paused a moment in the dance. "Why would I hate you?"

"Because of our fathers' past."

"Did you hate *me*?" Eleanor lowered her arm. "When we first met?"

He held her waist at a respectable distance—for the waltz, that was—and began to spin around with her. "I didn't know you."

The world whirled around and around and around in a heady rush. "You know me now," she said breathlessly.

"Yes, I believe I do."

The spinning stopped for a moment and they resumed their careful hold on one another, her hand atop his hard shoulder and his at the nakedness of her back.

His exotic scent was no longer foreign to her, and was uniquely appealing. Conversation was difficult to focus on when it was all too easy to let her gaze wander to his full mouth. And when he held her thus, lightly, almost in a caress.

She liked this, she realized. The closeness to his strong body, the wonderful smell of him, the enticement of intimacy. Was this what marriage would be? A blend of comfort and excitement?

It was far more than she'd ever anticipated a marriage could be.

"What I've learned about you makes me want to know even more." The Duke stared down at her, drawing her at-

tention from his sensual mouth. "Lady Eleanor, you fasci-
nate me."

Her face warmed in a blush. Was he intentionally trying to distract her?

Stay focused.

"How?" She spoke quietly, only half hoping he would
hear.

"You dress as an Ice Queen to force the *ton* into acknowledging their own gossip and yet you wonder why you fas-
cinate me?" He chuckled. "But that isn't all you want to
ask me, is it?"

The enormity of her previous anger and hurt crushed the
delicate mood of flirtation. She wanted to ask him why he'd
offered to court her. If he'd been sincere, or if he'd merely
been covering his appearance with a viable excuse. But she
realized she was not willing to hear the answer.

"What was your true purpose in calling on my mother?"
she asked instead.

They began to twirl once more, and the room whirled by
in a spinning array of resplendent gowns and murmured
conversation. Eleanor held tight to ensure she did not fall.
Their eyes locked, held, and she fell into the moment, tumbling head over heels into the palpable intimacy charging
between them.

It was more dizzying than the dance, and the rush of
emotion nearly overwhelming.

"I'm looking for a precious stone," the Duke of Somersville replied. "A ruby as large as a man's fist. It shines as
though a fire were lit at its center."

The spinning stopped, but Eleanor's rapid pulse did not
slow. Not when she was so close to Charles...not when her

body had grown accustomed to his touch on her back. On her skin.

"The Coeur de Feu," she whispered.

The Duke of Somersville stiffened. "You know it?"

"Of course. A magnificent ruby named the Heart of Fire for the way light flickers at its center. It's lost, from what I understand, though there was one person my father was certain knew of its location."

The Duke's gaze fixed more intently on her. "You know a great deal of it."

"Young ladies may be made to remain silent before their fathers, but it does not mean they do not listen. My father spoke of little else in the last year of his life. His inability to locate it consumed him. It was the one thing he could not control." Bitterness seeped into her tone.

"You know about the journals, then?"

The step the Duke of Somersville had been performing fell behind by half a beat, a move subtle and practically imperceptible. Had they not been so close she might not have noticed. There was something bright in his eyes. Excitement? Desperation?

He blinked, and recovered with a smooth smile. But it was too late. She'd seen exactly how important those journals were to him.

And she knew where they were located.

Chapter Eleven

Charles ought to be vexed by Lady Eleanor's lengthy silence. She glanced up at him with a coy look borrowed from Lottie and his heart missed a beat. While on Lottie he found the expression irritating, on Lady Eleanor it held a considerable amount of appeal. It also meant she knew something and was holding her cards close to her chest.

The snag of crystals against his fingers told him that her gown lay against his hand. The warmth of her seeped through into the tips of his gloves, reminding him of the nakedness of her back where the gown did not cover it, and how badly he wished he could stroke her silky skin.

She gazed up flirtatiously from beneath her mask and her full breasts rose and fell with her exertion. Despite all that had transpired between them she appeared to be at ease with him once more. Perhaps he had not fully ruined his opportunity. If that was indeed the case, he was an absolutely lucky devil.

"You know where the journals are, don't you?" he asked in a disaffected tone.

Deep down, he was anything but. He wanted those damned journals with such ferocity he could practically feel the smooth worn covers against his palm. He was too close to fail.

"I plan to read them," Lady Eleanor answered, with the simplicity of one discussing the weather. "To see what is so intriguing it would make a man lie."

The twirling began again, and he held her by her slender waist to keep them together. Their gazes locked, the way they might if they intended to kiss, and his blood raced with frenzied force through his veins.

He smirked at her confident reply. "You won't find what you need by simply reading them."

"Won't I?" She tilted her head.

"There's a key to decipher a careful series of coded letters," he said. "At least to obtain what is needed to locate the Coeur de Feu."

"I presume you have the key you're referring to?"

Her lips were pursed in a shrewd expression. He wanted to push his mouth against them and drag the tip of his tongue over her lower lip until she opened for him with a soft, eager breath.

Damn it. She was the daughter of his enemy, the keeper of what he needed. She was a means to an end, not a plaything.

"I do." His reply came out lacking the smugness he'd intended.

"Of course you do." She tossed her head, a haughty move so carefully blended into her steps anyone might assume she'd done it as part of the dance. "How very convenient."

There was something in their verbal *tête-à-tête* he was

rather enjoying. Her blend of astute observation and bold flirtation was enticing, and the glint of those green eyes certainly caught his attention.

"You look as though you are planning to make a bargain with the devil," he said.

"I very well might be."

His hand went to her waist again, while the other held hers at shoulder-height as they paraded around the dance floor, forced to regard one another from the side.

"Go on," he pressed.

"You have the key," she said. "And I have the journals."

"What do you want for them?" He spun her around.

"My request is twofold. Firstly, I want us to work together." Her voice was gentle, breathy...the way a lover's might be after a particularly passionate tryst.

"I'm a pirate, mind you—not a devil." He winked at her and reveled in her pretty flush.

The orchestra began to slow until the last notes faded away almost regretfully.

"And I'm not truly an Ice Queen." She curtseyed to him as he bowed.

She was indeed not an Ice Queen. The title of Ice Queen belonged to her mother, who now glared at him with all the hatred in the world. The Countess of Westix truly was a woman befitting a man like her late husband.

"What is the second part of your request?" he asked as he offered her his arm to lead her back to the watchful viper.

"If I am unable to find a husband you must agree to marry me."

His step faltered. Was she serious?

But the Countess of Westix was not the only person who awaited Lady Eleanor's return. Several men milled about the

Countess, chatting in idle conversation while keeping their focus firmly planted on the glittering form of Lady Eleanor.

They snapped to attention like well-trained pups at her approach.

"I do not think the latter concern will be an issue," Charles offered.

"Only because the elusive new Duke of Somersville danced with me." She tutted. "Besides, it should not be a true concern. And to think just this afternoon you were willing to court me."

The wry twist of Lady Eleanor's lips told him she had seen through his ruse. It also told him well enough how she felt about it.

"Think on it," Lady Eleanor said as he bowed a final time and released her to those so wholly unworthy of her company. "I'd like an answer soon."

"Tonight," he said.

It was an audacious suggestion, for it meant they would either have to be alone together at some point, in order to speak candidly, or he would be dancing another set with her. One or the other would certainly set a flame to the possible kindling of a scandal.

Charles turned from depositing Lady Eleanor among the pack of puppy-eyed suitors and all but bumped into an angel on his departure. But not truly an angel, for surely no celestial being had so robust a bosom as the one being tilted with obvious calculation in his direction.

The angel curtseyed. "Your Grace."

He nodded, unable to scrape up her name from his memory. Her face certainly was familiar, with its pink apple cheeks and bright blue eyes framed by a white feathered mask.

"You remember me, don't you?" She blinked up at him with feigned sweetness. "I came to Somersville Manor often."

Ah, yes, now he remembered. The Carston chit. The very one who used to dump dirt in Lottie's hair and rudely point out the quality of her worn dresses when they were all children. Charles worked hard to keep cultured impassivity on his face, when he wanted so badly to give in to a scowl of dislike.

"Lady Sarah." He nodded at the woman and hoped her costume was indicative of a bettered nature—for her own sake. "I trust you are well?"

She giggled behind her fan. "You *do* remember. And I'm quite well, I thank you." She leaned closer. "The other ladies are envious of our acquaintance. Many are clamoring for an introduction."

True enough, several faces were turned in their direction, all framed in a sea of curls and coiffures.

Dear God.

Attending Lady Covington's masquerade ball had been a dire mistake. In doing so he had publicly declared himself an eligible bachelor, with a new dukedom, and plopped himself squarely in the middle of the marriage mart. Invitations would be overwhelming Somersville House the following day, and no doubt all the mothers would be seeking to thrust their daughters into his path.

"This will be a very exhilarating set." Lady Sarah looked wistfully toward the dance floor and blinked up at him once more.

Charles gritted his teeth and made a silent apology to Lottie for what manners dictated he must do next. "Would you care to dance, Lady Sarah?"

She put her hand to her chest, as if the request had taken her by surprise. "I'd be honored, Your Grace."

She fluttered her lashes at him once more, with such vivacity he wondered if one of the feathers had come loose and was stuck in her eye.

Lady Sarah slipped her arm through his, tugging herself a bit closer than was necessary. While she paraded him through the ballroom like a prize won, Charles caught sight of Lady Eleanor, making her way to the dance floor on the arm of the notoriously eligible Marquess of Kentworth.

Charles had to focus once more on not scowling as he settled himself in front of Lady Sarah. He'd been wrong when he had declared himself merely a pirate. For now, being forced to dance with an angel while watching an Ice Queen with another man made him feel very much like the devil himself.

Eleanor's newfound appeal to the *ton* had more to do with the new Duke of Somersville offering to dance with her than the results of her social edification. However, her suitors made one realization glaringly obvious: not all men were like the Duke of Somersville.

Where he was warm and encouraging, sometimes even teasing, and with the most pleasant hint of flirtation, other men were—well, they were dull.

The Marquess of Kentworth was an exceptional dancer, and yet he'd prattled on so about his physical prowess that her eyes had nearly rolled from her head. The tall and awkward Viscount Rawley had come next, with a nervous bow, and during the course of their dance had dropped a scrap of paper with the dance steps written on it in blotted ink.

Following supper, which she'd been unfortunate enough

to be forced to attend with Viscount Rawley and his many dietary allergies, had come the very anticlimactic affair of unmasking.

It wasn't until she was subjected to Earl of Devonington, though, that she had finally had quite enough. She might have fallen asleep dancing the Scottish reel, with his boring chatter over his hunting dogs, had it not been for the many numerous times he trod upon her toes with his surprisingly dainty feet.

The final notes of the dance finally whispered through the air—far sweeter than any Eleanor had heard before. The Earl of Devonington gave a final deft leap and came down hard on her foot. The very one he'd crushed so often earlier in the dance.

He led her back to her mother with a comment on hunting that teetered precariously on the inappropriate and a promise to call upon her the following day. It was then Eleanor decided she needed a moment to herself, lest she go mad.

It had been wonderful, initially, to have the attention of so many gentlemen when she had previously been so woefully ignored. But easy conversation had not come with the others as it had with the Duke of Somersville. The carefree comfort she possessed when she spoke with him had not come as readily either.

The set she'd danced with him had set the night twinkling with promise and excitement. Everything thereafter had fallen rather flat.

Only when she was alone could she finally acknowledge the bold request she'd made of him: to marry her in the event that another man could not be found. She'd done it out of necessity, of course, to ensure her own financial security. At any rate, it did not seem likely he would need to follow through.

And yet she knew the offer had been unwise. Not only would her mother never allow such a union, Eleanor did not know what to make of the emotions swimming in her stomach when he was near, the sensation as exhilarating as it was frightening.

It was far too easy to recall the brush of his hand over her naked back, the way their eyes had locked while the world spun around them, as though their souls were joined. It was fanciful and ridiculous and altogether reckless.

She strode from the withdrawing room into the empty hall while thinking of the waltz. While thinking of him. They'd been so close—near enough for her to note the way his eyes crinkled at the corners when he smiled down at her, the way their bodies touched and how incredibly strong his broad shoulder had been under her hand. Even now the exotic spice of him clung to her skin and gown, the way the residual warmth of a good dream might linger into wakefulness—as if she could still savor him.

"What is it that puts such happiness on your face, Lady Eleanor?" a smooth, masculine voice asked.

Eleanor turned to her right and found the Duke of Somersville approaching her. "Your Grace…" Her heart fluttered like a freed moth in her chest.

The Duke tilted his head regretfully. "I'd ask you for a second set if you weren't so popular."

"You mean if it wouldn't be so scandalous?" she chided.

"I think I'd very much like to be scandalous with you."

He grinned at her, his lips parting over his perfect teeth and making him appear very much the pirate. Heat burned its way up from Eleanor's neck and scalded her cheeks.

The Duke of Somersville did not move closer to her, and yet the intimate glint in his eye made her feel as though he'd just closed the proper proximity.

"Why, Lady Eleanor," he said with feigned concern. "You appear to have overexerted yourself on the dance floor. Perhaps you ought to forgo this set and venture to the veranda for a bit of air?"

Her breath caught. Had the Duke of Somersville just suggested she meet him for a tryst?

And was she truly considering it?

Chapter Twelve

Charles did not wait for Lady Eleanor's reply before he bowed and took his leave. The suggestion of her joining him on the veranda hung in the air between them, ripe with temptation.

He let the stretch of time work in his favor and strode with a purposeful gait through the ballroom, nodding at the few attendees he recognized favorably and ignoring those he did not. Masquerade balls could be very convenient for avoiding unwanted social interactions.

And for creating enticing ones.

Everything in him wanted to turn and look behind him, to see if the sparkling Ice Queen of the ball followed, his invitation answered. He had to force his head to remain straight ahead, fixed on the doors to the terrace.

Several people milled about outside, in search of either fresh air, a moment unseen by an escort, or a liberating break for solitude. It was not improper for one to go outside alone at a ball, even less so at a masquerade ball, where minor transgressions were glanced over. It was his suggestion which had been improper, bordering on indecent.

Though it was not his place to crave it, he wanted a moment with her alone, somewhere she would be only his. Where suitors would not be present, seeking a dance or some of the attention she'd doled out with charming smiles and genuine attentiveness. The idea of her being solely with him eased some of the curious knots tightening in his stomach.

He stepped through the doors onto the veranda. The music was muted by the closing door, and the quiet of night overtook him.

The door opened behind him, but Charles did not look to see who had arrived. A tingling at the back of his neck told him that his senses had picked up everything he needed to know.

Lady Eleanor had arrived.

He didn't have to turn, but he did, for he would not miss the sight of her striding toward him.

"Ah, Lady Eleanor."

He'd meant to say more, but the words died on his tongue. Moonlight caught and twinkled in the crystals on her dress and hair, making her shimmer. The white cloth blended with the fairness of her skin, so only the pale blue fabric of the gown and slit sleeves showed, as delicate as a moonbeam across her skin.

"What a happy coincidence, meeting you here," he said, finally finding his voice.

She inclined her head respectfully and set the copper of her hair shining. "Your Grace…"

She stood beside him at the railing on the terrace and rested her fingers on the thick band of marble, a mere fraction of an inch from his own. How he longed for such separation to be closed between them, so he might delicately run a finger over the back of her gloved thumb. A slow stroke, easy and sensual—but one he would not make.

"I assume you've had a pleasant evening?" Her casual tone indicated no nervousness at being with him outside, alone.

"I have," he answered in earnest. For it had been so when she was dancing in his arms. "It would appear you have become quite popular."

Lady Eleanor's eyes danced in the night. "Is it not enough for you to be a humble pirate, but you must also be one prone to jealousy?"

Jealous? Him? It was so ridiculous a notion Charles could only scoff.

Eleanor lifted her brows and fixed her attention to the garden—a convenient distraction. He edged his hand closer, drawn by an unseen force, and grazed the back of her thumb with his forefinger before he realized what he was doing. The fine quality of their gloves glided against one another.

Eleanor gave a quiet gasp and met his stare, her eyes luminous. Blood rushed through his body and he found himself wishing to pull the gloves from them both, to caress the silky heat of her naked skin on his.

Gloves. Confound it.

He could have shaken his head at his own thoughts. He'd been too long abstinent from the fairer sex if he was thinking merely of removing gloves and touching hands.

No, not just gloves. He wanted to peel the dazzling dress from her body and watch the true beauty of her being unveiled in a way no crystal or diamond could ever rival.

She would be lovely. He needed only to see how the dress hugged her curves to know as much.

"Why are you looking at me like that?" she whispered.

Her breath was sweet and her lips were parted with innocence, with temptation...

The touch of their fingers was not enough, damn it. He wanted more—needed more.

Though he knew he shouldn't, he drew his arm around her waist, as he'd done when they'd danced the waltz. They stood together in the semi-darkness, far too close, with nothing between them but the sparking of mutual attraction.

Lady Eleanor did not pull back from him as she might once have done. She stared deep into his eyes, as if she saw every level of his soul...as if she could stay thus for hours.

He touched her cheek and cursed his gloves once more. Her lashes swept downward in pleasure at the caress. He shouldn't be doing this—holding her, wanting to kiss her. The right thing to do would be to release her and make his way back into the ballroom.

Even as he thought of the right thing his body acted on the wrong thing. He tilted the delicate edge of her jaw upward, turning her face to the moon, the better to see her beauty in the cast of silver light before he lowered his mouth to the warmth of hers in a delicate kiss.

Her body eased closer against him and her lips opened ever so slightly, granting him the opportunity to gently suck her lower lip. And the Ice Queen melted in his arms.

Eleanor was lost in the Duke of Somersville's kiss. His mouth was hot, and surprisingly soft, and the kiss was followed by the gentle drawing of her lower lip between his.

Despite the coolness of the night, her skin blazed with

the most delicious heat and settled into a low, eager throb between her thighs. His fingers trailed behind her head, cradling the weight of her hair. Then—dear God—then his tongue swept into her mouth and brushed across her own.

Sweet heavens.

Her nipples hardened with a pleasant needling against the silk shift she wore beneath her gown and every bit of her skin seemed to dance with awareness.

The Duke pulled away and gazed down at her in a way no man had ever done. "My God, you are beautiful," he said in a low voice.

"Will you kiss me again?" she asked breathlessly.

His gaze settled on her mouth and his lips lifted in a languid half smile. "Not here. Not now." He swept his thumb over her cheek. "I do not want your absence noticed."

She fought the urge to protest. She wanted to be kissed again. Again and again and again. Until the entire night faded away in the hungry pulse of heat still throbbing insistently through her.

"You shouldn't look at me like that," he said.

"Like what?"

"Like you wish I would kiss you again."

Her knees went soft at the deepness of his voice, at his obvious attraction to her. "You *could* kiss me again," she offered.

He put his hands behind his back and eased away to a proper distance, such as should exist between a lady and a gentleman. "I would not ruin your reputation, Lady Eleanor. I've seen the effects of ruination and would not wish it on a lady I hold in such high esteem."

A lady he holds in such high esteem. Her heart should not swell so girlishly at mere words, and yet it did, expanding in the most delightfully happy way until her chest seemed near bursting.

His scent hovered on her skin and mixed with the warm pleasure still tingling over her lips. It was divine—a heady, exotic combination of spices and adventure. The scent of a man who had seen the world she had only ever imagined.

A glance toward the door confirmed that the dancers were walking away from the finished set. She would need to return before the next began.

"Have you come up with your answer for me yet? Will we work on the mystery of the journals together? Will you...?" She flushed, unable to ask the most pertinent question aloud again.

"Will I marry you if no one else will have you?" he finished for her.

When he said it she realized how sad it sounded—how desperately pathetic.

"It would be my honor to work with you." His face was entirely earnest.

The very idea of working alongside him to solve the mystery left her pulse racing in her veins. The adventure...the excitement...

"And the other thing..." He paused. "I will need more time to consider."

Disappointment crushed in on her, but she suppressed the emotion with the stiffness she'd clung to for the better part of her life. This was a reminder not to allow herself to get too close to him, to remain at a distance no matter how he encouraged her to open to him.

"I shall bring one of the journals with me when I come to Lottie's tomorrow evening," she said. "But only one until the remaining terms can be met."

"Understandable."

He brushed the length of his forefinger over the back of her gloved hand once more. Her skin warmed at the caress.

Distance.

After all, she could not afford to be reckless.

"I do not wish to hurt you, Lady Eleanor."

He said the words so softly she almost did not hear.

"You must go." He bowed low. "Enjoy your evening, beautiful Ice Queen."

"And enjoy yours, jealous pirate."

She bobbed a quick curtsey to him and strode to the doors. It was a wonder she was able to walk at all with her legs trembling the way they did, with knees that seemed too weak to hold her upright.

But she did make it to the doors, and through the crush of people, until she practically ran into the chest of a man who did not move aside for her to pass. How very rude.

"Excuse me, please." Eleanor curbed the irritation from her words and looked up. Anything else she might have said died on her tongue.

Hugh looked down at her with a quiet smile on his lips. "Will you dance with me, Eleanor?"

In days past she would have readily accepted, maybe even harbored the hope that he might cast aside Alice, as he had Eleanor. But not now—not tonight. Not after the Duke of Somersville's searing kiss had relegated the memory of Hugh's kisses to a place of easy forgetting.

"Do forgive me, Lord Ledsey, but I am on my way to speak with my mother now." Her regret did not come across as earnest—not even to her.

Hugh's pale blue eyes regarded her carefully. Compared

to the rich depth of the Duke of Somersville's blue eyes, Hugh's appeared rather pallid.

"Perhaps later, then." He bowed to her, his tone cool. "You look beautiful this evening, Lady Eleanor."

While his words and actions were polite, there was an air about him that set little bumps of unease running down Eleanor's spine.

"I thank you." She was suddenly desperate to escape from Hugh, and found herself grateful for Lady Alice having interrupted their courtship.

At last Hugh moved aside and gave Eleanor leave to pass. Her mother was clearly waiting without patience, her face dour.

"You've certainly taken your time," said the Countess of Westix in a flat tone. "Was that Lord Ledsey I saw you talking to?"

Guilt prickled at Eleanor, but then memories of the pleasure of Charles's kiss wiped away any negative sensations. The kiss, the kiss, *the kiss*. She could swoon at the very thought of it, at the memory of the protective strength of the Duke's hands around her, the heat of his mouth on hers, his tongue grazing—

"Did you not hear what I said?" Her mother's brow rose. "I certainly hope you aren't imagining more kittens, or some other such nonsense."

Eleanor pursed her lips, thoroughly chastised despite the humor threatening to bubble up in her throat. The thing about the kittens *had* been rather amusing.

"Forgive me," she said. "The Earl of Devonington was not exactly light on his feet. I needed to recover."

She said it quietly enough, but her mother rebuked Eleanor with a sharp look.

"I have it on good authority that he was very taken with you." The Countess clapped her fan against the palm of her gloved hand. "You could do far worse than the Earl of Devonington."

She delivered a stare so pointed, it jabbed through Eleanor's daydreams.

"For instance, the Duke of Somersville."

Chapter Thirteen

If one measured success in such things as multiple callers, and flowers sent with heavy cream-colored note cards, it could be said the following day that Eleanor's appearance at Lady Covington's masquerade ball had been victorious.

And most intriguing of all the flowers she received were the brilliantly red tulips sent with a note stating only: *An admirer.*

The man who had sent the red tulips did not call, and nor did he send a servant so that she might guess who he might be.

The butterfly of hope in Eleanor's chest fluttered about. Surely it had been Charles.

While she ought to be simply pleased with her newfound suitors, she could not help but place him above others in her mind.

There were several others who did call—including the much sought-after Marquess of Bastionbury, whom she'd danced with later in the evening. Though following the magic of dancing with the Duke of Somersville, the Marquess of Bastionbury's appeal had regrettably been thin.

The Earl of Devonington called too, and took a short lifetime to finally depart, with the Countess of Westix practically tugging him back in.

The day trudged on, taking an eternity, until the sun finally began to sink behind the clouds. Most of it had been a blur—a background to the thoughts at the forefront of her mind: *an admirer*. The Duke of Somersville. And that kiss.

Surely he had sent those vividly red tulips which proudly spoke the love of their sender?

Finally night descended on London, and at long last Eleanor was finally able to slip into the domino and blonde wig with her black mask.

Amelia winked in the mirror at her mistress. "I don't think I've ever seen you beam so, my lady. Is it…?" She paused for a long moment before speaking. "Is it the Earl of Devonington?"

Eleanor's mouth fell open in horror. "Most certainly not!"

Amelia pressed her hand to her chest. "Pardon me for saying so, my lady, but I'm glad it isn't him who has you in a whirl."

"*Am* I in a whirl?"

"Your cheeks have been flushed all day and you've had a dreamy smile on your face, like you're floating through the world while the rest of us simply walk." The maid grinned down at her. "Are you going to confess to your trusted maid who it is?"

Eleanor's stomach clenched. As much as she loved Amelia, she couldn't bring herself to say the Duke's name aloud. Not when her mother's ears managed to extend through the entire house.

And a good thing too, for no sooner had Eleanor decided to keep quiet on the topic her mother strolled into the room in a glittering evening gown. Eleanor got to her feet and met the Countess's lifted brow as she regarded her daughter's masked appearance.

"What are you doing, Eleanor?"

Amelia bobbed a curtsey and left the room, silent as a mouse, the way a good servant ought to be. Oh, how Eleanor wished her maid was still there to share secret confessions with, rather than the Countess of Westix. Eleanor knew too well the determined glint in her mother's eye.

"We're going to Almack's tonight." The Countess spoke in a voice brooking no refusal.

The brilliance of Eleanor's excitement wilted into an ache of crushing disappointment. "I thought I was to go to Lottie's?"

Her mother waved her fan dismissively. "You needn't go there anymore. What she's taught you has evidently paid off. Several gentlemen are quite taken with you. Most especially the Earl of Devonington. He's asked to take you to supper later this week at Vauxhall Gardens."

"I don't want to go anywhere with him." Eleanor spoke the obstinate words levelly.

The Countess narrowed her eyes. "You are lucky to have his attentions, Eleanor. He's one of the wealthiest peers in London and would keep you in the lifestyle to which you are accustomed. Beyond it, really. While the others have merely flirted, he has spoken to me directly about his intentions to court you."

Eleanor said nothing. How could she? Her mother was right, of course. The Earl of Devonington was impossibly rich, and high in the instep as a result. He was clearly very interested in Eleanor, and he had the means to let her live even better than she did now. Her life would be just as the Duke of Somersville had predicted: an endless blur of soirees and luncheons until they were all strung together in a life without purpose.

Her stomach twisted at the thought of being wife to a man like the Earl of Devonington, with his pompous sneer and devastatingly painful little feet. While several months prior she would have been pleased with Devonington's interest, she understood now that she wanted more. *Needed* more. A suitor who matched wits with her—one who would turn her blood molten in her veins and make her melt with desire for intimacy.

"Nothing to say?" asked her mother.

Eleanor had much to say, but she had never given herself leave to allow her mother to see the depth of her feelings, to hear the truth of her opinions. Her blood rushed with such fervor through her veins it roared in her ears.

"Forgive me, Mother," Eleanor said. "I feel I would benefit from more of Lottie's instruction. I should like the opportunity to meet a suitor who appeals to me more than Devonington…one whom I might find happiness with."

Goodness, but her knees had begun to tremble, and she found herself wishing to be seated still.

The Countess's eyes sharpened with perceptible shrewdness as she regarded her daughter for a long, stifling moment. "You aren't dressed properly and your hair has not yet been done." She relaxed and sighed. "I daresay you wouldn't be ready in time. Almack's closes its doors to all patrons in the next hour. If you will agree to sup with Devonington at Vauxhall, I believe I might forgive your absence tonight."

Eleanor's heart leapt at the opportunity. "I agree."

Her mother gave a smug smile. Apparently they had both just won a victory.

The Countess of Westix brushed at her immaculate gown. "I shall inform Devonington tonight of your decision to dine with him, and convey your disappointment at not being able to attend Almack's. I shall say that you have truly been overly exerted by the events of today and last night. I will also see if Aunt Lydia and your cousin Lady Violet might be free to act as chaperons for you." She turned to leave and stopped. "You are smiling, daughter."

Eleanor pursed her lips to quell her blatant display of delight.

The Countess softened slightly and nodded. "I like it."

"Thank you, Mother."

The Countess of Westix swept from the room without further comment, letting the door shut quietly behind her. Eleanor rushed to her dressing table and pulled out the journal she had obtained from her father's study earlier that day.

But the eagerness of her joy was dampened by the presence of guilt. Her mother trusted her, and Eleanor intended to spend the evening with the very man her mother most despised. Eleanor bit her lip and slid the battered book into a bag. Her mother wanted Eleanor to be happy, though, and this made Eleanor far happier than anything else ever could.

Amelia appeared in the room once more and bobbed a curtsey. "The Countess has departed and the hackney has arrived for you." She glanced at the bag.

Eleanor resisted the urge to pull it behind her back.

Amelia winked. "You needn't worry, my lady. You could hide a body in here and I'd not tell a soul."

"You knew?" Eleanor asked.

"Nothing in your room goes unnoticed by me. It's my job, my lady. It's all part of protecting you."

Eleanor had never thought of Amelia as a protector. A maid, yes, but never a protector. The idea was a nice one—to know Amelia was on her side should she need her.

"Thank you," Eleanor said with genuine gratitude, before slipping away.

Only when she was inside the hackney did she notice a similar hired coach just pulling away from the home opposite her own, with a lone man sitting inside. Eleanor peered through the darkness at the face in the other coach's window. There, lit by only a sliver of moonlight, was a face she would recognize anywhere—Hugh, the Earl of Ledsey.

Charles arrived early to Lottie's by special request, and filled her in on the events of the ball—including Lady Sarah's preposterous costume of an angel. Lottie's smile wavered, however, at the mention of Charles dancing the waltz with Lady Eleanor.

The clop of hooves came to a stop outside and he glanced behind the window covering to see a woman in black slip out of a hackney. His pulse kicked up a notch in wicked delight. Lady Eleanor had arrived. And no doubt the journals with her.

Or one of them, at least.

Lottie twirled one dark curl thoughtfully on her finger and pursed her lips.

He dropped the curtain. "What is it?"

Lottie's brows lifted in feigned confusion.

Charles pointed to the hair curled around her digit. "You are twirling your hair and pursing your lips. Which you always do when you have something you want to say. So speak your piece and be done with it."

She sighed and spread her hands over the green silk gown she wore. "Have a care for why you're here, Charles. Why you're helping."

He frowned. "I am not following…"

The footman appeared at the door and announced the arrival of Lady Eleanor.

"Bring her in," Lottie said to the footman before turning back to Charles. "She is meant to wed, not to be distracted by you."

Something deep in Charles's chest gave a little snag. There was Eleanor's second condition, which he had not yet answered: his amenability toward marriage to her. He'd thought of it for a good length of time, and frankly did not see the possibility of her not being wanted.

"I'm well aware of that," he replied.

"Good." Lottie beamed widely at him. "Then I'll let you have your time with Lady Eleanor once we have had a chance to celebrate her success. Assuming she brought the journal."

Before anything further could be said Lady Eleanor entered the room, appearing unlike she ever had before. A gleam lit her emerald eyes, reflecting the grin on her face, and her cheeks were rosy with good health. She'd already removed her cloak and mask. Her bright red hair was tied back in a simple knot, and free of the ghastly blonde wig.

"Oh, Lottie," she breathed. "Thank you for your incredible instruction. Your tutelage has been invaluable."

Lottie gave a squeal of excitement and caught Lady Eleanor in a hug. "I'm so very delighted," Lottie gushed. "I heard how brilliant you were. Have you had any proposals yet?"

If Lady Eleanor had been surprised by the physical affection of Lottie's impulsive hug, she did not show it. Instead she returned the hug and laughed. It was a sweet, joyous sound that Charles found to be quite pleasant.

"It has only been one day," Eleanor said.

Lottie released her and put a hand on her hip. "Does that matter?"

"Well, I did have many callers, and Mother has stated that the Earl of Devonington would like to take me to Vauxhall. I also received several lovely flowers."

Lady Eleanor slid a glance at Charles and smiled, as if they had a shared secret. And perhaps they did—he knew how eager she had been to rid herself of the Earl's company. But even with the knowledge of her disdain for Devonington, he could not stop the gnaw of irritation grinding at him.

"Have your feet quite recovered?" Lottie asked with a chuckle.

Lady Eleanor rolled her eyes playfully. "Not enough to chance another set with Devonington any time soon. I was lucky to beg off from Almack's this evening, or I might have been in the same situation once more. But, I had something to bring tonight."

She hefted a bag from her side. Charles stepped forward and accepted the welcome heft of it into his grasp.

"One of the journals," Lady Eleanor said. "As promised."

He pulled the stiff leather handles of the bag, splitting it open at the middle to draw out a battered journal with an embossed gold compass on the front. A true journal of the Adventure Club.

Relief washed over him. *She had brought it.*

"You remember our agreement?" Lady Eleanor said.

Her sly glance indicated that she still anticipated an answer for her second condition. Charles's gut tensed. Surely agreeing to wed her if she had no other alternatives was no great deal. Her victorious night at the masquerade practically guaranteed that he'd never have to make good that promise.

He looked up from the journal. "I do," he replied smoothly.

He pulled the key from his jacket pocket. It had been worth the discomfort of its sharp edges jabbing against him to ensure it remained safe.

Lady Eleanor came to his side, teasing him with her delicate scent, which had clung to his clothes the night before.

"Shall we get started?" He handed her the key.

An impish smile touched her lips. "I confess I've read through a little of this one. Even without the key it made for interesting reading."

The flat metal sheet rested in her hands, held just at the empire waist of her evening gown. A mere inch below her bosom. Much as he wanted to delve into the contents of the journal, he could not stop his attention from glancing over the bounty of her creamy breasts, encased in a swath of pale green silk—the lucky cloth.

"Will you open it?" she asked.

"Yes." He pulled back the cover to the first page of neatly written script.

"It isn't my father's handwriting." Eleanor settled the key so it fit snugly within the page.

"Nor my father's." Charles studied the key. The letters revealed through the slits spelled out WDIFLSJSNLIDF-NEWSZDIJLBEK.

Eleanor shook her head. "It makes no sense—no matter how I try to combine the letters."

"It was the same with my father's journals," he replied.

"But there must be at least one or two pages where it works. It has to be here somewhere."

"This is so very interesting…" Lottie peered down at the book.

Charles knew Eleanor would prefer to be alone with him, to get his answer to her request. Part of him wished to be with only her as well, yet part of him feared it. Thoughts of Eleanor had burned through him since the masquerade ball, of kissing her and how much he longed to touch her.

Then there was the answer she still awaited.

He cradled the weight of the journal in his hands, its leather soft and cool against his palms, its secrets scrawled on fine paper. He knew he had to have them all.

He would have no choice but to agree to Eleanor's terms—and hope to God he was correct that she would never press him to make good on his agreement. And that he could stay his growing attraction.

Chapter Fourteen

Eleanor found using the key to be far less fascinating than reading the journals themselves had been. And Lottie found not a jot of it interesting, despite her initial claim. After only several pages she cast a flippant excuse and made her way from the drawing room.

Eleanor's pulse sped up a notch. She and Charles were alone. She would have her answer.

"We ought to forgo all the pages with images..."

Charles spoke beside her, near enough for his warm breath to tickle the sensitive skin of her neck. Each time he did so delightful prickles of pleasure danced over her, like the little bubbles of champagne floating up the sides of a glass.

"Good idea."

There would be no words on those pages, of course. Though she also suspected he feared some of the drawings would be too vulgar for her. And they were. She'd seen them herself, but she would not confess as much.

She tried to turn the page showing a roughly sketched tower, but it caught on her glove and she turned several pages rather than only the one intended.

"You should take off your gloves."

He took the book from her and set it aside with the key. Her heartbeat tripped over itself. Charles took her hand in his and slipped free the button at the heel of her palm. The blunt edge of his forefinger ran up her inner wrist. Eleanor sucked in a breath. When had the skin there become so sensitive as to make such a simple touch feel so terribly intimate?

"Your Grace..." she whispered.

"Charles." His voice was low, quiet—a silken caress in her mind. "Call me Charles, Eleanor."

Her mouth went dry and she found she could no longer speak. Instead her eyes remained captivated by his and she nodded. He pulled at the gloves and they slipped off, unveiling her palms to the cool air of the room one glorious inch at a time until her hand was bare and in his.

There were small calluses on his palms, but his long, tapered fingers were cool and smooth against the heat of hers. He held her hands between his, letting their skin press together.

Eleanor's breath came faster, and she wondered idly if he could feel the wild thrum of her pulse against his skin. His fingers moved over hers, restlessly exploring, including the carefully rounded edges of her nails and the highly sensitive dip of her palm.

Eleanor watched the graceful slide of his hands over hers and tried to keep from closing her eyes at the blissful sensation of their naked flesh against each other's. He put his hands to hers, palm to palm, so his fingertips extended an inch over her own, and slid his fingers between hers.

There was a sensuality in the act of joining them together which left her flushed and her insides trembling.

She gasped. "Your Grace, this is—"

"Improper." He released her and cleared his throat. "Indeed, it is. Forgive me."

He laid her gloves gently on the table and passed the journal to her. She took it with trembling fingers. Her skin still hummed with the tantalizing warmth of his caress.

"And it's Charles."

He winked at her, appearing unaffected by an encounter which had left her hot and flustered, with that strange thrumming racing through her veins. He reached over her and used those magnificent hands of his to find the page they'd last left.

"Do you have an answer for me?" Her voice had gone breathy and it made her sound altogether foolish to her own ears. "For my second request?"

"Say my Christian name."

His voice was a low, sensual purr that stroked over her. Dear heavens, he was going to make her faint dead away before the hour ended if he kept up with such intimate flirtation. Even still, her mouth went dry at the suggestion behind the command.

"Your answer, if you please… Charles." His name lingered between them and tasted sweet on her tongue, like tea cakes or marzipan.

"Yes, Eleanor." He glanced down, as though almost shy, and regarded the journal. "My answer is yes."

He lifted the key from where she'd set it aside absently and held it up, so they might work together again. The thin piece of metal fluttered in his grasp and giddiness charged through her at the way he too was clearly affected.

The idea that she was causing him to feel the way she did, shaking with excitement and breathlessness, served only to make every part of her tingle with awareness.

He leaned closer to her side with the key, close enough that their shoulders brushed as he moved the metal from one page to another. The warmth of his body seeped through his jacket and whispered against the exposed skin of her arm. She wanted to edge closer to him, until she was firmly pressed against his tall frame.

Eleanor turned the pages almost without seeing them, absorbed in his nearness, in the wonderful exotic spice of his scent. She hoped he was concentrating on the key, as she found herself incapable.

His gaze alternated between the book, and her. More specifically, her mouth, as though he longed to kiss her as he had the night of the masquerade.

She turned one more page and her gaze fell on a vivid painting of a woman wearing little more than scarves. A swath of red fabric was tied over her breasts and a long purple skirt was slung around her naked waist, with slits high enough to reveal her thighs. Her arm was extended upward, with her middle finger and thumb pinched together, and she stared directly out of the page with dark, fathomless eyes and long, enviable lashes.

The woman was beautiful, but the exposure of her person obscene. Far more so than any other image Eleanor had seen thus far. She would have dropped the book had Charles not grabbed it from her.

Too many questions whirled through her stunned mind

for her to fix on any one in particular, and she regarded Charles with a look of confusion. Well, perhaps panicked confusion, if she were being entirely honest.

"There are things in here a lady should not see."

She knew this, of course, but she hadn't expected such a state of nudity.

Eleanor swallowed. "Who was she? A…a courtesan?"

"Ghawazi." He closed the book and cast her a regretful frown. "Women who dance."

"She's so exposed…"

The horror began to fade and a raw curiosity pulled at Eleanor. She reached for the book. Charles did not stop her from taking it. She pulled it open to the page and stared down at the image once more—the image of a woman whose sole source of income relied on performing. Eleanor was not so foolish as to believe women such as her only danced. And yet there was no shame painted on the woman's lovely face. There was only pleasure and satisfaction.

Eleanor considered her own ungloved hands. How ridiculous to be so overwhelmed by bare fingers when this woman was nearly naked and seemingly glad to be so.

"This is not appropriate." Charles reached for the book.

"Nor is my being alone with you," Eleanor countered. "Or being in a courtesan's home, or reading through this journal, or having kissed you on the terrace, or our agreement. And yet I seem perpetually to do all the things I was taught long ago that a lady ought never to do. And I am enjoying it."

Her body trembled with the realization of what she'd said. It had burst from her with more emotional truth than she'd permitted herself to experience in a lifetime. It was powerful, this liberation. Powerful and euphoric. And she suddenly found herself craving more.

Charles had struggled for the whole duration of his time with Eleanor. It had all been so much easier when he had been able to regard her with distaste, as the daughter of the man who had destroyed his father's dreams.

But now, as he witnessed her determination to overcome her failings, and as she looked to him for his candor and advice, and after he'd sampled the sweetness of her lovely mouth, it was impossible to hate this woman.

What the devil had consumed him to have her call him Charles? And yet the way she said it, soft and hesitant and far lovelier than his name had ever been spoken before.

He'd been distracted by the closeness of her person to him—near enough for him to sense the heat of her, to breathe in the subtle jasmine notes of her scent—and that damnably low-cut bodice had distracted him every time he'd tried to read the letters in the key.

And after such a declaration from this woman, of her newly found enjoyment of life, he was drawn to her. He looked up and saw the passion lit up in the depths of her soul. He moved toward her as a moth to a flame, unable to stop his hands from caressing her lovely face.

He should stop. Leave. Call Lottie. Anything.

His mind raced with ways to free himself from the grip of his own temptation when Eleanor pushed onto her toes and pressed her lips boldly to his own.

He accepted the kiss, meaning it only to be a simple caress of her soft mouth on his own, something chaste and innocent. Just one and then he would back away, as he ought to. He needed to leave her for another man—one who would be a proper husband to her. And yet that first capture of her lower lip was swiftly followed by the greedy brush of his tongue.

A soft whimper sounded in the back of her throat and she sank against him, giving herself fully to the kiss, to him. His body roared with the want of her, the want to have her closer still, to remove so much more than her gloves. *But she was not his.* And then her lips parted and her tongue swept into his mouth.

His shaft strained against his fitted breeches and blinded all logic in his mind. He'd been a fool to allow so much time to elapse since he'd last had a woman. Too much of his focus had been spent on acquiring accolades and foreign treasures and not enough care had been paid to his person.

Everything in him begged he make up for the oversight now, with this pliant beauty in his arms and her wild vein of passion he'd helped unveil.

Charles trailed kisses down her chin to her slender, graceful neck and gently nipped the area just behind her jaw. Her moan hummed in his ear and sent pleasure rippling through him.

It wasn't enough. He wanted more. Needed more.

He needed *her.*

He should not, and yet he did.

His thoughts splintered apart his rationale and his lips wandered down the delicate line of her collarbone, lower still to the enticing swell of her bosom. Her fingers threaded through his hair and she gave a quiet gasp when his lips grazed the low neckline of her gown.

More.

He tugged gently at the silk until it slid low enough to reveal the tempting pink of one partially exposed nipple.

"Charles…" Eleanor whispered, her voice throaty with desire.

He didn't know if it was encouragement, but she kept a tight enough grasp on his head for him to be held in place and to assume it was not a protest. He pressed his thumb just above the pink nipple, popping it free from the confines of her stays, and closed his mouth over it.

Eleanor drew a sharp intake of breath and clung to him.

He held her more tightly, pressing her firmly against him, and drew the tip of his tongue around the pert nub. Her body writhed against him, implying that she wanted him every bit as much as he wanted her.

And, God, did he want her.

No. Need. He *needed* her. So much so he was swollen to the point of pain.

A single thought floated to the forefront of his mind: *her innocence*. Its loss would pull away the rest of life's opportunities for her, the way it had for Lottie.

No. Eleanor had need of a husband and it could not be him—not when adventure called to his blood, when he had unmet promises to fulfill.

Charles straightened and pulled her neckline back into place. "Forgive me," he said raggedly. "I forgot myself."

Eleanor glanced down, her lashes hiding not only the brilliance of those green eyes but also her emotions. When she looked back up her thoughts were closed off to him.

She lifted her head with the haughty elegance she'd exhibited weeks before. "Did I do something wrong?" she asked.

"No, thank God."

Her brow lifted. "I don't understand."

"Eleanor, that *couldn't* have gone further."

"I believe it could have."

He stared at her a moment, stunned beyond wit and words. "I'll not strip you of your virtue. Especially not when you are seeking a husband."

The small muscles of her neck tensed and she gave a stiff nod. "I understand."

She lifted the journal from where it had fallen on the ground, forgotten in the blaze of passion.

"I believe I will read through this on my own, as the key does not appear to have revealed any secrets to us."

He caught her hand and could not help but sweep the pad of his thumb over the incredible softness of her palm. "Are you sure you wish to do this? What is within those pages is not anything a lady ought to read."

She drew her hand from his. "I am not as fragile as you believe me to be."

She was sliding away from him emotionally, leaving him cold in her wake. "Will you be at Hyde Park tomorrow?" he asked.

"My mother did not know you in order to recognize you before," she replied. "I cannot believe she will be thrice fooled now that she's seen you enough to make the connection."

Devil take it, that was an excellent point.

"But you'll come tomorrow?" Was he bargaining with her?

She tilted her head, her expression sweetly pleasant. "Perhaps."

Footsteps sounded outside the door before Lottie entered, with Eleanor's cloak and wig draped over her arm.

Eleanor began to assemble herself for her immediate departure. "Thank you again for everything, Lottie."

Lottie pulled her into another gentle embrace. "The pleasure has been mine, Lady Eleanor. I hope our time together has been beneficial."

The footman appeared to announce that her hackney had arrived. Eleanor inclined her head at Charles and gave him a seductive smile that set his heart pounding.

"Thank you for the tulips, Your Grace."

And with that, she was gone.

The tulips?

"Did you teach her to smile like a coquette?" Lottie asked. "If so, I'm quite impressed with you."

"That was of her own creation," Charles replied.

"Well, then, I'm quite impressed with myself." Lottie winked at him. "Did you come to any exciting revelations?" she asked.

Too many to share.

"Nothing in the journal," he answered earnestly.

She nodded slowly and then smirked at him. "Tulips, Charles? Mind you do not lose your heart to the girl."

"Lose my heart?" Charles scoffed at the preposterous notion. "I merely have an interest in seeing her succeed. And I assure you the tulips were not from me."

Though, dammit, he could not help but sift through his memory to think on who might have sent them.

Lottie shrugged, as if she did not believe him. "I have a favor to ask you regarding Lady Eleanor."

He gave a tense nod, suddenly fearful that Lottie might suggest he never come back to assist Eleanor.

"Will you go to Vauxhall the night she is to meet Devonington?" Lottie wrinkled her nose with distaste. "I do not like the man."

"I'll be there."

Charles poured himself a finger of Scotch. He didn't much care for the man either. But then, he hadn't liked any of the suitors vying for Eleanor's affections. Not a one of them was worthy of such a woman as Eleanor Murray.

Least of all him.

Chapter Fifteen

The dinner at Vauxhall Gardens could not have been more terrible. Eleanor made her way to the carriage line through the thick crowd, desperate to be done with it all.

A day with the promise of heavy rain had left the London air thick with moisture. Her skirts hung with damp stickiness against her legs, her hair felt as though it were plastered against her brow and the evening chill seemed to have taken up residence in the marrow of her bones.

And, as if the atmosphere were not already uncomfortable, the company had been far worse.

The Earl of Devonington held tightly to her arm as he escorted her through the throng of people seeking to avoid the impending storm. It had been he who had been utterly deplorable. He'd eaten with relish at the carvings of ham, famously thin, apparently taking great quantities to satisfy his monstrous appetite.

Watching the glistening slivers of pink meat disappear between his wet lips had resulted in obliterating her own appetite.

And now he had allowed Eleanor's cousin Lady Violet and her Aunt Lydia to become lost in the crowd.

A clap of thunder sounded overhead and Devonington flinched on her arm. He patted her hand. "It's merely thunder. No need to be afraid."

Drops of rain trickled from the skies and the civility of the crowd dissolved quite suddenly into chaos.

A man lunged between Eleanor and the Earl, ripping her arm from where the Earl had gripped it.

Devonington looked down at his waistcoat and cried out. "The wretch stole my watch!" He bolted after the man without a backward glance to Eleanor.

She stopped in stunned shock. He had left her. Alone. She steeled her spine and pressed forward in the crowd, eager to get to her carriage and end the awful night.

A man further behind them in the crowd caught Eleanor's attention. He rose taller than the other men, his dark hair glossy in the subtle moonlight, with a profile all too familiar. Her breath caught.

Charles.

Rain pattered down with a vengeance and the crowd reacted in kind, becoming rougher and more forceful.

She blinked through the heavy droplets.

Was it truly him?

Had he come for her?

The man turned and she nearly cried out with joy. It truly was Charles. He scanned the crowd, his expression intense, before his stare came to rest on her. Eleanor's heart leapt at the connection, and pounded even harder when he fought through the wall of people, heading in her direction.

She shouldn't be so eager, of course. After their last discussion he had made it quite obvious he wanted her to seek another husband. He had agreed to her condition, but clearly did not intend her to remain unmatched.

The churning sea of bodies tugged her hard to the right, and for one cold, lonely moment Eleanor was at the mercy of wherever the panicked crowd forced her. Shouts filled the air as people cried out for lost companions, while others shoved for advantage. She searched the sea of faces but did not catch sight of Charles again. The glow of hope dimmed.

Then a strong arm settled around her shoulders, blocking the worst of the jostling, and Charles's familiar scent fell around her like a warm embrace.

"I have you, Eleanor."

The voice was smooth and confident. Immediately any distress with Eleanor's situation evaporated.

Charles was there with her and all would be well.

Charles shielded Eleanor from the crowd with his arms, taking on the worst of the bumps to protect her. He did so gladly, grateful for the opportunity to come to her aid, to see her liberated from the company of Devonington.

The arrogant ass of a man had been so loud while speaking that almost every word he'd uttered had reverberated around the expanse of the private boxes. Eleanor, her cousin and the older woman with them had appeared quite perturbed.

Now she was free of the Earl, and standing before Charles with a quiet smile hovering on her lips.

"I have had my footman bring my carriage around toward the back, where it might be less crowded," Charles offered. "May I escort you there?"

"It would be my pleasure to have you do so, Your Grace."

"Charles, please."

He led her away from the edges of the crowd. Those large green eyes flicked up at him and held his stare.

"Charles." She glanced to his mouth and quickly turned her head away, looking toward the direction they headed.

The rain had ebbed to a few trickling drops and the roar of the crowd faded behind them. Ahead, one light glowed in the distance like a brilliant ball of fire. Another lit up several feet away, followed by another, and another.

Eleanor stopped and Charles followed suit. "They've continued to light the lamps," she said.

"It would appear the rain is beginning to abate." He kept his hold on her. There was no longer a need to do so, but there was certainly a desire.

Several more globes of light lit up in the distance.

"It's amazing, isn't it?" she asked. "Like magic."

He looked down at her and found her lovely face awash in the gilded glow of those many lamps. "Indeed."

She shifted her gaze from the lamps in the distance to his face. Dots of rain had left a sheen on her skin, giving it an otherworldly, luminous appearance.

"Why are you looking at me like that?" she whispered.

"Because you're beautiful."

She did not lower her head in demure acceptance of his compliment. Instead she tilted her head up. "No longer an Ice Queen?"

The blazing memory of that kiss, her passion, scorched through him. "God, no. Rather the opposite." He dragged his fingertips over a wet lock of her red hair. "You are fire, and your kiss is quite unforgettable."

"Then you've thought of it?" She slid him that coquettish look.

"I have." Time and time again...until the tease of the memory became as unbearable as the aching in his groin.

She turned to him and set a hand on his chest. The rain had resumed its steady fall, pelting them with frigid drops, and yet so intense was the heat in her eyes he scarcely registered the cold.

"I've thought of nothing else."

Her voice was quiet, intimate, the same as it had been that day when he'd kissed her. He recalled it all too well now...taking the pinkness of her nipple into his mouth and reveling in her cries of pleasure.

"Nor have I," he groaned truthfully. It had even distracted him often from his task of finding the ruby.

Rain soaked them both, leaving their clothes clinging to them and giving shape to her curves beneath the loose-fitting gown she wore. He could see a narrow waist and full hips to match the breasts he knew to be round and firm.

Her gaze took on that boldness he so enjoyed. "Will you kiss me, Charles?"

Lottie's words came back to him at that unfortunate moment. *She is meant to wed, not to be distracted by you.*

Yes, he'd promised to marry her if there was no other interest, but he wouldn't be any more a good husband to her than his father had been parent to him. He should take her from this place. And yet even as he thought as much he found himself already leaning into her, drawn to the promise of her lips.

Her mouth was warm against his, despite the chill of her skin. Their lips met in a single chaste kiss before their tongues brushed one another's.

Charles's blood raced insistently through his veins, hot with need. Aware of the possibility of being seen, he pulled his evening cloak around her and held her gently to him as he led them both down one of the infamous dark paths of Vauxhall Gardens.

Once they were veiled in shadows, Charles kept his cloak over them both and tilted her face toward his. She licked her rosy lips. With a hungry growl he drew her more tightly against him and kissed her. He sucked her lower lip into his mouth and ran his tongue over it.

The feminine curves of her body arched against him, so the ache of his hard shaft pressed into the softness of her stomach with the most exquisite torment.

She trailed kisses down his jaw to the line of his neck. Her breath sounded loud in his ear and he felt the warmth of her lips parted over his skin as she gently nibbled at the sensitive skin there. He had to clench his teeth to keep from giving in to a long, hungry groan.

"Is that what you like?" she asked.

Dear God.

"Eleanor..." he said her name on a rough exhalation.

Her hot tongue touched his neck, followed by a delicate little nip and a sucking kiss. His body blazed with the tingles of lust. Did she know what she was doing to him?

He found her body under the cloak by touch, roaming his hands over her sweet shape. He reveled in the slenderness of her waist, the curve of her bottom, which he caught in his hands. She arched her hips forward and his shaft pressed against her stomach once more, causing friction against the intensely building pressure.

He murmured her name, though he'd intended to speak in protest. They should not be doing this—especially in a place they could be so easily seen. Yet even as he thought such things his hands did not cease their eager exploration.

She pulled her head away from him as his palms found

the weight of her breasts. Her lashes swept downward, her face registering all the pleasure she felt. Confound it, he could not help himself. His thumb brushed the swell of her breast until a moan told him he'd found her nipple beneath the thickness of her stays.

She was so passionate, so receptive. Had he ever wanted anything the way he wanted Lady Eleanor Murray?

Yes, he had. The stone.

Everything he'd sacrificed already and would sacrifice in the future. The stone, his promise—it had to be everything. Before the dukedom, before Eleanor. She needed a husband—not to be pawed by him.

It was for exactly that reason that he drew away and straightened. "We cannot keep on with this," he said.

Eleanor simply nodded. Her eyes sparkled with longing and her mouth remained reddened from the force of their kisses. She did not protest this time—perhaps because she understood that together they were far too dangerous.

Charles quickly adjusted his placket once his cloak had fallen back around him. He could only hope the raging swell of his manhood would soften quickly.

Eleanor took his offered arm, her hand trembling slightly when she set it atop his, and together they made their way to the waiting carriage.

The cool air cleared the fog of Charles's passion. He would not allow himself to ruin Eleanor—especially when he knew he could not in good conscience marry her.

Once he had the rest of the journals from her, he would unearth the whereabouts of the Coeur de Feu and then leave to reclaim the stone, fulfilling his father's promise. In the meantime he would have to keep his distance. For Eleanor's sake.

Chapter Sixteen

Charles couldn't take it anymore. Or rather he couldn't take the lack of progress anymore. He'd applied hours to searching through the journals from their country estate to no avail.

Placing the key on the page, reading something indistinguishable. Then placing the key on another page and reading something indistinguishable. And yet again placing the key on the page and reading something indistinguishable.

In truth, it was as he'd expected. He'd gone through every book and piece of paper in the stack of boxes. What he needed was doubtless in the other journals Eleanor had.

He would need to see her again in an effort to secure more of them. After all, he had said yes to her request to wed her if there was no one else willing to. The journals were his due.

And yet the very idea of being in the same room with her left his mind whirling with a stream of memories he could not shake.

Their secluded tryst under his cloak blended with that last time at Lottie's. When he'd kissed her. Actually much more than kissed. He had pulled down her bodice and drawn her nipple into his mouth. He almost groaned at the memory, for such a little bud it was—berry-pink compared to her alabaster skin, firm against his tongue. And the way she'd cried out and clung to him...

Regret twisted in his chest. He shouldn't distract her from the marriage mart. Especially when the only vow he truly intended to fulfill was the one he'd given his father.

He stared down at the great mahogany desk he sat at—his father's. Even the new chair Thomas had procured did not alleviate the sense of strangeness in the room, the sense that Charles did not belong there. Perhaps he never would adjust to this room being anything more than his father's study.

Charles lifted his gaze to take in the richly appointed room with its blend of luxurious furnishings and cherished artifacts, all amid the piles of opened boxes from Somersville Manor.

His father had seemed invincible, too vibrant ever to die. And yet he was truly gone. After a lifetime of seeking his father's approval, of wishing for the bond Charles had seen other fathers and sons share, it would never happen now.

Not that his childhood had been without privilege. Charles had been brought up with nothing but the best of everything, and his father had never asked anything of him.

Nothing until the stone. And in that one request Charles had failed.

He rose abruptly from the desk, unable to stand the crush of his father's success around him, the scalding reminder of how Charles was so very imperfect.

"Thomas," he said aloud. His valet appeared immediately. "Have my carriage readied. I'm curious to learn if I've been blackballed from White's yet."

As it turned out Charles had not been ousted in his absence, and was, in fact, welcomed eagerly into White's as if they'd known he was coming. No doubt Thomas's doing.

Upon entry he had a brandy in his hands and the hearty welcome of several members. Conversation centered on Napoleon's impending exile and the hardheadedness of General Thouvenot, who seemed to have a dogged determination to keep the fortress of Bayonne in French control, despite Napoleon's surrender.

The conversation fed an inner part of Charles he'd long forgotten he needed—a chance to come to a place like White's and let his mind relax, away from all of life's complexities. There was no mention of Lottie and her fall from grace, nor of unmet promises to dead fathers, nor even any reminders of a woman who set his soul aflame.

No, White's was about men. Sports. Drink. Politics.

"Somersville!" The Marquess of Kentworth waved him over from where he stood near the broad fireplace with the Viscount Rawley ever at his side. The volume of Kentworth's voice indicated that the man was thoroughly in his cups.

Charles sipped at his own ball of fire and made his way to his old university chums. They'd certainly had some fun together in their heyday, and he was more than ready to reminisce over those fond memories rather than dwell on the dismalness of his current life.

"How are you, old chap?" Kentworth smiled at him, revealing the dimple in his right cheek which had always set the ladies aflutter.

"Relegated to London society." Charles lifted his glass in silent toast.

Kentworth bellowed a laugh. "Aren't we all?" He drank deep from his overfull glass, sloshing some over the rim.

"Rawley." Charles nodded at the tall, thin man, who gave the shy half smile that had followed him into adulthood.

"Have you found all the gold in Africa yet?" Kentworth asked with a bleary grin.

The question rankled, teasing at Charles's already tense nerves. He hadn't gone to seek fortune. Fortune he had in abundance, thanks to generations of cunning investments and the well-known financial accoutrement of the Somersville ancestors. But then Kentworth's demeanor had always edged near the obnoxious when he was foxed.

"I don't believe gold is precisely what Somersville was seeking," Rawley said.

Kentworth squinted and nodded. "Of course, of course... Antiques and other things of the like—correct?"

Charles chuckled in an attempt to be more good-natured than he felt. "Mmm...other things of the like."

"I bet you found yourself a good bit of sport around the world, eh?" Kentworth said with a wink.

Before Charles could answer, or Rawley could intervene, Kentworth gulped more of his drink and put up a finger to indicate that he was prepared to speak again.

"You recall that bit of ice we danced with at Covington's masquerade ball?"

That bit of ice.

Charles clenched his jaw. "I might..." he replied slowly.

"The one with the glittering dress and the bright red hair?" Kentworth tilted his head as if the details weren't important. "She rather surprised us by being quite unlike the prim and prudish miss that Ledsey had led us all to believe she was. After all, the chap was once considering marrying the ewe."

"Lady Eleanor was quite impressive." Rawley nodded in agreement and took a measured sip from his own glass.

Kentworth lifted his drink in the air. Somehow it was already half drained. "If I were the marrying sort I'd make a bid for her myself. Though she won't be long on the market."

"Why do you say that?" Charles's stomach flipped. A ridiculous reaction. He should be grateful to be saved from having to work his way out of his promise.

"Devonington is going to make an offer." Kentworth snorted. "He may not be much of a boxer, but the old goat is full of spirit—I'll give him that. And I can't say she'll be inclined to refuse, considering she's got enough dust on her already to be lobbed on the shelf, and he's got enough wealth to make the heavens sing on command."

Charles's drink soured in his gut. Kentworth went on to prattle about some other such nonsense, but Charles had stopped listening.

Devonington was going to ask for Eleanor to marry him.

He was an earl with an unrivaled fortune. He had a strong name with titles that could be traced back to the Conqueror. The man was a bloated beast, and his conversation was a dead bore. But eligible ladies long on the market—ladies like Eleanor—might easily be pressed by their desperate families to accept such a proposal.

Kentworth was right. The odds of her refusal were low indeed—especially with the Countess of Westix shouting in Eleanor's ear.

Of course, she might refuse—but then she might do so

in order to come to Charles, for him to make good on his promise. And he could not follow through.

Either way, he did not like the outcome.

Charles finished off the rest of his brandy and excused himself to obtain another, eager for the slow burn and inevitable numbness of its embrace. Because apparently, no matter where he went, he was haunted by all his choices.

Eleanor was near bursting with excitement. She practically ripped off her cloak, mask and wig the moment she passed the threshold of Lottie's town house in Bloomsbury Square. She'd been forced to hold her news until now, as the prior evening her mother had insisted she attend Lady Bunton's soiree, which had been a wretched bore.

Certainly not as exciting as the night at Vauxhall. Not the time she'd spent with the Earl of Devonington, but the quiet moments stolen in the dark with Charles. Her face went hot at the memory, and she tried to still her pulse-pounding eagerness at the prospect of seeing him again.

Lottie's butler showed her inside and she all but ran into the drawing room where she had spent so many evenings. It was at that moment, when she was anticipating sharing her news with Lottie and Charles, that she realized that for the first time in her life she had friends. True friends whom she trusted.

"I have the most thrilling news to share!"

The words exploded from her before Charles could straighten from his welcoming bow. She clutched the bag of journals to her chest in her excitement.

He stiffened and rose slowly, his jaw locked in a tight grimace. Lottie cast him an odd glance and gave her a confused look.

Goodness, but Charles did look as though he'd put a vinaigrette under his nose. His lips were drawn together and the skin around his eyes was tight.

Perhaps he feared she might mention to Lottie their exchange at Vauxhall. But surely he would know she would keep such things to herself.

"I have the answer," Eleanor said breathlessly.

"Do you?" he asked, in a voice that could only be described as dispassionate. Holding much of the same cold detachment *she* had once been rumored to possess.

Now she understood how unwelcoming that demeanor could be, and why she'd had seven unsuccessful Seasons.

"Yes." She spoke more softly now. "The information we need is only in one journal."

Charles frowned at her from across the room. "What are you referring to?"

Lottie looked between Charles and Eleanor, frowning.

"The journals." Eleanor held up the bag. She'd procured the remaining five from her father's study, but knew there to be more at their castle in Scotland.

In truth, Charles had been correct—the contents in the journal were not for a lady's eyes. Amid lengthy stories of cracking ancient walls and dusty artifacts were lurid tales of what native women around the world offered by way of pleasure and sex.

One tale had gone into such detail on debauchery she had spent the better part of an evening woolgathering and wondering if such things could even be physically possible. So much so, she'd missed most of the Earl of Devonington's conversation about his new hunting dog while at the soiree.

Not that she'd minded terribly. At least not until she'd gone to bed that evening and the story in the journal had replayed itself in her imagination, and curiosity had caused a warm and hungry hum between her thighs…

The pinched expression on Charles's face relaxed. "The journals. Yes."

It was not only his face which relaxed, but the tension hanging thick between them.

Eleanor went on. "There was a final entry in a hand I did not recognize as your father's or mine. It alluded to another journal—one written only by this author—detailing his research on the whereabouts of the gem in light of growing unrest among them all."

"Yes, my father indicated there being only one we'd need the key for." Charles strode toward her. "Did you bring all the journals with you?"

"I did." Eleanor held out the black bag she'd brought with her. "Well, with the exception of the journals in Scotland, at our castle there."

Lottie peered at the journals, the twist of her lips indicative of her fading excitement. "While these *are* incredibly interesting…" She widened her eyes and looked askance with the exaggeration of a person intentionally lying. "I'll leave you to look them over. But this is the last lesson I give you permission to miss."

She wagged a finger in chastisement at Eleanor, but the threat behind her words were offset by the kindness of her sapphire-blue eyes.

Eleanor nodded obligingly and Lottie excused herself from the room rather than stay and be subjected to something she considered hopelessly dull.

Eleanor dug out the book she'd referenced, and flipped to the last page, where the author had written about the stone.

The door closed behind Lottie, and Charles came nearer.

The heady spice of his scent teased at Eleanor and swept her into a stream of memories. His hands on her, his mouth on her, the tug of her evening gown, the touch roaming over her body and coming to rest on her breasts... How she'd fantasized about what she'd read of in the journal transpiring between her and Charles, imagining it in every lurid, sweaty detail until she was dizzy.

She tapped the choppy handwriting with her fingertip, already having taken it upon herself to remove her gloves this time. She was nearly breathless with the hope that Charles would touch her again, kiss her again. "At least now we have the handwriting with which to identify the pages that will be needed to be compared against the key."

"Brilliant." He regarded her with a curious expression. "Is there any other news you intended to share?"

"Did you expect some?"

"Of course not." He chuckled.

The shift in his mood was notably odd.

"I'm assuming you've already sought out this man's handwriting throughout the other journals?"

He had known she would be thorough. The thought pleased her immensely. "I have," she confirmed. "There are several examples we can review with the key."

Silence blossomed between them, ripe with sizzling memories and wanting.

"I must thank you for coming to my aid in the crowd at Vauxhall."

Eleanor tried to push aside what had happened after his assistance, so she could fully focus on speaking. Only such memories were not so easily swept aside.

"I daresay the Earl was quite upset with my departure."

She almost laughed at how red-faced he'd been the next

morning, when he'd called. Even her mother was beginning to grow weary in her championing of him, despite his considerable wealth.

"Indeed?"

Charles studied her face with the intensity of a man who intended to kiss a woman. Was it wanton to wish so desperately that he would? Heat suffused her entire body in a vicious blush.

"In truth, I ought to apologize." He spoke in a quiet, intimate tone, impossible to overhear from the other side of the door. "I should not have kissed you."

Disappointment dragged at her elation. "You regret it?"

He ran a finger down her cheek and she found herself leaning toward him.

"Yes and no."

Her eyes closed, the better to appreciate the sensation of his touch.

"I've been thinking of you far too often…"

Charles's voice sounded gently in her ear, sensual and low.

"How you rob me of my senses…"

His small sigh whispered across her skin like a caress.

"I shouldn't have come tonight. In truth, I should never come again."

Never come again?

Eleanor's eyes flew open. "Charles, don't say such things."

He clenched his jaw and stroked the pad of his thumb over her lower lip. His touch against her mouth brought to mind a curious act described in the salacious tale she'd read, and a small flame kindled the fire.

Curiosity simmered through her.

Did she dare be so bold?

Chapter Seventeen

Charles knew he ought to walk away at that very moment. Leave London with the journals he did have and not return until he was certain Eleanor had been safely wedded and bedded and was forever out of his grasp.

And yet the idea of her marrying Devonington set his blood to boiling.

To imagine her in Devonington's bed…it was more than he could stand. Not that he hadn't imagined her in a bed—only it had been his own, her skin like hot silk under his hands.

She regarded him with a brazen stare, as though she could read his thoughts, as though she meant to entice them. It was getting harder and harder to walk away from the temptation that was Eleanor Murray.

So Charles did not walk away.

He did not even step back to break the inappropriate closeness between them.

He could not bring himself to, no matter how reason

played in his mind. His thumb brushed over her full bottom lip once more, reveling in the supple pliancy of her warm skin. Her lips parted—and then she drew in the digit with a hot, gentle suck.

His mouth fell open on a surprised exhalation and his manhood lurched to attention.

She tilted her head upward, releasing his thumb and capturing his gaze instead. "One of the journals proved to be most…edifying."

Charles swallowed around a dry throat. "I think you ought to have taken my advice and not read them."

Eleanor lifted an eyebrow in a show of naughty prowess. "Should I?"

This level of flirtation would make his shaft burst if she continued. Regardless, it did not stop him from speaking—from asking what he should not. "What was it exactly that you read?"

"Of the other things the *ghawazi* do." Her cheeks flushed. "Aside from dancing."

An image of her in swirls of near-transparent silk lodged in Charles's mind, the same image as had done so the last few nights. Ever since they'd looked at that image of the nearly naked woman together. His skin tingled with the nearness of her and his shaft raged against his breeches. Ridiculous, considering she hadn't even touched him. Well, save when she'd sucked on his finger as if…

He shook his head. "You should not have read them. They are not fitting for a lady."

"I have questions."

Walk away, Charles.

But again he did not listen to his own command, and instead found himself pressing deeper into the damning conversation. "What questions?"

She pulled in a deep breath and her bosom swelled against the red silk dress she wore. He thought of her nipples beneath, pink and perfect. His tongue longed to circle the sweet buds, to draw them into the warmth of his mouth and suckle her until the nubs grew taut.

Her lashes had lowered to a languid half-lidded gaze. "When a woman sucks a man's thumb, is it not in suggestion of her taking into her mouth…?" She paused, bit her lip and looked down to his breeches.

"Eleanor, this conversation is not—"

"Appropriate. Yes, I know." Her blush deepened to an even darker shade of red. "But there is much we have done that is not appropriate. Please answer the question. When a woman sucks on a man's thumb—"

"Yes," he gritted out.

Dear God, this conversation was becoming the greatest torture of the sweetest kind.

She nodded. "And if a man could be pleased thus, could not a woman?"

Sweat prickled on his brow. "A woman can be pleased in many ways."

"So, is it possible to please one another without penetration?"

The woman was going to kill him with such talk. "Yes."

"A man and woman can both be pleased while she continues to remain a virgin?"

Her line of questioning was suddenly apparent.

The room had grown far too warm, her gaze far too bold, and his willpower was far too damned weak. What man could resist such temptation?

Still, he knew he needed to try. "Eleanor, we shouldn't—"

"I know."

She stroked her fingertips over the lapel of his jacket before glancing up at his face. She rose up on her toes and pressed a kiss to his lips. There was no delicate innocence about her. No, this time her affections were those of a woman hot and hungry with need.

Charles ought to have resisted. God knew, he should have gently pushed her away. In truth, he had every intention of doing so—until she boldly sucked his tongue and gave a low, hungry moan. Her body melted against his, a delicious pressure against the strain of desire aching in his groin.

Dear Lord.

He was helpless against the lure of lust. His arms came around her, pulling her even tighter to him. Her hips pressed to his, against the impossible hardness aching here, and she gasped. Her hands slid up his back as she brought them closer still.

They kissed with lips and tongues and the careful grazing of teeth, until their panting breaths tangled with one another. He ran his hands over her body, gliding over the silk as he caressed her narrow waist and cupped the delicious curve of her bottom. She arched her pelvis against his and sent waves of pleasure through him from the hot friction.

She kissed his jaw, then his neck, and ever so delicately nipped the skin just below his ear. Prickles raked down him with an intense thrill. She writhed against him, her dance one of eager desperation.

Charles knew all too well the ravenous need plaguing her. He nudged his knee between hers and she parted her legs. Her skirts rode up to her shapely stocking-clad calves.

She held tight to his shoulders and rolled her hips in the

natural rhythm of lovemaking, riding his thigh in a way that made him want her to ride *him*. Her right leg was between his own, and her movements ground against his shaft. He drew down the neckline of her dress with a tug and her breasts popped free, full and firm.

Eleanor's hand moved up to the back of his head. "Yes. Please, Charles."

He bent his head to flick his tongue over her nipple, circling it several times before pulling it between his lips and into his mouth. She gave a quiet cry of pleasure and arched her back.

He moved to the other nipple while he cupped the weight of her silken breast. "Please what?" he ground out.

His mind whirled in a maelstrom of lust and burning hot need. He could barely think to breathe, let alone piece together what it was she asked for.

"Pleasure me." Her voice came out in a whimper.

Hell.

What man could say no to such a request?

Eleanor was so very near to exploding—as though she'd gone too close to the sun and all of her had been set aflame. Heat blazed through her veins and pulsed with such longing it was as if a pounding drum reverberated through her entire body. Her world focused on Charles—on those brilliant blue eyes and the wild passion he aroused in her.

He went still at her request. Would he deny her?

She put her hands to his chest and slid her fingers down his flat stomach, the way the woman in the journal's entry had done, down to where the thick column of his desire rose within his breeches. He choked in a breath.

She grazed the swell rising beneath the placket, tentatively at first. He gave a shuddered exhalation and tensed against her. She fixed her regard on his face and curled her fingers over the bulge. His brows flinched and drew together, as if the pain of his need was as intense as her own. He was hard under her touch, like iron or bone. *This* was the shaft the journal had referred to, engorged and heavy. It was the device from which a man drew his pleasure and gave it in return.

Charles cursed and pulled her touch from his body. Disappointment charged her at the thought of being forever without satiation from such powerful, painful longing. That was until he leaned her back onto the chaise and his hand swept up her calf.

Her breath caught.

She lay back on the smooth velvet as his fingers continued to move higher up her leg, inching up her gown and chemise. Her breath came faster as his touch proceeded, until his fingertips whispered past the edge of her stockings and caressed the nakedness of her thigh. Her core trembled in anticipation.

Yes. Higher. Closer. Almost…

Finally, at long last, he made his way up her entire leg. He eased her hem higher, over her hips, baring her most intimate place to him. She ought to have been embarrassed, but the lust hammering through her was too great. She could scarcely think, let alone feel shame.

He paused, gazed down at her, and brushed the juncture between her legs. A jolt of pleasure shot through her and she gasped at its intensity.

Charles closed his eyes like a man in prayer. "Good God, Eleanor. You are so very wet."

His words were appreciative, which must mean being

wet was good. She rubbed her thighs together in anticipation for more.

His chest rose up and down with his ragged breathing and he opened his eyes to watch her again as he drew his finger over her once more. Pleasure, marvelous and perfect, rippled through her.

"More," she whispered. "Please."

He did not disappoint. His finger moved with careful skill, up and down over her, before coming to a stop on a particularly sensitive spot. His stare burned into her as he rolled his digit in slow circles.

Heat spiraled through her. Eleanor covered her mouth to stifle a cry of pleasure and her head fell back. She was unable to focus on anything save the bliss of his stroke between her legs. Right when she felt as though she might explode, he drew his finger away and made the lazy path up and down, up and down over her once more.

Her hips strained toward him and she opened her eyes. "Please, Charles. *Please.*"

He leaned over her and captured her mouth in his, while his fingers found their way back to that delightful spot. His shirt teased against her nipples, his tongue tangled with hers, and his fingers moved and moved and moved, until Eleanor's entire body drew tighter, like a clock being wound to the point of breaking.

And break she did. Into splinters of color and light and heat and everything wonderful. She cried out with the overwhelming euphoria of it and her hips bucked upward. The sounds of her pleasure were muted against Charles's mouth as he continued to kiss her while his fingers worked, until she was too sensitive to stand another moment.

Charles pulled back slightly, his eyes intent on her. "That was beautiful, Eleanor."

This time a blush did heat her cheeks. "That was…incredible." Her voice trembled slightly. "I never knew…"

He gave her a lazy half grin and her heart flipped. "And now you do."

She couldn't help but smile. "And now I do."

The hardness of his manhood rested against her thigh, and called further attention to her curiosity. If his fingers could procure such delight, what might the organ made for pleasure accomplish?

She released her hold on his shirt, where she had apparently crumpled the fine cloth in her fist during the mindlessness of her climax, and let her touch wander toward his shaft.

"No." He spoke through gritted teeth. "Eleanor, do not tempt me."

Oh, but she wanted to tempt him. She wanted him to be as hopelessly lost in her as she'd been in him only moments before.

"I want to do for you as you've done for me." She continued her path downward. The bulge was hot to the touch.

"Eleanor." He wrapped his fingers around her wrist and pulled her hand away. "I cannot—"

Steps sounded outside the door. Footsteps muted by carpet until they were upon the wooden flooring in their last step before the door.

Eleanor and Charles stiffened as one in surprise, but both were too late even to attempt to move. The doors flew open and Lottie filled the doorway, witness to the full extent of their incredibly compromised position.

Chapter Eighteen

Charles had the presence of mind to shield Eleanor—at least as much as was possible in their precarious position.

Lottie stared in shock, her hand still poised on the door she'd thrown open. Her mouth hung agape, and her eyes were wide enough to indicate that she'd seen it all.

With a gasp, she jerked back from the room and slammed the door shut. The echo of the impact rang out for a solid second before either of them could move again.

Charles immediately turned to Eleanor and found her face as red as her brilliant hair. Her eyes caught his, sharp with guilt, before sliding away. He eased off her and reached to help her adjust her gown, but she brushed him aside. She quickly put herself to rights and stared regretfully toward the door. He didn't blame her. He wished to be gone from the room as well.

"Forgive me, Eleanor. I should never—"

He should never have what? Kissed her? Touched her? Wanted her? Were such things even possible to avoid?

"I should never have compromised you," he said at last.

Though she faced him, she kept her emotions masked beneath the sweep of lowered lashes. Her right eyebrow twitched upward. "I encouraged you." She pulled in a shaky breath. "I wanted you to do everything you did. So, you see, there's no transgression to forgive—except perhaps on my account. Forgive me for pressing you so firmly to…" She gave a shuddering exhalation.

He caught her under the chin with the tip of his forefinger. "Eleanor…" He hated seeing her like this, her pride bruised, her face colored high with shame.

"What's worse is that I do not regret what we've done, but only…" When she finally did look up at him, her eyes were wet with a sheen of tears. "Only fear the result of our being caught might mean Lottie will not allow you to meet with me again."

"Eleanor—" Damn, but words were hard to get out.

She lifted her brows.

"You should marry Devonington." He ground the words out as though they were glass splinters passing over his tongue. It was what he should say, he knew. For her sake.

A look of confusion puckered her brow, followed by a veil of emotionless apathy—the shield firmly lodged back in place. The knife in his heart twisted.

"I see." She lifted her chin in the haughty tilt she'd worn when he'd first met her. "You may keep the journals. You've earned them. Farewell, Your Grace."

She nodded her head politely, as was due his station, and opened the door, leaving the room.

Charles watched her departure, as he had most nights, and felt his heart twist under the duress of his shame.

Lottie appeared in the doorway and pushed shut the door behind her. "How dare you?"

Her voice shook and her glare skewered into his soul. She marched toward him and her silken skirt kicked out in angry thrusts.

"How *dare* you, Charles Pemberton?"

Before he could even open his mouth to speak, she pulled back her arm and her fist connected with his cheek.

He swallowed down the assault. It was deserved. His cheek stung.

"That was quite a hit, Lottie. Have you taken up boxing?"

"Do not jest with me." Her eyes flashed with a murderous rage. "How dare you do this to her? I care for her and you've left her ruined."

He reached for her. "You don't understand. I didn't—"

"*You* don't understand," Lottie hissed. "You've made her like me, Charles. You've ruined her life. Such a promising young woman…" She turned away and a sob choked out of her. "You've made her damaged…like me." Her slender back rounded and she cried with all the force of a broken heart.

But her heart was not the only one to break, for Charles's had surely shattered into a thousand pieces at witnessing such hurt in his childhood friend.

One step had him at her side. He put his arms around her and held her, even when she tried to tug away. "She was not compromised," he said insistently. "Our actions were certainly improper, but I assure you her innocence is thoroughly intact."

"Oh, Charles." Lottie turned into him and sobbed against his chest.

He held her in place and patiently waited for her tears

to ebb. At last they did, and she accepted the handkerchief he offered.

She dabbed her cheeks and regarded him with tear-spiked lashes. "It's for the best this way…letting her go. You could never marry her."

Charles gritted his teeth, hating how very correct Lottie's cutting words were. If he married Eleanor it would be a destined failure. If she remained in London while he traveled she would be miserable, and if he were made to forgo his travels he would be miserable.

He needed travel like air to his lungs. It pumped in his veins and brought light to his world. The first time he'd stepped off a ship…the first time he'd glimpsed what he had only read about before…the powerful force that made him feel that much closer to his father… It was an exhilaration he could never sacrifice.

A marriage between them could never be right.

Damn Lottie and her valid statement. And damn how much it piqued his ire.

"And how will she be better off with Devonington?"

"She will never love him." Lottie sighed. "So at the very least our sweet Eleanor will not suffer a broken heart."

With that, she left the room, leaving Charles alone with the weight of his own guilt and the echo of the painful truth.

The wait for Eleanor's hackney took the better part of what seemed like a lifetime. She stood stiffly, beneath the protection of her domino, wig and mask, hoping they were enough of a shield to blanket her mortification.

This was the price of wantonness.

Lottie had come to speak with her once Eleanor had disguised herself and begun waiting for her carriage. Their conversation had been brief, yet poignant enough to play out continually through Eleanor's mind.

She had tried to tell Lottie it had been her fault—which indeed it had been, shameful as it was to confess. Lottie had cast aside her admission with the counter that Charles had known well enough what he was doing and ought to have been in control of his person enough to decline her encouragement.

But it was more than just their conversation—it was Lottie's warning which resided in Eleanor's chest with all the comfort of a sharp stone.

Charles will never give up his travels...not even for you.

Eleanor hadn't expected him to give up *anything* for her, or to offer anything other than the pleasure she sought and a reprieve from the marriage mart. In truth, she hadn't even intended him to have to make good on his promise to marry her. And yet Lottie's words had pierced an area Eleanor had not realized was tender.

You should marry Devonington.

Charles's blunt statement echoed in her mind. Her eyes tingled with the threat of emotion, but she pulled deep on the strength she'd always fallen back on. Murrays were strong, after all. They did not give in to hurt.

Somehow the reminder failed to penetrate the haze of pain, where it glowed in her chest with a white-hot intensity.

The footman appeared and led her to her hired coach. She followed numbly, listening and speaking with mindless action. A similar hackney sat parked across the street. Its very presence rankled her nerves with considerable irritation. Was Bloomsbury truly so popular as to have such traffic dawdling upon its rain-slicked streets?

Eleanor turned her gaze from the offensive hackney and

directed her attention back to Lottie's town house, where it rose high and obstinate in the shadows. How would Lottie's conversation with Charles go?

The coach pulled away and Eleanor sat back in her seat. Worrying and wondering would do nothing. Considering how Lottie had spoken to her, Eleanor was sure she would not see Charles again—just as she'd feared. And it was her own fault.

Charles was gone forever—the man she'd somehow let in more than she'd thought. She'd hoped to meet another who could instill her with the passion he did, and yet she had been so dazzled by him the rest of the world had fallen into the shadows. Potential suitors included. She had squandered what precious little time she had.

It wasn't until she was safely home and in her room that she gave way to the crush of disappointment. She put her face in her hands, where her palms were cool against the blazing heat of her face, ready to let free her tears.

A knock sounded at the door—the gentle rap of her mother.

Eleanor snapped her head upright and sucked in a deep, calming breath before bidding her mother enter.

The Countess strode in with a smile. "I come with the most exciting news." Her mother clasped her hands together. "The Earl of Devonington has asked for my blessing."

Eleanor might have staggered under the news if she hadn't been standing beside her dressing table. She put her hand to its flat, steady surface. "I beg your pardon? Your blessing?"

"The Earl of Devonington. He is smitten with you, my dear." Her mother brushed a lock of hair from Eleanor's brow and frowned. "Are you ill? Your face is hot."

"Devonington?"

Eleanor shook her head. The events of the night whirled themselves into a tangle of thoughts and emotions too great to sort out. Charles had told her to marry Devonington. Actually *told* her to. Her stomach churned.

Frustrated desperation knotted at the back of her throat. "Mother, he is old and fat."

The Countess's mouth fell open in horror. "Eleanor Murray, you are not ever to say such things. The Earl is exorbitantly wealthy and his family well-established. With Evander gone…"

"I know."

Eleanor lowered her gaze from the starkness of her mother's stare. The topic of Eleanor's brother had always struck at a raw wound in them both. Her mother didn't need to finish what she'd intended to say. With Evander gone there was no way to increase the remaining funds in her mother's trust, nor to protect Eleanor from Leopold's avarice. And Eleanor's intention to find someone who made her feel like Charles had been terribly foolish and a shameful waste.

"The Season will be over soon," her mother said.

"I know," Eleanor said again, this time in a whisper.

The Countess stared at her daughter and her eyes softened. "I know you don't want to wed him, Eleanor. You're right—he is old and fat. But he is the type of man who will spend his days hunting and his nights engaged in activities which will keep him from your side. You need only see him occasionally, and he will likely die long before you."

"Mother!" It was Eleanor's turn to gape in horror.

The Countess waved dismissively. "Don't be so shocked, Eleanor. I'm being entirely pragmatic. Once he is dead you will be a widow with the bulk of his wealth. You will have freedom to do as you please without the obsessive scrutiny of the *ton*."

Her mother's words were hollow, but they were true.

"And the alternative is far more dismal," the Countess said with great gravity.

Eleanor nodded, unable to speak around the aching tightness in her throat. Her options were an abysmal marriage or a degrading, destitute existence. This was not how it was all supposed to turn out. She was supposed to have found a man who offered her a life of passion, of excitement.

The Countess patted Eleanor's cheek. "We are invited to a ball at Lady Canterbury's tomorrow evening. The Earl of Devonington will ask you to wed him. What will you say?"

Eleanor swallowed. Her heart throbbed with the weight of her burden and her ribs ached with every breath. "I will say yes," she answered dutifully.

It was not happiness or relief which showed on the Countess's comely face, but concern. "I think that is for the best." A smile twitched at her lips, but the display of discontent did not leave her features. And then her mother did a curious thing: she put her slender arms around Eleanor and embraced her.

Despite the chill of her mother's hands at her back, Eleanor leaned into the embrace and put her face to her mother's sharp shoulder.

"I should have done this more," her mother said on a choked whisper. "When you were a girl…before it was so very awkward." She laughed and leaned back. "I'm proud of you, daughter."

She gently kissed the top of Eleanor's head and left the room.

Eleanor stared at the closed door and tried to ignore the

dull pang in her chest. So this was her success, her grand victory. After working hard to allow herself to truly feel, to expect a brilliant life, she was now going to have to shove it all down deep within her once more so that she might become the Countess of Devonington.

Chapter Nineteen

Charles was in a devil of a mood when he returned home. So when Kentworth extended an invitation for a night on St. James's Street Charles was all too eager to agree. They started at White's, of course, with several rounds of brandy and a bit of faro. They played for over an hour before Kentworth decided the table's luck had run its course and they retired to one of the many tables to drink.

All night Charles waited with an anxious blend of fear and eagerness for Kentworth to mention Eleanor again. Thus far the conversation had not broached anywhere near women, let alone Eleanor.

Rawley glanced at his pocket watch—a habit he often employed prior to announcing his readiness to depart. Once Rawley departed, Kentworth would have no one to tame his crass commentary. If Charles meant to ask after Eleanor and Devonington, now would be the time to do it.

"Have you heard any further information about Devonington asking Westix's daughter to marry him?" Charles took a sip of brandy to cover up a grimace at his indelicate bluntness.

Rawley's perceptive scrutiny landed on him with too much interest. Kentworth, however, bellowed a laugh and put his drink onto the table. "You interested?"

Charles gulped down more brandy, his thoughts and tongue loose with drink. "I may be."

"In the wedding or the woman?" Kentworth waggled his brows.

Charles looked between Kentworth and Rawley. *Hell.* He'd opened the topic—he might as well see it properly closed. "The woman."

Kentworth chortled. "Would you even stay in London long enough to see her wedded and bedded?"

Irritation jangled Charles's nerves and he didn't bother to offer a reply.

Kentworth narrowed his eyes and his expression turned more serious. "You could do worse than her…" He tilted his head in latent consideration. "Far worse, actually."

"Are you going to ask her before Devonington has a chance?" asked Rawley.

"Always thinking ahead, this one." Kentworth reached across the table and ruffled Rawley's hair.

Rawley waved him off and brushed his hand over the mussed brown strands until they were swept neatly to the right, as he always wore his hair.

"It is merely a consideration." Charles leaned back in his chair.

"Are you considering when you'll ask or if you'll ask?" Kentworth probed.

Charles shrugged. He didn't know himself what he was

talking about. He only knew that the idea of Devonington taking Eleanor into his bed made his world darken.

Kentworth barked a laugh and got to his feet. "I need to attend to the call of nature. You gentlemen continue this discussion and I'll be back in a bit."

Rawley tapped a finger on the table as Kentworth strode away. "Do you love her?"

"What?" Charles asked, chuckling at the ridiculousness of the question.

"She won't increase your social standing, and while her family properties are substantial they're nothing compared to what you already hold. In offering to wed her before Devonington does you'd create a lifelong enemy. Why would you marry her for any other reason than love?"

That was a damn good question.

It was because Charles enjoyed her company and appreciated the frankness with which she spoke, and how she didn't make him guess as to her thoughts and desires as other ladies. Because a passion had been lit within her and it made her glow with a sensuality that drew him like the most attentive of moths. Because every time he thought of Devonington taking her as his wife, wearing her like an expensive bauble on his arm, undressing her and bringing her to his bed, it was like a punch in Charles's gut. But love...

Charles scowled and settled back in his seat. The aged leather under him creaked. "By God, Rawley, I daresay I had forgotten how damn insightful you are."

"It's part of my charm," he replied dryly.

Charles shook his head and chuckled at his old friend. More was the pity the chap couldn't find himself a lady he might be happy with. Many men weren't the marrying sort, but Rawley certainly was. Honest, dependable—a good man any way one looked at him.

"Another question." Rawley held a hand up in silent inquiry. "If I may?"

"By all means."

"Would you remain in London?"

Damn. Charles turned his focus to the cut-crystal glass in front of him.

Rawley continued before Charles was forced to answer. "I do not profess to know the hearts or minds of ladies. However, if you did intend to marry Lady Eleanor for love, I would venture to say she would not do well left alone while you seek adventure."

There always had been a gentle, considerate side to Rawley. Charles had forgotten that too. Perhaps it was because he'd been raised primarily by his mother, after his father had died within days of his birth.

Regardless, Rawley had brought up a point Charles already knew well enough. It was why he knew he could never have Eleanor in the first place. Charles's true love was travel—the same as his father. The idea of him even considering marriage was ridiculous.

And yet the idea of Eleanor wed to that pig Devonington coiled in Charles's gut like something cold and ugly.

Rawley tapped the flat of his hand on the table, severing Charles's ruminating, then got to his feet and nodded politely. "It appears Kentworth might have been waylaid by another faro game, and I have much to do in the morning. If you'll excuse me?"

Charles rose and nodded to his good friend as Rawley made his departure, leaving his brandy glass with several sips remaining at the bottom.

Kentworth was indeed at the faro table, where the conversation about Eleanor did not resurface. Once more he soon declared the faro table to be absent of luck, his tone boisterous with drink, and they found themselves in the West End, at a gambling hell of questionable reputation.

A smoky haze filled the room and the lights cast a low glow. Voices cried out in victory and defeat alike as dice rattled, cards snapped on tables and coin clinked from one hand to another.

Kentworth immediately made his way to the hazard table, sitting beside a woman who tossed him a coy glance as he called his bet. Charles stood several paces behind, not inclined at all to participate. He'd never been one to throw his wealth away.

"What's your pleasure, Your Grace?" a woman's voice asked.

Charles turned and found a red-haired woman in a crimson silk gown that had seen better days gazing saucily at him. She had green eyes, only not as green as Eleanor's... more of a moss-green, where Eleanor's were the color of vibrant emeralds or sunlit grass. Eyes that could penetrate the soul.

"I'll fetch you a drink if you like." The woman bit her lip in the obvious way women did when they wanted a man to stare at their mouths. "Or do you have other vices you'd like to see sated?" Her gaze wandered over him with interest.

A proposition. With a woman who looked like Eleanor. Would that quell the desire raging through him or only whet his appetite? Charles's mind was a sloshing jumble. He needed no more spirits.

"What would you do if you knew a lady was to marry a disgusting pig of a man?" Charles asked her abruptly.

The redhead's mouth pursed. "Depends on how you feel about her, I'd imagine." She gave a knowing smile. "Considering you're asking a woman who's all too willing to give you a night you won't forget a question about another woman, I'd wager you rather like her. And if I were in your position I imagine I'd try my damnedest to stop her."

Charles rubbed at a tense muscle along the back of his neck and nodded, considering her words.

She eased closer to him and the edge of one pert breast brushed his arm. There was a dry, powdery scent about her. "I can make you forget about any woman…"

Except he didn't want to forget Eleanor. Even if he should.

The redhead's words echoed through him. *I imagine I'd try my damnedest to stop her.*

Charles cleared his throat. "I think perhaps I should go."

The woman lifted a single shoulder, indicating that his refusal was of little consequence to her. "You know where to find me." She turned away with a suggestive wink.

He made his way from the gaming hell, knowing Kentworth would not notice his absence. Charles's mind was made up. He would speak to the very devil herself the following day and demand that Eleanor not marry Devonington. And while he was at it he would request the journals he knew to be in the Scottish castle. The journals Eleanor had given him that fateful day had yielded nothing of import.

Yes, in the morning, he would call on the Countess of Westix.

Eleanor stared down at the fresh bouquet of red roses on her dressing table. That made a bouquet every day from Devonington since they'd danced at the masquerade ball.

No doubt it was meant to entice her. Yet the delivery

served quite the opposite. The bright blooms inspired no affection in her. They didn't even hold a modicum of cheer. Rather they were a symbol of an ominousness that was far too imminent: her engagement.

It was through will alone that she did not give way to the threat of tears. After all, she'd yielded to the luxury of such emotion once she'd gone to bed the prior evening. Her eyes were still gritty with the aftereffects and slightly swollen.

The door to her bedchamber swung open abruptly and startled her into surprise. Amelia quickly closed the door and ran—truly *ran*—to Eleanor.

Amelia's hands fluttered anxiously in front of her. "My lady, he's here. I think to ask for Her Ladyship's blessing."

Eleanor's stomach dropped like a heavy stone. "But I thought I had at least until tonight?"

Amelia shook her head and her mobcap flapped around her narrow face. "Not the Earl of Devonington, my lady. The Duke of Somersville."

Eleanor stared at her maid, sure she'd heard incorrectly. "I beg your pardon?"

"The Duke of Somersville." Amelia bounced up and down in a bundle of excitement. "I think he's here to seek your hand in marriage."

Eleanor's pulse tripped and then wildly scrambled on at an erratic pace. Elation and excitement, pure and undeniable, thrilled through her. But surely he wouldn't truly offer. He had never expressed interest in marriage. As it was, he had needed time to consider her request even when he was not likely to have to honor it.

She shook her head, determined to tamp down the flame of insipid hope. "How do you know that's why he's here?"

Amelia grinned. "Because he's telling the Countess not to allow you to marry Devonington."

Eleanor leapt to her feet, unable to stop the foolish jolt to her heart. If there was a possibility of being with Charles she would not lose it—especially not for the likes of the Earl of Devonington.

"My lady, stop."

Eleanor stopped and turned back to Amelia. "Yes?"

"You shouldn't go."

Eleanor gawked at her maid. "You told me he was here to put an end to this dreadful engagement with Devonington. Why would you stop me?"

"This way if anyone asks you can tell them I told you not to go and not be lying about it." Amelia winked and shooed at Eleanor. "Go on, now."

Eleanor flew from her room and went as quickly as she dared down to the first floor, where she leaned her ear toward the crack between the double doors of the drawing room and strained to listen.

Charles's voice was the first she heard. "Your Ladyship, if you would only give me a chance."

Eleanor's heart soared with recognition. It truly was Charles. He had actually come here to seek her mother's permission to marry her. Just as Amelia had said.

"Your Grace, you demand my daughter not marry another, and yet you have no one else to recommend." The Countess's tone was on the verge of exasperation.

"I do have someone to suggest."

Charles's deep voice rumbled through the doors. Eleanor could scarcely breathe. Would he suggest himself?

The clink of a glass sounded. "By all means," said the Countess with some amusement.

Eleanor held her breath to ensure she would not miss a single word.

"Viscount Rawley."

Had Eleanor not been pressed to the door, she might have toppled over. *Viscount Rawley?*

"Viscount Rawley?" Her mother's incredulity matched Eleanor's own.

"He is responsible, mild-mannered, considerate." Charles rattled off the attributes like one might a list of items to obtain from the market. "He would be a loyal husband, and one with whom I believe Lady Eleanor might find happiness."

"Viscount Rawley has not asked for her hand but the Earl of Devonington has." The pause suggested the Countess was delivering one of her powerful pointed stares. "Will that be all?"

Eleanor closed her eyes to stay the prickle of tears. Charles had not come to ask her to wed him, but to suggest she to wed another. Someone *he* deemed adequate.

A lengthy silence followed. There was something else. She straightened, her curiosity piqued, her pathetic hope reignited with a miserable spark.

"My father had several journals," Charles began. "I believe you may be in possession of some. Possibly within your holdings in Scotland."

Eleanor clenched her fists. Blast him and his dogged determination to get those journals.

"I know nothing of such dreary things." The Countess sighed. "If there is nothing else…?"

There was another clink, more gently set than the other. "Thank you for your time, Your Ladyship. I'll see myself out."

Heavy footsteps sounded toward the door and Eleanor scrambled back to hide beside a large Oriental vase.

Charles had opened the door to a colorful life—one of feeling, of passion. All of that was now slipping through Eleanor's fingers. She would be left with nothing. Nothing but the memory of how life might otherwise be.

Her chest heaved and her mind spun with the beginnings of a desperate plan taking shape.

Charles emerged through the door, looking smart in a pair of polished Hessians with dove-gray breeches, a deep blue waistcoat and a charcoal jacket. She waited for him to walk partway down the hall, near the alcove by the stairs, and then she darted after him. After all, this might be her last chance to avoid marriage to Devonington and to truly live her life—especially when she had the very thing Charles needed: those damned journals.

Chapter Twenty

Charles was so enraged he almost did not hear the whispered call of his name. He turned cautiously, still unsure he'd heard correctly. Eleanor stood under the stairs in a white day dress, her lovely red hair bound back. Something hard thudded in his chest. God, but she was beautiful.

She pulled open a door in the wall beneath the stairs, revealing a narrow room within, and waved him over. A surreptitious scan confirmed that they were alone. For now.

She slipped into the darkness and he followed suit, ducking into the small space so he wouldn't bash his head against the low ceiling. She pulled the door shut behind him, plunging them into a darkness so great he could not see his hand in front of his face.

But he could smell her. Sweet jasmine, enticing femininity and all those memories, both tender and scorching.

"Charles…" she breathed. "I thought I would never see you again."

The familiarity of her voice, soft and intimate, pulled at

a place deep within him. He wanted to follow her words, to blindly locate her face. Devil take him, he wanted to do more than touch her soft skin. He wanted to press his mouth to hers, to be rewarded with her gasping cries of pleasure.

"I know you have no desire to marry me." Her tone pitched slightly and she paused. "You told me to marry Devonington, though clearly you do not wish for that."

His heart squeezed. How much of his conversation with the Countess had she heard?

"I do not wish to marry him either," she said. "And so I have one final proposition for you."

She rushed on before he could speak again, as though she were worried he would stop her.

"Marry me, Charles. Marry me and we will venture to Scotland, to Comlongon Castle, where the remaining journals are. I will give them all to you."

Marry her.

The boldness of this new offer should have shocked him. But it did not. He knew Eleanor far too well for that. She was determined, stoic in her resolve. Such very admirable traits. And yet he could not clear from his mind the thought of Eleanor alone in the vastness of Somersville House, surrounded only by the invisible presence of servants and loneliness.

A memory panged in his heart—one of the boy he'd been and how very enormous Somersville House had seemed when there was no one to fill it.

Could Charles do that to Eleanor? Leave her there, wondering what he was doing, as she stayed in that large, empty space, her imagination spiced with the readings of their fathers' journals. How could he confine her to such an existence?

"Am I truly so undesirable?" Her voice broke.

She bumped into him and the dull thump of her hand frantically patted the wall. Clearly she was seeking a way out. It was all too much—not only for her, but for him. The break in her voice, her desperation to leave. The knowledge that Devonington would have her, that the journals in Scotland could be his. Knowing he'd hurt her. Knowing that although he shouldn't, he *wanted* her.

"Eleanor, wait." He reached out for her in the darkness and sent something hard clattering to the floor.

The frantic sounds of her search for the door ceased. His hand found her shoulder. Using only the power of touch, he swept his fingertips over her fine cotton sleeve to the delicate hollow of her collarbone and up to her smooth cheek.

"I find you immeasurably desirable." He brushed his thumb over her lower lip. "I believe I have proved as much."

Her intake of breath whispered against his thumb. "Why will you not marry me?"

"Because I would make a terrible husband."

Confessing as much out loud made something in his chest give an unexpected wince. He shifted his thumb to stroke the softness of her cheek.

"Worse than Devonington?" she asked with obvious skepticism.

"I intend to travel, Eleanor, the same as our fathers did. First to find the ruby, and then to explore, once I've seen to the duties required of me as Duke. I have never considered myself a man to sacrifice the world for a family."

"You will have to marry eventually," she said softly. "As part of your duty. Why not let it be me?"

Her question squeezed at his chest. Why not, indeed? Perhaps because she was too intelligent. Possibly even too dear to him. Because, as much as he did not wish to admit it to himself, he did care.

More than he would like to.

"And why would you have to sacrifice your adventures?" Eleanor pressed.

He shook his head, though he knew she couldn't see it. He had lived a life without love for so long he did not know if he could ever create it, if he could ever give it. On so many accounts he would be a terrible husband and father.

"I wouldn't be able to live with myself if I abandoned you while I sought my own way in life. What sort of a husband would I be to leave you constantly? I refuse to do to my family what our fathers did to us." He spoke with quiet sincerity.

"I'm not a woman easily broken or swayed." Her voice was strong, with her usual show of tenacity. "And I can quite well take care of myself."

He chuckled. "Don't I know it?" He hated this darkness, and his inability to witness the determined flash he knew must be in those green eyes. "But I fear you would eventually hate me."

"I believe I would hate you less than my other option."

Her other option. Devonington.

A spike of discomfort shot through Charles.

Damnation, was that jealousy?

If he wed her he would have the rest of the journals. He would have her. Wholly and completely. His wife. In his bed.

It was then that he knew he could never truly have allowed her to marry Rawley.

"Hate me less, you say?" He couldn't help but grin. "Such flattery from an Ice Queen."

He couldn't stop touching her, letting his hands play over her cheeks, her neck, the graceful line of her collarbone. And she did not move to stop him.

"Your mother will be unhappy." He traced the edge of her collarbone. "And if we wed we ought to do so quickly. I could have a license in two days."

He stroked her neck and felt her pulse quicken under his fingertips.

"Then you agree?" Her question was breathless with anxious hope.

He would have her in his bed, the journals would be at his disposal, and part of his ducal agreement fulfilled. How could he say no?

"Yes." He drew her to him, unable to stop himself.

"Will you be attending Lady Canterbury's ball this evening?"

"I have an invitation, but have not yet accepted it."

This earned him a playful tap on the arm. "You ought to respond to your invitations. Preparations must be made for intended guests."

"I've always been bad at such things. Fortunately for me that task will pass to my wife in the future."

"You're hopeless." Laughing joy was evident in her voice. "Attend tonight," she said. "We can announce our betrothal and the banns can be called later this week. We could be married in a month, easily. It will all be proper, which will please my mother, and she will eventually forgive me, I'm sure. After the announcement is made and the banns are called she will not have me beg off our engagement. Not when it would cause a scandal."

It was an underhand plan, but a solid one nonetheless.

"Are you certain, Eleanor? Your mother may not forgive such a deception."

"I cannot imagine my life with Devonington."

Nor could he. The very idea of winning her from the buffoon made Charles want to puff out his chest. Instead, he cradled her face and brought his mouth down to meet her lips. Except he met something decidedly not her lips.

Eleanor gave a little laugh. "You've kissed my nose."

He kissed her lower, touching his lips to her warm mouth. However, once he had managed one kiss he knew it would never be enough again. He anticipated the future with something deeper, more passionate—an ignited lust that would not have to stop.

He straightened, pressed his lips chastely to the top of her head, and breathed in the floral scent of her. Soon he would bury himself in that perfume, tangle in it amid tossed sheets and naked limbs.

"I shall see you tonight."

A crack of light showed at the door and he realized she had pushed it open. She hesitated, her face cast in that slice of light, revealing her beauty to him and, more importantly, where her lips were located. He bent over her and gave her a kiss he was sure she would not forget.

He lingered a moment longer than he should, hesitant to leave when he wanted nothing more than to deepen their kiss. "Tonight."

Finally, he slipped into the brilliance of the empty hall, making his regretful departure as he'd promised the Countess he would.

At last, he would have his journals—and he would also have leave to fully taste Eleanor's passion.

* * *

It wasn't until Eleanor and her mother were announced at Lady Canterbury's ball that nerves finally got the better of her. Not necessarily because of the public declaration of her engagement to Charles, but her anticipation of declining Devonington's offer.

Lady Canterbury had always possessed an affinity for roses, and red blossoms now adorned every surface. Why, it almost looked like her own home, after all her hothouse deliveries from Devonington.

Suddenly she recalled Lord Canterbury's support of Lord Devonington in parliament, and her blood went cold.

These roses weren't there to reflect Lady Canterbury's predilection for the flower. Good heavens, they were there for Eleanor. For Eleanor and the Earl of Devonington.

No sooner had she thought of the man than he appeared before her. His thinning brown hair was slicked back against his scalp and he had a quizzing glass raised to one eye, so that it appeared three times its size within the lens. Beneath his black evening jacket he wore a red waistcoat.

"Lady Eleanor."

He bowed over her hand, revealing the balding patch at the back of his head. His mouth pressed to the back of her glove and she found herself grateful for the barrier between her skin and his lips. He straightened and openly admired her, running his gaze down the length of her sapphire gown overlaid with black lace.

His chest puffed out. "You look stunning."

Eleanor murmured her thanks—a difficult thing to do around the weight of her guilt. Devonington, while not the man she'd wanted to wed, had gone to great lengths to make the evening memorable.

"My Lord." The Countess inclined her head in a generous nod and held out her hand.

Eleanor waited for the Earl to bend over her mother before her gaze swept the room for Charles and met only disappointment. He had not yet arrived.

She glanced to the entrance, where Lord and Lady Canterbury were still receiving their guests, but did not find him there either. The music would begin soon. Surely he would want to be there for the opening set?

The Earl of Devonington grinned down at her. "Lady Eleanor, would you do me the honor of allowing me to lead you out for the first set of the evening?"

It was on the tip of her tongue to decline, or at the very least offer some form of an excuse that might afford her some time to allow Charles to arrive. But the Earl's smile wavered and she realized she was taking too long to reply.

"How very flattering of you to consider me," Eleanor said, as genuinely as she could muster. "I would be happy to."

All too soon Lady Canterbury was asked to declare the first set. She cast her sly consideration upon Devonington and announced that it would be the waltz.

The Earl offered his arm to Eleanor, who had no choice but to accept. Her glance around the room turned desperate, but all she found were the same familiar faces of the attendees and too many blasted roses. *Where was Charles?*

"This time have a care not to miss your steps as you did when last we danced," Devonington said under his breath to Eleanor.

"I beg your pardon?" she asked, distracted.

"Your dancing could use some improvement, and as you

are dancing with me I want to ensure you perform perfectly."
He touched her shoulders. "Straighten your back more."

The pressure of guilt in her chest lessened—especially
as he'd nearly crippled her last time with his oafish steps.
But if nothing else, the dance would help pass the time.

However, it was also a revelation in her understanding
that she could never have gone through with a marriage to
him. From the closeness of his overwarm body to the unend-
ing stories of his hunting dogs and having her feet crushed
again and again, she knew she could never have a life with
him. Not a happy one.

Finally the dance finished and he escorted her back to
her mother while Eleanor searched the sea of faces. Without success.

No sooner had they arrived at her mother's side than the
Earl grinned down at Eleanor. Fine red veins crossed like
embroidery thread over the tip of his bulbous nose. "I'd
like to dance the next set with you as well, Lady Eleanor."

Eleanor turned sharply to her mother, who simply nodded. Suddenly the air seemed too thin to breathe and all the
blood in her body rushed to her head.

"But a second set would imply…" Eleanor's mouth went
dry.

Devonington smirked and wriggled his shoulders, very
much like a cat about to pounce atop a poor unsuspecting
mouse. Except that Eleanor did suspect.

He took her hand in his. "Lady Eleanor, I'd be honored
if you would join me in the next set, and be by my side as
the Countess of Devonington."

"P-pardon me?" Eleanor stammered, though she'd heard
him quite well enough.

"Don't stammer—it sounds common." Devonington's eyes were hard when he spoke. "I want to marry you."

Eleanor's search around the room became frantic—a drowning victim seeking a rope. But Charles was not there. Why had he not shown? He should have been here to save her from having to reject Devonington. Had he changed his mind?

"You do not want to wed this woman."

A masculine voice spoke up. While familiar, she knew at once the man was not Charles.

Eleanor turned in surprise and found Hugh standing before Devonington.

"Ledsey, what the devil are you going on about?" The Earl puffed up, seeming to draw the girth of his prominent belly into the expanse of his chest. "You had your chance at her. Leave her to your betters, boy."

"This has nothing to do with me." Hugh gave a smug grin. "And everything to do with the courtesan who has been training her each night."

Chapter Twenty-One

Eleanor stared in horror at Hugh. Had he truly said aloud that she had been visiting a courtesan at night for training?

Her stomach sank as she remembered seeing him in the hackney by her house. Had it been him in the hired carriage near Lottie's house as well? Eleanor had been so distraught when she'd left that night, so preoccupied with having been caught with Charles, she had not given the threat the attention it was due.

Now she would pay the price for her careless folly.

Devonington took a threatening step toward Hugh. "That is quite the accusation you make against the woman I intend to have as my wife."

Hugh regarded her, his nose wrinkled with distaste. "I'm sure she'll make for a *wicked* wife…based on the lessons she has been given."

"This is a preposterous accusation," the Countess said, her tone sharp.

"I assure you it is no accusation," Lord Ledsey said with

a smirk. "I saw her leave your town house wearing a blonde wig after you had departed for Almack's. I followed her to Russell Square and waited while she was in the town house of a courtesan known as Lottie. I didn't think it was Lady Eleanor at first, but then I questioned the servants and I got the whole story about how Lady Eleanor has been instructed by Lottie these last few weeks in 'special lessons.'"

It *had* been him. Heavens!

Eleanor's stomach swam with something vile and her mouth filled with water, as if she might be sick. To have her secrets bared thus was almost more than she could stand.

"Did you know?" Hugh tilted his head toward the Countess and tapped his chin in mock contemplation. "Or were you blissfully unaware of your daughter's misdeeds."

The color leached from the Countess's face. Eleanor would be ruined no matter how the conversation turned. Too many had been witness to the accusation. Too many were still listening.

The Countess opened her mouth, but Eleanor stepped forward. "She didn't know. I didn't tell her as I feared it might give her an apoplexy. Look now at her face—at the shock you've given her."

Eleanor's mother shook her head, her face falling with disappointment, though only Eleanor knew the truth behind the breaking of the Countess's composure.

"*You* told everyone how cold I was," Eleanor said to Lord Ledsey. "Do you have any idea how difficult it is to attract new suitors while saddled with the moniker Ice Queen? I wanted to learn how to be kinder, sweeter, more likeable— the way your lovely Lady Alice has always been."

A sad, despairing part of Eleanor bade her skim the room for Charles once more. But truly she did not need to confirm what her heart already knew. He had not come. He had abandoned her to this fate.

It would appear she had been too aggressive in their conversation earlier that day. She had badgered him into agreeing to marry her.

The Earl of Devonington turned to Eleanor, the quizzing glass firmly lodged against his owlish eye. "Are you saying this is true, Lady Eleanor?"

How could she deny it?

The attention of all attendees fell on Eleanor. "It is true," she whispered.

Hugh folded his arms over his chest, satisfied with her answer.

Lady Canterbury strode forward and placed herself between Eleanor and Devonington. "Your Ladyship, kindly escort your daughter from my home. She is no longer welcome here."

Eleanor's mother opened her mouth and shook her head. "It was—"

"Forgive me, Mother," Eleanor rushed in. "I should have told you."

Her mother gave a small nod and reached for her with a trembling hand. Eleanor took it and pulled her mother close. Together they slipped behind their societal shields, their faces devoid of all emotion despite the torrents driving through them.

The music had stopped and the silence of so many people lent a surreal presence to the room. A wall of jewel-toned gowns and waistcoats parted to make way for Eleanor and the Countess as they made their shameful departure from the rose-laden ball.

Their last ball. And not just for this Season.

Charles had not come and now even the possibility of wedding Devonington was gone. Eleanor had lost her prospects and damned them to a life of poverty, all in one awful evening.

The Murray women were completely and utterly ruined.

Charles's head ached like the very devil himself. He groaned, and even the rasping growl in his throat set off a pain in his brain so deep the sound might as well be a sharpened weapon plunging through his skull.

Good God, what had he drunk to leave him so ill?

He hadn't been this stale drunk since his university days. Well, aside from perhaps that one evening with the bottle of absinthe, after a French import had been impounded on the coast of Africa.

"Thomas…" The valet's name came out in a slur.

Regardless, Thomas appeared beside the bed. "How are you feeling, Your Grace?"

"Like I've gone for a jaunt on the Thames and then been stampeded by a herd of elephants."

Thomas tsked to himself and helped Charles sit upright.

The room spun and the sun streaming in through one window seared into Charles's eyes.

Thomas pushed a glass of something murky and foul-smelling toward him. "Drink this. It'll help."

Charles grunted. "Isn't it drinking which has got me to where I am presently?"

Thomas smirked in that obnoxiously optimistic, affable way of his. "One would assume so…though I find it odd that only one drink would cause you such misery."

"Only one drink?" Charles slugged the bitter mixture

down. It was thicker than he had expected and stuck in the back of his throat, no matter how many times he swallowed.

Thomas, angel that he was, passed Charles a cup of tea. He gave his servant a grateful look and let the hot liquid scald away the remnants of the foul concoction. His tongue prickled with the effects of a righteous burn, but it was a far cry better than that awful unpleasantness.

"You had a glass once you returned from the Countess of Westix, Your Grace." Thomas took the empty tea cup. "More?"

Eleanor's mother.

Charles's mind snagged on a troubling thought. Why had he gone to see that devil of a woman?

The single thought tugged and the rest came tumbling back in a great rush. He had finally agreed to wed Eleanor. He would have her *and* the journals. Their engagement was to be announced that night.

"Reply to Lady Canterbury, if you will, Thomas." Charles sagged back against his bed. "Inform her that I will be attending the ball tonight."

"Forgive me, Your Grace, but the ball was yesterday."

Charles jerked upright. "Yesterday?"

Thomas nodded. "You fell asleep in your study after having called upon the Countess of Westix. I left you sleeping as I found you for two hours, then finally brought you to your bed. You slept on through the night." Thomas frowned. "I don't understand it. The bottle only appeared to have one measure taken from it."

The blood drained from Charles's face and left him cold. They were not yet married and already he had left her abandoned.

"Eleanor. The ball. I have to go to her."

Charles swung his legs over the bed. When he rose his legs did not seem steady enough to support him, and he had to catch himself on the mattress to keep from falling.

"Not like this." Thomas shook his head. "Whatever was in that bottle did not agree with you."

"Damn it—what bottle?" Charles growled.

"In your study. The one you received as a gift. I thought you knew who had sent it?"

The memory swam up in Charles's mind now. The fine bottle of brandy…the note welcoming him home and signed with the stamped gold Adventure Club insignia of a compass. He'd thought it a lark—a jest from Eleanor.

Unease blared through the fog in his mind.

Something wasn't right.

In fact, something was very, very wrong.

He staggered to the edge of the bed and held onto the bedpost for support.

"Please, Your Grace." Thomas rushed to his side. "You are not well."

"I daresay I was drugged, Thomas." Charles staggered to the door and burst through it. "I have to go to my study."

Thomas was immediately beside him and he slid Charles's arm over his steady shoulders. They made their way thus to the study, where everything appeared as Charles had left it. He pulled his arm from Thomas, steadier now that the valet's brew had begun to take effect. The liquid had been dreadful, but it apparently worked miracles.

His study was perfect. Too neat. Especially his desk, which all the servants knew better than to touch, even for cleaning.

The five journals strewn haphazardly over Charles's

desk were missing. Only the bottle Thomas had mentioned remained.

Charles's stomach plunged to his toes, for the journals were not the only items missing. So too was the key.

Charles gave a groan of despair and sank to the floor.

"Your Grace…" Thomas tried to pull him from where he'd fallen to his knees.

"The journals…the key. All of it." Charles stared dismally at the desk. "Gone."

Thomas regarded the expanse of empty desk. "The key… You don't mean that bit of metal with holes in it, do you?"

Charles dropped his head to his chest. "Yes. It is the only way I'll ever know where the location of the stone might be." Thomas snorted a choked laugh and Charles glared up at him. "What's so damnably funny?"

The valet's face immediately smoothed. "Forgive me. Only it was stuck to your face when I pulled you up to stand. I tried to peel it off and had quite a time extracting it from where it was plastered to your cheek." His mouth twitched and went straight, then twitched again. "You had dots all about your face where the holes had settled for so long they'd left marks."

His face contorted into an exaggerated frown before curling up into a smile, and he covered a laugh with a very unconvincing cough. As he described it, the scene did sound rather humorous. But the most important fact of all from the story was that the key was still in Thomas's possession.

"Do you have it?" Charles asked. "Were the journals gone when you found me?"

Thomas helped him to his feet. "The journals were not there, but I do have the key." He pulled open one of the drawers and withdrew the flat bit of metal. "Here it is, Your Grace."

He approached the desk, lifted the bottle and sniffed.

He scowled. "Laudanum."

"Are you sure?" Charles asked.

"My mother was stuck to the stuff when I was a boy. I'd know the smell of it anywhere." He grimaced toward the bottle. "This was no accident."

Accident or not, Charles had failed Eleanor when it was most important that he be at her side. His heart slithered into his roiling stomach.

"An investigation will have to wait for later," Charles said grimly. "Get me dressed—and quickly. I must go to Lady Eleanor."

"Your Grace, you need rest."

But Charles would not listen to protests. Not when Eleanor no doubt assumed he'd thoroughly failed her.

Chapter Twenty-Two

By the time Charles made his way to Westix Place it was long past an acceptable hour for morning calls. In fact the ladies were most likely readying themselves for their constitutional in Hyde Park. He could recall Eleanor so vividly from those times they'd walked together, with the outdoors making her green eyes sparkle and her cheeks rosy…

He waited in the foyer for the butler to announce him, despite the servant's discernible disapproval. After a worrisome length of time had passed the butler reappeared.

"Forgive me, Your Grace. I have been told to advise you that Lady Eleanor will not be taking callers."

Charles's stomach knotted. She was home, then. "I understand," he said at last.

But, damn it, he did not. He couldn't bear the idea of Eleanor being there and his being unable to see her. He had abandoned her, and now he was without the opportunity to offer an explanation.

By God, he would *not* let this be the end of everything they'd pursued together.

The butler held open the door for Charles to leave. But Charles did not leave. Instead he dashed through the foyer to where the stairs arced up to the second level.

The butler was amazingly fast for his age, and sprinted ahead of Charles to block the stairs.

"I don't wish to fight you," Charles said between gritted teeth.

"And I won't have you harming the ladies of this house." The butler did not move.

Charles tried to force his way around the older man—to no avail. *Damn.* But there was another way around the older man.

"Forgive me." Charles pushed the servant to the right, careful not to hurt him. The butler staggered through an open door, which Charles swung closed, twisting the key and pulling it free. The butler began banging on the door, but Charles did not wait to see if it drew attention and instead quickly dashed up the stairs.

"Eleanor?"

He shoved through the first door to find a water closet. Empty, thank God, for that might truly have been an unforgivable offense. He tried a second door and found a room filled with trunks strewn about, bursting with colorful gowns and simple day dresses.

Eleanor's maid appeared, screamed, and threw the slipper she was holding at him. The red satin dancing slipper bounced ineffectually off his chest and landed soundlessly on the carpet.

"Please," he begged, ignoring the inept assault. "Lady Eleanor. Where can I find her?"

The woman gaped at him. "Your Grace, you most certainly—"

"I have to see her. *Please.*"

Desperation scrabbled over him. For all he knew the Watch had been notified of his forcible entry. He might have only minutes to plead his case.

"I was drugged last night. Robbed. I couldn't come. I only woke up an hour ago. I fear… I fear I have let her down."

The maid's face lost its harsh resentment and she pressed her palms to her heart.

"I have most certainly let her down," Charles muttered, more to himself than the woman.

"You have indeed disappointed me."

Eleanor spoke from behind him. He whirled around to find her standing in the doorway of what seemed to be her dressing room. The mass of her gorgeous red hair was bound in a simple knot atop her head, with several loose ringlets spilling over her shoulders like fine silk.

"Your presence here is unwelcome and highly inappropriate." She pointed to the open door to her chamber. "I'm asking you to leave."

Charles didn't bother to move. He wouldn't—at least not until he'd said his piece. "I had to see you, Eleanor. I was drugged last night." He shook his head. "Yesterday afternoon. Before I was to prepare for the ball. For seeing you."

Eleanor folded her arms over her chest, her stubborn chin set decisively.

"I thought *you'd* sent me the brandy," he rushed on. He looked toward the door, expecting a small army of footmen to appear and haul him away. "It was a gift and it had the Adventure Club's compass on the card. I thought... I thought it was from you." He grimaced, knowing his story made him sound mad. "When I awoke only an hour ago the journals were gone."

She straightened. "Gone?"

"Stolen," he amended grimly. "And I've the devil of a headache. Apparently the brandy was laced with a heavy dose of laudanum. I don't remember much after arriving home from here yesterday afternoon. It's all hazy."

Her shoulders relaxed somewhat. "What about the key?"

"It was hidden, and thus was not taken." Hidden under his face, that was, but he was not about to share as much. "They most likely didn't know to look for it."

He drew the stiff metal key from his jacket pocket and looked around the room once more, really noticing its state of disarray for the first time. The drawers of her dressing table were pulled out and the trunk beside it half full of various bottles and pots. Gowns and shoes were laid out over the blue silk coverlet on the bed, arranged in neat order beside yet another trunk.

"We won't be staying in London." Eleanor's tone was solemn. "Charles, we're ruined."

"I beg your pardon?"

"Lord Ledsey saw me going into Lottie's and warned the Earl of Devonington away from me during the ball. Everyone heard, of course." A pained look creased her face. "We were asked to leave."

Charles winced. He had not been there to protect her from what had to be the worst night of her life.

She strode to the bed and let her fingertips sweep over the delicate beadwork along the sleeves of one of the gowns. "We're going to Westix Manor, where we will most likely remain. This was to be my last Season anyway. Most likely this is my last day in London."

She was leaving? Everything in Charles went on high alert. Damn it, he had not come all this way to see her slip through his fingers.

"Eleanor, this does not change anything for me."

"I am a pariah, Charles. There will be no grand wedding at St. George's, nor banns read." She shook her head. "This was all just...ridiculous."

Her voice caught and she turned away from him.

This was all his fault. If he had been there he could have protected her somehow. He had to make it right.

He gritted his teeth. "It was not all ridiculous, Eleanor. Not to me." Charles closed the distance between them and drew her toward him. "We can leave on our own. Now. We can go to Gretna Green. No one there will give a fig about Lady Canterbury's ball or the damned gossip." He stroked a hand over her face and reveled in how her green eyes softened when they met his. "You need not be ruined."

Eleanor cast him a chagrined expression. A lock of red hair had slipped from the loose knot and now fell becomingly over her forehead. "Gretna Green... Of course. Because it is near the castle."

"The castle?"

"Comlongon Castle." She lifted an eyebrow. "Where the journals are. The entire reason you even came here. They're the only thing you ever think of."

Yes. Of course. The journals. Though the thought came as a surprise, for it suddenly struck him that in all his panic over having abandoned Eleanor he had not once thought of those journals in Scotland. Yet again, he had thought only of her.

* * *

Was Eleanor mad? Was she truly trying to dissuade the Duke from continuing with their agreement? Marrying Charles was the only option she had, aside from being ruined.

Charles watched her with a curious expression, one set somewhere between concern and—dared she think it?—*tenderness.*

"I was not there to protect you," he said. "Let me make this right."

"It's not your responsibility to make it right, Your Grace."

Though even as she said the words her voice faltered. What was it about this man that drew out her emotions? They rushed through her veins unbidden and left her thoughts scattered. This man who had promised so much and made her experience life with more color, more vivacity than she had known possible.

She put a hand to her brow to still the chaos churning within. "Charles. Please…"

He stepped toward her and tentatively reached for her hand. She looked up at him, reminded again of how very tall he was. And how terribly appealing, with his brilliantly blue eyes. The tenderness there was unmistakable now, far outweighing the concern, and it threatened to undo her.

If she were a smart woman she would offer to sell him the journals at an exorbitant price. And yet here, held in his gaze, she found she could not properly speak. Nor did she pull her hand away when his fingers met hers, gloveless and naked. His touch sent a tingle of warmth up her arm where it radiated outward.

"Marry me, Eleanor. Not to save yourself from ruin but for our mutual compatibility." He slid a side glance at where

Amelia stood, clutching her hands over her chest in rapt attention. "In all things," he added with discreet intimacy.

Eleanor's breath quickened. How could she deny the passion between them, and the candor they'd shared? And yet could she live with the riot of feelings he set loose within her? He would leave often, as her father had done. She would have to expect it and ward off any swaying toward love. To protect herself. She had previously assumed love to be something of stories. She knew now its existence as well as its danger.

"Yes, Charles," she answered in a quiet voice.

Amelia gave a little squeak.

Charles glanced to the side once more, this time with mild irritation at their spectator, who was now fanning her glossy eyes.

"But we will have to leave now," Eleanor said. "Before Mother learns of it. Amelia, please pack a bag for me."

"And quickly," Charles added. "I believe your butler may have sent the Watch for me, if he does not appear himself, armed with a pistol."

Eleanor turned from where she was pointing to several garments for Amelia to pack. "What happened with Edmonds?"

"I locked him a room," Charles answered. "The library, I believe. It was not my intention, but the man fought like the devil to keep me from entering."

Eleanor held up one hand and pinched the bridge of her nose with the other, belatedly realizing it was an action her father had done many times. "You locked Edmonds in the library?"

Charles grimaced. "To see *you*. I will compensate him for his troubles and beg his forgiveness."

The very thought of Edmonds battling Charles to protect her endeared her to the overly formal servant. It had been valiant. She would be personally thanking him as well. Once they returned.

A giddy bubble of excitement tickled up within her, despite her attempts to tamp it down. For when next she returned to London she would be a duchess.

"I expect no less." She only hoped Charles's efforts would be enough for Edmonds after what he'd been through, the poor man. "It was quite brave of him. Please ensure you provide restitution."

The doorway remained thankfully clear during the short time it took to get a simple trunk packed and compose a hasty note to her mother. Within several minutes Eleanor and Charles were racing down the servants' stairs to avoid being seen.

Soon they would be wed. And finally, after all the frustration and pain of their precarious situation, Eleanor and her mother's troubles would be over.

Chapter Twenty-Three

After Charles had packed his own trunk at Somersville House, they had only one stop to make: Lottie's town house.

"We needed a second witness," he said, in reply to Eleanor's confused expression. "Aside from Thomas. I trust you approve?"

She beamed up at him and accepted his proffered arm. "Most assuredly."

Charles and Eleanor were shown into the drawing room, where Lottie rose to greet them. The neckline of her red gown was a bit low-cut for Charles's taste. Well, perhaps a *lot* low-cut for his taste. Her hair fell in a heavy curtain of glossy curls down one shoulder and she'd applied a thin layer of kohl to her eyes, giving her a dramatic, seductive appearance.

Charles did not much care for that either.

She ran to Eleanor and embraced her in a heartfelt hug. "Lady Eleanor, I am terribly distraught over what happened at Lady Canterbury's ball."

Lottie did indeed appear distraught. The dark smudges under her kohl-lined eyes indicated a lack of proper sleep. And, now that he looked at her, the flush to her cheeks appeared to have been put there by cosmetics rather than good health.

It was no wonder Lottie took Eleanor's distress so personally. He knew Lottie saw her lessons as a personal failure. However, it also meant she would need to return to the life she'd led before her attempt at educating the daughters of London society.

Lottie looked from Eleanor to Charles and her eyes narrowed. "Is there a reason the two of you have arrived together, without a chaperon?"

"We require a witness." He lifted his brow. "For our marriage."

"Well." Lottie's face remained blank for a moment, before she gave an overzealous clap and beamed a mite too brightly at them. "I am overjoyed for you both. Felicitations on your upcoming nuptials."

"We will leave as soon as you pack a trunk," Charles replied. "We need an additional witness when we get to Gretna Green."

"Please, say yes," Eleanor implored. "We will stay for a few days at Comlongon Castle, which is nearby. It will be such a delightful break from all the wagging tongues."

Lottie folded her hands in front of her. "Charles, may I speak with you a moment in the library?"

Charles glanced at Eleanor, who nodded. "Go on," she said. "Though if you still have those kittens, Lottie, I'd very much love to see them."

"I am certain they would very much love to see you as

well," Lottie said. "Once they're a bit older you may choose one to keep as your own. As a wedding present."

She rang for one of the footmen to fetch the kittens and motioned Charles to follow her. She did not speak until the door to the library was closed behind them.

"Tell me this is not all in the pursuit of those damned journals." She glanced to the closed door, as if she could see Eleanor through it. "That young lady has been through so much already. The rumors of what happened last night are dreadful. I am ashamed that her association with me has left her so besmirched. I cannot in good conscience allow you to further use her."

"Lottie, I…" He ran a hand through his hair. "Yes, we had made an agreement for the journals, I confess."

An enraged snarl sounded from Lottie's throat.

"However," he rushed on, "when I missed the ball where I intended to announce our agreed-upon arrangement I was in a frenzy to see her, to explain. It was only when she brought up the journals herself that I realized…" He shook his head at his own confused thoughts. "I realized I hadn't even considered them. I had only been thinking of her."

Lottie's frown melted into a slow smile. "Very well. I will come. Only I have one request." She curled a length of dark hair around her finger. "I wonder…is it possible to leave tomorrow?"

"Do you need so much time to pack?"

She was silent long enough for concern to scrape at the back of Charles's mind.

"What is it, Lottie?"

"I have an…engagement this evening," she said softly.

The confession hit him like a slap. Charles swallowed around a suddenly dry throat. "A lesson?" he asked with hope.

Lottie's stare slid from his. "No."

Hot anger flashed through him. "Lottie, you said you were done."

"I said I was trying a new venture." Tears filled her eyes. "It didn't work."

"Let me give you money to live on. Eleanor will understand. In fact, she'll encourage it."

Lottie put up her hand. "Stop. Please. You know I won't accept your charity."

It wasn't charity. Charles bit back the argument, knowing it would do no good. "We must go now," he said instead. "The Countess is unaware of her daughter's departure— or perhaps she is aware now. At any rate, we cannot risk being stopped."

Lottie gave a deep sigh. "Very well. I will send my regrets and hope we can meet once I return."

Charles didn't move, overwhelmed at his own self-hatred for having abandoned her all those years ago, when she'd needed him most. "I despise that you're doing this."

"And yet you love me enough to understand I must live my own life." She regarded him in silent search of confirmation.

His shoulders sagged. "Yes."

Lottie rose on her tiptoes and kissed his cheek. "Give me a moment to pack."

"You were more of a success with Eleanor than you realize," he said, before she could turn away. "You brought a light to her world she never would have had without you."

Lottie's smile touched her eyes. "And that is enough for me."

Charles nodded and left her to pack. For now he had everything he needed. Even though Lottie was forgoing a potential protector—at least for the time being. Eleanor's reputation would be salvaged once they were wed, and he would be getting the remainder of the journals. Thomas would even stop haranguing him about his ducal duty to wed.

For the first time since his return to London everything was going exactly right.

In all, the exceedingly bumpy trip took the better part of six days—primarily due to Eleanor insisting on several occasions that they stop at an inn for the night, to sleep in a real bed rather than endure another stiff slumber on the narrow seats of the coach.

It was a curious thing to reconcile herself in those six days to the idea of having a husband. After seven failed seasons and a botched courting only two months prior, Eleanor had become resigned to a spinster's future. Never had she thought she would be on her way to Gretna Green to wed an incredibly handsome duke.

During those days she sat beside the man who would be her husband, very aware of every part of him. His intoxicating scent and the heat of his thigh touching hers. In truth, all of him was impossible to ignore. He gazed at her often, in a manner she believed he thought discreet, and glanced away each time she met his stare, perhaps accepting the idea of marriage to her very much the same way she was doing with him.

Late into the afternoon of the seventh day, they arrived at the small inn near the blacksmith's at Gretna Green where many clandestine marriages took place. As with all their prior stops, Charles got them each their own room, which were well-appointed and comfortable.

Regardless, Eleanor lay awake, her body and her mind on fire with curiosity and anticipation for what the next day would bring, when they were wed.

When the sun had finally risen high enough to deem the day worthy of waking, Eleanor was more than ready.

Lottie helped her dress in a white gown of Brussels lace and silver beadwork that twinkled at her sleeves and hem when she moved.

Lottie herself wore a pale blue gown of a much more demure fashion than any other garment Eleanor had ever seen her wear previously. The clothing made her even more beautiful, with her silky black hair and those large blue eyes.

It was Charles, however, who took Eleanor's breath away. She saw him first when she began to descend the stairs of their quaint inn. He stood on the first floor, waiting for her, wearing champagne-colored silk breeches, white stockings and a blue waistcoat Eleanor had never seen him wear before, in a deep blue brocade set against a paler background. All of this was quite nicely complemented by his navy jacket.

He stopped his conversation with his valet as if he'd sensed her approach, and looked up the short flight of stairs to where she remained in observation of him. His gaze moved slowly over her, devouring her like a delectable treat. He did not wait for her to descend to him, and instead climbed the stairs to be at her side.

"You are stunning." Charles offered Eleanor his arm.

"And you're the most handsome man I've ever seen."

And he was. His face was clean-shaven, his dark hair swept smoothly back, and the brilliance of those blue, blue eyes was shining as it rested on her.

"Are you ready to become my wife?" he asked.

"I daresay I would not have engaged in such a journey if I were not."

Charles chuckled. "I'm inclined to agree with you. I'm eager for a few days' escape in Scotland." He led her down the stairs and spoke in a low and intimate voice. "Alone. With you."

The breathlessness came rushing back, and the decadent torment of hot temptation. *The journals*, she reminded herself. Despite what he said, she knew what they meant to him. She would do well to keep that at the forefront of her mind.

He led her outside to where an endless sky spread over the lush, rolling green hills. Eleanor closed her eyes and breathed it all in—the sweetness of the sun-warmed grass, the moisture in the air suggesting it might later rain, and the wonderful spice of Charles's scent. Then together they walked to the squat white building where the infamous anvil awaited them.

With Lottie and Thomas behind them, Eleanor and Charles strode through the wooden door of the simple blacksmith's. The whitewashed walls were pocked and smeared with soot, and various odds and ends of the trade hung from pegs.

A large man tottered into the room. Sweat dotted his brow and stained the leather apron he wore. His head seemed screwed down into the bulk of his neck and he eyed them for a considerable length of time.

"Could you direct us to Joseph Paisley?" Charles asked.

The man nodded. "'S me. Ye are here to get married, then?"

A prickle of alarm washed over Eleanor. The man didn't look like he'd bathed in some time, and there was a sickly pallor beneath the layer of sweat glistening on his skin.

Joseph Paisley scoffed before Charles could answer. "Of course ye are, or ye wouldna be here. Let me make the necessary preparations."

Eleanor took the moment of his absence to look to Charles, who must have seen evidence of her concern for he nodded to her in silent comfort.

Joseph Paisley staggered back into the room and grabbed a book off a nearby shelf. The odor of stale alcohol hit her and his lurching gait suddenly made sense.

Joseph Paisley, the man who would see them wed, was entirely sotted.

Chapter Twenty-Four

It was indeed fortunate that Charles held his bride in such high esteem, for truly the venue for their marriage was abysmal. Mr. Paisley leaned to the right and then to the left before swaying back to the center. For a tenuous moment Charles thought he might be forced to catch the man.

A younger man appeared, thin, and wearing a dark jacket of some elegance. He approached them immediately and waved Mr. Paisley away. "Ye've been unwell. Have ye a rest. I'll take care of these two."

Lottie stepped forward and gave an encouraging nod. "If he's unwell, perhaps that might be best."

"I'm fine," Mr. Paisley said firmly. "Stay to help if ye like, but I'll wed them."

Content, the young man clasped his hands at his back and stood resolutely at Mr. Paisley's side.

Eleanor tensed against Charles's arm.

Mr. Paisley drew in a deep breath and braced his stance wide, his belly thrust out like a barrel. "We are now gathered here in order that I may solemnize your marriage in the presence…"

He did not look down at his book as he read, and his words slurred together, thick with drink and bored memory.

"Before ye…" He pointed at Charles.

Charles stared back blankly, unsure what the man intended.

"Please state yer name, sir," said the younger man.

"Charles Christopher Pemberton." Charles nodded to the younger man in appreciation.

"And ye…" Mr. Paisley pointed this time to Eleanor.

Eleanor, having the great benefit of learning from Charles's folly, replied promptly, "Eleanor Susan Murray."

Charles looked down at his soon-to-be wife. He hadn't known her full name before, and it pleased him to know it now.

Mr. Paisley cleared his throat and waggled a finger between the two of them. "Before ye're both joined in marriage, it is my duty to remind ye—"

The man's face suddenly went bright red and he bent over with a hacking cough.

Charles's arm shot out to pull Eleanor back at a safer distance from the ailing man—for all the good it might do. "Good God, man. Are you unwell?"

Mr. Paisley continued to cough, his face having gone nearly purple.

The younger man led him to a bed set near the back wall, which Charles hadn't noticed until that exact moment. Mr. Paisley continued to cough in great racking waves while the younger man tucked him into the bed with soothing tones.

Eleanor glanced up at Charles, her brows lifted with concern. He was beginning to share her apprehension. As distasteful as London had become, they could at least have been wed there without fearing the spread of disease.

"This is preposterous," Charles conceded.

His mouth twitched in a tickle of laughter and Eleanor's did the same.

"Truly disastrous." Then the humor in her eyes shadowed. "Are you quite sure this union will be considered valid?"

"Very." He looked to where Mr. Paisley was being fed a posset of some kind by the younger man.

"I now require that ye make a declaration!" Mr. Paisley bellowed from across the room. From his bed.

Truly, it was shocking.

He waved them over and they obliged, walking closer.

The man eased himself into a sitting position and breathed heavily with the effort. "I would ask that everyone present please be upstanding," Mr. Paisley continued. He indicated them each in turn. "Charles Christopher Pemberton and Eleanor Susan Murray. Before ye're joined in marriage, it is my duty to remind ye…"

Mr. Paisley's voice rattled on and on, reciting words he had clearly spent a lifetime saying.

Charles's attention, however, was on Eleanor—the woman who would become his wife, the daughter of his father's greatest enemy. There was a twinge in his chest as he regarded her, a sharp affection that had crept up on him through their lessons with Lottie, on those promenades through Hyde Park, in the quiet, intimate moments shared between them.

"Charles Christopher Pemberton!" Mr. Paisley called. "Will ye take Eleanor Susan Murray's right hand in yers?"

Charles took Eleanor's small, delicate hand in his and stared down into the eyes of the woman he was giving his name to, sharing his title and his life with. "I, Charles Christopher Pemberton, am taking Eleanor Susan Murray's hand."

The young man quietly rushed over, took their joined hands and carefully pulled them in slow shuffling steps until they were directly over the anvil. He nodded, then dashed back to his place beside Mr. Paisley's bed once more.

Mr. Paisley proceeded to shout out the most important words of Charles's life—the vows which would bind him to Eleanor and have him see her forever cared for. It was a series of "wilt thee" and "wilt thou" Charles could barely understand with the man's slurred and shouted speech.

"I will," Charles replied when the man stopped talking.

Mr. Paisley asked the same of Eleanor. The mirth quieted in her eyes and turned into something warm and affectionate. "I will," she answered with reverence.

"The ring?" Mr. Paisley barked from where he sat.

The younger man ran over with his hand outstretched. Charles pulled from his jacket pocket the emerald ring he'd taken from the safe at Somersville House—his mother's. It was the one his father had given her on their wedding day. The green stone glittered against the fashionable gold setting, almost a perfect match to Eleanor's eyes.

The younger man took it to Mr. Paisley, who muttered over it a moment.

"We won't have to kneel, will we?" Eleanor asked in a quiet whisper, with a grimace toward the dirty floor.

Charles had only time to shake his head before the younger man brought back the ring and he was advised to present it to Eleanor. Complying, Charles slid the ring on her finger and smiled as it fit perfectly.

"Oh, Charles, it's perfect," she whispered, and stroked the emerald with her thumb.

Mr. Paisley hiccupped and then continued with the ceremony, until at last he uttered the final words they had all been waiting to hear. "I now pronounce ye man and wife."

The young man rushed over with his quiet steps once more, hefted a hammer and struck the anvil with a resounding smack. He grinned up at them. "Felicitations on your union."

Felicitations, indeed.

Charles pulled close his lovely bride and kissed her full on the lips for all to see. It was a slow kiss, with the parting of mouths and the tantalizing skim of tongues—a tease for what would certainly come soon. Very, very soon. Thank God.

His body roared with an eagerness to fulfill his wedding vows. Eleanor melted against him with matched expectation.

A male voice splintered through the moment.

"Are you Joseph Paisley?"

Charles broke off the kiss and regarded a young couple, standing anxiously at one another's side.

"I believe our time is up." Charles led Eleanor from the building with Lottie following them. Thomas remained behind a moment longer to collect the marriage lines.

No sooner had Charles stepped into the freshness of clean air, away from the prevailing heat and sickness in the building, Lottie threw up her hands in exasperation. "What the devil was *that*?"

Eleanor threaded her bare fingers through Charles's and laughed. "The most outrageous wedding of all time."

Charles reveled in the silky warmth of her palm resting

comfortably against his. Eleanor was now the Duchess of Somersville. His wife.

The poignancy of that moment was not lost on him, and suddenly he found himself possessive of her, and eternally glad to have her at *his* side and not that of Devonington, or even Rawley.

She was his.

The celebration of their union was a quiet affair, and one that ended quickly—much to Eleanor's delight. Or rather to her delight, excitement, anticipation, nervousness, and everything else that loomed in her expectation of impending intimacy.

Charles led her to his room at the inn by a gentle hand, his gaze locked on hers as he opened the door. Though he had been there only one night, his wonderful scent of rich, foreign spices lingered in a room identical to her own. He closed the door and plunged the room into total silence.

Her breathing came fast and her body buzzed with heady anticipation as he approached her.

"My wife." His mouth lifted in a charming half smile. "Do you have any idea how long I have wanted you?"

Her heart leapt at such words. "I believe I do have an idea."

He grinned and pulled her to him. His mouth lowered to hers in a slow, sensual kiss that told her they had all the time in the world, and that he planned to savor every second of it. His fingers skimmed down her gown and began to work at the delicate line of buttons going down her back.

"As beautiful as you are with this on, I imagine you are far lovelier with it off."

A soft sound of longing hummed from the back of her

throat as each button fell open in turn under his subtle touch and widened her gown further and further. He watched as he undressed her…as the fabric began to loosen and gape.

Wanton though it might be, there was a part of Eleanor that *wanted* him to disrobe her, to leave the hot tension of her skin exposed to the open air. And, if she were being entirely honest, a wickeder part of her longed to see him as well.

At last the gown slipped off one shoulder and Charles eased it carefully down to the ground, so she stood in only her unmentionables. Her heart pounded in her chest with an intoxicating blend of expectation and excitement.

Charles paused for a long, slow breath and then pulled free the tie holding her petticoat in place. It shifted from her waist and puddled on the floor. He immediately set to work drawing the bow from her corset, where it was laced up at the front, one loop at a time. Within mere seconds the strings hung limp at her sides and Charles swept his hands over her shoulders, caressing her as he pushed the corset from her body.

"Your chemise," he said in a deep, smooth voice. "Take it off."

Eleanor paused then. For it was one thing to have her husband undress her, and entirely another to do it herself as he watched. Heat singed her cheeks and the warmth in other places grew hotter still.

She took the smooth fabric between her fingertips, carefully pulling it up her body and over her head. She let it float to the floor and stood before him wearing only pale silk stockings tied at her thighs. He took his time taking her in, lifting his steady stare up her legs to her breasts, then settling on the thatch of red hair between her legs.

"Stunning," he said. "It would appear I was right. As lovely as you were in your gown, you're far lovelier out of it."

He closed the distance between them and delicately ran a finger from her shoulder down the side of her breast, along the curve of her hip to her thigh.

Her breathing grew faster and her skin burned where he'd touched her. The pleasant throbbing between her thighs increased its tempo in eagerness to experience more of the pleasure they'd shared.

His hand curled around the swell of her bottom, feather-light, and he caught her lips with his own. The kiss was tender at first, until his tongue touched hers and the embers were fanned to flames. Eleanor lifted her arms to his shoulders and tilted her face toward his, her own tongue seeking and stroking.

His delicate touch at her bottom became more inquisitive, more restless, roaming up to her waist, up to her breasts, where he teased at her sensitive nipples, and then down, down, down to where he'd stroked her before.

At the first sweep of his finger over the source of her need Eleanor's knees buckled. She pushed at his jacket, shoving it from his shoulders so it fell unceremoniously to the floor.

"I want to see you, too." Her voice was husky with lust.

She moved to the buttons of his waistcoat. Her fingers trembled, fumbling in her impatience to have him as naked before her as she was to him.

"Relinquish your stockings," he said against her mouth. "And I'll remove my waistcoat."

She obliged, rolling her stockings down her legs. Her skin was alight with intense sensitivity, so that even her own touch along her thighs left her flesh prickling with pleasure.

Charles unbuttoned his waistcoat with expertise. And he did not stop there. He next removed the collar from his shirt, revealing a hint of curling black hair, before tugging the cloth over his head. Lines of muscle showed along his stomach in tight bands, and the power of his chest swelled beneath a smattering of black hair.

Eleanor drew in a soft breath.

He pulled off his boots and stockings while the strength of his arms flexed and bunched in the most fascinating of ways, powerful muscle working under firm flesh with each movement. He worked at the buttons of his breeches, where the thick column of his shaft showed under the fine fabric.

She made a little sound in her throat before she could stop herself. She'd thought of this for far longer than any respectable girl ought to have. The memory of what his fingers could do mingled with the lurid tales from the journal, swirling into hot lust in her mind.

He pulled the loosened breeches from his narrow hips and stood before her in his full, powerful glory, the proof of his need jutting toward her.

No sooner had she begun to admire him than he drew her into his arms, his warm skin on hers and his shaft pressed hot against her belly. The hair on his chest scratched pleasantly against her nipples and Eleanor's pulse fluttered with erratic, wild beats.

For this time there was no innocence to protect, no barriers to keep them apart. There would be no stopping until all her curiosities had been thoroughly sated.

Chapter Twenty-Five

Charles held his wife against him, skin to skin, pounding heart to pounding heart, and knew there was no place in all the world he'd rather be. Every inch of Eleanor was wonderfully silky and supple, and her mouth was eager beneath his.

Her legs parted around his thigh and he knew all too well what it was that she wanted. He skimmed his fingers over her inner thighs and reveled in the eager intake of her breath. He found the wet heat between her legs and slid the pad of his middle finger over her core until he reached the little bud. Her hips twitched upward reflexively and she gave a sigh of pleasure.

Charles bit back a groan and his shaft flexed against her. At this point the greatest feat of his life would be remaining in control and not throwing himself upon her as he so desperately wanted to.

He continued to stroke, teasing the little knot of her desire. He carefully dipped his finger inside her, fearful of causing her discomfort. She was impossibly tight, slick with wet heat and promise. Charles gave a long, low groan of anticipation.

Eleanor gave a breathless cry and swayed slightly. "Yes…" she whispered. "Please. More of that."

His manhood lurched. There was not much more that Charles could take. He needed her on the mattress, spread before him. He wanted to touch her, tease her, ready her. Taste her.

He caught her parted legs and spread them over his waist, lifting her in order to carry her to the bed. She moaned and ground her body against his. The heat of her rubbed over the length of his shaft and the decadence of such temptation was so much that he damn near dropped her.

He clutched her to him, carrying her the few feet to the four-poster, where he lay her down on the firm mattress and bent over her. She did not uncurl her legs from his waist. She locked her heels against his buttocks and continued to grind against him with a frustrated craving that readily echoed in the ache of his tight balls.

God, but she was a sweet enticement. It would be so easy to shift his shaft against her and glide in. The very idea made his nerves jangle with insistence.

But when he did finally take her there would be a virgin's pain. He had to be gentle, careful. Slow.

She panted against his mouth and let her touch wander over him with abandon, hot hands making an exploration that damn near drove him mad. Over his naked back, across his chest, raking over his nipples before driving down his stomach.

He'd managed to kiss her throat on his path to her nipple, when her fingers curled around his shaft. His world stopped and his mind plunged into utter blankness, forgoing any thought but the excruciating pleasure radiating through him.

"Will you teach me?" she asked, her voice low. "To pleasure you? To take you in my mouth?"

She sat up slightly and regarded him. Her carefully crafted coiffure had become mussed and several long tendrils spilled down her shoulders.

She pursed her reddened lips. "Like in the journals. It seemed to bring the author great pleasure. And if it brings you pleasure I'd like to try."

Charles swallowed. "Eleanor..."

She slid out from underneath him and off the bed, so she stood at its side. Charles turned to watch her, still too damn stunned to come up with a polite answer.

She was his wife.

And yet the idea of her hot mouth surrounding his shaft...

With careful precision she pulled the pins from her hair and let them plop to the thick carpet one by one, until the glory of her red hair spilled down her shoulders and breasts like she was some mythical mermaid. She bent over him and kissed him, her tongue expertly finding his. Her breasts arched to his chest and she whimpered against his lips.

His body lit with wanting immediately, insistent and demanding. Her fingers brushed over the head of his shaft and a groan tore from his throat. She explored him, touching, stroking, cupping. His world was pinpointed on the the sheer pleasure of it all, where it radiated out from his shaft and coursed through him.

"Teach me to take you in my mouth."

She looked up at him with an expression both sultry and imploring. To hear his wife speak so intimately, and with such base words, drove him absolutely mad with wanting.

"You'll need to get on your knees," he heard himself say.

She gracefully obeyed, and gazed at him for further instruction. Her attention shifted to his shaft and she licked her lips.

"Take me in your hand and guide me into your mouth..." Charles somehow managed to get the words out.

Her fingers curled around the base and her lips parted just over the head, the most sensitive part. His shaft disappeared several inches into her mouth.

"Close your lips," Charles instructed. "And suck."

Her mouth closed around him, hot and wet, and she drew him in with an obedient suck. Charles's balls tightened and he knew he would not be able to take much of this before she unmanned him. Sweat gathered along his brow and his entire body trembled with the effort to stave off his climax.

"Move your head. Up and down. Over..." God, he could barely talk.

Eleanor slid the suckling warmth of her mouth toward the head and then sank back down again, halfway down his shaft. She did this three more times, bobbing her head over him until he was near bursting.

"Enough." It came out as a growl. On his honor, he truly could take no more.

Eleanor released him with a startled expression. "Have I hurt you?"

He swept her onto the bed and braced himself over her. "I've been ravenous for you for too long without having you, Eleanor. I cannot take much more before..." He smiled. "It's your turn."

"My turn?"

He was already kissing a path down to her breasts, where

he paused to flick his tongue over her nipples before descending to her slender stomach.

"I'd be willing to wager this wasn't in that journal."

Before she could offer any protest he kissed his way down to the fiery curls between her legs and ran the tip of his tongue over her glistening center.

Eleanor's awareness blazed with pure bliss.

Charles watched her and traced his tongue over her sex.

Pleasure tingled through her and prickled at the tips of her nipples. A soft cry escaped her mouth and she was only mildly aware of Charles spreading her thighs further apart.

He flicked his tongue where his fingers had been before, sliding it over her, circling the part of her that made everything quiver, plunging it inside her. The hunger and the longing all knotted together, and wound her into a deliciously tight ball of glorious feelings.

Something entered her, long and deep, while the caress of his tongue twirled over the little nub that brought such breathtaking euphoria. Eleanor cried out at the sheer exquisiteness of the blended sensations, and glanced down at him to find his finger thrusting into her while he continued to lick and tease.

Her body wound in on itself, tighter and tighter. So close, so close, so close...

But then, just as she was fully prepared to careen over, Charles withdrew his attentions and rose over her. Those brilliant blue eyes of his found hers, unfocused and heavy-lidded with lust. His body was hot and hard against hers, and the length she'd so eagerly loved with her mouth now pressed with heavy insistence against her inner thigh.

Eleanor arched her hips upward, eager for Charles to satisfy the maddening, thundering want raging through her.

He braced himself so his weight did not crush her. His powerful body flexed with the effort, and she could not stop herself from stroking his beautifully corded body.

He remained locked in place, unmoving.

Her hips rolled of their own volition, undulating in a primal dance she hadn't needed to be taught. "Please, Charles…"

He kissed her, long and sweet. But Eleanor didn't want sweet. Sweet wouldn't quell her ferocious craving.

"Please, Charles…" she panted again.

He rested his damp forehead against hers and clenched his eyes shut, as if he were in pain. "I don't want to hurt you," he said raggedly.

She knew there would be pain. She'd overheard the conversation of recently married ladies.

"You won't," Eleanor ground out. "Please. You must do this or I'll go mad with wanting."

He opened his eyes and flexed his brows in consideration. Finally his shaft shifted from her inner thigh to the throbbing ache of her need. He pushed into her gingerly.

More. She needed more.

She spread her legs wider and he pressed forward, until the very entrance of her stretched around the girth of him.

He clenched his jaw. "Are you ready?"

Eleanor nodded, and opened her mouth to speak just as he thrust into her. A flash of pain burst through the haze of her lust.

Charles froze where he remained, still buried in her depths. He was large within her, slightly uncomfortable, and the feeling was foreign and awkward.

He touched her face. "I've hurt you…"

She shook her head, unable to speak. Her body would adjust, and then there would be gratification.

He pulled out and a ripple of pleasure went through her. She drew her legs around him and rocked her hips with the same natural motion as before. He followed the slow pace she set, slowly easing deeper inside, and deeper still. His breath came fast against their shared kisses.

Just as Eleanor had known would happen, her sex became accustomed to him—not only accustomed to the invasion of her intimate place, but welcoming it with slick, wet heat. His hand moved between them and found the spot where he would drive her to the edge of ecstasy. He circled it with his thumb in time with his thrusts, until Eleanor's body tensed with impending release.

"Yes…" he breathed against her ear. "Yes, come for me."

He didn't need to ask. She couldn't stop it even if she tried. Her body clenched until she feared she would begin to tremble, and then the pleasure exploded around her like the flashing fireworks of Vauxhall Gardens in the night sky.

The spasming of her core gripped around Charles's length repeatedly, further heightening their bliss and prolonging their satisfaction. Charles pushed firmly inside her and gave a tight grunt. He twitched within her depths and a delicious wave shuddered through her.

Unwilling and unable to move, they remained in their joined position for a long moment, both gasping to catch their frantic breath.

Eleanor's heart raced harder and faster than it ever had before, frenzied with the excitement of their intimacy. And as her breath began to calm, a quiet contentment swept over her, bringing total and complete satiation.

Charles slowly pulled away from her and motioned her to remain where she was while he strode across the room in all his nude glory. She watched his form appreciatively, enjoying the play of light and shadows over the powerful planes of his back.

When he returned he carried a wet cloth and gently cleaned her. Though the heat and pain of his initial intrusion had ebbed, the coolness of the cloth against her sensitive area was most welcome.

He regarded her tenderly. "Are you all right, love?"

Love. Her lips curled into a dreamy smile. "It was beyond words, Charles. Truly, in every brilliant way."

Eleanor stretched back onto the bed and Charles pulled her into his arms.

She could lie there forever at his side, she thought. Listening to his heartbeat, wrapped in his embrace and trying not to fall in love.

Chapter Twenty-Six

The following day Eleanor found herself in the confines of a carriage once more—but this time she hardly minded. It was only for a short time, while they made their way to Comlongon Castle, and she was with her new husband. The one who had kept her up the better part of the night with another round of teasing and satiating and loving.

Her body hummed with the languid warmth still thrumming in the slight tenderness between her thighs.

As if he were considering similar thoughts to her own, a soft smile touched Charles's lips where he sat across from her in the private carriage they'd taken. Once more they were blissfully alone, with Thomas and Lottie having remained to see to their effects at the inn so Eleanor and Charles could arrive at Comlongon together.

Charles's brilliant blue eyes were fixed on Eleanor's. It would be hard not to love a man who looked at her so, and yet she knew it best to guard her heart.

"You look radiant, my Duchess." He settled back in his

seat with a contented grin. "I am the luckiest man in all of Christendom."

"To have had so fine a wedding?"

Together they laughed over the episode at Gretna Green. It was the kind of shared joke they would tell in the years to come.

The trees cleared away around them to reveal a large span of lush green grass with the powerful form of Comlongon Castle rising at its center. It wasn't so much the sight of it that robbed Eleanor of her speech, but the memories which crashed into her with such alarming clarity it rendered her quite overwhelmed.

For many summers her mother had taken her and Evander to Scotland. To familiarize them with their roots, she'd said. To learn to be strong Murrays, her father had clarified.

Either way, when they'd been in Scotland, beyond the watchful gaze of their father, who'd used the time to travel abroad, her mother had released the control she'd held over her children.

Together, Eleanor and Evander had run free about the castle and its grounds. They had been two scamps, romping and playing like hellions every one of those summers, until Evander had been sent away to school. He didn't return home often, and when he did, they both treated one another civilly, coolly, with all the love and laughter stripped out of them.

Pain squeezed at Eleanor's heart. For *she* had been the cause of his abrupt departure. She had been too excitable, her father had said, too desperate for affection. It was lowborn and improper. When once she had tried to stop her father from leaving on yet another trip, and had dared to shed tears, the Earl had shown his disappointment with blows and with the most crushing punishment: sending Evander away.

While she'd never regarded her childhood after that with fondness, she *had* cherished the years before. She'd tucked them somewhere private within her, and locked away the pleasant memories of those summer days with Evander.

They rose up within her now, sharp as a familiar scent, and tore through her with bittersweet joy.

Evander had possessed a high-pitched laugh when he was a boy—an unfortunate attribute he'd luckily outgrown as an adult—and he'd been quite a sight as a youth, or "a lad," as they'd called him in Scotland, with his shock of red hair and his silly laughter.

And, oh, they'd had such times for him to laugh. Such as the afternoon they'd set a frog loose in the kitchen and it had propped itself on Cook's large rump for the better part of an hour before she'd even noticed. Or the summer they'd released all the foxes caught by the hunt to liberate them from their terrible fate. Or the time—

Charles sat forward. "Eleanor? Are you crying?"

Was she?

She touched her fingers to her cheek and pulled it away to see they were indeed wet. "It would appear I am."

Concern showed in his eyes. "What is it?"

The carriage bounced along, carrying them past the woods Eleanor had run through with Evander, and past the lake where she'd swum on days when the weather had been warm enough to make the loch only slightly less than freezing.

"I came here with my brother when I was a girl." She shook her head. "I haven't thought of those memories in years. I haven't thought of…him."

"Loss is never easy."

He shifted in his seat and she recalled his own father's recent death.

"I'm very sorry you've had your own loss as well," Eleanor said gently.

His gaze was fixed on the gray face of the castle, growing larger as they made their way closer.

"It doesn't seem real, does it? As if by not acknowledging it, somehow that might result in it never having happened. Which is foolish."

"No, it's not."

The closer they got, the more Eleanor's heart ached. For the young brother she'd played with and loved, for the serious grown man he'd become and the cold rift set between them. For his absence without reconciliation.

"I believe my mother feels similarly," Eleanor said. "She seldom discusses Evander. Though I think we both expect…" She shook her head. "I cannot even say it."

The carriage drew to a stop before Comlongon Castle and a ball of dread tightened in Eleanor's stomach at the thought of the ghosts which might linger in those ancient halls. Not of Murrays long dead, but of the Murray too long missing. Perhaps it had been a poor decision to suggest the castle.

"We will heal with time, my dear Eleanor," said Charles, and exited the carriage and waited to help her down.

Eleanor stepped down onto the familiar crunch of gravel. Her heart pounded in her throat and there was a headiness inside her which made her feel quite faint.

She hadn't been honest when she'd told Charles she hadn't ever had a confidant. When she was a girl, it had been Evander. And, although the years and their father's demands had spread a gap of silence and maturity between them,

Evander had gone off to reclaim the family fortune, to save her and her mother from ruin, and it had most likely cost him his life.

Eleanor clasped her hand tightly on Charles's arm to keep her trembling legs from pitching her to the ground.

Charles knocked on the door and waited.

A butler appeared and lifted his bushy gray brows. "May I help you?"

"I am the Duke of Somersville and this is my new bride, formerly Lady Eleanor Murray." Charles smiled down at her before continuing to address the butler. "We are here to spend several days in Scotland and to celebrate our marriage prior to returning to London."

The butler bowed. "A moment, if you please, Your Grace. I must notify the Earl."

The Earl? Eleanor's mouth fell open in outrage as he showed them inside, where they were left momentarily blinded by the absence of sunlight behind the block of thick castle walls.

The butler disappeared before she could offer protest.

"Charles, someone is masquerading as Evander!" she hissed.

"I'll see to this. Don't concern yourself."

The butler appeared once more. "If you'll follow me, the Earl of Westix will see you now."

Eleanor had to force her steps to the pace of a well-bred lady, for all she wanted to do was run to the room at the end of the hall, push her way through the doors and demand to know what scoundrel would dare impersonate her lost brother for his own personal gain.

She would let Charles kill him in a duel and not lose a wink of sleep. No, she would kill him herself. With her very own hands. Her body blazed with the fire of her rage and her jaw ached from clenching it so ferociously.

The butler opened the door and saw them in. Eleanor looked at the tall figure standing beside the fireplace and only just managed to smother her cry behind the press of her fingertips.

For there, looking as handsomely young and strong as he had when he'd left for his expedition, was her long-missing brother: Evander Murray, the rightful Earl of Westix.

Chapter Twenty-Seven

Eleanor couldn't take her eyes off her brother, standing so casually before her. As if he hadn't been missing for years. As if they hadn't all assumed him to be dead. And then he smiled. *Smiled!*

Eleanor's hand was pressed to her mouth and her eyes filled with tears. "Evander…" She pulled free from Charles and staggered toward her brother. "Is it truly you?"

"Eleanor." He strode to her. "My butler has informed me you are a new bride. Felicitations on your marriage." His gaze slid toward Charles, all emotion masked.

"We thought you were dead!" She fell then, pitching toward the ground.

Evander caught her and gently held her upright. "Why ever would you think that?"

The weakness in Eleanor's legs strengthened with the force of her ire. "Why would we think *that*?" she demanded. "Because you have been missing all these years without

any word of where you were or when you would be home
or even—" Her voice broke. "Or even if you were alive."

He frowned. "I confess I did not write as often as I should
have, but there have been at least two letters sent."

"Two?" she gasped. "In four years?"

"I gather they did not make it to you."

Evander had the good sense to cast his eyes downward
at her admonishment.

"Have you been here in Comlongon the entire time?"
Eleanor drew herself away from him, fully able to stand
on her own once more. "While we have feared the worst?"

Evander shook his head. "No."

It was then that she finally noticed the room, crowded
with many items—relics and tomes and crates. In truth,
it was cluttered with such mess it looked not at all like a
proper receiving room, but rather one meant for storage.

"I do not wish to betray our family troubles to you, sister."

He cast a glance toward Charles. Which meant he did not
wish to discuss such matters in front of Charles. She looked
between the two. Did they recognize one another? Did they
know each other to be the son of their father's enemy?

Neither one's expression gave any indication.

"You mean our dire financial situation?" Eleanor pressed.
"It was the reason you left."

While Charles hadn't been offered the details, it was apparent that he had already worked out the finer points on
his own—or at least was playing the part of knowing ad-
mirably.

Evander narrowed his eyes at Charles with a flash of dis-
trust. Maybe they were acquainted after all.

"Yes, well…what I anticipated only taking several months

took several years." He gave a mirthless chuckle. "It would appear that our fathers told rather grandiose tales of their travels without recounting the liberties they took when obtaining their treasures."

Charles lifted a brow.

"What do you mean?" Eleanor asked.

"They were not moral," Evander scoffed. "Were I as unscrupulous, my task would have been over in six months' time and I would have been home with those I love."

He nodded to Eleanor before claiming a glass of amber liquid from a nearby table.

Eleanor shook her head, not comprehending. "But if you were here—" Her throat tightened around her words and cut them off.

"I have only recently returned, Eleanor. I confess that I was so focused on selling the goods I had accumulated to rebuild our wealth that I did not wish interruption. And I did not send correspondence until I had reestablished our wealth. I assumed the letters I sent were enough to allay your concerns. I realize now how very wrong I was."

Confusion and anger and…yes, hurt—mostly hurt—blazed like a glowing coal in her chest. "Why did you not come to London to sell the items?"

Evander took a sip of his drink. "We all know how gossip spreads through London like fire. As no one visits Comlongon anymore I expected it to be safe to come here without rattling hope and inciting rumor. I did this to protect you and Mother." He lifted his glass to Charles. "Would you like one?"

"Dear God, yes," Charles replied promptly.

Eleanor followed her brother to the small table of cut-crystal decanters. "I think I would like one as well."

She wrestled with the power of her emotions as he poured two glasses, handing one first to Eleanor and then to Charles.

Eleanor cradled the cool glass against her palms and took a shuddering breath. "Evander, we thought..." Her throat clenched tight around the words. "We thought you were dead. Do you think we value fortune over love?"

"*Everyone* values fortune over love," Evander said simply.

Was that what he thought? That she and her mother were so keen on an abundant fortune that they would rather wealth than him?

"That isn't true," she protested. "We would rather have had you with us in London. Mother is overwrought at your loss, and I..." Tears blurred the room and a sob choked from her throat. "I tried to push aside my memories of you, but when we arrived here, when I recalled all those summers when we played together—Evander, you have broken my heart."

And it was true. He had indeed left her heart broken.

"Eleanor..."

There was a catch to Evander's voice, and it snagged at a deep, wounded part of her. Without saying more he rushed to her, his arms open, and pulled her into a solid embrace. It was the way he'd done when they were children and she was upset. Before he'd gone to school—before the emotion had been strapped out of them all.

She curled into the embrace and let the truth of it all wash over her. Evander was alive. He had tried to let them know he was safe. He had tried and he had done all this for *them*. The tears came in a flood: relief that he was alive, happiness to be having this incredible reunion, and sorrow for the years they had lost.

"I only wanted to help…" Evander's voice rumbled around her. "I never expected it to be like this."

Eleanor took a shuddering breath. Evander smelled different. When he was a boy, he had smelled of wet grass and sweat—now, as an adult, he smelled of shaving soap and Scotch.

"Will you forgive me, Eleanor?" he asked softly.

She looked up, gazing into a face she had often thought never to see again. How could she not, after all he had done for her and Mother?

"Yes, of course," Eleanor replied, and tightened her grip on him, never wanting to let him go again.

Charles had slipped from the room to give Eleanor and the Earl of Westix privacy in order to discuss whatever it was siblings discussed after a reunion in which one had been presumed dead. He didn't imagine it would be an easy conversation to have, let alone in the presence of one's enemy.

Except he did not consider the new Earl of Westix an enemy—not in the way he once would have. If Charles had had a sister, wouldn't he have done something similar to see her well cared-for?

He took a long draught of Scotch. It was good-quality, and the burn in his stomach was smooth and pleasant.

Westix being alive added complications—and Charles could not help but consider the impact of such a change.

He now understood that Eleanor's reason for offering her original request had been financial necessity. Now, with Westix returned, with their fortune restored, she had no need of this marriage.

Except it had already been consummated. There could be no annulment.

Then there were the journals. They were no longer Eleanor's to give, and Charles doubted Westix would willingly offer them to his enemy.

He regretted not having brought the key with him to Scotland. He'd left it behind for two reasons. The first being to prove to Eleanor and to Lottie that this marriage meant something to him. The second because he had been worried that if he did find the answer he sought with the key he would be chomping at the bit to leave immediately. He knew several day's difference would not matter on his departure to find the stone, but that these few days at Comlongon would matter to his new wife.

If he'd had it with him now, however, he and Eleanor could have searched for the journals and used the key without Evander being the wiser. *Damn.*

The butler strode down the hall, cast him a curious look, then pushed through the door of the room where Westix and Eleanor were.

"Forgive the interruption, My Lord, but it appears there are two more in their party who have only just arrived."

"Show them in," the Earl replied.

That must mean that Lottie and Thomas had arrived. Charles waited for the butler to bring them in and then followed them into the room.

Eleanor's eyes were red-rimmed but dry, her tears having ceased. She removed herself from her brother's side and approached Charles. For one tense moment he did not know how she would react to him now that she truly did not need him any longer.

He put his arm around her shoulder and was awash with relief when she melted against him.

"This is charming," Lottie said in the affected manner she'd always possessed.

She looked around at the stacks of wooden crates and ancient artifacts before her eyes fell on the new Earl of Westix. The smile drained from her lips, along with all the color from her face.

And it was not only Lottie looking at Westix, for he was staring as intently at her, his face equally pale.

"Lottie?" Charles asked, from where he stood holding Eleanor's shoulders.

Westix opened his mouth and closed it, then opened and closed it again.

Lottie was not so indecisive. She marched forward, drew her hand back and slapped him across the face.

Westix touched his cheek. "Lottie, I'm so sorry..."

Lottie. Charles was rankled. The Earl was uncomfortably familiar with her.

"You lied to me," Lottie said sharply. "You swore to come back for me and you never did. I waited—" Her voice cracked.

Realization slammed into Charles with the suddenness of an unexpected punch to the gut. He recalled Lottie's refusal to discuss the man who had ruined her, the insistence she'd placed on helping Eleanor. And now here was Westix, standing there, saying Lottie's given name when he hadn't been in London in four years.

Good God.

Westix was Lottie's lover.

Charles's hands rolled into fists, ready to exact vengeance

for the woman whose life had been ruined—whose good prospects had been dashed by the Earl's lust.

Without so much as a passing thought Charles released Eleanor. He lunged with his arm cocked back and let his fist slam into Westix's face.

Eleanor and Lottie screamed in unison.

It was Eleanor, though, who grabbed Charles's coat in an effort to draw him away. "Charles, explain yourself."

He let himself to be pulled away—for Eleanor's and Lottie's sakes. Certainly not for the piece of rubbish standing before him with a reddened cheek on one side of his face and a blackening eye on the other.

"He ruined Lottie, Eleanor!" Charles snarled. "She was a vicar's daughter—a woman with many prospects. Your brother seduced her and abandoned her. If he hadn't robbed her of her virtue when her father died she wouldn't have had to—"

"Charles." Lottie put a hand on his tense arm. "I believe this is a conversation I ought to have with the Earl myself, rather than see my scandal aired so publicly."

Charles's anger clenched into a searing knot in his gut. "Very well."

"You and your wife ought to be shown to your rooms." Lottie's smile didn't reach any part of her face but her lips. "You and I can leave this discussion for later. For now, I would like a moment alone with the Earl of Westix."

Thomas indicated the closed door. "Shall I summon the butler to show you to your rooms?"

Charles glanced behind him to find Eleanor's cheeks had gone quite red. She gave a subtle nod, and he realized she was agreeing with Lottie and Thomas. The door to the room clicked open and Thomas disappeared.

Westix bowed to Charles. "If you'll excuse me, Your Grace? I would very much like to speak to Lottie alone."

Charles gritted his teeth. "If you hurt her, I'll kill you."

Westix did not so much as blink at the threat. "If I hurt her in such a way again, I'll kill myself."

"Evander!" Eleanor gasped in horror.

Her brother shook his head. "I have committed many egregious wrongs, sister. And for all of them I'm heartily sorry."

The Comlongon Castle butler entered the room and politely asked Charles and Eleanor to follow him.

This time Eleanor did not protest, and neither did Charles. They obligingly followed the butler from the drawing room, leaving Westix with Lottie and the ugly truth about what his abandonment had cost her.

Eleanor was unsurprised to find they were shown to her girlhood room at Comlongon Castle, with its billowing white curtains framing a cherrywood four-poster bed.

"We have several maids who can see to your unpacking," the butler said in a drawl of regal nonchalance, and nodded to the small pile of their effects.

"Perhaps later." Charles nodded his thanks and the butler took his leave.

Then Charles turned toward her, his gaze full of concern. "Eleanor…"

The way he said her name was tender, and weighted with all the sorrow of what had transpired. Laughter bubbled up in Eleanor's throat. Or was it a sob? By her word, it was impossible to tell at this point.

Evander was alive, in Scotland, at Comlongon Castle.

And he had tried to send letters. If they had got through, how many years of heartache might have been avoided?

Her throat grew tight.

"Eleanor..." Charles said her name again and strode toward her, his arms open.

She needed no further encouragement and ran into his embrace. His body was strong, protective.

Once she'd confessed to Evander why she'd married Charles he had offered to allow her to stay there in Scotland. It would be so easy to set herself free of the entire mess of it. Even the scandal they'd caused in London would soon be buried beneath something more salacious. Fortune, after all, did have a way of encouraging acceptance.

Except that her marriage to Charles could not be annulled.

It would be safer for her to stay in Scotland—for her heart at least. This last day with Charles had pressed upon her with more difficulty than she'd imagined. How could she be with him and not fall in love? And if she lost her heart in her attempt to live a true life would that be a worthy sacrifice? Or would it only bring a greater misery?

Her head ached at the torrent of thoughts smashing around in her skull.

"The journals are no longer mine to give you." She was grateful her face was buried in Charles's chest, so she did not have to see his face when she spoke the horrible truth.

"I'm well aware." Charles rubbed a gentle circle over her back.

"My side of our arrangement is woefully short." She squeezed her eyes shut, as if she could as easily close off her hurt.

"I still needed a duchess," Charles replied. "I am glad to have you as my wife."

A wife he would soon leave in pursuit of the ruby. For she knew he would never abandon it. No doubt he would approach Evander about the journals the first chance he got.

The ache in Eleanor's chest became palpable.

"I want you," Charles said softly. "As a confidante, to continue our candid discussions, as a beautiful woman on my arm, and to share my bed and explore the passion we share."

Eleanor's breath caught and her body immediately reacted with a low, warm pulse between her thighs. She drew her arms around the back of his neck, eager to give in to the pull of passion and liberate herself from the chaos in her mind. For right here, right now, she would allow herself the luxury of unfettered longing and the beauty of being sated.

And for this one blissful spot in time she would allow herself to be swept into the sweet oblivion of his embrace, where she didn't have to think of the challenges ahead—including the very precarious state of her heart.

Chapter Twenty-Eight

Eleanor's fine warm glow cooled as she descended the stairs for an early dinner. Evander and Lottie awaited them.

It had been all too easy to put her brother from her mind when she was upstairs with Charles. Evander. But not only was he alive, he was the scoundrel who had destroyed Lottie's future.

The very thought settled as an ache in Eleanor's chest.

As if sensing her unease, Charles put his hand to her lower back and carefully guided her down the stairs. The touch was intimate and surprisingly reassuring. She looked up at her husband and hated the tightening of her chest and what it meant.

She'd seen those blue eyes alight with passion. She'd kissed those lips and experienced the pleasure they could bring. And it was because of this knowledge that the most handsome man she'd ever seen was suddenly all the more so. Dangerously more so.

They reached the bottom of the stairs and Charles leaned in close. "All will be well, my Duchess."

Together, they approached the dining room, where Lottie and Evander sat at the long, familiar table with the blue runner down its middle. Their voices were impassioned with a loud whispering that went silent when Eleanor and Charles entered.

Evander rose immediately in welcome. At least he had not lost his manners.

Lottie got to her feet as well, her cheeks stained with a deep flush. "Excuse me. I find I am without an appetite this evening."

She did not give anyone a chance to reply and all but ran from the room.

"What did you say to so offend her?" Charles asked Evander, with an edge.

"The offense was given long ago."

Evander pushed a hand through his hair and a tuft of it jutted out over his right temple. That particular bit of hair had always been stubborn, even when he was a boy. It was a stabbing reminder of the young brother Eleanor had loved, and it endeared him to her, in a deep place in her heart, where her affection for that young boy could never be uprooted.

Evander sighed and motioned for them to sit. A muscle worked in his jaw. "It is an offense for which I will never be able to make amends," he said. "And I believe the cost is no more than I deserve."

Charles scoffed and then helped Eleanor into her seat before taking his own.

The footman came forward and presented them with a delicate savory soup.

Evander stared into the distance, forgoing his soup in favor of the wine at his side. A crease showed on his brow, similar to the one their father had often had when he was disappointed.

"Will you tell us of your adventures?" Eleanor asked. "The journals make everything seem so very fascinating."

Charles stiffened at her side at the mention of the journals.

Evander turned his gaze in her direction. "You have read them?"

She lifted her chin. "I have."

"Elly…"

He said his childhood nickname for her in a sad, slow tone. There was a tired look about him that made her want to coddle him.

"Those aren't appropriate for you. There's so much in them…"

"I am well aware." Eleanor slid the spoon into her soup. "I am no longer a child."

"But you are still a lady."

"We have more journals here, do we not?" She kept her gaze from gliding toward Charles. He had accepted her without the journals, but she knew what they meant to him regardless.

Evander settled back in his chair, with no interest in the food before him. "Our fathers were men without honor."

"Not both of our fathers were," Charles replied evenly.

"Both of our fathers." Evander steepled his fingers and touched his forefingers to his lips in contemplation before speaking. "They stole their treasures. They looted the wealth of poor countries without any means to stop them. Reaping treasures from religious and holy sites. One of the other members of the Adventure Club was apparently exceptional at discovering artifacts in a way they were not. They stole from him as well."

Charles slapped the table and set the wine glasses trembling. "Ridiculous!"

Eleanor stared in shock at her new husband. After some of the hideous entries she'd read in the journals she possessed, Evander's claims did not seem unlikely. Unfortunately...

Evander regarded Charles. "I assure you it is not ridiculous. I followed the path detailed in one of the journals I had with me. There were many villages with starving people whose temples had been plundered."

Charles simply stared at Evander.

"You know the truth of it even if you don't want to accept it." Eleanor's brother gave a wry twist of his lips. "I was trying to rebuild my family's fortune, but I could not bring myself to take what belongs to others. I dealt primarily in the purchase of spices and silks—a task made difficult with the war, which appears to have finally ended now that I've established enough wealth."

"My father was honorable. A man determined to bring ancient cultures to London for all to experience," Charles countered. "He was admired for his relics...for the care he took with them."

Eleanor knew that Charles had also admired his father, and held him in the highest esteem. Therefore she also realized it was not rage behind his words, but fear.

And with good reason.

From what she'd read in their own hand, their fathers had *not* been good men.

If Evander had other journals here, and if he gave them

to Charles, Eleanor had a strong suspicion that in getting exactly what he most wanted Charles would also be learning exactly what he most feared.

Charles no longer had an appetite. Who could with such dinner conversation?

Westix pushed away from the table and rose, giving up all pretense of attempting to find interest in his own food.

"I know you don't want to hear this, Somersville, but our fathers spent more money on acquiring their treasures through bribery than any profit they might have generated. Tell me, did you not encounter the situations of which I speak in your own travels?"

He pulled his glass from the table by its rim and strode toward the window to stare out into a field of vibrant green.

Charles knew the Earl was giving him a moment to contemplate what he'd said. It was true, there had been great poverty in the foreign countries where Charles had traveled. And there had been rumors of treasures taken from those countries. But those had been by thieves—not English gentlemen. And certainly not Charles's father, whose acclaim had grown with each unique discovery.

Charles himself had acquired treasures on his travels, all accumulated through morally correct avenues. Indeed, there had been the opportunity to bribe, but Charles had not permitted himself to be drawn into such temptation. He'd assumed his father would never have engaged in such immoral actions.

"I have something to show you," said Westix.

He opened a drawer in a large chest near the window and withdrew a journal. Its battered binding was of similar appearance to the ones Eleanor had given him in London.

She sat higher at Charles's side. "You *do* have them here..." she breathed in wonder.

His heart smacked his ribs. Damn him for not having brought the key.

Westix tossed the book unceremoniously on the table beside Charles. "Look for yourself."

He turned and requested the footman bring more wine.

Charles picked up the journal. The script within was choppy, written in the same hurried hand as the one Eleanor had shown him.

"That's the handwriting we need," Eleanor whispered. "Get the key."

"I don't have it," Charles muttered.

"Read it." Westix nodded to him.

Charles ignored Eleanor's questioning look and read aloud. "'Avarice has pervaded the Adventure Club, rendering it rife with treachery and perfidy. What was once a group of morally sound men has descended into a group of men committing the sins of debauchery, bribery and blatant theft. The taking is done without regard to the owners, or to the deficit such losses will press upon the cultures they have plundered. It is ironic that the greatest offenders are none other than the esteemed men of good breeding who conspired to instigate the club's institution—a certain earl and duke whose names I will not put to paper.'"

Charles stopped, unable to bring himself to read more. The author did not have to put such names to paper—not when Charles already knew.

His father had been a thief. A great man brought down by the force of his own greed.

The soup churned in Charles's stomach.

The footman placed a glass of wine before him. Charles

reached blindly for it and drained it in one gulp. The alcohol burned a path down his chest and pooled in his unsettled stomach, assuaging the need to retch.

If only the pain in his chest could be so easily quelled.

The foundations of Charles's life—the greatness of his father and the accolades surrounding his incredible findings—had all been built on a lie.

Chapter Twenty-Nine

Charles grappled with what he'd read in the journal. In fact, with what he'd read in several more journals. All of which Evander had gladly turned over to him.

Dinner had gone largely uneaten and they had all retired immediately afterward, overwrought with the events of the day.

Now Charles made his way to the room he shared with Eleanor, weighted with the burden of newfound knowledge. No, with the confirmed knowledge of what he hadn't allowed himself to consider previously. It settled like a rock on his chest, rough-hewn and heavy.

Eleanor didn't say a word until they were in the privacy of their room. Then she turned to him, held out her arms and drew him into a tender embrace. "I'm sorry for what you have learned of your father."

Charles let himself be cradled against her perfumed warmth, breathing in that lovely jasmine smell of her. "I'm sorry about your father as well."

Eleanor released him and shook her head. "My father was never held high in my esteem. He was not…not kind."

Charles bristled. "Not kind?" he repeated.

"He did not like what he could not control, and that meant me and my emotions." Eleanor slid her gaze away and walked toward the vanity, where she sat and began to pull the pins from her hair, her back ramrod-straight as she spoke. "He did not like us to show emotion of any kind. Not happiness, for it made us too excited, and certainly not rage or fear, for that made us weak. Except I did feel, and it was a visceral ache when he left so often."

Charles approached Eleanor and helped pull the small pins from her beautiful hair.

"I missed my father when he was gone," she said quietly.

Something in Charles's chest went tight. He would need to be gone soon too, the way her father had been gone. This was the truth he had not wanted to face—the reality of the critical issue of their marriage. He would need to leave, to put the calamitous piece of his soul to rest with travel, while she remained in London, alone. He slid a pin free and gently uncoiled the length of red hair it had held in place.

"Once I asked my father to stay. The thought of him leaving again was too great." Eleanor dropped her hands from her hair and clasped them together in her lap. "He ignored me and I started crying. I begged him and he…he…"

"He what?" Charles tensed, knowing innately he would not like the answer.

"He struck me." Eleanor lowered her head. "It happened so fast…and he was so strong… Evander was sent away soon after that. The soft affection I'd once been afforded went hard and I was given a rigorous education in its place."

"He struck you?" Charles growled. If her father were

still alive, Charles would strike *him*—repeatedly. Stand up for the girl who had not been able to stand up for herself.

Eleanor pressed her lips together before speaking again. "He did not have the extensive lineage my mother had, and he'd always overcompensated for his new acceptance into the nobility. He wanted us to be iron, emotionless, strong."

Charles clenched his jaw with restrained rage. He reiterated in his mind, if the former Earl of Westix were still alive Charles would kill him. To think of Eleanor being so helpless against the power of a grown man...

"The loss of love was far more painful." She turned her face up to him. "And all for treasure."

Charles's heart flinched.

"Charles..." She met his gaze in the mirror.

His stomach sank. Would she ask him to forgo his travel? "Yes?"

"What if the only way for you to get the ruby you seek is to employ the tactics they used?" Her brows pinched together. "Would you still reclaim the stone?"

He didn't respond. He couldn't. His final promise to his father had to be fulfilled. Experience had taught him that not all treasure could be legally acquired. In the past Charles had let it be—it was unnecessary to bring everything back. But the Coeur de Feu...

It was the one thing he knew he could do in his life that would have made his father proud.

"I shall endeavor to keep my morals intact," he replied slowly, diplomatically.

"And if they cannot be kept intact?" she pressed. "How great is your desire to possess the stone?"

Again, he hesitated, hating this part of himself, hating the burden of his father's dying wish.

"Did you ask Evander if you could use the key on the journal?" She resumed the task of pulling pins from her hair and unraveling her long, glossy hair.

"I didn't bring the key with me."

The pin in Eleanor's hand pinged onto the table.

"This trip was about our wedding." He put his hand to her shoulder.

"We ought to return to London soon, then." She gave him a cool glance over her shoulder. "So that you might get the key and have your journey underway. And Mother will want to know Evander is safe."

Charles said nothing. How could he when a fire burned in the pit of his stomach? Eleanor had not asked him not to leave, and yet he knew she did not want him to go. It would be on him to make the decision to stay in London, and he could not do that. Not when he was so close to redeeming himself with his father.

Except he would have to do it knowing that in making good on his father's dying wish he would be hurting the woman he cared about more than any other.

It was not only the aggravated silence between Lottie and Evander that was growing in the carriage upon their drive back to London—there was a length of silence between Eleanor and Charles as well.

Eleanor knew it to be of her own making. After all, when she'd agreed to marry him she'd known he would be going after the Coeur de Feu, no matter the cost.

Why, then, did she feel so hollow inside when she thought of him leaving?

It was more than just the possibility that he might have to employ immoral practices to get the stone. It was the idea of being left alone. *Again.* Every man in her life had left her to experience the world. She had subsisted as they'd *lived.*

And it would be happening again with Charles.

She'd anticipated that the empty feeling would dissipate, but it had only grown like a festering wound inside her, hot and red and raw with powerful emotion.

And while Eleanor had tried to convince herself that she could keep her heart guarded, its pathetic leap every time her eyes lit on his handsome face suggested otherwise. Which was why it was better to cut her emotions to the quick and rely on older, safer habits—the habits that protected her from feeling.

Finally, after a tense and interminable ride back to London, and dropping Lottie at her town house, they returned to Westix Place so that Eleanor and Charles could offer their apologies to her mother. And witness Evander's homecoming.

By the time they made their way up the steps Edmonds was already pulling the door open. He looked first in surprise at Eleanor, then glowered at Charles. But when his gaze caught on Evander his mouth fell open, and the older man could only stare before stammering out an acceptable welcome.

No sooner had they crowded into the receiving room than the Countess approached, fanning herself to ward off an apparent flash of heat. "Eleanor Susan Murray, you—"

Her mother stopped, and the fan fell from her hand and dropped to the marble floor with an audible smack. Her fingers trembled where they hung in midair before coming to rest on her partially opened mouth.

"Dear God… Evander." She blinked, and a tear rolled down her cheek. "My son."

She reached for a small table near the wall to brace herself and missed.

Evander caught her before she could fall. "Forgive me my prolonged absence, Mother."

She gave a choked sound, as if it had been wrenched from the depths of her soul, and then touched his face, her fingers shaking. "It's you. It's truly you, my sweet boy. You've come home. You're…safe."

She turned away abruptly and the room was filled with the soft gasps of her weeping.

Evander put his arm around their mother's slender shoulders. "I won't be going away again. I've accumulated enough wealth—we shall not have to worry for generations to come."

"I don't care about the fortune. My children…both of whom I'd thought lost forever…have returned."

The Countess looked to Eleanor and held one arm out to her daughter. Eleanor took her mother's hand and found herself pulled into the extremely rare embrace of her family.

She smiled at Eleanor through her tears. "I am not pleased with your decision." Her mother jabbed a glare at Charles. "But I am pleased to have you home."

Pain twisted at Eleanor's heart. Was she herself glad for her decision? Or would she come to regret it in a wash of loneliness and hurt?

The Countess pressed a kiss to each of her children's foreheads, going on tiptoe for Evander, and then pulled away. She swept at her cheeks and smoothed her immaculate blue day dress.

"Yes, well…" She sniffed. "Excuse me a moment. I must freshen up. And then we will all take tea."

Eleanor sat silent and stiff through tea, letting her mother and Evander do the talking. Charles remained at her side, equally quiet, his constant glances at her the only indication that he suspected something might be wrong.

She should tell him, and yet she could not quite work out the best way to say the words.

How could she possibly ask him to forgo the stone and stay with her in London?

Chapter Thirty

Charles was not so foolish as not to know something was
amiss with Eleanor. Nor was he daft enough to wonder at
the cause, when she had said it so plainly herself prior to
their departure from Comlongon.

The loss of love was far more painful. And all for trea-
sure.

He knew he should not go on his journey, and yet how
could he forgo his opportunity to find peace with his father? How could he sacrifice the excitement of the world to
simply stay in dreary, dull London for the rest of his life?

And love... What was love? It was not what he had felt
for his father—that had been respect. Nor was it what his
father had felt for him—that had been obligation. Perhaps
it was what he felt for Lottie—but surely even that was sis-
terly affection?

He knew he enjoyed Eleanor's laughter and her smiles,
that they made his heart swell when he elicited them. He
knew he'd never once hesitated at the thought of traveling

until he'd known her. And he knew he was frightened that he might somehow lose her.

Later, upon their arrival at Somersville House, and after a brief introduction of Eleanor to the household staff, she immediately went up to her rooms with her maid. It was then that Grimms informed Charles that Lottie had sent over a letter, in the short time he had been at Westix Place. He expected to read of Lottie's heartache, considering what had transpired between her and Westix.

Charles made his way to the library, where he firstly extracted the key from the safe and then opened Lottie's note. His heartbeat quickened with delight as he read.

It seemed Lottie had received a considerable amount of mail in the short time of their travel—all of it from mothers, and even some fathers, with daughters in the *ton* who might benefit from her instruction. She would no longer need a protector.

Smiling, he set the letter on his desk beside a bottle and pile of unopened letters.

Bottle? The smile faded from his lips.

Why the devil was there a bottle on his desk when he hadn't been home long enough to have put anything there? The last one had been thrown out with the rubbish. He'd seen to that.

But there it was, with a card dangling from its thin neck, glinting with the imprint of a compass.

This bottle was full—new. Which meant that whoever had put it there had been in the house—and most likely very recently. A shiver of warning went up Charles's spine and he felt an immediate and sudden need to ensure Eleanor was safe.

For in his gut he feared she was in danger.

* * *

Eleanor had not expected such grand rooms—though, considering the vastness of Somersville House, she ought to have known the Duchess's chambers would be glorious.

Amelia had agreed to come to Somersville House to ready the rooms when Eleanor had left for Scotland with Charles. Now she fluttered about like an excited child while she detailed every feature of her new residence.

"And the best part, if you don't mind my saying, Your Grace…" Amelia pushed at the wall. A quiet click sounded and a portion of the wall popped out to reveal a hidden door. "It leads to the Duke's chambers."

Eleanor pulled at the hidden door. It slid easily toward her on silent hinges. She looked at Amelia, who grinned and nodded toward the passage.

"Go on," Amelia said. "I believe your Duke said he'll be joining you soon."

"He did…"

Eleanor kept the trepidation from her voice. She had known that the closer they had drawn to London, the sooner Charles would be leaving. It was unfair to ask him not to go, and yet… And yet it had been impossible not to soften her heart to him even in her ire. How could she possibly do it while they lived together? Shared a bed together?

She slipped through the hidden door, which immediately clicked closed behind her. The chamber she stepped into was powerfully masculine, with heavy mahogany furniture and artifacts used in its decoration throughout. The familiar exotic spice of Charles's scent filled the room and set her pulse pounding.

A creak sounded behind her. Eleanor was startled from her thoughts and spun around.

At first she saw nothing, and then she noted where the wall had parted to reveal yet another hidden door across the room. Not the one she'd entered through.

She swallowed down a prickle of fear. Surely Charles hid behind it, in an attempt to surprise her? She pulled it open and found the passage empty. A chill crept up her spine. She frowned to herself at her childish fears and closed the door firmly.

The chill did not abate. In fact, her skin practically crawled with primal apprehension. Not silly, nor foolish, but a true and persistent warning.

She turned slowly—and choked back a scream. A man stood not more than ten feet in front of her. Not Charles, but a man she recognized nonetheless.

The Earl of Ledsey.

"Hugh…?" she managed.

He curled his lip. "I heard he'd married you. The servants talk, you know." A muscle worked in his jaw, where he clenched his teeth. "*I* could've married you."

"You have Lady Alice." She backed away from him.

"Everyone wanted her. How could I resist?" Hugh smirked. "But then you came in as an Ice Queen at the masquerade ball…and you were magnificent."

He stepped closer and Eleanor realized she had no way to back up further.

"And then *he* began sniffing around you and I *knew* you had them still."

Her mind reeled. *Had them still?* The Earl had lost his mind. She edged to the side and he followed her step in a mocking, macabre dance.

"Did you like my tulips?" he asked. "You never once even looked outside to see me there, watching you. Imagine my

surprise, though, when you went to that whore's house."
Hugh laughed—a scoffing, snort of a sound.

"Don't you dare call Lottie that!" Eleanor concentrated
all her fear and her anger into grabbing a statue of a gold
elephant and hurling it at him. The thing was heavier than
she'd anticipated and veered wildly off course, before landing with a muted *thunk* on the carpet several inches from
his feet.

Hugh tilted his head at this inept attack. "A whore is exactly what she is. And you're no better—married or not."

Eleanor spun on her heel and darted away from him.
She'd only taken a few steps when she felt a sharp rip of
pain at her scalp, and found herself wrenched backward
by her hair. She gave a surprised scream and was thrown
to the floor.

Hugh stood over her and placed the sole of one immaculately polished Hessian on her chest. "This will all be over
soon and I'll finally have what I have needed from you since
the beginning—the journals."

He drew a pistol from his jacket, then lowered it and
aimed it directly at her face.

Chapter Thirty-One

Charles took the stairs two at a time and broke into a sprint on the landing, racing toward Eleanor's rooms, where he bolted through the door.

Her maid shrieked and dropped the ivory-handled brush she held. At least she hadn't thrown it.

"Did you hear that?" Charles asked. "A heavy thud."

The maid shook her head.

"Where is she?" he demanded.

"N-next door, in your room."

Charles ran back into the hall and found his own door locked from within.

His heart was sucked into his throat.

He darted back into Eleanor's room, not stopping until he was at the concealed door.

Amelia followed behind him. "Your Grace...?"

He threw open Eleanor's secret door, then his, and stopped.

Lord Ledsey stood on the opposite side of the large bed, looking down at something Charles could not see.

What the devil was Ledsey doing in his chambers? The Lord's attention snapped to Charles. "Come any closer and I'll kill her."

Her.

Eleanor.

Dear God, no.

The maid's gasp sounded behind him, followed by the pattering of her footsteps over thick carpet. She had evidently made the same assumption as him, and would surely be going for help.

Ledsey nodded at Charles. "Close the door and lock it behind you."

Charles hesitated. He didn't want to close the door, or lock it. He wanted to spring across the room like a savage lion so he could tear the blackguard's throat out and ensure Eleanor was safe.

But he was no lion. He was only a man, helplessly standing too damned far away to protect her.

"Do not test my patience, *Your Grace*." Ledsey sneered out the title. "Close the door."

Charles pushed the secret door closed, but did not lock it, and hoped Ledsey would not notice. Charles put his hands up in surrender and moved deeper into the room.

"What is the meaning of this, Ledsey?"

He was nearly around the bed when his gaze fell on the splash of vibrant red hair against the blue carpet and the glint of the pistol held in Ledsey's grip.

Anger erupted through Charles with brilliant intensity. "Let her go."

He stalked around the bed and drew to an abrupt halt when he came to Eleanor, lying with her back against the thick carpet, rigid and stiff.

Eleanor. His wife.

A panicked jolt shot through his heart. He could not lose her. He *would not* lose her.

"I want the journals. And the key." Ledsey's stare flicked to Eleanor, but he did not appear nervous, merely watchful.

Charles had opened his mouth to reply when Eleanor spoke.

"You couldn't have known about the journals...or the key...unless..." She gasped.

The realization slammed into Charles at exactly the same moment. "It was you who drugged me that night. You took the journals. You put that bottle—"

Ledsey smirked. "Yes, it was me. The previous Duke made it so easy, with all these passages and hidden rooms. I was able to wait for you to fall asleep, then I crept in and took them. Clever of you, though, hiding the key."

"How do you even *know* about the journals?" Eleanor's voice was sharp with demand—certainly not the voice of a woman being held at gunpoint.

"How do I know about them?" Ledsey stared incredulously down at her. "My father was in the Adventure Club. He's the one who found most of the artifacts. Your fathers took them from him. They basked in public adoration while he was relegated to the shadows."

His upper lip curled back in disgust.

"Who do you think wrote about their misdeeds? He told me about the journals, about the Coeur de Feu, but I didn't know about the key." His face twisted wryly. "He must have written the journals and made the key on his last trip to India, just before he died."

Charles didn't answer. In truth, the names of the members of the Adventure Club were kept anonymous, with the exception of his and Eleanor's fathers. The other members hadn't been as wealthy, as famous or as influential, and clearly their names had faded, leaving no connection to the acquired accomplishments.

"The Duchess and I have recently learned the sordid details of those discoveries," Charles answered. "But sinking to this level, where you are threatening a woman, will never elevate your standing with anyone. Least of all me."

"I want the Coeur de Feu." Sweat was beginning to bead on Ledsey's brow.

"You can have it."

Charles reached into his jacket to claim the key without thought. Damn the journal, damn the key, and damn his promise to his father. Eleanor. She was all that mattered. His wife. The woman he loved.

"No!" Eleanor said sharply. She kicked her foot out at Ledsey, catching him in the shin. The blow sufficed to knock him back half a step.

Ledsey grunted in pain and again pointed the gun down at Eleanor. "It would appear I need to ensure I'm taken more seriously."

His arm tensed and the gun went off.

An extreme pressure slammed into Eleanor's arm and she was vaguely aware of a salty taste in her mouth. An acrid odor hung in the air, stinging her eyes. Her ears rang with the explosion and Charles's voice bellowed in the distance—outraged, horrified, undecipherable.

She pushed up and nearly fell to her right. Her arm seemed somehow inoperable. The room swirled around her. She looked down to where an ache blazed with insistent pain. Blood bloomed like a violent flower over the pale pink of her sleeve and spattered the rest of her gown.

Blood?

Her mind reeled with confusion at the dark, bloody hole in her upper arm.

When did that happen?

Her heartbeat throbbed too fast. Her breath was too shallow. Her lips tingled.

Charles lunged forward, moving as if very slowly, but before he could reach her, a heavy object landed by her feet. A pistol, with a stream of smoke still curling up from its barrel.

And yet hard metal jabbed into Eleanor's temple, shoving her head savagely to the right.

"If you come any closer I'll shoot her in the head this time."

Hugh's voice.

Suddenly it all rushed back to her and dislodged the addled freeze of her brain. Hugh was holding her hostage, demanding the journals and key, claiming them to be his father's. And he'd shot her.

He'd *shot* her.

Her mouth was dry. She tried to swallow and found her throat stuck against itself rather than finding relief.

Blood soaked through her dress, intensely opaque and red against the gentle pink. The agony of it rushed through her arm, blazing.

Charles stared at her, his eyes wide, his face completely white as if he'd been shot as well.

"Good thing I loaded a second gun," Hugh said in a mocking tone.

Pain mingled with the metallic taste of fear and left her stomach whirling with nausea. The barrel of the pistol dug into her scalp, forcing her to crane her neck. Emotion clogged her throat, but she kept herself from crying out.

"Give me the journals and the key," Hugh demanded.

"Don't hurt her." There was pleading in the strength of Charles's voice. "I swear to God if you hurt her, I will kill you."

"The journals and the key," Hugh repeated.

Charles set the key on the ground and withdrew the journals from the trunk he'd had in Scotland.

A ball of frustration welled in the back of Eleanor's throat. She knew what those journals meant to Charles. He was sacrificing them, sacrificing the fulfillment of his father's wish—*everything*—for her.

The dam in her heart holding back her emotion broke then, and overwhelmed her with the very truth she'd been trying to ignore for far too long.

No matter how desperately she tried to deny it, or to shield herself from the truth, she loved Charles. She loved him with every nook and cranny of her heart.

Charles shoved the stack of books toward Hugh. "Let her go."

Hugh didn't reach for the journals. Instead he pushed the pistol barrel harder into her head.

A cry rasped from Eleanor's throat despite her attempt to maintain her composure.

"Do you truly think I'd let you both live after this?"

Hugh's feet were so close to Eleanor they pressed against her thigh where she sat in a daze on the floor. Panic raced through her. They couldn't die. Not now. Not like this.

She put the hand of her good arm to her brow, as if mopping the layer of sweat there, then drove her elbow down with all the strength she could muster.

It connected sharply with the side of Hugh's knee, exactly where she'd intended to strike. Her aim had been true and Hugh's legs folded against themselves as he fell to the ground with a shout.

Charles did not hesitate. He ran at Hugh and kicked him square in the face. The sound was hollow and wet, like a melon breaking against a hard surface. Then Charles bent and retrieved the gun before dropping to Eleanor's side.

He gathered her in his arms and the pulse of pain splintered into mindless agony. The world swam in a wavering light in front of her, threatening to pull her under.

"Eleanor..." There was alarm in his voice, a quivering pitch she'd thought never to hear from a man as brave and strong as Charles.

She was of a mind to answer him, to tell him she was fine and cry out at what he'd sacrificed to save her. And she wanted to tell him that she loved him, more than life itself.

But her voice did not correspond with her mouth any longer. An intense fatigue washed over her and left her with a thick and lazy sensation.

"Eleanor." Charles caught her face in his palms and stared down at her with wild eyes. "Please. I love you."

I love you.

The words floated above her pain and smoothed over her heart like a balm.

"Don't leave me." Charles stroked her face, his eyes red-rimmed.

Tears leaked from her eyes at his admission, and her heart gave a weak flutter. The room began to fade.

"Please," he begged. "Focus."

Yes, focus.

She squinted her eyes at him and did exactly as he bade.

Her thoughts centered on watching him, on resisting the urge to succumb to the sweet lure of oblivion, on wanting him to say he loved her again and again and again.

A shadow rose over them and Charles's head snapped to the side. He collapsed to the ground the way a marionette might do if its cords had been cut. Eleanor fell to the ground too, and pain shone bright anew.

Helpless, she could only watch as Hugh bent over Charles and grabbed the gun. Charles did not stir. The darkness pressed around Eleanor. She tried to blink it away. She had to do something. She had to help.

There came a loud crack at the opposite side of the room. Still Charles did not move.

"Halt!" The voice was authoritative, coming from where Eleanor could not see. "Put the gun down, my lord, or we will have no option but to use force."

In answer, Hugh raised the gun, pointing it at Charles's face.

The fog of exhaustion dissipated for a brief moment.

No. Not Charles.

Eleanor struggled to stand, drawing from a waning well of strength. Black dots swam in her vision and her body went limp. She fell to the ground, only vaguely aware of the agony in her arm when the hurt in her heart was so great. Too weak to even save Charles.

The pounding of footsteps thundered for only a scant second before the popping of gunfire filled Eleanor's ears and she could no longer fight the pull of darkness.

Chapter Thirty-Two

Charles's head throbbed with pain and his ears shrilled with a high-pitched whine.

A sharp scent hung in the air—thick and unpleasant and redolent of gunfire. He tried to turn his face from the odor, but his scalp screamed in protest. He blinked his eyes open and found Ledsey lying on the ground beside him, holding something wet with blood, his face twisted in agony.

Footsteps and shouts came from nearby, distorted as if Charles were listening underwater. Men appeared around and over him. One in particular pointed next to Charles's head.

"You've got the angels on your side, Your Grace," the man said. "That bullet was meant for your head."

Despite the pain of doing so, Charles turned his head and found a scorched hole in the carpet, directly in front of his face.

"Come along, my lord."

Another voice spoke this time, followed by an anguished scream from Ledsey.

Charles looked up in time to see Hugh being led from the room, with a mangled hand clutched against his chest. Only when he was gone did Charles see Eleanor, lying on the ground.

The whole world faded away, leaving only the horrific sight of his wife in a pool of blood.

A man appeared in front of him, reaching down to help him to his feet. Charles leapt up on his own and ignored the way the world tilted. He had to make his way to Eleanor, to confirm she was not...

He couldn't even think the word. Not when it made his insides blaze with incomprehensible loss.

Eleanor, his beautiful wife, with all her boldness of character, so passionate and vivid in his life and in his heart. He couldn't lose her.

He staggered to her and dropped to the floor at her side.

She lay unmoving, her face pale.

"Eleanor?" Her name caught in the tightness of his throat.

She wouldn't answer him—he knew that in his soul. The massive puddle of blood welling under her told him all he needed to know, all he hated to acknowledge: she had lost far too much blood. Surely one couldn't lose so much blood and...?

But she couldn't be...

Surely she wasn't truly...?

He couldn't even think properly.

It wasn't possible. Not when they had just started their lives together. Not when he loved her.

The well of agony burst in his chest and became so damn unbearable his vision blurred.

"Eleanor…" he said again, unable to stop himself.

Only this time when she did not answer he felt a visceral crack as his heart broke.

A man bent over her and attempted to gather her in his arms.

"Stop." Charles glared at the man. "I will have your skin if you touch her again."

The man gave an efficient nod. "Forgive me, Your Grace. But I'm an officer, aye? You must understand we need to make her comfortable. The physician was summoned when we were called and he needs to see to her."

Charles stared at him dumbly. "I…" He cleared the knot from his throat. "I beg your pardon?"

"Your Grace, please."

"You mean, she's…?"

The man nodded. "Alive. Please, Your Grace."

Charles backed away quickly and nodded, nearly choking on his relief. He would do anything in his power to ensure Eleanor lived. Anything.

The man lifted her easily, minding to hold her arm over her chest, so it did not dangle and cause further injury. Charles tried to get to his feet once more and stumbled, his legs too weak to support him. But he had to follow Eleanor. He had to make sure she would truly be all right.

Eleanor—his Eleanor. His love.

Thomas appeared at Charles's side. "Let me help you, Your Grace." He clasped Charles at his elbow and pulled an arm over his shoulder.

Charles managed to stand upright, albeit a bit wobbly. The world swirled in a dizzy rush around him, but Thomas's hold did not relax and he managed to keep him solidly in place.

"Give it a moment, Your Grace. You took quite a knock to your head."

"Eleanor—" Charles gritted out.

"The physician is seeing to her." Thomas guided Charles to a chair beside the fire.

Charles pushed against his valet's hold, forcing them both to move back to the secret door connecting the rooms. "I must go to her."

Thomas shifted direction once more. "After you sit for a moment. Please, Your Grace."

The room swirled and Charles's knees buckled, nearly sending him to the floor. "Very well, but for a moment only."

He sank into the chair and sat until the room ceased its spinning and his breath was sufficiently restored. Until he could take the waiting no longer.

Charles pushed to his feet and walked on his own across the room, with Thomas hovering like an anxious hen at his side.

Amelia appeared in the doorway, her face drawn. She twisted a hand in her skirts. "You can't come in, Your Grace. The physician is with her. Thank Heavens the servants summoned him at the same time they went for the Watch when I told them. Or else…" Her eyes welled with tears.

"By God, I *will* see my wife." It took all he had in him not to roar at poor Amelia, who already appeared quite ready to drop.

She chewed on her lower lip.

"I want only to be with my wife." Charles spoke with a gentleness the urgency raking through him did not warrant. By God, he wanted to see Eleanor, and no man or woman would stop him. "Please. I love her."

Amelia's face softened and she put her hands over her chest. "I'm sure the physician would not complain if you remain quietly to the side."

She stepped back and allowed Charles to enter the room. The door clicked closed behind him, shut by either Amelia or Thomas, and Charles was left in the silent room, where a physician bent over the bed against the opposite wall.

"I assumed I'd be seeing you." The older man's voice grated out.

Charles approached the bed where Eleanor lay, unmoving and pale. His heart sank lower than it had ever fallen.

He had expected...what? That she would be awake? Speaking?

"The bullet passed straight through." The physician spoke as he wound cloth carefully around Eleanor's arm, where the fabric of her sleeve had been cut away. "We are fortunate for that."

"And she will recover?" Charles's throat was so tight he could barely force the words out.

The aging man looked at him from behind wire-rimmed spectacles. "Her Grace will need rest, but she will recover. I recommend broth to strengthen her and laudanum for the pain." He indicated a clear bottle on the bedside table. "The healing will be more uncomfortable than a lady can bear."

"I think you underestimate my wife," Charles said.

After all, Eleanor was no ordinary lady. In the face of danger she'd first kicked Ledsey, in an attempt to keep the journals from him, and then had knocked him to the ground when he'd rounded on Charles to shoot him.

Had she not been given to such bravery Charles might very well be dead. Certainly the officers would have been seconds too late to see him saved. No, Eleanor was not an ordinary woman at all.

Her eyes blinked open and met his. The corners of her lips drew up in a soft smile and his heart soared with relief.

The concern on the doctor's face faded and his wrinkles pulled back in an affable expression. "I think she will recover quite nicely, Your Grace."

With that, he gave a bow and left the room, leaving Eleanor and Charles alone.

"Charles…" She opened her eyes fully and pushed against the bedcovers, as if trying to sit further upright.

"Please stay where you are." He rushed to her side and stopped short.

Her skin almost perfectly matched the white sheets of the bed, but the sharp brilliance in her eyes remained. Even tired and battered, she was the loveliest sight he'd ever seen.

An ache returned in the back of Charles's throat. "Eleanor."

Her gaze went glossy. "Charles. I thought he'd killed you." A tear slid down her cheek. "I thought I'd lost you."

"I thought I'd lost you, too, Eleanor." He knelt at her bedside and took the hand of her uninjured arm. "My God, woman, I love you."

She drew in a sharp breath and squeezed his hand.

"I do." He kissed her knuckles. "For your bravery and your warmth and your incredible passion."

"I love you, too," she whispered. "I thought I'd lost you, that I'd never see you again or have you in my life."

"You have me." Charles eased up onto the bed. "It is why I've made the decision I have."

He took a deep breath and said the words he knew had to be said. For the sake of keeping her, of loving her.

"I will not be going after the Coeur de Feu. Never again will I do anything that means I might lose you."

Eleanor jerked as though she'd been struck. For surely she had. After everything Charles had done to get the journals—everything he'd sacrificed in the pursuit of his father's dying wish—no, he could not give it up. Not for her.

"Charles, no."

He shook his head, his face lined with concern. "I cannot risk losing you again. I do not want to be separated from you for months, sometimes years at a time, any more than I want to abandon you the way our fathers did us."

"Perhaps there is a way you can fulfill your promise and have me at your side." She smiled coyly up at him.

His brow furrowed and then smoothed as understanding dawned on him. "Surely you don't mean—"

"That I join you?" Her heart raced a little faster at her own bold decision. "Of course I do."

He frowned and opened his mouth, but she began speaking again before he could protest.

"I have read the journals, Charles. And in them I found a taste of a life I've never known. Excitement and adventure unlike anything London can provide. I confess I loathed the idea of being here by myself while you traveled, but I realized that was because I envied you the opportunity to see the world."

Charles leaned closer and the bed creaked beneath them. "It isn't always safe, Eleanor, nor clean or hospitable."

"I'm a Murray who has married a Pemberton." She lifted her head with pride. "Adventure surely runs in my veins."

"You certainly can hold your own. You never told me you were an accomplished bruiser."

He smiled and his eyes crinkled at the corners in that way she loved.

His gaze flicked toward her bandaged arm. "Will you agree to wait until your arm is healed?"

"Of course."

She kept her voice even, but her pulse thrummed wildly in her veins at the prospect. Imagine! Witnessing the world herself, sampling its cuisines, meeting its people. And, though she knew she shouldn't care, she couldn't help but wonder if her father would have been proud.

"Though I will demand a higher moral integrity than our fathers had," she said resolutely.

Charles nodded. "I would never do anything to compromise us the way our fathers did. Even for the stone." He searched her face with his beautiful blue gaze. "I've learned there is so much more to life than treasure."

Tears tingled in Eleanor's eyes. He truly did love her. She blinked her emotion away. "We cannot go anywhere if we do not know where we're going." She grinned up at him.

"Shall we examine the journals with the key?" Charles asked with a twinkle in his eye.

"Yes!" It came out far louder than she'd anticipated.

"It's driving you mad, is it?" He laughed, the rapscallion, and then called for Thomas to bring them the journals and key. "I confess I'm eager to know as well."

Eleanor wriggled in her bed to sit higher up, for a better position to view the journals, and tried to ignore the sharpness of discomfort in her arm.

Thomas did not leave them waiting long, and brought the three remaining battered books to the bedside. He passed them crisply to Charles and left them alone in the room once more.

Charles took the flat piece of metal and opened the first page of the first journal. It held no information. The second journal, however, revealed squares that fit neatly in spaces with no writing. This appeared several times until about the seventh page, when the holes matched perfectly over a series of letters.

Eleanor held her breath and tensed. Those letters formed words.

DECCAN PLATEAU CLIFFSIDE ON R

Charles drew the key up and turned the page.

"Do you know where that is?" Eleanor asked.

"I do. It's in India. I've even been there once." He put the key to the second page.

IVER WAGHUR WHERE THERE IS A U

Charles shifted the key to the opposing page. Again and again he did this, until the entire message had been spelled out.

Deccan Plateau cliffside on River Waghur
Where there is a U-shaped gorge
A door will open to a large room
Seek the hollow stone

Eleanor's heart raced faster and pulsed in the injury of her arm. "Charles, this is it."

"It might be. There has been much speculation for years on what became of the stone. This is one of many assumptions."

But even as he spoke with such skepticism, his eyes were alight with the joy of their discovery.

"We've deciphered the code! Charles, we did it." She flushed with their accomplishment.

"Indeed we have." He folded the key into the journal. "And it couldn't have been done without us working together. I think we make a fine Adventure Club on our own."

A pleased blush warmed Eleanor's cheeks at his praise. "That we do. Do we leave soon?"

His brows rose. "When you're well."

"I could heal on the boat while we journey." She beamed up at him in the way she knew he liked.

He chuckled and shook his head. "You truly were born an adventurer, my Duchess."

Epilogue

Deccan Plateau, ten months later

A trickle of sweat ran down Eleanor's back and the heavy fabric of her skirt continued to catch at the brush. The oppressive heat was ubiquitous, pressing and suffocating. Loose tendrils slipped from the knot of her hair and were left to curl about her damp face.

Mad though it might seem, never had Eleanor been happier than when she was hiking through the wilds of India with Charles at her side while they followed their guide. The young boy was named Sahil, and he had a mop of dark hair perpetually falling into his soulful brown eyes.

Every day took them on a new adventure. Even if they had not yet discovered the Coeur de Feu, she was happy to continue to search every inch of India to find it.

At present they were staying in the opulent rooms of an Indian inn decorated with lights that shone through cut sheets of fashioned metal. They ate food spiced with flavors that tingled on Eleanor's tongue, and they slept and loved on a bed heaped with pillows and felt decadently colored silks against their bare skin.

Charles's hand found hers and he threaded his fingers between her own. He moved through the mass of twisting vines and overgrown trees without pause, his confidence evident in the ease of his stride. This was the element in which her husband thrived.

He smiled at her, his teeth a flash of white against his tanned skin, which had become all the more golden in these past two months of their searching.

"Why are you grinning at me like that?" she asked, smiling in return in spite of herself.

"Because you're lovely."

Eleanor self-consciously brushed at the sweat-slick curls plastered to her face. She was quite sure she was *not* lovely, with her cheeks flushed beneath a new smattering of freckles and spots of perspiration darkening her dress.

"I fear you may have touched some poisonous plant." She slid him a glance. "You're delusional."

Charles chuckled. "It's no poison, my Duchess. You are the most beautiful woman in this entire jungle."

Eleanor laughed at that—a clear, bright sound that carried unabashedly around them. And she didn't give a fig that it wasn't a bit ladylike. "I believe I am the *only* woman in this jungle at present."

"Yes, but you're the loveliest woman no matter where we go." He stopped and gave her an appreciative glance over. "By God, you make me a happy man, Eleanor."

Sahil appeared behind them suddenly and began speaking rapidly. Eleanor had only just begun to learn the exotic language but managed to recognize the words for *cave* and *near.*

He pulled at Charles's sleeve and then ran forward into a deeper portion of the jungle.

Charles glanced back at Eleanor and his blue eyes flashed. "I think this is it."

Together they followed the boy, their pace fast despite the thickness of growth.

Sahil gave an excited squeal and leapt into the air. *"Yahaan."* He pointed vigorously. *"Yahaan."*

Here.

Charles moved forward and pulled at the vines covering the bulk in front of them. They fell away to reveal a wall of rough-hewn stone. Eleanor's pulse quickened. Perhaps this truly was it.

Charles pulled a flat metal bar from his pack, slid it into a crack at the side of the stone and pulled with all his strength. It gave with a grinding, popping sound and slowly slid open. The sound echoed within, indicating a large, empty depth.

"It's a chamber," Charles said excitedly, and stuck his head inside. The air whooshed out from his lungs as he pulled Eleanor to his side.

She stared into the vast darkness with awe. There, lit by a sliver of sunlight, was a vast room lined with columns along either side and a massive structure toward the back. Clumps of color showed on the columns.

"Go in," Charles encouraged. "I'll ready the torch."

Eleanor shook her head. "We go in together."

He smiled proudly at her and captured her hand in his. "I've never been so eager to see a discovery in all my life."

"It is the Coeur de Feu," Eleanor said with a lift of her brows.

He shook his head and stared down at her in wonder. "No, it's you. It's us. I've never had someone to share this with before. You give this experience a power and excitement it never before possessed."

Eleanor found herself blushing "Shall we?" she asked.

Together they entered, and bore witness to the remnants of colorful paintings along the columns, where colors were still recognizable as gold and russet and white and blue. The ceiling arched high overhead and echoed their scraping footsteps back at them.

An intense feeling of reverence fell over Eleanor. For what care must have been placed in creating such a structure, what love and time spent on each carefully sculptured and painted bit of wall.

Charles gazed at the splendor before them. "Our fathers would have wanted to break this room into pieces and transport it back to London."

Eleanor regarded him and his thoughtful expression. "And what will *we* do?"

"My father wanted the stone, not the chamber." Charles took her hand in his and kissed her knuckles. "And I believe this is where true adventure lies. To know of its existence, to experience it, and to leave it for future generations to enjoy in its entirety. I think our fathers never understood as much."

"I am grateful that we do."

"As am I, my love. As am I."

He tilted her head upward for a kiss. His lips were salty and warm and completely enjoyable. A low pulse of longing hummed between her legs and she found herself looking forward to their return to their room.

He must have been of the same mind, for his tongue dipped into her mouth and brushed hers.

Eleanor pulled away slightly. "If you continue to kiss me thus I do not know that I can wait for our return to the hotel," she whispered, even though she knew Sahil did not speak English.

"That may result in bug bites in unfortunate locations." Charles grimaced comically and began rapping on the stone, in search of the Coeur de Feu's hidden location.

Eleanor chuckled and knocked on a piece of stonework herself. They all worked thus, including Sahil, gently thumping at every sound piece within the room. Until at long last Eleanor's raw knuckles struck against a particular square of stone behind one of the many columns. Its hollow sound echoed within and rang out against the high ceiling.

"Charles." Before she had even completely got his name out he was beside her, kneeling and studying the piece. "Do you think this is it?" she breathed.

Sahil appeared with the torch, his large dark eyes fixed with fascinated wonder on the square.

"We can but hope."

He put the edge of a pick to the stone and gently tapped it with the hammer. A crack showed immediately. He hit it a second time and a corner crumbled inward. A third careful blow created a fist-sized hole.

Charles lowered the tools and reached in, his eyes narrowed in concentration. His face cleared, and a smile stretched over his mouth. He drew his dusty hand from the hole, revealing a massive red stone clutched between his fingers.

The ruby glinted in the torchlight, despite the coating of

dust atop it, and sent sparks of color dancing around the walls of the cave.

They had found it. Together. The Coeur de Feu.

"Be careful, Eleanor. Nothing will melt an Ice Queen like the heart of a fire." Charles winked at her.

She closed her hand over his and kissed him. "I think you mean the heart of a duke."

* * * * *

HOW TO START A SCANDAL

Author Note

One of the things I enjoy the most about writing historical romance is the research involved. Sometimes that research leads me to a character I get in my head and know with certainty I have to write. Seth's character was one of those.

I had to research the Battle of Waterloo for a previous story. As I dug deeper into the details of the battle, it put into perspective for me how grisly it must have been for those men. The battle took place on June 18, 1815, and in that one day, forty-seven thousand men lost their lives and even more were left wounded. I won't go into detail on this, but it was pretty horrific. In the Regency era, while celebration of the victory was all the rage, the descriptions of what was seen and experienced there were considered vulgar.

I couldn't get out of my head how difficult it would be for a gentleman to go from the horrors of the battlefield to the glittering ballrooms and flirtatious conversations of daily London life. Many men did actually suffer from post-traumatic stress disorder (PTSD), though it wasn't given that name until 1978. During the Regency era, it was simply referred to as "melancholy."

I wanted to write Seth's character to bring to light the existence of those who suffered in silence and pull back the curtain on the difficulties they faced upon their return home, even in the glow of having been the victors.

To my mom, who has always been my biggest
supporter. I love you beyond words and am
grateful for you every single day.

Chapter One

June 1815—London, England

Lady Violet Lavell had been summoned to the Earl of Hollingston's study, which never boded well, and was settled precariously upon the chair her eldest sister had once dubbed the 'squeak seat'.

Her father cut an imposing figure with his large, square-shaped face and eyes that held the potential to bore into one's very soul. There were moments of tenderness, of course, but now was not one of them.

'You have four older sisters who are married with children of their own and a brother who has spent his life preparing to assume the title in addition to having his own family as well.' Lord Hollingston's brown eyes lifted from a piece of paper. Several stacks of paper, that was.

'All my children have gone on about their lives,' her father continued. 'With one exception.'

His stare jabbed into her as though she was one of the

hapless butterflies pinned into frames on his wall. 'You,' he said.

She shifted on the chair before she could stop herself. *Squeak.*

Drat.

'You are three and twenty, Violet,' he continued. 'Nearly "on the shelf" as it's said these days. Yet you certainly spend money as if you are still seeking a husband.' He tapped the stack of papers with his fingertips.

Her bills, no doubt.

'You have no plans for an unexpected windfall, do you?' He lifted his brows.

Actually, she did. But certainly nothing she meant to share with him. Not just yet, at least. Not until she built up the readership of her *Lady Observer* column in the *Society Journal* to the point where it generated a decent income. And by 'decent income', she meant the ability to afford more than a new dress once a year and a few sweets each month.

She sat quiet as a mouse, unmoving on the dreaded squeak seat.

He took her silence as surrender to his sound logic and proceeded. 'Violet, I have indulged your desire to remain unwed long enough. It is high time you were married.'

Violet's heart knocked hard in her chest. 'Please do not make me, Father.'

He pinched the bridge of his nose, then laboriously lowered his hand back to the desk. 'I anticipated that might be your response. If you refuse to wed, I'm afraid I will have to insist that you retire to the country.'

Violet nodded slowly. Retire to the country. It was not ideal, but she would readily take it over marriage.

'As it happens, your sister is seeking a governess and

would appreciate assistance with the children until she finds one.'

Squeak.

Drat.

'Which sister?' Violet asked quickly to cover up the groan of springs.

Please don't let it be Sophie. Please don't let it be Sophie. Please, please, please, be anyone but Sophie.

'Sophie,' her father answered.

At that, Violet's insides withered with dread. Sophie had four children. They were an unruly, spoiled lot, resorting often to screaming fits as well as biting and all manner of awful habits.

Violet shuddered. 'They've been through four governesses already. This year.'

Lord Hollingston's expression was implacable. 'Which is why I suppose she requires another.'

'I would prefer not to, please,' Violet said as prettily as was possible.

Her father remained unmoved. 'Your only option, I'm afraid, is to either wed by the end of the Season, or retire to the country and assist Sophie.'

Violet's mouth fell open. 'Papa, it is most likely only three weeks until the end of the Season. Perhaps a month at most.'

He steepled his fingers. 'So it is.'

'Might I have the summer to think it over?' The chair cried out beneath her, but she didn't care. 'Perhaps next Season—'

'You've had six already.' He spoke drily as his fingertips found their way to tap against the stack of bills. She didn't have to look to know they were from the modiste, the milliner and other various shops she frequented.

She had needed that clothing. In order to glean gossip for the *Lady Observer*, she had to move freely among the *ton*. How was such a thing possible in an old frock?

'There will be no negotiation.' Lord Hollingston got to his feet and indicated the door.

She had been dismissed with the worst of choices laid out before her.

He walked around the desk and followed her out of the study. 'I am not doing this to be cruel.' His tone was gentler. 'You cannot simply exist in life like this, Violet. You need purpose.'

She pressed her lips together. She did have purpose. The *Lady Observer* occupied all her free time. Except no one knew she was the author of the column and she didn't care for them to know. Instead, she simply nodded and made for the stairs. Her feet hesitated as she got to the landing and considered her options.

Going up the stairs would lead her to her chamber. Walking down the hall in the opposite direction, however, would lead to the kitchen where Cook had made the most delicious pastries earlier. Violet knew well enough that Cook made more than would ever possibly be eaten in only one day.

She shouldn't, she knew.

Except that she could practically taste the sweet, tart strawberry jam against her tongue. Her teeth longed to press down into the flaky dough and meet the delicate crunch and pop of the sugar crystals that glittered over the top like frost.

Yes. To the kitchen. She shifted.

'I wouldn't bother.' Lord Hollingston lifted his gaze over the top of a paper he held in front of his face as he walked. 'Your mother anticipated you might be emotional over this and had Cook lock away all the pastries.'

Emotional? All of them?

She tried to swallow her sorrow, but still a squawk emerged. It was bad enough to be given such dismal choices. It was entirely another to be deprived of consolation.

Tears blurred her vision.

'Good evening, Violet.' Her father's gaze swept up the stairs, a silent order to proceed to her chamber.

She nodded, unable to speak, and backed away from him, this time climbing the risers as she was bid.

As her feet trudged upwards in a slow march, she concocted an article in her mind.

Scandal-sheet writer disappears from society rather suddenly. Speculation abounds, but rumour has it she's gone to take on the menial task of unpaid governess to her sister's four children. A scandal, indeed!

Not that anyone would truly even notice if she was gone. What was one less wallflower floating in the background at a ball? The knot in her throat tightened and she almost burst into tears right there.

She couldn't, just *couldn't*, act as governess to Sophie's children. Not when countless others who had far more experience and patience than she had given up the task as hopeless. But marriage…

Well, she couldn't do that either. She pushed through the door to the bedchamber and glanced at the silver-tissue gown on a dressmaker's form propped at the side of her room. To some it might be considered a fashionable form of decor.

For Violet, it was a painful reminder. Of what she had lost, of how she had failed. That she always needed to try harder. A surge of anger overtook her.

A pox on trying harder.

She shoved past the gown to the small box in the drawer behind it, the one filled with toffees. She snatched one up, unfurled the crinkly wax wrapper, popped it into her mouth and practically moaned as the decadence of sugary confection dissolved against her tongue.

She shouldn't be doing it, she knew, but could scarcely help it any more than she could stop breathing. After all, food was a way of remembering for her. Well, for remembering and for forgetting and, at that moment, she wanted to forget it all.

Even if it was fleeting.

A sob choked out around the sweet in her mouth, a pitiful sound to be sure. She put her face into her hands and gave way to the desolation ringing hollow in her chest.

What was she to do?

Seth Sinclair, the Earl of Dalton, entered the town house located on Grosvenor Street for the first time in nearly six years. In his absence, the old brick front had been stuccoed over, the layer of plaster smoothing out all the chinks and seams.

He had left as a second son with little purpose beyond his purchased military commission. He now grudgingly returned, fresh out of a major battle, as an unqualified earl who would rather continue his life as a soldier. Especially when he'd been only months away from being promoted to major, a rank he'd worked damn hard to achieve.

Gibbons was still the same, the old butler not looking a day over ninety as he always had. Pleasure flushed the aged man's cheeks as he offered a warm welcome.

Despite the external alterations to the town house, the

interior was unchanged with a shining marble floor in a checked pattern and a pale green silk brocade on the walls. Paintings from centuries of Sinclair ancestors stared down at him with bland expressions. Disappointed with him, no doubt. Most Sinclairs generally were.

Though everything was as it had always been, Seth did not have the sense of having returned home. But then Dalton Place never truly had felt like a home should. At least not for him.

His feet echoed on the hard floor as he made his way back to the morning room where Gibbons had informed him his mother was taking tea. Seth stopped in front of the grand double doors, loathing the trepidation tightening the back of his neck. He had sent his mother a missive to inform her of his impending arrival. No doubt she was expecting him.

'Seth?' Lady Dalton's voice came from the other side of the door, pitched with what almost sounded like desperation.

He opened the door at last and stepped inside. His mother had already risen from her favourite blue-velvet sofa and stood poised with a foot set forward as if she'd meant to go to the door herself. Though it had been over a year since William's death, she still wore a black gown, indicating her full mourning.

Of course she did.

Had Seth been the son to have died, doubtless she would be outfitted in a pastel sprigged muslin.

'Are you injured?' she whispered.

For that one moment—that wrenching and sadly fleeting moment—she actually appeared to care. He hated the wrench in his chest. After all these years, he should be beyond hope.

'No, I'm not injured,' Seth replied steadily. Many of his

brethren at Waterloo, however, had sustained debilitating injuries of those who had the good fortune to even come away with their lives.

But he couldn't think of Waterloo. Not now. Not when it had been less than a fortnight since the battle and the stink of gunpowder and blood still clung to his nostrils. Not when the images left were lodged like nightmares in his mind.

He clenched his teeth.

His mother straightened and, all at once, her expression smoothed. 'You are home then? For good.'

'I'm selling my commission,' he replied. He had to, lest he be tempted to return. The life of a soldier had suited him far better than one wiled away tediously in drawing rooms and Almack's. 'I am home.'

She nodded and considered him for a long moment. No doubt comparing him against William. Seth would come up short. He always had.

Her forehead crinkled and he almost thought she might express some concern for his well-being during the six years he had been away fighting. First on the Peninsula, and then at Waterloo.

Many of his fellow soldiers had died in that time. Though Waterloo had easily claimed the most lives, wreaked the most carnage.

The beginnings of sweat prickled along his brow. He clenched his hand into a fist.

Stop thinking of it.

'It's been over a year,' his mother said, emotion clogging her voice for the first time in perhaps Seth's entire life. She swallowed. 'It's been over a year since William—' Her words choked off and she dabbed at her eyes with a handkerchief she pulled from her long, black sleeve. 'You didn't attend his funeral.'

'I was escorting Napoleon to Elba when it occurred and was then required to attend the Vienna Congress.' Seth kept his response absent of emotion despite the ire nipping at his nerves. 'I didn't even receive notice of his death until well after the funeral had passed.'

'And yet still you did not return home.' Her words were accusing as her tears fell in earnest.

'I was fighting for England,' he countered.

'You were fighting for glory,' she scoffed and pushed past him, not bothering to close the door behind her as she left.

Seth sighed into the empty space. That had gone exactly as poorly as he had anticipated.

'Seth?' a soft feminine voice spoke up from behind him.

He turned to find his younger sister, Caroline, standing in the open doorway. She was no longer the little girl he'd left behind, but now a woman of nineteen, recently come out. He'd missed her debut, too, though he'd read about it in the papers some months later when they were finally delivered.

'Caroline, I'm sorry I wasn't there for you,' he said.

She raced over the thick Turkish carpet and threw her arms around him. 'You've nothing to apologise for.' She squeezed him fiercely. 'You're home. That is all that matters.'

Home. The word was so easily thrown about. But it wasn't his home. It wasn't his title. He didn't even have his own bloody valet. Everything had all belonged to William. Seth was merely a figure standing in place for a ghost.

He gave a half-hearted smirk. 'You may be the only one pleased with my return.'

Caroline released him and stepped back. She'd grown

into a lovely woman. She had the same dark eyes and hair as him, but where his features were hard lines and sharp angles, everything about her was soft with femininity.

'It's been terribly difficult on Mother.' Caroline glanced behind her and lowered her voice. 'The solicitor who was handling our affairs stole all her jewellery. Mother tried to keep it quiet, but…' Caroline pressed her lips together. 'Word got out. It was quite the scandal to weather.'

Seth winced. 'And I wasn't here.' For the first time, he truly did regret his absence from London.

'You were fighting for our country.' Caroline gave a little shrug. 'And you're here now. That is all that matters. I'm so pleased to have you home, Brother.'

'I intend to fully take on the earldom and see to all our affairs. Neither of you will ever have to worry again,' he vowed. And by God, he meant it. No matter what it took, he would do what was necessary to be every bit as good an earl as William had been.

Or at least he'd be the best he could.

Chapter Two

Though Seth had attended the Duchess of Richmond's ball prior to the battle breaking out, returning to such opulence so soon after having been mired in dirt and gore practically left him reeling.

The ballroom glittered with an undeniable splendour. Beeswax candles emitted a golden glow, made brighter by the backing of opulent mirrors. Hothouse flowers were arranged into perfect displays giving splashes of colour throughout and sweet music floated effortlessly beneath the hum of conversation.

It was all such a beautiful waste. Soldiers had gone without pay, sacrificing their lives while the *ton* nibbled on food they didn't intend to eat and threw money about with reckless abandon. Profligates, the lot of them.

More than the unnecessary extravagance of it all, what struck Seth again and again was how clean everything was. It was the same at his home with the polished wood furniture and the dust-free notions and floors.

His life as a soldier had been one of fighting and death. Sometimes this had brought injury, other times hunger. There had been wet chills from rainstorms, oppressive humidity that hummed with insects and thick, sucking mud.

Never had there been luxury.

Not like this.

Though he looked very much as though he belonged in his surroundings with his black tailcoat and silk breeches, he felt worlds apart. He glanced down at his hands encased in white gloves. His cuticles and fingernails were still stained with the grime of war despite his inherited valet's valiant attempts. The hours that Bennet had worked to make Seth look presentable had made him feel like the town house—chipped, broken brick smoothed over with an attractive facade. It didn't mean the cracks weren't there any more, only that they were covered up.

'Dalton.' A hand clapped him on his shoulder and sent him spinning around.

The Marquess of Kentworth grinned at him. 'I dare say it's been ages since I've seen you about. Still looking quite the soldier, I see.' He indicated Seth's red waistcoat.

The colour had been intentional. Seth could no longer wear his uniform. He'd given up that honour when he decided to sell his commission. But by God, he could still wear the colours of a proud soldier.

'Rawley, look who is among us once more.' Kentworth tapped the arm of the man beside him.

Viscount Rawley turned and gave a rare and broad smile. 'Lord Dalton. Good to see you've returned home safe.'

Seth inclined his head in thanks.

'Now I'll finally have someone to drink with me.' Kentworth winked at Seth. 'After the necessaries of the ball have concluded, what do you say we go and find ourselves some gin and a bit of muslin?'

While the offer would have been appealing years ago, Seth now shook his head. 'I'm afraid I cannot. I have a meeting with my new solicitor early tomorrow morning.'

Kentworth's blue eyes widened. 'I heard about the perfidious cretin who pilfered from your accounts while you were off fighting for England.' He scoffed. 'A shabby show of loyalty for one's King and country, I say. Truly despicable.'

'Did they find him yet?' Rawley asked.

'Find him?' Seth narrowed his eyes. 'He is still at large?'

Rawley smoothed a hand over his brown hair as though worrying it had somehow been mussed out of place. The action was one he carried with him from his youth and had apparently not yet dropped. 'It was my understanding that he absconded with nearly all of Lady Dalton's jewellery and was never heard from again.' He offered an apologetic shrug. 'I could be wrong.'

'No,' Kenworth confirmed. 'You're not. The wretch buggered off to who knows where.' He waved at someone across the room.

Seth's mind spun at the news. Not only had no one been there to protect his mother and Caroline from theft in his absence, no one had even seen to the arrest of the man who had done it. The notion was unfathomable.

But then, Seth had put the whole business of his family from his mind, hadn't he? He hadn't taken the time to reach out to friends and ask them to look after his mother and sister. He hadn't ensured someone was nearby to offer support should it be required.

No, he'd tucked away the news of William's death as though it was a missive he could read later. Except while

Seth let the responsibilities of the earldom slip from his care, his family had suffered the consequences.

His stomach clenched. Such a failure was unforgivable. He would not make so grave a mistake again. Not ever.

He'd start making up for his transgressions immediately. Starting by finding the bastard who'd had the temerity to steal from the Sinclairs.

'Do excuse me.' Kentworth slapped a hand on Seth's arm. 'Meet me at White's later for a nightcap, then a trip to Kings Place. You won't regret it.' The Marquess lifted his eyebrows with the bawdy suggestion of visiting the area that housed his favourite brothel.

The ballroom had become thick with people. Someone bumped into Seth and murmured an apology.

Seth's head spun with sudden lightness. The crowd was too thick, too close, the lights too bright.

Seth shook his head. 'I have already told you that I cannot accompany you tonight.'

'Please,' Rawley hissed in a whisper.

Kentworth laughed at his friend. 'What does it matter to you, Rawley? You'll have a finger of Scotch, glance at your watch and be gone before my grandmother is in bed.'

Rawley gave a long-suffering sigh. 'It doesn't mean you won't harass me to join you.'

'Harass?' Kentworth scoffed. 'One day you might actually allow yourself to have some fun.'

With that, the two were off to chat with another university chum whose name Seth couldn't recall. The press of people was even closer now, stealing his air, making it overwarm.

The battle had been the same way. Worse. The blasts of gunpowder, the cannons detonating, raw firepower igniting the fields of Mont-Saint-Jean into a damned inferno.

He fisted his hand at his side and focused on the pressure. *Don't think of the battle. Not here. Not now.*

He needed a distraction. *Any* distraction. He scanned the room, desperate for someone he might know that wasn't Kentworth.

A woman with dark brown hair in a blue dress caught Seth's attention. She was nestled among the spinsters and old women, tucked towards the back of the room, too beautiful, too vibrant to fade into the background as she was so obviously attempting to do.

The woman was one he would recognise anywhere— his neighbour's daughter and childhood friend, Lady Violet Lavell.

Death at a ball!
A beleaguered soon-to-be spinster has passed on from sheer boredom at the most gossip-free ball there ever was.

Despite her early demise, it was widely considered that her fate was a gracious deliverance from the burdensome obligation of becoming an unpaid governess.

Violet tapped her slipper in time to music she would not dance to and kept a pleasant expression on her face even as she penned the sardonic header to the *Lady Observer* in her mind. To anyone who might notice her, she simply appeared to be enjoying the orchestra playing for the dancers. But it was not instrumentals to which she tuned her ear.

It was gossip.

Salacious, enticing gossip. Whispered words dominated any ballroom and tonight's gathering was no exception. Unfortunately what was said was all redundant, information easily gleaned through the papers that prior week. She nearly issued forth a painstaking sigh.

Even watching those around her had proven to be lacklustre entertainment. No gentlemen danced with women they were not supposed to, no one appeared to have imbibed too much wine to the point of behaving foolishly. But then, supper had yet to be served.

She'd heard there would be beefsteaks with sautéed onions and a rich oyster sauce. How she loved a good beefsteak. It always made her recall the time she'd attended Lady Norrick's supper party and had the grand idea to begin the *Lady Observer*.

In any event, any food would be preferable to crayfish in jelly, which was also rumoured to be served that evening. The poor creatures were heartily unappetising in such a plating where they hovered, boiled red and suspended in jelly, with their beady black eyes gazing out at those who would eat them. She shivered and hoped she did not sit near that plate.

For the time being, she surveyed the ballroom for a possible sighting of the Earl of Dalton. Gossip had indicated he would be in attendance.

Violet had not yet caught sight of his face in the crowd and found herself grateful for that small mercy. No, that was a lie. She was both grateful and disappointed. He was a charming man, enticing in every way she should find displeasing, but did not. No, she certainly did not.

Something in her chest gave a little twist, one she chose pointedly to ignore.

'Lady Sarah has been rather popular with the gentlemen,' a woman in a feathered turban whispered to the woman beside her.

Violet's ears perked up at the conversation—a refreshing deviation to the direction of her unwanted thoughts.

'I hear she is the newest pupil under that woman's tutelage.'

Violet feigned interest at something across the room and stepped closer towards the ladies.

'How a courtesan ever put herself in a place of edifying the young, impressionable ladies of the *ton* is beyond my realm of comprehension,' the woman with the turban replied in a haughty tone. 'It's disgraceful.'

Unfortunately, two ladies strode in front of Violet, engaged in a very enthusiastic, very loud, conversation on the latest trend of spencers. With a ripple of irritation, Violet abandoned her attempt to overhear the conversation about the newest student in Lottie's care.

For though they had not mentioned the courtesan by name, Violet knew her well. Or at least, knew of her. After all, it had been her own cousin Lady Eleanor—now the Duchess of Somersville—who had first gone to Lottie for assistance in wresting herself free of the dreaded moniker of Ice Queen.

After the scandal of her instruction was made known, Lottie's clandestine lessons became quite popular and very sought after, ironically by the very people who had bemoaned their affectations of its vulgarity.

For all the repugnance pervading the topic of 'Lottie's Ladies' as they were called, rumours continued to spread of noble daughters seeking her instruction. What was more, it was not unheard of for ladies to spread their own false tales of attending such tutelage when they had not, in the hopes of drawing the attention of male suitors.

Because the male suitors *were* interested in Lottie's

Ladies. Very, very interested. To such an extent that any woman who was even said to be attending those unmentionable lessons was almost always married within a month's time.

The curiosity of what possibly could transpire in those meetings with the famed courtesan briefly flitted through Violet's mind when an idea slammed into her.

What if she went to see Lottie herself? Not to try to obtain a husband, but to glean information for an article. No, an exposé.

The *Lady Observer* was a column read by some of the *ton*, but not all. However, if Violet penned a story revealing what truly went on in Lottie's parlour, the *Lady Observer* held the potential of becoming a tremendous success. It would propel the *Society Journal's* subscriptions and they would pay her significantly more. She would make the *Society Journal* esteemed enough for every household to purchase one.

Which would give her the income and purpose that would hopefully impress her father to the point she would no longer be required to choose between such unsavoury options.

Violet was so overcome with delight at her idea, she did something she never allowed herself to do on an ordinary night at a ball. She went to the refreshment table to permit herself a small cake. Well, not so small.

In truth, she selected the largest one on the platter. One with a beautiful marzipan rose adorning its sugary frosted top. Before she could talk herself out of the indulgence, she plucked it from the tray and popped it into her mouth.

'Lady Violet.'

The voice made her go still. It was unfamiliar and it was masculine.

She pressed her lips together to contain the cake and covered her mouth as she hurriedly chewed.

Of all times for someone to approach her. A man, no less. Heavens.

'Forgive me,' the man said. 'I didn't mean to interrupt.'

She shook her head and waved her hand as if it was no bother. It was, though. Very much. She never allowed herself those small dainty treats from the refreshment table. Indeed, she'd hear about it from her mother on the way home.

She hastily swallowed what she'd intended to savour, turned towards the gentleman who had so rudely curtailed her enjoyment and froze. Even the cake lodged itself uncomfortably midway down her suddenly dry throat.

Mr Sinclair.

No, that wasn't right. He was no longer Mr Sinclair. He was an earl.

Lord Dalton.

She put her fingers to her mouth to cover an unseemly gulp and hastily brushed at her lips in case any crumbs or frosting remained. He watched her with a half-smile, as handsome as ever.

Perhaps even more so.

His dark hair had a habit of being unruly, but rather than giving him an unkempt appearance, it lent him a boyish, rugged charm. His time at war had chiselled his face and his body, carving with time and experience what had once been soft with youth. And it only made him all the more alluring.

More than the appeal of his appearance, however, his eyes were always what had left Violet totally and utterly captivated. With irises so dark one could not make out the pupil, his was a gaze that held all the emotion his features repressed. Right now, that stare was bright with interest and genuine delight.

At her?

Truly, it was unfair how intensely attractive he had always been. His were the good looks that made one recall every deficient attribute in themselves by comparison.

Soon-to-be spinster, nearly on the shelf, dies from the sheer handsomeness of newly minted Earl upon his return from war.

'Lord Dalton,' she said at last. 'Forgive me.'

'I intruded upon you,' he replied.

At least they could agree on that.

'What are you doing among the spinsters and old women?' he demanded.

Violet's eyes widened. 'They might hear you.'

'They know what they are,' he said, but did so with at least a lowered voice. 'Why is your husband not sweeping you across the dance floor?'

She wanted to close her eyes and truly fade back into the wall until she turned entirely invisible. But such a thing was impossible. Instead, she squared her shoulders and met his gaze despite the heat burning her face. 'I am unwed.'

He lifted a brow. 'You can't be serious.'

This is where she ought to say something witty and poignant. Except that she had dulled the point of her humour over the years, grinding it away in an attempt to slip unseen into the background where she would not be noticed. No doubt she'd come up with a charming reply somewhere between three and four in the morning when it wouldn't serve her a whit of good.

Instead of an intelligent reply, she offered a helpless shrug and inwardly rolled her eyes at the action. Could she be any more of a dullard?

'It's been six years since you came out,' he said. 'That would put you nearly on the shelf.' His gaze reflected something she didn't care for. Was it disgust? Pity?

In that moment, she was able to remember more than just how his handsome looks stole her attention and how his flirtation made her pulse stutter. Times when they were children and he had crushed her spirits with words that sliced deep. Like referring to her as hearty or commenting that she wasn't skinny like other girls.

The angry hurt swirled around the small cake in her empty stomach and snapped some steel into her spine.

'Perhaps it's because I'm so *hearty*,' she shot at him. She wished she had been completely calm when she said it, that her heart wasn't hammering with frantic, erratic beats when she ripped those painful words from her memory, but she'd be lying.

His eyes narrowed at her. 'I feel as though you're being cryptic.'

'I assure you, I'm being quite blunt,' she replied. 'You said that to me when we were children.'

He lifted a brow. 'You remember that?'

She met his eyes. 'I recall many things you said to me when we were children. And even when we were older.'

A muscle ticked in his cheek, and he shifted his weight from one foot to the other in a show of apparent discomfort. 'I believe,' he said slowly, 'that I was rather an idiot in my youth.'

'And you're a better man now?' The disappointment of that night slammed into her anew, tearing open the old wound she'd thought long since scarred over. He'd held her heart by a string then, dangling it, toying with it. And she'd so readily handed him the end of that string, so eager for love, so desperate to be seen as more than a minor flirtation. Perhaps that was why she'd been so easily swept off her feet later.

'I certainly hope to be a better man.' Lord Dalton's gaze softened and he regarded her with such earnestness, such heartfelt emotion, that her defences relaxed.

'You're home now, then?' she asked. 'From the war?'

Though she hadn't meant the question to be a barb, the skin around his eyes tightened briefly, almost a flinch.

'I am,' he replied. 'I do hope I'll be seeing more of you now that I'm returned?'

The inflection at the end of his statement turned the words into a question. An invitation. She would do well to break out a whetstone and sharpen her wit back to rapier precision. For even with her shield up, it was always best to be armed when it came to a man like Lord Dalton.

Chapter Three

Seth had nearly forgotten how beautiful Lady Violet was. She fixed him with her ice-blue gaze. Her eyes had always been lovely, pale blue like a winter sky, ringed in a darker, deeper blue set beneath her black, expressive brows. The effect was stunning, especially with her long, dark lashes.

Though he shouldn't, he let his hope that she might be interested in seeing him more often hang for a moment between them. Surely he didn't deserve the attention of a woman like Lady Violet Lavell. Not when she was so beautifully pure within and he was so horribly damaged.

She tilted her head and offered him a contemplative look as if studying him in a manner he rather liked. Earlier that day, he'd been irritated at Bennet for the hours of attention he'd given Seth upon his return from Waterloo. Now, however, Seth was grateful for his valet's efforts.

'Perhaps,' she replied at last.

'A bit coy for a wallflower, aren't you?'

She flushed prettily. 'Perhaps I'm full of surprises.'

It had doubtless been meant as innocent banter, seasoned with a dash of flirtation, but, good God, how it set his mind wondering. Every thought that flitted through his mind was entirely too wicked for the likes of a ballroom. 'Indeed,' he simply replied.

He considered her for a moment, really taking her in for the first time since seeing her. The blue silk of her gown was overlaid with a bit of gauzy thing that had ribbons sewn all over it. But that wasn't truly what caught his interest— it was the hint of her body beneath, her voluptuous curves.

She'd always enticed him with that body, the one society forced her to try to hide beneath the high-waisted hideous gowns in fashion. Now, though, the lower-cut bodice of her ballgown cradled her generous breasts, full and sensual where the gentle, creamy swells teased him.

It took nearly every ounce of his control to keep from letting his gaze fall to her bosom.

'How the devil are you not married?' he asked aloud the question that he probably ought to have kept silent.

'Not every woman wants to get married.' She lifted her chin in a prideful manner, in a way that suggested she defended her position often. She always had been one to play up her false bravado. But then, didn't they all?

That was one of the things he'd always liked about her, how very real she was. It made her instantly likeable and wonderfully relatable.

'Of course every woman wants to get married or men's lives wouldn't be as difficult, attempting to thwart matches and debutantes.'

He shouldn't be having this light-hearted conversation with her any more than he should allow himself to be swept away by her. Not when he had his family to care for and his demons to tame.

She gave a little laugh at that and he couldn't stop the surge of victory swelling through him at the warm sound. She had a beautiful smile, her lips full and pink, her teeth white and straight. He'd fantasised about kissing her when they were acquainted as youths those years before the wars.

That was a lie, actually.

He'd fantasised about doing far more with her than just kissing.

The orchestra tinkled to life in preparation for a set.

'Would you care to dance?' he asked.

Her smile faltered. 'Forgive me,' she said in an apologetic tone, 'but I don't dance.'

He should take her rejection and walk away. But he remembered the young woman she'd been and how her eyes had always lit up when she danced.

'Nonsense. Yes, you do.' He waved aside her protest and offered her his hand. 'I've danced with you several times in my life. You performed adequately with your feet moving in the appropriate steps and in perfect time with the music.'

Her brow lifted in a bemused expression. 'How flattering.'

'You were quite graceful as well,' he offered. 'As I recall.'

Though he gave the praise flippantly, he felt the words in his bones. Or at least some part of him that was below his waist. He'd very much enjoyed dancing with her in those earlier years. Her eyes had a way of sparkling at him every time they came together and some of the more vigorous steps in the dance had made her breasts give an enticing bounce.

'I'm sorry, I...' She shook her head even as her gaze found the dance floor, her expression longing.

False bravado indeed. Why wouldn't she give in to her desire to dance?

He was certain it had something to do with how she'd nestled herself among the wallflowers. A brilliant violet standing out boldly in the garden no one paid mind to.

'Perhaps the next set, then?' he offered in an attempt to give her time to yield to her own desires.

A drum was struck in the orchestra, a deep resonating tone that thwacked him dead in the chest.

All at once, he was marching towards the enemy at Waterloo, heart hammering in time with the pulse of that bloody drum, energy and anticipation crackling all around him.

Sweat prickled at his brow.

This. This was what he had dreaded the most in striking up a conversation with Lady Violet. He curled his hand into a fist and squeezed in an attempt to gain control of his thoughts.

When the devil had they started incorporating drums into the orchestra at a ball? Or was it for this victory celebration commemorating the defeat at Waterloo?

It didn't matter. All that concerned him was how his mind had flickered back to things best left forgotten and how his skin suddenly prickled with sweat.

Lady Violet's mouth moved, but he didn't possess the wherewithal to understand a single word emerging from her lips.

The drum sounded again and echoed in his brain.

The first shot. The shouts that followed. The cannons. God, the cannons.

He gritted his teeth.

The drum pulsed again. Its rhythm echoed in his temples and drowned everything out except memories he could not push away. Being shoved by Brent and how it had sent Seth sprawling. The cannonball that would have ended Seth's life if Brent hadn't so bravely saved him.

That cannonball.

Bile rose in Seth's throat. His cravat was too damnably tight. He wanted to dig his fingers into the bound silk and rip it from his neck.

Except he was in a ballroom where etiquette prevailed. Where men were men and not cowards whose minds were plagued with the horrors of war.

Lady Violet regarded him, as though expecting him to speak.

He shook his head. 'Forgive me,' he said. 'I can't...' He backed up and bumped into someone.

It was all he could do to mutter an apology, to keep from letting the breath escape his chest in heaving gasps. He was a man, damn it. A soldier. He was no coward to fall prey to these memories that haunted him during the day. Especially not at a simple ball.

He managed to keep his gait slow as he made his escape to the door leading out to the veranda. The cool night air was a balm against his blazing skin and the darkness eased his aching head.

The reprieve did not last long.

What kind of a man was he to buckle under thoughts? They were only memories, after all. He'd spent years in battle. Years.

But none had been like Waterloo.

A shiver raked over his skin.

Waterloo had been bloody. He'd lost more men in that

one battle than in the whole of his career. Men exposed to fighting for too long did not always fare well in the long of it. He'd seen them himself. Soldiers with hollowed eyes and gaunt expressions, their minds shattered by memories.

Was he becoming such a man?

He leaned against the stone railing overlooking the garden and dropped his head forward. Perhaps it was a good thing he had been forced to sell his commission. As much as he'd dreaded facing the unfamiliar obligations of an earl, they might be the very things needed to save his sanity.

He lifted his head and glanced behind him, through the glass-paned doors and into the ballroom. Violet was in there somewhere, abandoned by him in the middle of their conversation.

He pulled in a deep breath and forced himself to make his way inside once more. To face the social responsibilities of an earl and to face his error with Violet.

Except she could not be found, not even among the wallflowers.

Violet made her way up Fleet Street with her maid, Susan, and a sack of coins secured in the confines of her reticule. Her collections from the print shop were larger than anticipated. Of all times to receive such a boon, she was most glad for it now—when she had true need of funds.

She had secured an audience with Lottie for that evening, well past the time her parents would have retired, an hour that seemed to come earlier as they grew older. It would be easy to sneak past the servants, secure a hackney, and make her way to Lottie's residence at Russell Square in Bloomsbury. Surely the money Violet had collected, as well as what she'd been setting aside, would be sufficient to afford her a proper number of lessons.

A giddy flicker of excitement rippled in her chest at the idea of putting her plan into motion. She, Violet Lavell, muted wallflower, plump spinster, would be attending the highly coveted lessons with Lottie.

Two gentlemen were approaching them in the opposite direction and she nodded politely as she and her maid passed.

Yes, she could have had the carriage bring her directly to Fleet Street rather than pretend to have turned down the road while out shopping. Except the carriage driver was not as discreet as Susan.

Part of Violet—a tiny, minuscule part of her—wondered what Lottie's edification might do regarding her interactions with the men of the *ton*. Or, at least one in particular.

Lord Dalton.

No sooner had the thought entered her mind than she tried quickly to push it away. He had been rude the evening before, abandoning her after having invited her to dance. Granted, he had not looked well.

Regardless, he was a man who did not keep his promises. Not six years ago. And not last night when she changed her mind and was finally giving in to the temptation to accept a dance for the first time in nearly six years.

Then he'd walked away.

Just like the night of her debut.

But she wouldn't think of him and his dark, soulful eyes or how the way he looked at her made her knees go soft. She wouldn't think about how he'd returned from the war with a hardness to his masculinity she shouldn't find appealing. Which she did. Oh, she did.

She was so busy not thinking of him that she actually heard his voice in her thoughts. 'Lady Violet.'

Violet could have rolled her eyes heavenwards if she weren't on the streets of London. Would she never be free of Lord Dalton's grip on her?

'Lady Violet, may I walk with you?'

That voice was apparently not in her head. Her cheeks went hot as she glanced over her shoulder to find Lord Dalton walking towards her at a brisk pace.

Susan caught her eye and suppressed a smile. The maid had been with Violet long enough to understand the impact of Lord Dalton on her mistress.

'What are you doing on Fleet Street?' He caught up to her and offered her his arm. He wore a black jacket with a brown waistcoat and buckskins. The latter fit him perfectly against his snug thighs and muscular calves, as if the entire fad of wearing the more casual clothing had been designed entirely for him.

Heavens, if every man wore buckskins like he did, even Almack's might be willing to soften their dress code.

Violet pulled her musings, and her stare, from his well-made legs and held up a folded copy of the most recent instalment of the *Society Journal*, which had been turned to the *Lady Observer* column. 'You've caught me.' It was the excuse she always had prepared in case she did get caught on Fleet Street, an occurrence that had not happened until that very moment. 'I was at Fleet Market and figured I might wander down this road to obtain a paper.'

He peered at it as though she held up a dead rat. 'A scandal sheet, Lady Violet?'

She let the flirtation in his tone burn her cheeks in an effort to allow herself to look slightly remorseful at the guilty pleasure. 'Well, it is rather a nice day to be out walking.'

And that was her folly. For even as the words were emerging from her mouth, she glanced up at the grey sky as flecks of rain spattered at her face. 'Or rather, it was nice earlier.'

'It was storming earlier,' he offered with a smirk.

'I meant, after that.' Her reticule was terribly heavy and cutting into her wrist. She fiddled with the strap while considering a way to spin the conversation on him. 'It's quite fortunate to run into you in any event. I'd intended to thank you.'

He looked at her, wary, clearly smelling the trap she'd laid at his feet. 'Thank me?'

She hummed in soft agreement. 'For the dance last night.' It was snide of her, yes, but she wasn't feeling especially generous. The wonderful thing about being beyond caring about marriage was not having to always tiptoe so delicately around her words.

'Ah, yes.' His brow furrowed slightly. 'Forgive me for my abrupt departure. I'm afraid I suddenly felt rather unwell.'

His gaze was so earnest with remorse that she was left feeling very much like the idiot in the conversation this time. Whatever witty retort Violet might have had at the ready died on her tongue. He would never have looked thusly, so sincere in his youth when he'd been wild and unrepentant.

Maybe he had changed.

'You did appear unwell,' she offered by way of apology. 'I trust you are quite recovered.'

'I am in better spirits.' He gave her a genuine smile that nearly knocked the low-heeled slippers from her feet with its charm. 'Especially now.'

Heavens, but he could turn on his allure when he wished to.

'I believe this is your carriage, is it not?' He stopped.

Regret pinched at her. Though the sprinkling of rain had increased as they strolled and the humidity in the air promised a proper and thorough storm, she could have spent the rest of the afternoon at his side. 'It is,' she conceded. 'Thank you.'

He didn't wait for the footman to scramble down from his perch. Instead, Lord Dalton put his gloved hand to the handle of the door and opened it for her, first assisting Violet into the small cabin and then Susan. This set both ladies flushing with pleasure as he bid them good day and snapped closed the door once more.

'Well,' Susan said with an exuberant exhale. 'He seems to have changed.'

'Indeed he has.' Violet peered out the window at his departing figure.

'And he appears to be rather taken with you.' Susan lifted her thin brows at Violet as her hazel eyes twinkled with delight.

Violet scoffed. 'A war hero returning home to an earldom and a ballroom filled with available debutantes would hardly pull a spinster from her shelf and dust her off for the wedding of the ages.' She sighed. 'I don't see that tale headlining any articles of the *Lady Observer*.'

Susan appeared nonplussed. 'It's not impossible. I'm sure your cousin the Duchess's situation seemed just as hopeless. More so, perhaps.'

Violet adjusted her skirts rather than watch Lord Dalton sweep past the window. 'It's of little concern regardless,' she said. 'I have no intention to wed.'

Susan did sigh at this, a soft resigned sound. 'Pity, that. You'd be a fetching pair if I do say so myself.' Silence fell over the carriage before her voice continued. 'If it wasn't for Lord Fords—'

'Don't,' Violet choked out. 'Don't say his name.'

Susan immediately pressed her lips together to still her words. It didn't matter. Violet needed only hear his title and her folly the night of her come out rushed back at her.

Lord Fordson. He'd happened upon her when she was freshly wounded from Seth's dismissal and her mother's disappointment. He'd filled that first dance of her debut that Seth had left open, as well as another towards the end of the ball.

Afterward, they'd gone out on the veranda for a bit of fresh air and received far more than a little rosiness in their cheeks from the outing. Violet had been wholly taken by him, by the way he'd gazed as her as though she was the only woman in the room. He had made her feel worthy of love. He'd made her feel beautiful.

All the way up until the next day when he did not call. He hadn't as much as sent flowers. When next they saw one another, he avoided her. It had taken a moment for her to realise he was intentionally edging away from her, but once the understanding dawned on her, it came with a fresh wave of hurt. And the truth of exactly what a fool she had been.

It still cut now, even six years later.

Now, Violet looked up too quickly in the carriage and caught Lord Dalton's gaze on her as they rolled away. Her heart, silly and stupid as it was, gave a little leap.

And though she could not bring herself to even hear his name any longer, Violet found herself agreeing with Susan. It was indeed a pity Violet was not going to wed, but it was certainly nothing that would change.

No matter how tempting the man.

Chapter Four

After Seth delivered Lady Violet to her carriage, he made his way back to his own where it sat idly on the street waiting for him to return. He'd insisted on stopping so he might attend to Lady Violet whom he'd seen walking with her maid in what promised to be a violent summer storm.

He'd meant to smooth over what he'd rumpled the night before. Judging from the faint colour touching her cheeks when he saw her into the carriage, he'd succeeded.

His intention in speaking to her had been to apologise and now he had done exactly that. There would be no further need to speak to Lady Violet in the days that followed. He would leave her to her life of feminine pursuits—watercolour paintings and shopping and the like. And he would continue salvaging what bits of his life he could scrape into a semblance of wholeness once more.

'To White's,' he told the footman.

The man, Burton, was a slender soldier who'd fought alongside Seth in the Peninsula. He'd previously worked as a builder prior to becoming a soldier. Unfortunately, the bullets to his leg had shattered his bones and left him with a terrible limp, one that rendered him unemployable. At least, to all but Seth.

He'd hired Burton as well as Harold, a burly soldier who had lost an arm and could no longer work with horses as he'd done before his time as a soldier. One arm or two, there was no one in all of London who cared more for the chestnuts than Harold. The man tended to the beasts as if they were his children. What's more, Harold was a genius with maps. If it weren't for his inability to gently stop a carriage, he might be the most perfect driver there ever was.

While Seth had no desire to be an earl, he would at least concede that it allowed him the opportunity to offer employment to those society would otherwise cast aside.

'While I'm at White's,' Seth continued, 'I'd like you to pick up a paper called the *Society Journal*.' He regretted the request as soon as he'd made it. Whatever Lady Violet found interesting within those printed pages ought to be of no concern to him. He set a foot upon the small stair leading into the carriage and hesitated. 'For Lady Caroline, of course,' he added.

Burton's lips quirked in a ghost of a smile. 'Of course, my lord.'

The ride to White's was short. Regardless, rain began pattering at the windows, fat droplets that melted against one another and ran down the expanse of the glass pane. Had Lady Violet decided to pursue a lengthier walk, she would have got soaked.

What a shame that would have been.

An image of her dripping wet immediately sprang into

his mind. Her hair falling around her shoulders, tousled and damp, her gown clinging to those luscious curves, the fine, thin fabric made practically transparent by the thorough dousing. Rain would sparkle on her creamy skin like diamonds and those blue, blue eyes of hers would practically glow in contrast to the grey sky above.

Oh, yes, what a shame indeed.

His body responded to his imagination, growing warm and, well, rather hard. The carriage stopped abruptly, knocking him from his thoughts and giving him a solid thump on the back of his head. Served him right for thinking of Lady Violet again. Even the fates were telling him to leave her be. She was not for him. Or, as was more likely, he was not for her.

He rubbed at the sore spot as Burton pulled open the door with an apologetic smile.

'He's getting better at the stops.' The footman winced as he noted Seth rubbing at the back of his head. 'I think...'

Seth lowered his hand. 'I did stay in my seat this time.'

Burton grinned. 'You see, m'lord?'

Seth didn't bother to nod as he removed himself from the carriage and made his way into the opulence of the most exclusive gentleman's club in all of London. In the past, Seth would never have dreamed of belonging to such an elegant establishment. Now though, as the Earl of Dalton, there were plenty who sought to sponsor his membership.

Money, of course, had a role to play in all of it. Money *always* played a role. And Seth had a considerable amount. A ridiculous amount, really. Enough to summon notice.

All in all, it was still a gentlemen's club and one he hoped could provide a strong lead as to what had become of the solicitor who had stolen from Seth's mother.

He had a name, at least. Mr Charles Pattinson, Esquire, as well as the description of an older chap with thick dark hair and fine white teeth. No doubt he had exerted his charms on Lady Dalton which had led to the embarrassment of her having been duped. Why else would she have allowed him to get away without repercussion?

Viscount Rawley stood by a window on the second floor of White's with a cup of tea in his hands as he gazed out into the street in quiet contemplation. A quick glance confirmed his counterpart, Lord Kentworth, was decidedly absent. What good fortune.

'Good afternoon, Rawley.' Seth approached the studious man.

The Viscount turned with a friendly expression and the two exchanged the usual pleasantries, health and the weather and all that, performed with careful haste on Seth's part before Kentworth could invade on the conversation.

When the usual polite chatter fell away, Seth broached the topic he'd most wanted to discuss. The missing solicitor.

Seth scanned about once more to confirm Kentworth was not nearby. 'I was wondering if you might be able to assist me with providing a contact to locate the solicitor who took advantage of my family in my absence.'

Rawley's forefinger tapped at his teacup in consideration and slowly nodded. 'I have a man for such a thing.' He, too, looked over his shoulder, as though concerned Kentworth might interrupt. 'He's a former Runner who now operates on his own. He's devilishly smart and hasn't failed me yet on any matter I've brought to him. What's more, he's discreet.'

Seth nodded. 'Perfect.'

'I'll have him reach out to you.' Rawley went silent as a pair of men strode past them and did not speak again until they were out of earshot. 'You're forewarned, he can be rather rough around the edges.'

Seth was undeterred. 'After so long being a soldier, that is certainly the least of my concerns.'

'What have we here?' Kentworth's voice filled the conspiratorial space between them.

Years ago, Seth had enjoyed the good times shared with the Marquess, but now the man's boisterous presence rankled at Seth's nerves.

'You missed quite the time of it last night.' Kentworth lifted his glass in silent salute. 'The ladies love a man with war scars to show for his efforts.'

Seth offered a stiff nod in an attempt to be polite despite the lack of consideration on the other man's part.

'You should come with me tonight, I'll be—'

'I'm afraid that's impossible.' Seth braced his feet wide on the soft carpet. A soldier's stance. 'I have matters to see to the following day.'

'Matters that no doubt require a clear mind and good rest.' Kentworth rolled his eyes and nudged Rawley with his elbow. 'He's sounding like you.'

Rawley merely lifted a brow.

'Seeing to one's estates and family is a noble occupation,' Seth responded.

'Stewards.' Kentworth took a swallow of brandy. 'They handle the lot of it. Well, them and solicitors.' He paused, tilted his head and cast an exaggerated grimace in Seth's direction. 'Well, most of them, that is.'

Sweat sheened Seth's palms. A sleepless night filled with horrible memories was exacting its toll.

'Kentworth,' Rawley said in a low tone.

'Don't, Rawley.' Kentworth pushed at his friend's shoulder to put him off. 'What happened to you?' He frowned at Seth. 'Rawley's always been a puddle of mud. But you... You used to be able to drink more than me, you'd take two ladies when I took only one, you didn't care a whit for anything. And now look at you. Your *joie de vivre* has died.'

Rage whipped hot and reckless through Seth in a wave that immediately overwhelmed him.

'No, my men died,' he bit out. 'In front of me.' Images flashed in his mind, broken and violent.

Red and white flickered at the edge of Seth's vision.

Blood. Chaos. The acrid odour of gunpowder. The screams...

'Sounds as though you need a tup more than the rest of us.' Kentworth chortled and lifted his glass.

Seth flew at him, pinning him against the wall, forearm to neck. 'A tup won't remove what I've seen and it won't bring those men back.' He pushed himself harder against Kentworth. The glass fell from his hand and landed on the soft carpet with a *thunk*.

'They were good men,' Seth growled into Kentworth's face. 'They were hard-working. Brave.'

'Lord Dalton.' Rawley spoke quietly as he put a hand lightly on Seth's shoulder.

The Viscount stepped back to reveal the sea of faces turned towards them, aghast with horror. Seth uttered a curse and released Kentworth, who rubbed at his cravat.

'I'll handle this,' Rawley said quietly. 'I think it's best you take your leave.'

Seth nodded and backed away. He put up a hand as he did so, in silent apology, in acknowledgment for what he'd done. He hadn't been back for a week and already he was on the cusp of most likely being blackballed from White's.

The quiet room erupted into a buzz of voices as he departed. The incident had rattled him. His own reaction had rattled him. It was more than the sleeplessness that had led to him exploding as he did, it was the awfulness in his head, the way he could never clear the smell of blood and smoke from his awareness. It was the paralysing fear that the horrors he'd witnessed had left his mind broken.

Despite what he'd been through, despite the years he'd aged and the man he strove to be, he was still an idiot and he was still making mistakes. He was an earl now, however, and his errors no longer only affected him. It was his family who would suffer.

At least the visit to White's had revealed what he needed: someone to aid him in finding the runaway solicitor. Seth would make certain he did not err in bringing the bastard to justice and making right the wrongs he had caused his family by leaving.

The sky had opened up into a veritable deluge by the time Violet arrived at her town house on Grosvenor Street. She declined the proffered umbrella, put the *Society Journal* over her head and dashed through the rain to her home, nearly tripping over the cat in the process.

The cat?

She spun around and squared off against the offended animal, both gazing with incredulity at the other. Her with dripping hair and a sodden newspaper and it with… Was that a bonnet?

She blinked.

It blinked.

'What—?'

The thing hissed abruptly and tore off, causing Susan to let loose a startled shriek.

'Good thing you were wearing a bonnet,' Violet called after the large cat. 'Or I might have dripped water all over you.'

Small footsteps tapped over the marble entryway. Violet turned towards the sound and was met with the sight of a little girl with blonde hair, large blue eyes and a slightly upturned nose. Violet blinked again.

'May I help you?' she asked. 'Are you lost, perhaps?'

'I'm Felicity.' The girl folded her arms over the frilly front of her pink smock. 'Lady Erstworth's eldest daughter.'

Lady Erstworth. Violet wanted to clap a hand over her face and groan. *Sophie*.

'Oh, yes. Felicity,' Violet exclaimed with as much brightness as one could when dripping with rain water and having recently tripped over a well-dressed cat. 'Goodness but it's been so long since I've seen you. I scarcely recognised you. Is your mother here?' Dread shivered along Violet's damp skin. 'And your sister and brothers?'

'Just me.' Felicity gave Violet an expression that mixed scepticism with blatant irritation.

Only Felicity, then. Thank heavens. Even if she was the worst of the bunch. Being the eldest, she was a ringleader of sorts, encouraging naughty behaviour and revolts.

The girl peered around the corner where the feline had fled. 'Was that Hedgehog?'

'It was a cat,' Violet replied helpfully.

Felicity rolled her eyes. 'I'm perfectly aware that he's a cat. His *name* is Hedgehog.'

Violet pursed her lips. 'Why ever would you do that?'

'Do what?'

'Name a cat Hedgehog.'

Felicity strode across the entryway, her shoes clacking noisily, and peered around the corner. 'Because his body is grey, but his belly is fat and pink. Like a hedgehog.'

'Ah, well, when you explain it like that...' Violet handed Susan the sodden newspaper with an air of apology.

Susan silently wished Violet luck with a look and departed to dispose of the ruined news sheet.

The butler, Wilson, took Susan's place and collected Violet's gloves and hat. 'Lord Hollingston would like to see you in his study, if you please, my lady.'

Violet almost groaned aloud. That was all this day needed. First the meeting with Lord Dalton where she'd acted like a mindless dolt, then nearly running down a poor cat with a rather unfortunate name, followed by the disagreeable meeting with her niece. And now, the squeak seat. Again. For the second time in only one short week.

Violet swallowed her chagrin and nodded in thanks to the butler.

Clothes still damp from being caught in the rain and on the lookout for an errant beast scurrying about the carpet, Violet made her way to her father's study. He was waiting, his elbows perched on the expansive desk on the opposite side of the tyrannical chair.

She tried to give a happy smile and act as if everything was perfect, which, of course, it wasn't. 'Hello, Papa.'

He lifted his eyes at her, his face impassive.

Drat.

His expression didn't bode well. Her spirits sagged like sails whose wind had suddenly died.

'Wilson said you wished to see me.' Violet entered the room and hesitated before the squeak seat.

He gestured for her to sit down. She complied, bracing herself for its protest.

And protest it did, in a grating squawk of irritation and pressure of her ample rump upon its surface.

'You recall Sophie's eldest daughter, Felicity?' Lord Hollingston lifted his bushy brows.

'I do,' Violet replied.

'She's come to visit. For you to become better acquainted with her prior to removing yourself to the country this summer.'

'Oh, yes.' Violet kept her face from showing any of her emotions. 'I saw her. As well as Hedgehog.'

Lord Hollingston's composure rumpled in a furrow of his bushy white brows. 'Good God, she brought a hedgehog?'

'It's a cat.'

He held his hands wide, opened his mouth, shook his head, and continued. 'Your mother and I would like for you to spend some time cultivating a relationship with your niece while she is in town.'

Violet pressed her lips together to still her protest, then thought better of it.

If she had only weeks of freedom left, she would not spend them beleaguered with a condescending child and a cat adorned in frippery.

'I had hoped to spend the remainder of the Season enjoying my time in London.' She widened her eyes in the way that always worked on her father. 'After all, it will be my last opportunity to do so.'

Her father stared at her for a long moment. 'Violet, you have a choice to make. Whatever the devil you choose, I'd like you to know it well before you settle on your decision.'

A smile nearly erupted on Violet's face at his word selection. She tried to squelch it and instead sent the chair crying out in displeasure.

His forehead crinkled in question.

Violet swallowed her laugh. Or at least attempted to. 'Did you just call your granddaughter a devil?'

Lord Hollingston sat back in realisation and his lips quirked as a snort of a chuckle escaped him. 'Well, it would appear I did. But you well know that is not what I meant.'

'I know, Papa.' Violet grinned at him.

'Go on, you imp.' He waved at the air playfully in dismissal. 'And know I'll not change my mind on this.' His final words were laden with seriousness that left no room for argument.

Violet closed the door and suppressed a sigh. There would be no escape from this task. An unhappy beast hissed from somewhere in the house and Violet steeled herself for the task at hand. After all, how awful could a seven-year-old girl and a bad-tempered, ill-named cat be?

Chapter Five

Violet discovered exactly how awful a seven-year-old girl and a bad-tempered, ill-named cat could be.

There had been a game of hopscotch that had gone horribly awry when Violet tripped over Hedgehog and went sprawling into the perennials. Inside the home was no better when a game of dressing dolls had changed focus and poor Hedgehog became the object of Felicity's styling. Following all that had been the upset tea table in the creature's haste to run off, leaving his dignity behind. Violet couldn't fault the beast.

And it was best not to even think about Felicity's attempt to bring the cat to the dinner table. Lord Hollingston, fortunately, was far more firm in his orders and Felicity had been forced to sullenly deposit her hapless feline in another room before a fine roast could be spoiled by a dusting of cat hair.

By the end of the day, Violet was heartily exhausted. If she didn't have plans, she would have collapsed in her bed and not roused until well after noon the following day. She did, however, have plans. Or at least one very grand one.

Her parents retired earlier than usual, not long after Felicity, coincidentally, which gave Violet plenty of time for Susan to help her into the domino and summon a discreet hackney to the back of the house.

Violet slipped into the carriage and noted a similarly discreet coach at the house beside hers, taking off in the opposite direction. She craned her neck to see the passenger. The chiselled profile confirmed her suspicions. Lord Dalton. And whatever he was doing apparently required that he leave through the back of his home in secret.

A changed man, indeed.

Perhaps it was for the best Violet had no interest in marriage. Surely there was nothing guaranteed but heartbreak. And she had already been well acquainted with that pain.

She drew the curtain closed over the window to ensure there was no possible way for her to be seen. Especially when Violet's parents were unaware of her intention.

Violet remained thus in her seat for the duration of the journey, stock still, heart pounding, until at last the hackney rolled to a stop. The door opened and the driver held out his hand before leading her down.

'Busy address, this is.' He gave a grin that bordered on a grimace and showed splotches of rot in his teeth. ''Specially when it's at the back o' the 'ouse.' His threat was thinly veiled and his intent apparent.

Violet took one of the precious coins from her reticule and deposited it into the driver's grimy palm without touching him. He winked at her and let her pass.

Not wanting to linger on the street or in his presence, Violet rushed to the back door of the town house where she'd been instructed to go. She had just lifted her hand to knock when it opened before her.

A butler welcomed her in. He led her through the clean, neat kitchen and into the drawing room where Violet noted the curtains had been drawn tight against any prying eyes. Only then did he take her domino, which she relinquished with shaking hands.

He bowed low upon receiving the item and left her to take in her surroundings. She'd only time to notice a harp in one corner set atop the Brussels weave carpet when the double doors opened and one of the most beautiful women Violet had ever seen stepped through them.

The woman's hair was thick and dark, glossy with becoming curls, her skin was smooth as cream with high, elegant cheekbones and a generous mouth. She had a slight tilt to her blue eyes which lent her a sensual, intriguing air.

Violet hadn't been certain what to expect from Lottie. She knew her to be a courtesan, but this woman was dressed in a lovely periwinkle-satin evening gown that opened at the centre to reveal a panel of demure white muslin. The sleeves were short, revealing slender arms and the bodice was low, but not indecently so. In fact, the entire ensemble was nothing more or less than what Violet would expect to see at any dinner party.

'Lady Violet?' the woman prompted in a soft, sweet voice.

Violet's cheeks flamed at the realisation she'd been staring. And who would not? Lottie was the epitome of what a woman dreamed of looking like. Her slender arms and impossibly small waist. Violet wouldn't have a body like Lottie's even if she starved herself and she knew that from experience.

'That's me.' She hated the timidity of her voice and how much she wanted to crawl inside herself to disappear from the presence of the lovely courtesan.

'I'm Lottie,' the woman said. 'I can see the resemblance between you and the Duchess of Somersville. You both have such flawless skin and expressive eyes.'

Violet nodded dumbly. All this had seemed such a good idea from the outside. But being in Lottie's drawing room, staring at the exquisite beauty Violet could never dream of attaining, Violet felt the terribleness of it all come crashing down around her. She wanted to dash through those double doors and race the whole way back to Hollingston House.

'I know this is uncomfortable.' Lottie stepped closer. 'You're probably regretting your decision and wish to leave.' She gave an understanding smile. 'Please know that I put your privacy and the discretion of my tutelage at the forefront of everything I do. My staff is well paid and loyal and I take personal responsibility for every one of the ladies who passes through my doors.'

Her acknowledgement of Violet's discomfort relaxed some of the tension from her shoulders.

Lottie poured a glass of wine and held it out in offering, which Violet accepted with gratitude and sipped with more ease than she felt. The rich, ruby liquid was decadent, the alcohol like velvet as it warmed a path down her throat.

'Tell me, Lady Violet—' Lottie levelled her gaze '—why are you really here?'

All the tension clenched back into Violet. Did Lottie suspect her?

The woman reached out and gently rested her fingertips on Violet's arm. 'You needn't look so frightened. I merely wished to know what you hope to receive from our lessons together if I agree to take you on.'

Violet almost gasped in relief. 'I... I hope...' she stammered.

Truthfully, she hadn't put much thought into what she had expected to learn.

'The usual, I suppose?' Violet said in a very non-committal fashion and sipped at her wine.

Lottie smiled patiently. 'Every student is different. There is no "usual".' She regarded Violet appraisingly. 'You've been a wallflower for years with no mind towards marriage despite your beauty and the family you hail from.'

Despite her beauty.

Violet almost issued a bark of laughter at that and instead swallowed her mirth with a bit more wine. 'I am not noticed,' she managed to say.

Lottie studied Violet as though she was peering straight through the veneer Violet had long since donned. As though Violet was transparent and Lottie could look clean through her and put her finger on where the issue lay. 'I'm afraid I disagree. You are a woman who is not noticed because you do not wish to be,' Lottie said. 'You are aware that any instruction I might offer will encourage attention.'

'My father wants me to wed.' The truth burst from Violet. 'If I do not marry, he insists I retire to my sister's country estate to help care for my nieces and nephews. He thinks I require purpose in my life and this is how he means to see I have it.'

Lottie smirked, a wry twist to her pretty lips. 'Men often do not see women's lives as having purpose.' Her gaze lowered to the empty wine glass clutched in Violet's grasp. 'I have only one more question.'

Her words hung in the air while every nerve in Violet's body went taut.

Lottie looked imploringly at Violet. 'Do you want to be here?'

Violet's heart slammed so hard in her chest, she feared it might be audible. Was she up for the challenge? Could she force herself back out into the attention of others to properly pull off this charade?

'Yes.' Violet nodded with resolve. 'Yes, I want to be here.'

The concern on Lottie's face smoothed. 'Then I shall see you tomorrow evening for your first lesson.'

And there it was: Violet had secured a space in Lottie's highly sought-after, extremely secretive lessons.

Seth met the former Runner in a dodgy public house that smelled of hot bodies and smoky tallow candles and stale spirits, and sat apart in a shadowed corner where they wouldn't be disturbed.

The man, known simply as 'Nash', was entirely the sort of man Seth had predicted he would be: grizzled, with a beard that hadn't been trimmed in some time, a straight, humourless mouth, clothing that looked as though it hadn't been washed in an age. He was the kind of man who could blend into a tough crowd and disappear. Unmemorable. At least until one glimpsed the sharp intensity in his eyes, bright with intelligence and heavy with a haunted expression Seth had come to know well. He'd witnessed it in his men, after hard battles or too many years on end without cease. Worse still, he sometimes even saw it in himself.

Seth handed him a leather portfolio containing all the information gleaned on the solicitor, Mr Pattinson, which sadly, wasn't much. The perfidious solicitor had managed to lay low for the duration of his time in London prior to weaselling his way into Lady Dalton's employ. Then again, a widowed countess who had recently lost her son was surely an easy target.

'No one knows where 'e's gone, eh?' Nash peered into the portfolio, his brow crinkling.

Seth leaned forward to be heard over the raucous crowd without having to speak too loudly. 'It's as though he's simply disappeared.'

Nash snapped the portfolio closed and curled the string around the supple leather. 'No one just disappears.'

'And that's why I have come to you, my good man.' Seth took a sip of the porter at his side. It wasn't a proper drink for a gentleman and certainly the glass was far from clean. But it was the kind of libation he'd often found himself enjoying during his time in the military, alongside his men.

An ache clutched at his heart. Too many of those men were now dead.

He tightened his grip on the glass.

'If anyone can find 'im, it'll be me.' Nash spoke with the confidence of a man who knew his worth.

A man who would get the job done no matter the cost.

Seth swallowed down the rest of his porter and got to his feet. The room had become increasingly crowded since he'd arrived. The hour was late, the ideal time to drink, gamble and visit brothels.

Six years ago Seth would have been meeting up with Kentworth, eagerly anticipating the night's sport—in whatever fashion it happened to be enjoyed. Now, exhaustion pressed on him and the only thing he looked forward to was morning, when another night of haunted dreams would come to an end.

He nodded a farewell to the Runner and took his leave. The ride home was swift, as it often was with so few carriages about. Curiously, there was one arriving at Hollingston House next door when Seth drew closer to his home.

He peered into the darkness. Lord Hollingston was a man well known for his morals. He cared for his children, remained faithful to his wife and served in Parliament with steadfast determination to right the wrongs of England. And indeed it was not Lord Hollingston who alighted from the carriage. It was a woman.

Seth sat forward in his seat. The mysterious lady wore a full-length black domino and a concealing mask over her face. Surely it was not Lady Hollingston, who watched the world with a tight-lipped frown of disapproval. And no servant would dare risk ruining the Lavell name by bringing scandal to their doorstep. Quite literally. Especially not servants as loyal as those serving at Hollingston House.

Which left only one potential lady who might be out at such a damning hour.

Lady Violet.

He remained fixed with riveted fascination as she rushed through the back gate and garden. The door opened before she even arrived, shooting a streak of light out over the moonlit grass. She slipped into the house and the door closed. Darkness resumed once more.

Lady Violet, out alone and wearing a domino. What was the little wallflower doing?

The thought teased at him throughout the night as he tossed and turned on his fine mattress that had taken several nights to readjust to.

There were many reasons a woman might don a mask

and cloak in the dead of night. The gaming hells ladies frequented beneath the obscurity of anonymity, a lover whose arms she might secretly fall into. There were even salacious parties where couples loved freely among one another while wearing only those masks.

Suddenly there she was in his mind's eye, naked save for a fitted mask that framed her startling blue eyes and thick, sable lashes. While Seth had never been to one of those parties, he'd heard enough to know what went on. Enough to consider what she might do if they were in attendance at one together and she was entirely free to come to him.

That night, for the first time since his return from Waterloo, he wasn't tormented by images of his men dying, but ones that were far sweeter and left him hot, hard and aching the following morning.

Through it all, he could not liberate the thought from his mind: What if Violet was not as innocent as he'd initially presumed?

Chapter Six

Violet had been playing with spinning tops for the span of a very long, very monotonous afternoon that involved a tedious amount of flicking her wrist. Lift the top, twist it to spin, wait for it to roll to a stop. On and on it went: lift, spin, wait, lift, spin, wait. And throughout the excruciating duration, Hedgehog darted about madly in an attempt to pounce upon the small, whirling objects.

It had been rather funny at the start. The first several dozen times at least. Then Violet began to feel rather sorry for the poor beast. Surely he was getting as tired as she.

'Would you like to play another game?' Violet asked.

Felicity stared at a final spinning top with a smile hovering on her lips in expectation. Hedgehog, adorned in a blue-sprigged cap with bits of lace at the edge, flew into the air with a sprightliness his corpulent frame would not suggest him capable of and landed upon the top with an audible *thunk*.

Felicity threw her head back with laughter. Her glee was such that Violet found herself chuckling at the child's mirth.

'I believe Hedgehog will grow weary if we keep making him run about,' Violet said.

Felicity reached for her cat and drew him towards her. He allowed the action with the bland expression of complete resignation at his fate.

'Are you getting tired, my dear one?' Felicity cooed.

The cat hung in her arms without moving. She hugged him closer to her like a doll and kissed the top of his head.

'We could change his bonnet.' Felicity fingered the lace edge of his current adornment.

Hedgehog issued forth a soul-deep sigh.

'I believe he looks fine as he is,' Violet said quickly to spare the creature another ridiculous hat. Felicity had been eyeing a feathered hat that looked as though it might drive Hedgehog to distraction.

'Do you think so?' Felicity lifted the cat into the air and scrutinised him. For his part, Hedgehog dangled from her hands by the undersides of his arms, his pink belly jutting out, exposed.

'Quite,' Violet replied. 'The blue flowers are very fetching.'

Felicity gave a quiet hum, suggesting she did not agree with Violet's assessment. Regardless, she set him down where he promptly rolled on to his side and nestled against her knee.

Felicity scratched under his chin and the sawing purr of his contentment filled the room. 'Why don't you have children, Aunt Violet?'

The question was so bold, so beyond anything ever considered polite in a child that it took Violet aback.

'I'm not married,' she replied without thought.

'Why aren't you married?' Felicity looked up from the cat.

'Such questions are not proper for a child to be asking,' Violet scolded in a gentle tone. They were hardly proper questions for *anyone* to be asking.

'I'm hardly proper and we both know it,' Felicity stated matter-of-factly. 'Are you afraid to answer?'

Foolish irritation nipped at Violet's nerves. She shouldn't let a child get to her and yet she hated the challenge hanging in the air. 'Of course not. I simply haven't met the right man.'

'Do you want to get married?' Felicity fired the question almost as soon as Violet replied.

Violet hesitated in her answer. To be truthful and say no would doubtless result in a new barrage of questions. 'Some day I think marriage would be nice,' she lied.

Never would it be nice, especially when it would require that she empty the contents of her heart on to the table prior to any discussion of marriage. Even if she wanted to wed, no gentleman would want her. She was completely ruined.

Felicity's unwavering stare remained fixed on Violet. 'Mother says you haven't wed because you're too plump.'

Violet swallowed down an indignant gasp. 'I beg your pardon?'

'Men don't like plump women.' Felicity lowered her attention to Hedgehog once more and scratched her fingers over his bonnet just behind his ears. 'That's why Mother said I'm not allowed to eat more than one sweet at a time, lest I end up like Aunt Violet and be too plump to ever wed.'

'I see,' Violet replied. And she did see. So clearly that it made tears sting in her eyes.

She was being used as an example for her nieces.

*Self-relegated wallflower who put off marriage after
her debut deemed too plump to wed.*

In the next instalment of the Lady Observer: *How
not to attract a sought-after suitor...*

Now, that would be a headline.

Violet's throat felt thick suddenly and the threat of crying in front of her niece seemed like a very real and awful possibility.

'Please excuse me a moment.' Violet did not bother to wait for Felicity to acknowledge her statement or offer any indication she had heard her.

Violet didn't rush to her room where her footsteps would clatter noisily and give away her location in the quiet house. No, instead she sought her solace in the one place where she'd always sought comfort: in the garden.

Away from everyone, even the servants.

Violet let her head fall back against the closed door and breathed in the summer scents of the garden. Rich dirt mingled with the sweetness of sun-warmed grass and the delicate perfume of flowers in bloom. A balmy breeze brushed her face and drew her from the tiled steps, out into the narrow garden. She sank on to a marble bench under the shadow of an elm tree and let her ears feast on the blissful nothing around her.

Carriage wheels rumbled over the streets in the distance, a clattering of dishes came from within the house, somewhere a dog barked a high, pitching yap. She closed her eyes and let herself be pulled in by her senses, yielding to it for reprieve.

Another sound entered her awareness—the distinct click of a door being shut.

Her eyes flew open and she glanced back towards her town house, but no one was there. Movement over the hedge separating her property from the one next door caught her gaze and her heart went still.

Lord Dalton.

He was alone as she was. The same as when they were children and would speak together between the hedges. Sometimes even skirting the small gap between the foliage that never quite closed all the way between the two properties.

She doubted he remembered such childhood romps.

But she did. In fact, she recalled them fondly, with the exception of when he'd referred to her as hearty. Of course, that was all before his rebelliousness when he grew a bit older. It was then he alternated between pretending she didn't exist and flirting with her so keenly, he robbed her of breath.

Suddenly, she did not want to be there, to be seen by him. She carefully slid down the bench to put herself from the line of his gaze.

'Lady Violet,' he called. 'Is that you I see under the tree?'

Violet hissed a soft exhale. Not this. Not now.

But all the wishing in the world wouldn't change the situation for what it was: she'd been caught.

There was nothing for it but to swallow down her trepidation and speak to the man. She peered around the elm's peeling trunk and saw his dark gaze fixed on her.

Be still her pathetic heart.

Seth thought he'd been imagining things when he first laid eyes on Lady Violet in the garden next door. He stepped closer to the hedges separating their properties and found himself searching to see if the narrow gap between the dense green leaves was still there.

'Lord Dalton.' Violet watched him from the bench where she sat like a forest nymph.

She got to her feet and approached the hedge. 'What brings you into the garden?'

His mother. Her waspish words. A respite from the verbal assault. A reprieve from a conversation about—of all things—Almack's.

Because being outside cleared his head of the nightmares that threaded through the dark recesses of his mind like ubiquitous cobwebs.

He said none of this, of course. In fact, he should say nothing beyond bidding her good day and returning inside.

His curiosity at his neighbour's nocturnal activities, however, kept him locked in her presence.

He put his hands behind his back and stood at attention like the soldier he'd been. 'I don't strike you as the type to peruse a garden for its simple enjoyment?'

'You do not, my lord.' A smile teased at her lips.

'Then I may surprise you.'

She lifted her brows. 'Oh?'

'Yes, I often come out to admire the...' He turned to a patch of pink flowers on long pale green stems. 'Uh...the...'

'Peonies,' she supplied.

'Yes, of course, the peonies.' He gestured to the white flowers. 'And the, uh...well, the...'

'Daisies.'

He nodded. 'Yes.'

'I never realised you were a connoisseur of flowers, then.' She nodded her head as though thoroughly impressed. 'Do you have a favourite?'

Ah, now there was an answer he readily knew. 'Violets.'

'Flatterer,' she chided. Yet, even as she did, her cheeks coloured with a pretty blush.

He'd had it in his mind to nudge their conversation towards the late-night carriage he'd seen, but then their eyes met and he thought better of it. There was something tender beneath her flirtation, something shy and perhaps wounded.

Suddenly, he recognised himself as the cad he was. No doubt she was still upset over his abrupt departure from the ball.

'I apologise again for not dancing with you,' he said earnestly.

Her eyes widened and her mouth fell open. 'Well, I suppose you were eager to join your regiment,' she replied in a halting stammer.

He paused, uncertain what the devil she was talking about.

Her cheeks went scarlet. 'I thought you were referring to my debut.' She touched her hands to her face as though she could press away the flush of embarrassment. 'Forgive me.'

At her debut? He concentrated, driving his memory back six years, and recalled that yes, he had promised he'd dance with her first at her debut. Had he not?

'You don't remember.' A look of pain flashed on her face and she quickly turned her head to the side to break the connection between them.

Without thinking, he reached over the narrow hedge and touched her cheek to turn her pretty face back towards him. It was a mistake to do so. Her skin was soft and warm beneath his touch, no doubt scented with a delicately feminine fragrance. The slight connection made him want to touch her more, to lift her face up to his and kiss her deeply.

He half-hoped she would draw away, but she did not.

She allowed the gesture, looking up at him in supplication, her stare brimming with hurt. A hurt he had placed there.

And the worst part about it was that he'd been too foxed at the time to remember what had even happened.

'I was an idiot, as I've said.' His thumb moved against her jaw, stroking the smoothness of her skin. God, she was sweet. Tempting. Perfect. 'I'm not that man any more and never want to be again.'

She swallowed. 'It's fine.'

'It's not,' he countered. He had to make it right with her. 'Will you dance with me?'

He wanted to regret the words once they had left his lips, but he could not. After all, it would only be one dance. To put things right between them once more.

She exhaled a nervous laugh. 'Here?'

He laughed with her and dropped his hand from her lovely face lest he give in to the temptation to kiss her. 'When the next opportunity presents itself. Most likely at Almack's on Wednesday night.'

She gave him a shy smile that made him want to draw her towards him and wrap his arms around her. 'Almack's?' She put a hand to her chest. 'My, you have changed.'

He'd tried not to glance down at her bosom, but with her fingertips resting lightly on her fair skin, his gaze wandered of their own volition. Her breasts were high and round, supple skin rising over the modest neckline that made his imagination take over.

His stare lingered for only a second, a glorious, tantalising second, before he met her eyes once more.

'My mother,' he grumbled. But he stopped himself. He

didn't want to talk about his mother right then, or the fight they'd had over her planned discussion with the patronesses of Almack's to get him permitted back in.

And though he shouldn't admit it, he was exactly where he wanted to be: in the garden, alone with Violet, and wishing the hedge between them wasn't there so he could pull her into his arms and kiss her. Even as he thought it, he leaned closer. The hedge dug into his waist and pressed at his stirring arousal.

'Dance with me,' he said. 'The next chance you get.'

If she rejected him again, he would not protest. In truth, even in making it right, he knew better than to dance with her. A dance couldn't be enough. Even though it ought to be.

He half-hoped she would say no, yet part of him wanted desperately for her to say—

'Yes.' She licked her lips. Pillowy soft and pink and wholly tempting.

He nearly groaned his relief in her reply.

God, he wanted to kiss her. To taste the sweetness of her mouth and sample the smoothness of her skin with his tongue. Especially along the length of her graceful neck and over the tops of those beautiful breasts.

He kept his gaze fixed on hers to avoid letting it drop to her bosom again. It was too easy to admit to himself how badly he wanted to cup his hands over the generous swells, to tease at her nipples with the pads of his thumbs until she cried out beneath him. He leaned further still, practically bending over the hedges to close the gap between them. Sharp sticks dug into his thighs and stomach, but he paid them no mind.

He cared of nothing but the woman in front of him.

There was a delicate powdery perfume about her. Violets. She smelled like her namesake and was just as lovely, just as delicate and sweet as the flower.

'Seth.' She whispered his Christian name, one she hadn't spoken since they were children. She said it in a breathy voice, one laced with intimacy and desire.

'Tell me to walk away,' he said.

She gave a shaky sigh. 'I can't.'

'Tell me not to kiss you,' he cautioned.

She licked her lips again, slower this time. 'I can't.'

He reached for her face once more, this time tilting it up towards his. Her lashes swept to her cheeks just as his own eyes closed. She was silk under his fingertips and fire in his veins. Had he ever wanted anything more than to kiss this woman?

He lowered his mouth, expecting to encounter warm, sensual lips. But that was not to be.

Before the slight breath of distance between them could be fully closed, a door banged open, Violet was forcefully flung away from him and a high-pitched shriek pierced the air.

Chapter Seven

One moment, Violet was locked in the anticipation of an impending kiss, her heart pounding, head spinning, and the next, she was sitting hard upon the grass in total bewilderment.

There had been a bit in between, of course. When a cat wearing a pink bonnet collided at an impossible speed against her shins with the force of a stone and sent her sprawling backwards. How ungainly.

'Don't let him run away,' Felicity shouted in a most unladylike manner.

Violet wanted to drop her face into her hands and die of the humiliation burning through her. Instead, she sneaked a glance upwards at Lord Dalton.

He stared down at her, his brows furrowed with concern. 'Good God. Are you quite all right?' He cast a chagrined glance at the hedge between them.

'Yes.' Violet floundered on the ground in an effort to haul herself to her feet as gracefully as possible. There was no grace about it, however. Not when one wore several layers of skirts while attempting to extricate oneself from the grass without allowing any indecent flashes of unmentionables.

Dalton shoved through the small gap between the hedges, the very one they'd used as children. He *did* remember. It almost brought a smile to her face, except at that very moment he pitched forward and fell as well. Right alongside her.

He landed on his side with an *oof*.

Violet stopped struggling and immediately turned her attention on him. 'Are you hurt?'

'I assure you, after the years of fighting and battle, it will not be a gap in a hedge that will best me.' He righted himself in a far more fluid motion than her fumbled attempts and held his hand out to her. 'What the devil was that?'

'Hedgehog.' Violet put her hand into his and found herself gliding upwards with incredible ease, as though it were no effort on his part whatsoever to lift her to her feet.

'Found him,' Felicity cried out in victory somewhere in the garden.

'A hedgehog?' Dalton's hand remained locked with Violet's even though she was properly standing. 'It looked rather like a cat.'

Violet, self-consciously and yet reluctantly pulled her hand from his large, warm one and brushed at her skirts in an effort to smooth the crumpled muslin. 'He is a cat. His name is Hedgehog.'

Dalton narrowed his eyes. 'Is he wearing a bonnet?'

Violet turned to where he stared at Felicity carrying the rotund creature by its armpits.

'I almost lost you,' Felicity cooed. 'That was very naughty.'

Hedgehog glowered up at her from beneath a layer of pink organza this time.

'Yes,' Violet confirmed. 'He is wearing a bonnet.'

'The poor wretch,' Lord Dalton muttered.

Felicity marched her way over to them, Hedgehog swinging in her grasp. 'Aunt Violet,' she said in a chastising tone. 'You ought to know better.'

A chill trickled down Violet's back. Had Felicity seen her almost kiss Lord Dalton? The hellion of a child would tell all of London with boisterous tone.

If such a thing fell on the *ton*'s ears, it would be quite the scandal. And Violet was keenly aware of what a scandal could do to one's standing in society.

'I beg your pardon?' Violet asked in a manner she hoped did not reveal her horror.

'To be outside without your bonnet.' Felicity lifted Hedgehog in indication of Violet's face. 'Look at how red your cheeks already are. You'll have freckles soon for certain. Mother says freckles are most unbecoming.'

So great was the force of Violet's relief, she could have laughed aloud. It was such an innocent offence compared to the one nearly committed. The one Violet wished she could still commit.

Even now, she kept her attention averted from Lord Dalton lest the 'the sun' hasten the redness of her face further.

'Thank you for your concern,' Violet said. 'This is our neighbour, Lord Dalton. Lord Dalton, this is my niece, Lady Felicity.'

'My parents are Lord and Lady Erstworth.' Felicity's small chest puffed with importance. 'Do you know them?'

'I've not had the pleasure of an introduction,' Lord Dalton said.

Felicity nodded in understanding. 'They are very busy. I hardly see them myself. Isn't that right, Hedgehog?' She nuzzled the cat to her face and rocked him so his dangling feet swung back and forth. The look on his face was not one of amusement or joy.

'I think we should get Hedgehog inside,' Violet said in an effort to intercede on the creature's behalf. 'Lest he end up with freckles.'

Felicity peered under Hedgehog's bonnet. 'Do cats get freckles?'

She didn't wait for the answer before carrying the feline from the garden and into the house, leaving only Lord Dalton and Violet. Except this time, he was in her garden with her. Alone.

It was improper. And delicious.

Would he try to kiss her again?

She truly hoped so.

Alas, he did not. Instead, he stepped back to put space between them and his lips twitched in the hint of a smile. 'It was a pleasure, Lady Violet.'

It was a fortunate thing she could not get freckles from blushing or she'd be covered with them on every inch of her body by now.

'For me as well,' she said quietly.

He backed towards the gap in the hedgerow while facing her, as though he could not bear to look away. 'Wednesday night, then?' he pressed.

She ignored the nip of trepidation. After all, it was far from a marriage proposal. Her secrets could remain safe and she could enjoy at least one more dance before finally entering the futility of spinsterhood.

'Yes,' she replied. 'Wednesday.'

He glanced over his shoulder and pressed through the gap in the hedges. It apparently did not yield easily to him, for it took several jerking steps and a bit of a struggle on his part before he was on the other side.

He smirked at the wayward hedge, then bowed in her direction. 'I look forward to seeing you, my lady, without the barrier of shrubbery between us.' With that, he made his way back into Dalton Place.

She waited for him to go inside before replying, 'As do I.'

And indeed she did. Far too much.

She slowly walked towards her own home, preferring to relish the idea of the impending dance rather than face Felicity once more.

If Hedgehog had not scampered outside at such an inopportune time, would Lord Dalton have kissed her?

Violet was sure he would.

Would she have let him?

Of that, she was even more certain.

And it was what scared her most.

It also was not where she ought to be focusing her attentions. That evening, she would be attending her first lesson with Lottie and had to compose a list of discreet questions to ask. Violet would have to be strategic, not only to avoid arousing suspicion, but also to glean the most information as possible. The Season was drawing to a close and there was most likely only little more than a fortnight remaining.

For the first time since Seth's arrival in London, he felt lighter. Happier.

It had every bit to do with Violet and her promise to dance with him at Almack's. This time he knew there would be no drums in the orchestra. The patronesses of Almack's would never allow such a deviation from the social norm.

Which meant he would be able to dance with Violet in peace, without terrible images nudging into his mind.

Then he would be able to stop seeing her. The dance would make up for having abandoned her the other night, as well as during her debut six years prior.

Resolved, he made his way to his study to tend to the daily correspondence and tried to put Violet from his mind. It would be too distracting to think about the shy way she'd looked at him when he'd leaned in to kiss her, and how that reticence had slipped away as her lashes fluttered in preparation for their lips to meet.

He sat down in the chair behind his desk. God, how he'd wanted to kiss her, to taste her lips with his own. And how dangerous it had been to attempt. Were it not for the cat, he might have ruined her reputation. Had anyone seen them in that garden, kissing over the hedges...

'Seth?' Caroline's voice came from the doorway to the study. 'Do you have a moment that we might speak?'

'Of course.' He pushed aside the correspondence so he could offer her his undivided attention.

She smiled her appreciation and approached. 'I know you aren't eager to be attending Almack's so soon upon your return and with so little time left in the Season. But Mother is only doing what she thinks is best.'

Seth bit back a retort. After all, Lady Dalton had suggestions for everything she thought was best. How he ought to vote in Parliament, as if he didn't have his own opinions, who he ought to dance with to attract the right quality of woman for a wife, how he ought to hold his brandy glass to make him look most debonair, how to tie his own cravat, et cetera, et cetera...

'I'd hazard to guess she did not do this with William,' Seth surmised.

Caroline sank slowly on the chair, clearly weighing her words before speaking. 'It was different with William.'

'I'm quite aware of that.'

'Will you please reconsider allowing Mother to speak to the patronesses at Almack's?' Caroline asked patiently.

She always had been the peacekeeper among them, the one who interceded on their mother's behalf with him and the one who went to her to make apologies for Seth. Not that he'd ever supported a single one of those apologies. It had been a role Caroline handled with grace and dignity, without ever making Seth feel like the horrible person he knew himself to be.

'She can speak with them today,' Seth replied.

'You see, there are a great many reasons why attending Almack's could benefit you—' Caroline stilled. 'What did you say?'

'I said she can speak with them.'

Caroline straightened. 'Oh. Well. That was far easier than anticipated.'

'Contrary to what others may believe, I want to be a good earl.' Seth glanced at the stack of correspondence. It was larger than he'd been expecting, but he would address it as he had the days before. One missive at a time. 'And that extends beyond our holdings and those we employ. I know I have been...difficult in the past.'

Caroline shook her head, brushing off his castigation. 'You weren't always so bad.'

'Now you're being kind.' He settled back and regarded his younger sister with a frank stare. 'Do you remember the night before I left to join the military?'

Caroline fiddled with the hem of her sleeve, as though finding it intensely fascinating.

It was all the response he needed. He hated the answer he feared she might give, but he had to ask the question regardless. 'Do you recall if I attended Lady Violet's debut?'

'That was all in the past.' Caroline smoothed at the lace on her sleeve. 'It needn't be brought up now.'

Was it all that bad, then? Seth grimaced. 'I'm relying on your good memory and honesty, Caroline. I confess I cannot remember much of that night.'

'That doesn't surprise me in the least. You were sufficiently foxed by mid-afternoon that day.' Caroline's mouth pulled down in a slight frown. 'I only remember because Mother made a point of grousing about you being in your cups and missing Lady Violet's debut.' She pursed her lips.

Seth winced. 'Go on if there's more.'

Caroline lifted a shoulder in a partial shrug. 'I was not yet old enough to be invited, so I cannot vouch if you were indeed in attendance or not. I only know Mother did not see you there.'

That gave Seth pause. *Had* he gone? He tapped his finger on his knee in thought.

'There is another matter I'd like to speak to you on,' Caroline said.

Wary, he lifted his attention back to her. 'Yes?'

'You said you wanted your care to extend beyond your property and those you employ, meaning Mother and myself, correct?' An anxious expression pinched her face.

'Is there something amiss?'

She shook her head vigorously and a furious blush stole over her cheeks. 'No, not at all. It's only that, well, there is a certain gentleman of your acquaintance whom I have found rather interesting in the last few years. I had hoped he would notice me after my come out, but three years have passed...' She toyed with the lace on her sleeve again. 'And he has not.'

Seth lifted his brow in a silent prompt for her to continue. 'Would this have to do with your rejection of so many suitors?'

She nodded and bit her lip. 'I wondered, if it was not too much bother...' She gave Seth a hopeful smile. 'If you would consider speaking to him. About me. To perhaps gauge his interest in me.'

'Who is the fortunate gentleman?'

'One of your university friends.' Caroline wriggled her shoulders, the way she did when she was a girl and couldn't contain her excitement. 'One you used to run about with before you joined the military.'

Seth's stomach went into a tight knot. Surely she was not referring to Kentworth. He'd just as soon offer his sister to the devil himself rather than allow Kentworth anywhere near her. Though truly, they were most likely one and the same.

'Who is it?' Seth repeated, his tone cold.

Caroline took in a deep, gulping breath. 'Lord Rawley.'

Seth stared at her, dumbstruck. 'Viscount... Rawley? With his perfectly combed hair and the pocket watch at his side?'

'Yes, isn't he just a dear?' Caroline bounced in the chair. 'He's more a gentleman than any other I've met. Will you please find a way to see if he has any interest in me whatsoever?'

'Yes, of course.' The answer came automatically and without any indication as to the thoughts jumbling in his mind.

Caroline popped out of her seat, ran to him to deliver a kiss on his cheek, then dashed from the room with a distant squeal following her departure.

Lord Rawley?

Women never noticed him. If ever a man could be a wall-flower, it would be the Viscount. Indeed, in the entire time Seth had known him, Lord Rawley had never once visited the light skirts in a brothel or made advances towards any woman. He'd looked, of course. What man did not? But any attempts at trying to court a woman had been disastrous.

Contrarily, Caroline was a lovely young woman who was accomplished and vivacious. Her dowry was substantial and her lineage could be traced back several hundred years. Any man would consider himself lucky to have the good fortune to catch her attention.

Seth leaned back in his chair and actually chuckled. Of all the challenges he faced upon his return to London, this would be by far the easiest.

The mirth died on his lips as he considered his own re-lationship. What had he done on the night of Violet's ball? He glanced out the window to where he could see the small garden at the back of Hollingston House. Violet was not out there.

Not that he had expected her to be when they both had only recently returned inside. However, he would remain vigilant. If she went out once more and he had the good for-tune to catch her alone, he fully intended to ask her exactly what had happened the night of her debut.

He had to know, even though he suspected it would be excruciatingly terrible. Something that would require more than a single dance to make reparations.

Chapter Eight

Violet slipped out in the dead of night once more, this time with a different driver who Lottie had recommended. And this time with five questions that were carefully selected from a long list she'd composed earlier that afternoon. If she divided them between her lessons, she could glean everything she needed from Lottie for her exposé.

The list had taken the better part of her afternoon, pieced together in the shreds of time when Felicity was otherwise engaged. It would all be worth it.

When she arrived and the butler showed Violet into the drawing room, she did not hesitate as she removed her domino and mask. The gown beneath was blue silk with a tulle overlay on the skirt where whorls of silk ribbon had been stitched. It was perhaps too fine for the occasion, except the last visit had left Violet feeling shabby by comparison to Lottie's beauty.

While Violet could not change her body shape, much to her chagrin, she could at least choose a more flattering frock.

Lottie entered the room, carrying the glass of wine herself, which she handed to Violet with a sweet smile. 'It is so good to see you again.' Her gaze skimmed over Violet. 'You look positively radiant. That colour suits you.'

The compliment was genuinely given, but even with the exuberance of Lottie's words, Violet's attire was nothing compared to the plain green gown Lottie wore. Unadorned and simple, it served to only call attention to her perfect figure.

Just beyond her was a bouquet of hothouse flowers the likes of which Violet had never seen. It was the perfect deflection from compliments, physical appearances and painful failures. 'Goodness, those are lovely.' She indicated to the bunch of lilies and roses with bits of ivy woven between them.

Lottie glanced at them and a wounded expression flickered in her eyes. She recovered with a quick smile. 'Thank you. They're from an old friend.' She redirected her attention to Violet. 'Shall we begin?'

Violet nodded, fully prepared with her carefully selected questions lodged in her mind.

'I realise you may have concerns about me,' Lottie said by way of opening. 'I also realise you are taking a significant risk in coming here.'

Violet opened her mouth, but hesitated, unsure of how to respond to such a bald statement.

Lottie put a hand up. 'You needn't say anything. It's only that I want you to know, so you understand where I've been and why I am doing this now. You see, a lifetime ago, I was a vicar's daughter.'

Her claim took Violet aback. How did a vicar's daughter become a courtesan?

'It was foolish, I know.' Lottie's cheeks coloured prettily. 'But I fell in love and I gave too much.'

It was Violet's turn to feel her face grow hot. She was quite aware of what Lottie was speaking. Violet herself had once given too much.

'The man I loved promised he would come back,' Lottie continued. 'He did not. My father died shortly thereafter and I had no means of support. I tried as best I could to work in an opera house. Not the most esteemed of professions, I'm well aware, but then there are few options for women. I could not wed and found myself unable to support myself on the pittance of an opera dancer. I tried to resist the advances of men, but finally had to concede. For if I was to eat, I had to accept the new profession forced upon me.'

Violet ought to have been grateful for the candid story, for the words that would drip salacious details like the juices from tender cooked beef on to the column of the *Lady Observer*. Except Lottie's confession knotted like a ball of ice in Violet's stomach. How close had she herself been to such a fate as Lottie's?

'I'm so sorry.' The words slipped from Violet's mouth before she knew she meant to say them.

Lottie shook her head. 'I'm not looking for sympathy by any means. I only told you for two purposes. First, I want you to understand why I became what I did. Second, I want you to know something deeply personal about me.'

The former courtesan took Violet's hand in her delicate grip. 'What we discuss in these lessons will require an unquestionable trust between us. It is unfair to expect you to share, yet know nothing of me in return.' Her fingers squeezed against Violet's. 'Can you trust me?'

Guilt bit hard into Violet's awareness and did not let go. Lottie was giving far more of herself than anticipated. Before Lottie could sense any hesitation on her part, Violet forced a nod. 'You can trust me.'

And in that exact instant, Violet made the vow to never reveal Lottie's own personal story in any part of the exposé for the *Lady Observer*. Such secrets were meant to be kept between women.

Lottie pulled Violet into a companionable embrace. 'I'm delighted to hear it, my darling. Now, let us find you a husband. Is there a man you have your heart set upon?'

Lord Dalton's image flashed in Violet's mind and seared something deep in her chest. The way he'd bent over the hedge to touch her, his hand firmly set against Violet's face, how his dark eyes had become pools of ink before he closed them in preparation for a kiss that never came.

'I'll take that as a yes.' Lottie's eyes sparkled. 'We ladies don't become that thoughtful over the idea of any man. We only do so at the idea of one man in particular.' She tilted her head and her glossy curls shifted over her shoulder. 'Am I wrong?'

It was so tempting to lie, but Lottie's request that they be honest with one another stilled Violet's tongue and she found herself shaking her head.

'And what do you think keeps him from noticing you?' Lottie queried. 'You're far too lovely to be ignored.'

'He does notice me,' Violet replied.

Lottie put a slender finger to the bottom of Violet's chin and tilted her head up to better meet her eyes. 'Then what is the problem, dearest?'

'I...' Violet faltered, her fears sticking fast in her throat.

Lottie's slender brows pinched together. 'Tell me so I can help you. What is keeping you from him?'

Because she was spoiled for any man, because she would never have a body like Lottie's, because he was a war hero and an earl and she…she was nobody.

Tears stung at Violet's eyes with a force that surprised her. 'Because I'm not worthy of a man such as him.' A sob burst from her, harsh and ugly and unexpected.

'Then I think I know what we need to work on.' Lottie had a handkerchief at the ready in a flash and extended it to Violet.

'Making me worthy?' Violet asked miserably.

Lottie smiled and shook her head. 'Making you understand that you already are and that you always have been.'

There were more tears as the night went on, when Violet peeled away the first layer of her heart as she explained her countless inadequacies and all the various ways she was entirely deficient.

Lottie listened carefully and with a patience that somehow managed to bring on more tears. What was it about the realisation of finally being listened to for the first time in a lifetime that rendered one a soggy pile of emotional mush?

Yet as the lesson drew to a close and as her tears dried, Violet discovered that even just discussing her past hurts made her feel exponentially better.

Her initial suspicion of what Lottie's instructions would entail had involved advice in flirting, kissing and seduction. What Violet had thus far received was something far beyond those things. It scored deep and penetrated the very heart.

And made her completely forget to ask even one of her prepared questions.

* * *

Seth did not see Violet in the garden again, though he had looked for her. Two days later, however, when the weather was far too fine to sequester oneself in a carriage, he happened upon her in Berkeley Square.

She was with her maid and little Lady Felicity, who was pointing excitedly to something in a shop window.

'Not now,' Violet said as he was walking up. 'You must be well behaved or you'll get none at all.'

'I want it now.' Felicity's face turned pink with outrage and she opened her mouth to wail.

'Lady Violet.' Seth tilted his hat to her. 'Lady Felicity.' He winked.

The little girl's petulant rage dwindled and her mouth closed before she could let loose a squall.

For her part, Lady Violet appeared quite flustered, her own cheeks red and her mouth pinched at the corners.

'Good day, Lord Dalton.' She attempted a smile. 'I trust you're well?'

'Even better now.' He grinned at her.

'You may not say that for long,' Violet warned under her breath. 'Felicity, please bid Lord Dalton welcome.'

The little girl narrowed her eyes. 'Good day, Lord Dalton.'

If everyone wished each other good day with the same vehemence, not a man under the sun would have a fine day ever again.

Except he was not irritated by her poor behaviour, not when her actions were ones with which he was so very familiar. Children did not misbehave without purpose. This particular child was afflicted by something Seth understood better than anything else: a distinct lack of attention.

It had been the same with him as a boy when his attempts at being the best at everything had slipped beyond his parents' notice. They had praised William constantly, commending his accomplishments, no matter how mundane or mediocre they might have been. It was then Seth had stopped trying. And it was then that his parents had actually paid attention to him.

Even displeasure was acknowledgement that he was alive, that he was an active member of the household. Better unhappiness than indifference.

He considered the little girl now and knelt down beside her. Eye to eye, giving her every ounce of his focus.

He tilted his hat to her as he'd done with Lady Violet. 'How are you today, Lady Felicity?'

She scuffed her toe on the ground. 'I'm well, thank you. And you?'

'Quite well, thank you.' He made a show of looking about. 'Where is Hedgehog? I am quite eager to see what bonnet he's sporting today.'

A smile edged into her pout. 'He's in the carriage, wearing a yellow bonnet. There's a feather on it and it's driving him half-mad. He keeps rolling about in an effort to get at it.' She giggled.

It *was* rather a funny image. 'I imagine he'll have it removed by the time you return,' Seth said.

'I imagine so.' Felicity grinned at him so widely he noticed she'd recently lost a bottom front tooth.

'I was on my way to get an ice at Gunter's,' he fibbed. In truth, he'd been on the way to White's. 'Would you ladies care to join me?'

Lady Violet cast a longing glance towards the shop. 'I shouldn't...'

Felicity turned her face to her aunt. 'Mother says ices aren't for ladies who—'

'We should be on our way,' Lady Violet said in a rush. 'Thank you kindly for the offer.'

Whatever Felicity had meant to say had evidently rattled her.

'Nonsense,' Seth said. 'A man cannot eat an ice alone. Especially when he has the opportunity to do so with a lovely young lady and a well-behaved girl.'

'I'm not especially well behaved,' Felicity conceded.

'Truly?' Seth raised his brows. 'I'm sure that's not correct. Tell me something good you've done recently.'

Felicity scrunched her face in deep thought. 'Hedgehog was making a sound as though he was going to evacuate his stomach into Aunt Violet's slippers, but I moved him away before it happened.'

Lady Violet gave a squeak of surprise.

'That was very good of you,' Seth agreed. 'And quite deserving of an ice.'

Felicity beamed up at him.

'Shall we, ladies?' He rose, brushed off his trousers and escorted them both to Gunter's.

They ate their ices in the sunlit afternoon with laughter and good conversation. The unexpected detour left a warmth in his chest.

These were the simple moments in life, the ones he had missed during his time as a soldier. Moments where there wasn't danger lurking around him, where he didn't have to plan where he might hide in the event of an attack.

This was a slow reclaiming of pieces of a life he'd once lived, a life he had not truly appreciated. He only hoped he might gather enough to eventually be whole again.

* * *

When the ices were finished, he bid farewell to Lady Violet and her niece before making his way to White's. His pocket watch informed him he was nearly half an hour late for his meeting with Rawley, an offence he knew the Viscount would notice, but would forgive.

Seth entered White's and immediately found Rawley sitting beside a window with a fresh cup of tea in front of him and a steaming one in the empty seat across from him. He got to his feet when he saw Seth approach.

'Dalton.' He nodded in greeting. 'I see they still let you in.'

'Thanks to you, I'm sure.' Seth took a seat opposite his friend.

Rawley shrugged as if smoothing ruffled feathers so Seth wasn't blackballed was inconsequential. 'Is everything fine with Nash?' He settled back into his chair.

'Yes, of course,' Seth replied. 'I met with him and he is looking into the matter regarding the solicitor.'

Seth considered his friend objectively for the first time. Viscount Rawley was not an unattractive man. He had warm brown eyes, the same colour as his hair that was combed immaculately into a crisp side parting. His outfit complemented his colouring with varying shades of brown and green. While not the height of fashion by any stretch, it was finely made.

Seth was aware Rawley had been raised by his mother with not a single male influence in the home, leaving his demeanour, well, a bit gentler than most men of the *ton*.

No man in all the world was worthy of Seth's sister. But if he had to choose one who would be a good, kind husband to Caroline, it would be Rawley.

The Viscount smoothed his hair with the flat of his palm. 'Dare I ask why you're looking at me in such a manner?'

'You're not a bad man by far. Do you know that?'

'I should like to think so,' Rawley replied slowly. 'What is this in regard to?' He lifted the teacup to his lips.

Seth leaned forward in his seat. 'My sister.'

Rawley gulped at his tea, then sputtered out a cough. 'L-lady Caroline?'

'Yes.'

'What of her?' Rawley set the cup back into the saucer with a rattle of porcelain.

'What do you think of her?' Seth pressed.

'She's…kind. Friendly.' Rawley kept watching Seth as he spoke, as though closely gauging Seth's reactions to his stuttered words.

'Is that it?' Seth grimaced. 'Kind and friendly? Come, man, tell me what you truly think of her.'

'She's…' Rawley swallowed. 'She's very lovely.'

Seth nodded. That was better. 'What would you think about courting her?'

Rawley's eyes bulged.

'Come now, she isn't all that bad.' Seth held his hands out. 'She's actually rather a wonder with the household. She's always loved children and would probably make an agreeable viscountess.'

Rawley shook his head vehemently, and Seth's stomach dropped. He had thought the Viscount would have been elated to have claimed Caroline's attention. Rage flickered in the bowels of Seth's patience.

How dare Rawley think himself better than Caroline?

'It isn't her,' Rawley said with heavy insistence. 'It's me.'

Seth narrowed his eyes. 'You?'

Rawley leaned forward so he and Seth were bent together like school children mid-scheme. 'Look at Lady Caroline... and look at me.' The Viscount scoffed. 'I'd never be good enough for her. She's exquisite. Stunningly so. She's...'

Rawley exhaled. 'She's the most beautiful woman in the entire world.' He paused, reverent for moment, then leaned back and helplessly gestured to himself. 'And I'm me. I know nothing of romance or wooing or courtship.'

Seth shrugged. 'Regardless, she claims to have always been attracted to you.' He took a sip of tea and muttered into his cup, 'For whatever reason.'

Rawley bolted upright at that and pulled at his cravat, as though it had suddenly become too tight at his throat. 'I can learn all of those things,' he vowed.

Seth grinned and slapped his friend on the shoulder. 'Damn right you can. We'll be at Almack's tomorrow evening. I trust we will see you there?'

Rawley's face went pink, and he nodded. 'Yes. Yes, of course.'

Seth got to his feet. 'Wednesday it is, then.'

For all that Seth had failed at, he was finally setting his life to rights. First with the solicitor who had stolen his mother's jewellery, now with Caroline in taking the first steps to securing her preferred match. And soon with Lady Violet by making up for the dance he had missed so many years ago. Finally, after all this time, he would stop being such a damn disappointment.

Assuming it all went according to plan, that was. And it had to. He could not let everyone down. Not again.

Chapter Nine

As expected, the patronesses granted Seth a voucher into Almack's. He sat across from his mother and sister on the carriage ride, as dandified as he would allow Bennet to make him. The valet would have worked meticulously for hours if Seth had let him. Which Seth did not.

Caroline's fingers restlessly smoothed over her dress. Then fidgeted with her reticule. Then patted over her hair to ensure it was perfect. That done, she crossed her ankles, first one way, then the other.

'Heavens, Caroline,' their mother exclaimed. 'What vexes you, child?'

Seth's sister cast him a helpless expression.

He gave Lady Dalton his best bored look. 'Maybe it's another tedious assembly at Almack's.'

He'd said it in an attempt to pull their mother's attention from Caroline and, judging from the Countess's pinched lips, it had worked.

'Attending Almack's is what earls do,' she said firmly.

'I'm well aware of that, Mother.' He gave her a tight smile.

Caroline tilted her head in a silent plea, clearly not wanting them to fight. Seth swallowed down his next retort, for whatever good it might do him. Especially when his mother's mood was ostensibly peevish.

At that moment, the carriage drew to a hard stop. Lady Dalton spilled out of her seat with a shriek and crashed into the unoccupied space beside Seth.

Seth grasped her arm and helped haul her upright once more. 'Mother, are you injured?'

She popped up with a sniff and immediately brushed her hands over her coiffure. 'I am unhurt, despite your new coachman's efforts.' She jerked herself from Seth's grasp. 'You must hire another one. This armless friend of yours won't do.'

'He has one arm,' Seth retorted. 'He is learning to work around the injury and will be competent in time.'

'Competent in time?' Lady Dalton repeated, her tone snide. '"In time" isn't good enough.'

Seth frowned. 'He lost his arm for you, Mother.'

The Countess rolled her eyes. 'Don't be so theatrical, Dalton.'

Seth's heart thundered in his chest. 'It was for you and every other citizen of England. He made sure you could keep your fine home on Grosvenor Street, and your gowns with all their frippery and all the freedoms you take for granted every day of your life.'

Seth should stop. He knew he should, but the rage inside him went white hot and took control. 'While you were sipping tea and shopping on Bond Street, men were fighting. *Dying.*'

Caroline put a hand to his sleeve. 'Seth, please.'

He ignored her. 'Do you know that I almost died, too? There was a cannon aimed right at me, primed to snuff out an English officer. One of my men shoved me from its path and took the full impact of the cannon shot. Do you know what the blast of a cannonball does to a human body?'

'Don't be vulgar,' Lady Dalton snapped.

'It's not vulgar, it's reality.' Seth narrowed his eyes. 'Men explode when they're hit like that. In pieces, fragmented into nothing. It happened right in front of my eyes, even as I realised it should have been me.' The memory was too vivid in his mind. The horror too great.

Suddenly, he was on the wet ground of Mont-Saint-Jean with the cannonball moving in slow motion towards Brent, connecting with his body in a violent collision of gunpowder and gore.

'I could taste his blood in my mouth,' Seth whispered, more to himself.

'Seth.' Caroline's sharp cry snapped him from his trance.

He jerked his attention to the present.

Caroline gaped at him with large eyes, bright with tears. 'Please. Stop.' She blinked and one ran down her cheek.

He turned to his mother whose face was entirely leached of colour.

Too far. He'd gone too far. Damn it.

'Forgive me,' he muttered. 'I shouldn't…' He swallowed, unsure of what to say. He was spared having to come up with something when the door to the carriage slowly opened and Burton peered hesitantly at them.

'Eh, we've arrived.' The footman indicated over his shoulder where Almack's stood, its many windows lit with golden light against the inky darkness of night. 'If you're ready, that is. If you require a moment…'

Lady Dalton pushed towards the door. 'I assure you, I've had quite enough.'

Seth quickly alighted from the carriage to help his mother down. She ignored his proffered hand and swept past him. Caroline emerged next, putting her fingers lightly to his palm. She hesitated and shook her head, her mouth working without a single word emerging.

He nodded in the direction of the door. 'Go on.'

'I'm sorry,' she whimpered and slid out behind their mother.

Seth watched them go without moving to follow. Above them, figures in black jackets and resplendent gowns were visible behind the panes of glass, dancing to music that travelled out into the open night.

'Will you be joining them, my lord?' Burton asked.

Seth glowered at the building, opulent, decadent. Frivolous. Who cared who was important enough to warrant a voucher to Almack's? Who cared who wore aubergine or chartreuse or whatever ridiculous colour was in fashion now?

It was all a waste of damn time. It might be what earls did, but the existence earls lived was absent of any substance.

Seth whipped off his chapeau bras and tossed the hat on to the seat of the carriage. 'I can't do this, Burton.'

The footman looked to his left. 'There are carriages behind ours, m'lord.'

'Then park elsewhere while I figure out where I want to go.' Seth climbed back into the cabin.

Burton nodded and the door clicked closed. The carriage took off not even a second later. Only when Almack's rolled away from sight did Seth recollect the one reason why he had wanted to go there in the first place: Lady Violet. He'd promised her a dance.

Bloody hell.

He didn't want to dance. How could he when Brent's death was so fresh in his mind? So vivid?

It should have been him. Brent should be the one at home with his family, with his boys and his wife. It should have been Seth who received that cannonball.

The carriage slammed to a hard stop. Seconds later, the door popped open and Burton slipped into the empty seat beside him.

Seth didn't bother to reprimand him.

The footman looked around the cabin with a slow nod. 'It's fine in here.'

Seth scowled. 'I'd trade it all to be back with my soldiers.'

'You are with your soldiers.' Burton leaned back and adjusted his injured leg in front of him. 'And besides, there are others here who are countin' on you.'

'I know,' Seth replied tersely. 'It's the only reason I bothered to return at all.'

'Harold'll take you wherever you want to go.' Burton screwed up his thin lips. 'He is trying, Captain.' He shook his head. 'I mean, m'lord.'

'I know,' Seth said gently. 'I don't intend to sack him, so you can put that from your mind. My mother can grouse all she wants, but I'm the Earl and what I say goes.'

The footman's shoulders relaxed. 'I suppose there are quite a few good bits about being an earl, then. Where do you want to go, m'lord?'

'Where do I want to go?' Seth repeated the question aloud. 'I *want* to go to a gaming hell and lose myself in a glass of strong spirits.'

Burton brightened at that.

'Where *will* I go?' Seth rephrased the question. 'Back to Almack's, as it is what earls do.'

'I'm certain Lady Dalton will be pleased with your decision.' Burton stroked a hand over the velvet cushion, grinned and slipped from the carriage.

But Seth wasn't going back because of his mother. He was going back for Violet. Though God knew her life would be better without him, he could not bring himself to hurt her again. Not when she was expecting him.

He was admitted to Almack's with his esteemed voucher three minutes before eleven o'clock and was led into the small, overcrowded room glowing gold with gilded pillars and small flames enhanced by gilt mirrors. The patronesses sat upon their dais at the upper end and regarded him with scrutiny before inclining their heads in a grudging welcome. He'd nearly been too late to enter, a point of fact they were all well aware of.

It was hot within the ballroom, oppressive with the heat of all those bodies. He eyed the refreshment tables in the supper rooms. Bowls of nearly clear lemonade and crustless bread with glistening smears of butter sat in an unappetising offering.

No wonder men drank before they arrived at Almack's. All this would be at least a modicum above abhorrent if only one were seasoned with a finger or ten of brandy.

A sweet, powdery scent caught his awareness and drew his attention from the insufficient fare.

'Lord Dalton.' The familiar feminine voice rose above the din of conversation and music around him.

He turned to find Lady Violet standing before him in a pink gown that made her cheeks and lips appear pleasantly rosy. It was the high-waisted sort of frock that hugged at her generous breasts and made his stare long to fall into them.

He kept his eyes on hers and tried to speak through the fumble of his mind. 'Forgive me for being late. I confess, I did not actually want to come.'

He winced inwardly. That was certainly *not* what he'd meant to say.

Violet couldn't help the crush of disappointment at Lord Dalton's statement.

'Oh.' It was a simple response. A stupid one that was really no reply at all.

Soon-to-be spinster forces war hero Earl to attend Almack's. He begrudgingly attends, to placate the poor, insipid fool.

Which might well lead to something rather like:

Soon-to-be spinster gorges self on stale bread and butter at Almack's, dying soon thereafter. Her last words were cited to be, 'I wish it had been cake.'

'I mean, I want to be here.' Seth glanced around them. 'Actually I don't. But I have been anticipating the opportunity to see you.' He grimaced. 'That was bad, wasn't it?'

She laughed, relieved they could both agree it was indeed. 'It wasn't particularly good,' she conceded.

Lord Dalton lowered his head. 'Shall I try again?'

Violet held out her hand in invitation. 'By all means.'

To her surprise, he turned around, then spun about to face her once more and lifted a single brow in a debonair manner that made her heartbeat skew. 'Oh, Lady Violet. Imagine seeing you here.'

'Imagine.' She pressed her lips together to hold back a laugh. 'And what a wonderful surprise to find you in attendance as well, Lord Dalton.'

He cocked his chin at an arrogant angle. 'I believe you promised me a dance.'

Heat suffused her entire body. She had been anticipating this moment since their conversation in the garden when he'd first asked. Then even more so since having ices with him, when he'd been so kind to Felicity.

Violet hadn't been the only one impressed with him. Felicity had commented more than once on the Earl's kindness and might have mentioned a time or two how handsome he was.

Nervousness left Violet's stomach swirling. 'I believe I did promise you a dance.'

Dangerous. He was dangerous.

For her situation. For her heart.

'I have to ask.' He looked about as though ensuring no one could overhear their conversation.

She leaned closer. He smelled of shaving soap. No costly cologne or scented pomade, just clean male. And it was heavenly.

'What did you wish to ask?' she whispered.

His dark eyes fixed on hers, so fathomless she could fall into them and get lost. 'Did Hedgehog have his bonnet removed once you returned to the carriage?'

Violet couldn't help but smile at the silliness of the question. 'Yes, he did. The feather was torn to bits.'

'I don't blame the wretch.'

Violet laughed. 'I don't either, the poor creature. I am, however, quite impressed with you.'

'I don't know what I did, but I am glad to have done it.'

'Felicity,' Violet explained. 'I cannot seem to get the child to be well behaved. But you immediately curled her around your little finger in the space of a single afternoon. How did you do it?'

'I believe, based on what she's said of her parents, that she feels somewhat unwanted and abandoned by them. The best way to handle someone in her position is to make them feel wanted again. She just needs the right sort of attention paid to her.'

Violet had heard Felicity say the same things, but apparently had not listened to the same extent Dalton had. 'How do you know that?' she asked.

'If you recall, I had my own qualms with my parents, or rather they had theirs with me. As a result, I was quite rebellious as a youth.' He flashed her a devilish smile that made the air go thin.

'You were quite the rogue.' And, oh, he had been. Drinking, carousing and flirting so shamelessly with Violet that she lay awake many a night, imagining what it would feel like to have his mouth on hers, his hands on her body.

Dalton tilted his head. 'That's not too bad, then.' He slid a wink towards Violet. 'Rogues are charming, after all.'

'Oh, you certainly were.' Too charming.

He leaned closer. 'And now?'

The final notes of a country dance tinkled to a close.

She studied him, noting the crinkles at the corners of his eyes even when he wasn't smiling, the hard lines of his jaw that had been etched there by war. He'd been a flirt before he left, a wild, wicked second son with too much time at his disposal and an eagerness to fill it with salacious activities. He'd come back weighted down with the burden of responsibility heaped on his square shoulders, claiming to be different; a better man. *But was he?*

'Confusing,' she answered honestly.

'Confusing,' he repeated.

Attendees took their places on the long dance floor.

'And dangerous.' She put a hand to her brow, wishing she could draw those words back. 'Shall we dance now?'

He hesitated before offering his hand. 'Dangerous?'

'Do you intend to repeat everything I say?' she asked. 'It will be quite a dull conversation if so.'

They stepped on to the dance floor, taking their place with three other couples. The opening notes of a quadrille began.

'I would never hurt you, Violet,' he said softly.

She sucked in a breath at his words, but it did not abate the ache yawning open in her chest. Because he had already hurt her. Terribly.

And because she was foolish enough that everything within her longed for him still.

The first pair of couples met in the middle and stepped in time with the music.

'I did hurt you, though, didn't I?' he said perceptively, almost inaudibly from her side. 'Tell me what happened during your debut.'

She suppressed a wince at his request, but it still sliced deep. 'Not here.'

'It was egregious.' His gaze followed the couples pairing up and gliding over the floor as he spoke.

She was glad etiquette dictated they keep their eyes on

the dancers, lest he see the pain on her face. 'Do you really not remember?'

'I was in my cups.' He sighed. 'I was lost in my own world of selfish melancholy before departing for a life in the military. No one cared that I was leaving and I let it get the better of me. Or the worse of me, as it were.'

'I cared.' Violet broke propriety and looked up at him.

It was a brief moment, one broken by the quadrille that had them dancing forward to meet the couple opposite them. But it had been enough to see the raw emotion etched in his eyes. Regret.

The music brought them together long enough to take a turn, but nothing substantial enough to allow conversation. Violet's stomach clenched with anticipation when their part was done and they could once more return to the side while the other couples made their way into the centre to dance.

'Please, Lady Violet.' There was a pleading note in Lord Dalton's tone. 'I must know. Tell me what I did.'

'I... I can't.' It was hard to breathe suddenly, with the press of her raw heart against her lungs. 'Not here.'

'Where, then?' he asked. 'The garden?' His suggestion came in a lowered voice, meant only for her. As it should. What he suggested was no chance encounter, but a request to meet alone. Unchaperoned.

Such things could ruin a lady's reputation and she'd worked too hard to keep hers intact regardless of whether it was deserved or not. She should say no.

But she didn't.

'Yes,' she whispered.

Her pulse quickened at her audacious agreement to his brazen invitation. She would be alone with him. Again.

Except this time, instead of a kiss, he was asking for her

to bare her soul and put one of her deepest scars on full display. And she would do it. For him. Regardless of the nip of worry in the back of her mind. She'd been honest when she'd confessed to him that he was dangerous.

Even knowing this, she could not stay away.

Chapter Ten

Seth's heartbeat slammed with a tangle of eagerness and nerves and fear. Violet would be with him in the garden later, alone. To finally share what he had done the night of her debut. His energy ran high with anticipation, like when he charged on to the battlefield with his men behind him and the enemy in front.

Only this time, he was the enemy. Or rather, the man he used to be was. The egocentric wastrel who was content to throw his coin away and into dirty pint glasses, weighted game tables and painted women. That man was the one who had hurt Violet.

The current man was the one who walked the tenuous line between making it right and trying to keep his distance. All for her benefit.

And as he'd faced his enemy, he would now face what he'd done and endeavour to do what he could to make it right.

The remainder of his conversation with Violet through

the dance had been lighter by comparison, comprised of Felicity's latest antics, Hedgehog's many dashes for freedom and rather agreeable shared recollections on their childhood antics. It was by far one of the most enjoyable conversations Seth had shared with anyone since his return to London.

The elevation to his mood remained after he returned Lady Violet to Lady Hollingston, who practically oozed with flattery upon his arrival. It was then he saw Rawley on the opposite side of the room from Caroline.

Seth had anticipated the two would be near one another constantly. If not dancing, then flirting. Why else would anyone attend Almack's if not to participate in one of those two activities?

He made his way through the crowd towards Rawley. The exertion of bodies dancing combined with the candles lit throughout the room left the air hot and thick. The ghosts of war whispered at him from the shadowed corners of his mind and sweat tingled at his brow.

He balled his hand into a fist.

Damn it. He was a soldier. A man who'd fought for his men's lives, for his country—and lived. Memories would not defeat him. For that was all they were: memories. Things of the past.

He breathed in slowly and concentrated on thoughts of Violet. The way she'd looked in her garden when he'd been about to kiss her, eyes closed with her long, dark lashes fanning across her cheeks, her supple pink mouth soft with expectation. How he'd wanted to pull her against him, to allow years' worth of desire to consume him. In his mind, he trailed his mouth down her throat while cupping a full breast in his hand, his thumb grazing a naked nipple.

His groin stirred and he brought his fantasy to an abrupt

halt. Damn it. He'd almost gone too far. The last thing he needed was to lose his voucher to Almack's for offending the patronesses with an obvious erection.

His mother would certainly never let him live that one down.

Rawley stood only a few feet from Seth. A perfect distraction. He waved to his friend and approached. 'I'd have wagered you'd be spending most the evening with Caroline,' Seth said.

Rawley glanced away and brushed at the lapel of his jacket, as if it was not already perfect. 'Yes. I meant to approach her.'

'Meant to approach her?' Seth frowned. 'So you've not even bade her good evening yet?'

Rawley dipped a finger into his cravat and pulled it from his throat. 'I meant to,' he repeated.

'Why the devil have you not?'

Rawley seemed to shrink into himself. 'I'm afraid I… I won't know what to say. That I'll miss a dance step.'

'You've done these dances dozens of times.' Seth glanced at the open floor where a country dance was now in full tilt. 'Go to her now so you might speak at length before the next set begins.'

Rawley shook his head. 'I forgot my card.'

'What card?' Seth asked.

'The card he carries with dance steps upon them so he doesn't forget them.' Kentworth threw a hand over Rawley's shoulder.

Rawley, who usually tolerated Kentworth's obnoxious behaviour more than most, scowled at his friend and shrugged the Marquess away.

'Come now, Rawley, you needn't be so missish about the

whole business of it.' Kentworth drank so deep from his lemonade, Seth was certain he had added a flask of flavouring to it. 'Why did you do this to him, Dalton?'

'Do what to him?' Seth demanded.

Kentworth rolled his eyes. 'Pulled him from the comfortable shell of his life. I've never seen the poor bastard in such a state. Look at him. He's gone all pink about the face.'

Seth turned his attention to Rawley, who indeed had become a bit discoloured.

Kentworth kept his hand wrapped around the glass of lemonade and removed his forefinger long enough to point at Seth without releasing the beverage. 'You should apologise.'

Was Kentworth truly the man Seth had once considered one of his closest friends? Had Seth really acted similarly in his youth? The answer tightened into a ball of self-disgust in his gut.

He glowered at Kentworth. 'Forgive me, Rawley. I apologise for hand-delivering you the knowledge that one of the most sought-after ladies of the *ton* is infatuated with you. I'm sorry to have placed the burden of an easy, agreeable match upon you.'

With that, Seth departed and made his way to the person who he truly did owe an apology to for how the evening had gone thus far. Caroline.

She stood in the supper room with a bit of dry cake.

'You must be forlorn to be eating that.' He indicated her plate.

She sighed and set it aside. 'Is it my gown?'

Her...gown? He looked down at the white frock adorned with red ribbons and silk twisted things he assumed were meant to be flowers. It wasn't unattractive.

'What's wrong with your gown?' he asked.

'That's what I'm asking you.' She sighed again.

He gave a helpless shrug. 'I...think... I mean...'

She watched him, her brows raised in expectation.

'It's a gown.' He spread his hands wide. 'It's...pretty.'

Her head fell back in exasperation. 'You're no help at all.'

Good God, what did she expect from him with this conversation?

'The flower things are a nice touch.' He waggled a finger at one of the silk ribbons. 'I dare say.'

She gave him an incredulous look and chuckled. 'Thank you for trying.' She shook her head and her dark curls swayed from side to side. 'What did I do to put him off?'

Him.

Rawley.

It was Seth's turn to sigh. 'The man is inept at handling himself around women, I'm afraid. I assure you, the fault is not with you.'

'You spoke with him?' Caroline gave Seth her clear and undivided attention. 'Did he say why he had not asked me to dance?'

Seth caught sight of Rawley across the room, hugging a wall as dearly as any wallflower. Perhaps Seth ought not to be so honest with Caroline. Except that his sister regarded him with wide, desperate eyes. If he didn't know her better, he'd swear she was on the verge of tears. Placating her with a lie would not do.

Forgive me, Rawley.

'He lost his card with the dance steps on it,' Seth conceded.

'He has a card with dance steps on it?'

'Well, he *had*.' Seth stressed the last word. 'Or he would be swirling you about the dance floor by now, I wager.'

Caroline pressed her hands to her chest and her face took on a dreamy expression. 'Oh, he is just too precious.'

For the first time since his return to London society, Seth found himself wishing for a visit from Kentworth. He could use some of that lemonade.

'Seth, I have one more favour to ask of you.' Caroline folded her hands in front of her waist.

'Go on.' He nodded.

She glanced about to ensure no one was near enough to hear them. The supper room, however, was absent of anyone but them.

'I want to take lessons,' Caroline whispered.

What an odd thing to whisper about.

'What sort of lessons?' He matched her volume by way of teasing her more than in sincerity. 'Water colours? Bonnet making? I confess, I know of a cat who would benefit well from your handiwork.'

'No.' She giggled. 'Seduction.'

Seth straightened and looked through the crowd for Kentworth in earnest. He could truly use some of that bloody lemonade.

The house had gone silent the following day. Which is exactly what Violet had been waiting for. She had never set a time with Seth to meet him in the garden and they'd had to leave before she'd managed to arrange it. That had been an oversight on her part, a detail she'd been too rattled by nerves to adequately consider.

Lady Hollingston had taken Felicity to Gunter's for an ice. Violet had been invited to join them, but had declined. Not only because she wanted this opportunity to be alone to venture into the garden, but also because she tried to avoid eating any sweets when around her mother.

If she accepted a treat, she would be lectured on how she ought to avoid them. If she declined a treat, she would be lectured on how good it was to avoid them. Regardless, it always resulted in a lecture and the feeling of utter self-hatred for her plump, impossible body.

Violet leaned against the window to look out into the small formal garden behind their home, most of which was obstructed by the large elm tree. No one appeared to be outside. If memory served correctly, the gardener came on Tuesdays. Definitely not Thursdays.

Violet allowed Susan to secure a straw bonnet to her head with a perfect bow tied just by her right ear. She wouldn't be caught without a bonnet again. Once done, Violet quietly slipped from the house, making doubly sure no naughty feline followed. As she had assessed, the garden was empty. Unfortunately, so was Lord Dalton's.

In an effort to appear normal, she strolled along by the flowerbeds, mainly in areas she thought might be most visible from Dalton Place next door. She marvelled at the roses and the heady, sweet jasmine. She was just getting to the peonies when the click of a door opening pulled her attention to Dalton Place and the very handsome dark-haired gentleman entering the garden.

He grinned at her and approached the hedge, scanned quickly about and navigated the gap between their properties with considerable ease. Violet smoothed a hand down her white muslin day dress and belatedly realised she ought to have picked a more vibrant gown. At least something with a bit of colour to it.

'Lady Violet.' He bowed. 'Imagine finding you out here.'

'Imagine.' She sauntered to him and glanced up from beneath the brim of her bonnet.

He was immaculately turned out, as always, with his hair slightly mussed in a way that made her want to run her hands through the short strands. 'I enjoyed our dance,' he said in a low voice.

Her cheeks went hot. Heavens, was she blushing already? 'As did I,' she replied in a voice too shy for her own liking.

'I'm sorry it was six years late.' A muscle worked in his jaw.

She shook her head. 'Think nothing of it.'

'It's all I have been thinking of.'

'Truly?'

His eyes always were a perfect mirror of his soul, sharp with his emotions. Right now, his gaze reflected painful regret. 'Tell me,' he said. 'And spare me no details.'

'You did not come to the ball.' She shrugged as though it was a small matter to be easily pushed aside.

He took her elbow and gently led her to the shade of the elm tree, where no one would see them from any floor in either home. 'I want to know what happened that night.' His brows pinched together with sincerity. 'Please, Vi.'

Vi.

He hadn't called her that in years. First he'd used it when they were children, then when he got older, he used it as a form of flirtation, as though teasing her with her own name. And how it had made her heart flutter.

The same as it did now.

Her heart raced with such ferocity, it hardly left her lungs with the capacity to draw breath. Was she truly considering doing this?

Of course, not all the details could be shared. Not Lord Fordson. And especially not what had transpired with him.

No one would ever know that.

'You didn't come to the ball,' she said again, this time in an opening to the painful tale. She swallowed. 'I had expected you, it's true. You always had a way of talking to me that no one else did. It made me feel special. *You* made me feel special. And when you asked if you could have the first dance at my debut, I hoped—' She stopped short. She was saying far too much.

'You *are* special.' He watched her with a look of intense concentration. 'You always have been. Tell me, what did you hope?'

She shook her head, refusing to say what she'd meant to. How she'd imagined he might consider her for marriage. The idea was laughable now, but then it had been entirely plausible in her mind. Far too plausible. And foolish.

That was what she'd been—a foolish girl with a fragile heart, too eager to settle it into someone's palm.

A man like Seth, as the object of her affection, was guaranteed to bring her pain. One moment, he would rain compliments down upon her, the next he was out carousing with Kentworth.

She had been innocent then, but not ignorant. She'd heard the rumours of where they went. Of the women of ill repute. Better perhaps that he had broken her heart then in one swift blow rather than chipping off small shards and pieces over the course of a lifetime.

'You came to the house before the ball and told me that you would not be in attendance.'

'I was thoroughly intoxicated,' Seth said flatly.

'Yes.' Humiliation burned through her, as fresh and hot as it had been that fateful day. 'You came into the town house—I have no idea how you entered as none of the servants had admitted you. But you stopped when you saw me and you stared at me for some time. I could see you taking me in, my hair, my gown.' She bit her lip, hating the emotion tightening in her throat. 'You clearly didn't like what you saw, because it was then you announced you would not be attending my ball, or dancing with me.'

Her eyes stung with tears, but she swallowed them down. She'd spent far too long weeping over the mortifying incident.

'Did I say anything else?' he asked.

'No,' she replied. 'But you didn't have to. I knew exactly why you didn't want to come to my ball.'

'Because I was stupidly drinking myself into oblivion before joining the military and drowning myself in my own selfish loathing?'

She blinked. 'No, because of my gown.'

'Your gown?' He squinted his eyes in confusion. 'Why is it women always think it's the bloody gown?'

'Because it was hideous.' A sob rose in her throat at the admission.

'Why the deuce would you select a hideous gown for your debut?'

Ah, and there was the rub of it. Her shame. Not as bad as Lord Fordson, of course, but mortifying none the less.

'It wasn't the gown I had chosen,' she admitted. 'That one was far lovelier with silver tissue glittering over the skirt and sleeves with small silver beading stitched into the bodice. It was lovely.'

'Yet you didn't wear it.'

Violet looked down at the ground, stinging with fresh hurt. 'My mother had the gown made in a smaller size. I know I'm not a slender woman and it has always been to my mother's chagrin. She had hoped the desire to wear the gown would be great enough to make me lose the extra bit of weight I had gained the prior year. There was a second gown made, in case I failed. The hideous one.'

He stared at her blankly. 'Surely you jest.'

'I couldn't do it.' Violet blinked, but it was too late. Her tears had overcome her resolve and one fell from her eye like a dropped crystal. 'I tried so hard. I didn't eat for nearly a week. Then the first dinner party we attended, I ate so much, I made myself ill.' She'd been dizzy with hunger and the second something other than tea or water had hit her tongue, she'd lost all control. To this day, roasted pheasant tasted like failure. Rich with crisped skin, succulent meat that fell from the bone and a gown she would never be able to wear.

It had been disgusting how much she'd eaten and she'd paid the price for it after. Not only with the retching protest of her offended stomach, but also the scorn of her mother.

'I failed,' Violet whispered.

'And the other gown was your punishment?' he surmised.

Violet nodded miserably, alight with the blaze of her humiliation.

'Good God,' Lord Dalton said. 'That's…'

She winced, expecting his agreement at how pathetic she was and that even the promise of wearing that lovely gown hadn't been enough of an enticement to achieve her goal of slimming down.

After all, he'd always been well aware of her size. Certainly, he'd called attention to it on several instances when they were children, like telling her that she could climb trees because she was solid, or that she could survive any illness because she was so healthy.

She held her breath and waited for the words that would irrevocably cut her to the deepest part of her core.

Chapter Eleven

Seth stared incredulously at Lady Violet. His mind reeled with the story she'd told him. How could any mother be so cruel?

'That's dastardly,' he said finally, able to dislodge the words from his thoughts.

Violet blinked in surprise as though expecting a different response. God, he must have been truly awful for her to assume he'd agree with something so vile.

'You thought I would agree with her?' he asked in horror.

'You've always thought me plump.' She pressed her lips together and another tear ran down her cheek. 'You called me things like "healthy" and "substantial" and "solid". And I'll never forget how you looked at me before my ball when I wore that hideous gown.'

He shook his head. 'I meant those as good things,' he protested.

'Good?' She gaped at him. 'How could such phrases possibly be good?'

'Because you're—' He broke off before he said something crass.

'You made it clear how you felt about me the night of my debut.' Her eyes flashed with the depth of her wounds from that fateful moment.

'Tell me,' he said in a tone far steadier than he felt. 'Tell me what I told you that night, how truly awful your gown was. I want it all.'

She plucked a leaf from the elm tree and put all her attention on it as she twirled the stem between her fingers. 'It was pale lavender and made me look as though I was in half-mourning. The waist came too low and showed how round my hips were and the top was cut to reveal my shoulders.'

The description nudged at his memory. Perhaps gowns did truly have some impact. 'Did it have laces crisscrossing the bottom of your skirt?'

She startled. 'Yes. You do remember, then.'

'Only a bit.' He shook his head, detesting himself for the thickness of his intoxication back then that clouded his memory now. 'What did I say to you to let you know how much I hated it?'

'You stared at it for a long time and you didn't say anything.' She bit her lip. 'I hoped that meant maybe you liked it, perhaps it wasn't as bad as I had suspected. I asked what you thought of my gown.'

A memory formed in Seth's mind as Lady Violet spoke.

A memory of Lady Violet Lavell coming down the stairs to discover him standing in the entryway. She'd glowed with pleasure at his arrival, but his eyes had only lingered on her face for a moment before gliding down to her body.

God in heaven, that body.

Her frock had been a creation beyond anything he'd witnessed before. It had hugged her nipped waist and gone broad at the sensual curve of her hips. His fingers had itched to caress the feminine swell there.

He'd crept his gaze upwards slowly, savouring her. The drink had made him heedless of social propriety and time had left him ravenous for the voluptuous lady who lived next door. He'd wanted to take her in, one glorious inch at a time.

Her breasts… Firm with rounded cleavage, tempting as they rose above her neckline. Her shoulders had been bare and gleaming like pearls.

She'd fingered the silk of her skirt and watched him with an anxious stare. 'What do you think of my gown?'

What had he thought?

He'd wanted to kiss her until her lips were red, stroke his tongue against hers, give this sweet woman a taste of wickedness that would make her toes curl. He'd wanted to grasp her round bottom in his palms and grind the hardness of himself against the softness of her innocence. He'd wanted to shove her against the wall, tug down her neckline and take her nipples into his mouth to tease with his tongue and teeth until she cried out.

'You don't want to know what I'm thinking,' he'd muttered.

She had swallowed, her eyes wide and innocent. She had been innocent and he the epitome of sin. His body had swelled with a longing for her curves, with a need he could not sate. Not with her. She'd been meant for another—someone who would be a better fit for her. Not some useless second son who wasn't good for anything more than being cannon fodder for the enemy.

'Is it that bad?' she'd asked, a little laugh in her words.

He hadn't even wanted to make love to her in that moment. Not in the sweet, tender way men were supposed to do with their wives. He'd wanted to pin her to the wall and rub at her most intimate place until she was dripping with need for him. He'd wanted to ravish her. Hard. Deep. Thoroughly. So they were both glistening with sweat after.

'Oh, God, yes,' he'd ground out.

Then he'd turned away before she could make out the rigid outline of his manhood in his breeches.

He couldn't dance with her. Not like this. Not in that gown.

She was continuing the story now. 'I asked if it was so bad and you said...'

'Oh, God, yes,' he said for her.

She winced. 'You do remember.' She wiped a tear from her cheek. 'You were gone the next day. You never even said goodbye.'

Seth ran a hand through his hair. 'My meaning was wildly misconstrued that night. I didn't mean that I thought your frock was ugly. It was that you were...'

Luscious. Sensual. Titillating. Tempting.

God, he couldn't say that. Not to a wallflower who remained unwed at three and twenty. He'd mortify her.

'Beautiful.'

'Beautiful?' Scepticism laced her voice.

'I wanted to...'

Grab you to me. Stroke your tongue with mine. Make you cry out in passion. Taste you.

'To kiss you.'

Her lashes fluttered. 'The way you almost did recently?'

No. Deeper. More passionate. Greedier. Hungrier. Thoroughly and completely until you feared you might die without me inside you.

'Yes.'

She shivered. It was an almost imperceptible movement and told him in every wonderful way how much she had longed for that kiss as well.

Violet was a wonder of sensuality. A woman who would never have need of lessons from a courtesan like Caroline had mentioned the night before. The notion of seeking lessons in sexuality was truly preposterous and nothing Seth wanted to think of now. Not ever, really, except that he'd promised to consider the ridiculous notion and give Caroline an answer later.

He pushed the thoughts of the courtesan and his sister from his mind and instead focused on the lovely woman in front of him. The object of his desire for the last decade.

Violet.

He wiped at the bit of wetness on her cheek from a tear that never should have been shed and left his hand cradling the smoothness of her skin.

She gazed up at him with wide blue eyes. 'Are you going to kiss me now?'

He pulled her closer to him, putting her lush body fully against him.

Inappropriate. Vulgar. Sheer perfection.

'I am,' he said in a low tone.

Her breath caught. 'You aren't going to warn me off like last time?'

He should.

'God, no.' He grasped the blue silk ribbon of her hat and gently pulled the bow free. 'Last time I did, the offer was taken up by a cat.' The straw bonnet slipped off Violet's head and was caught by the ribbons Seth still held. 'This time there will be no one to intervene.' He paused. 'Unless, of course, you do not want this. If so, simply say no.'

He held his breath, waiting for her rejection. It was what he deserved. God knew that. Violet knew that. Hell, even he knew that.

But she didn't say no. Instead, she stretched up on her toes, closed her eyes and whispered, 'Yes.'

Violet breathed in the delicious scent of shaving soap and warm male. Her skin practically hummed with heightened sensitivity, aware of the strength with which Seth held her to him. How very powerful his body was, a wall of muscle.

And the incredible hard, heavy bulk of his very obvious arousal.

That she had brought him to such a state made a steady pulse of need thrum between her legs. She wanted to arch her hips against him so that thick length of him pressed between her legs.

Sinful.

She was so sinful. This was wrong.

His mouth lowered to hers, a tender brush at first, then more firmly pressing to hers, his lips warm and surprisingly soft.

Even if this was wrong, it was also so wonderfully right.

A hungry whimper sounded from the back of her throat. Before she could even feel a flash of embarrassment at the sound, he gave a growl and he flexed against her. It was a wild, primitive display of lust that made her tingle in all the right places. She gave a breathy exhale, and his lips parted hers as his tongue brushed into her mouth.

There was a spiciness to him that encouraged her kisses,

made her long to give more, take more. She could kiss him for a lifetime and still be unsated.

His hand shifted to the back of her head, cradling her in his palm while he tilted her head back and deepened the kiss. Her pulse escalated to something uncharted and erratic.

She had been kissed before by Lord Fordson. But it had never been like this.

Lord Dalton pulled her lower lip down with his thumb and sucked on it, teasing it slightly with the tip of his tongue. No, never like *this*.

She moaned, the sound quickly dissipating between their mouths as he kissed her once more. His free hand brushed over her neck, her collarbone, down to skim the sides of her breasts. Her nipples tingled at the nearness of his touch. Without thought, Violet arched her chest towards him. His hand hesitated next to her breast, then his thumb tentatively swept over the swell of it.

She let her head fall back with a moan. His mouth descended on her throat, kissing with hot panting breaths while his hand closed fully around her breast. He uttered a curse against her skin and swept a finger over her taut nipple. Though layers of cloth separated his digit from the little bud, pleasure danced up through her torso and spread through her entire body.

The pulse between her thighs had become an insistent ache, demanding, needing satisfaction. The bulge of his arousal pressed against her stomach and only intensified her longing. She arched against him, flexing her hips upwards so their pelvises met.

He groaned, a low, deep sound that touched her at her

core. She lifted her face and kissed him with all the lust thundering through her veins.

He broke off the kiss and rested his brow to hers, his chest rising and falling with his frantic breathing. 'We must stop.'

Violet's mind spun, dizzy with desire. She didn't want to stop. She wanted to kiss and touch until the hum of desire throbbing an insistent beat between her legs had been sated. It had been six years since the time with Lord Fordson. She had been ill prepared for that encounter.

But now her body knew. And it craved.

Oh, how it craved.

But hers was a secret that must be guarded no matter the cost. She pressed her lips together to savour the memory of his mouth and nodded.

Seth backed away and stared hard at her, his eyes deep pools of reckless emotion. 'I shouldn't have kissed you.'

His words plunged into her like a dagger. 'Please don't,' Violet said.

'Don't kiss you?' The corner of his mouth lifted.

Lust was so hot in her blood, it was difficult to breathe, to think. 'Please don't regret it.'

He closed the distance between them once more, but did not pull her back into his arms. 'Selfishly, I could never regret it. I only want to ensure your reputation remains intact.'

Her reputation was a sham hidden behind a veneer of reticence. She was a fraud. But she couldn't say as much aloud. How could she confess such shame?

He stroked his thumb down her cheek, tender and affectionate. It was all she could do not to close her eyes and lean into the caress.

'How is it you're not yet wed?' he murmured.

He had asked her that before. She shifted her weight,

unsure of what to say. How did one explain the lack of interest in marriage when in her heart that was exactly what she had wanted? Once upon a time, long ago, before she'd met Lord Fordson. She'd longed for someone to love her wholly and completely and without condition, who truly thought she was beautiful and made her feel the way Lord Fordson had with his lies.

Seth's hand fell away and he backed away to give her more space. 'You've had suitors, though, surely.'

'I prefer the company of spinsters,' she replied staunchly. It was a prim response, one meant to discourage further conversation on the topic. But Seth was a man unlike any other, especially since his return.

'What if a man did wish to court you?' he asked. 'Would you still prefer the company of your fellow wallflowers?'

Violet's breath caught. Did he mean to ask if he might court her? If so, how was she to answer such a request?

'I suppose it would depend on the man,' she stammered.

He tilted his head in concession. 'That's a prudent response.'

The sun had begun to sink into a bed of fluffy clouds overhead and cast the sky in myriad hues of purple, blue, pink and orange.

'I have a rather odd question to ask you,' he said suddenly.

Violet's heart nearly seized in her chest. If he meant to ask if he could court her, would she agree? One was not courted by a man without the intention of marriage if they were compatible.

And what if they were? What if he asked for her hand in marriage? He believed her to be pure.

It was too much. A tension gripped her chest and air was suddenly difficult to draw in.

'May I ask it?' he asked.

She nodded even as her pulse raced faster than Hedgehog fleeing a new fashion accessory.

Seth took a breath, paused in apparent contemplation, then opened his mouth and continued with what appeared to be a difficult question to compose.

Violet's whole body went stiff as he finally spoke. And it was not at all the question she had expected. In fact, it was almost worse.

'What do you know of a courtesan who instructs young ladies?' Seth queried.

'A courtesan?' Violet squeaked.

'Yes, apparently there is a woman named Lottie who instructs the ladies of the *ton* on seduction or something of the like.' Seth cleared his throat. 'It is rumoured the women who go to her marry quickly as men are eager to wed those women who have received such edification. Is this true?'

Violet nodded. 'So I hear.'

'What is your opinion on it?'

Violet gathered her thoughts and answered his question with slow, careful words. 'I believe it to be helpful to the women who require such assistance.'

'Interesting.' Seth nodded to himself. 'And you don't find it at all appalling?'

She studied the rough striations of the elm's bark and hoped he couldn't detect the guilt clenching in her stomach. 'She doesn't debauch young ladies as I understand it. If such a thing does, in fact, exist. I believe she helps ladies become more attractive to men. They are still innocent. And isn't that all that matters?'

She held her breath and waited for his response.

'Yes, of course,' he answered quickly. 'When you put it that way, I suppose it is not so bad.'

And there it was, his agreement to the importance of innocence. A purity she no longer possessed. That she'd been so stupid to have given away with the first set of compliments to breeze in her direction.

She was doing it again now—falling for a man's praises, giving in to clandestine kisses in a garden. Alone. Putting her reputation on the line after having just managed to salvage it after the first transgression.

Had she not learned her lesson already once before? Suddenly she felt foolish. A ridiculous girl who had endured a lifetime of inadequacy, willing to do anything to feel important. Wanted, needed, anything.

Violet turned to the town house. 'Forgive me, but I must be going.'

'Will you be at Lady Cotsworth's ball tonight?' he asked.

That night, Violet would be meeting with Lottie. It had been a hard decision to make. Lady Cotsworth was a known gossip and juicy titbits ran free as a stream through the ballroom of her home. But if Violet did not make time to meet with Lottie, she would never have enough information for her exposé.

Violet shook her head without offering an explanation, swiftly bid him good day and returned to the safe quiet of her home. Her heart slammed with deep resonating thumps that left her breastbone practically vibrating.

She should not meet with Seth again. She shouldn't have danced with him and certainly should not have kissed him. Except that even as she thought these things, she lifted the curtain to view the garden behind the town house and felt a pang of disappointment to find it empty. He was gone, but the memory remained. Of his touch, his kiss, the press of his arousal against her. How desperately she wanted him.

Violet's sigh fogged the glass. She would do well to stay away from Seth, for though he'd returned from war with stronger morals, he was far more dangerous now than he'd ever been before.

Chapter Twelve

Violet spent the remainder of the day alternating between a dreamy state of remembering Seth's kiss and crippled by self-castigation.

After all, what would a man like him want with her? He was wealthy, titled, a war hero and beyond handsome. He could have his pick of any woman he wanted in the *ton*. Surely he was not interested in her beyond that kiss and what he thought he might be able to encourage from her.

How could he be?

She'd excused herself to her bedchamber the moment Felicity and her mother had returned, citing a vexing headache. She'd laid down to rest, but had been unable to do so, even when the warm weight of a furry grey cat plopped down beside her. And while she did not sleep, the feline was a quiet comfort.

Hours later, when the house had gone still and amid a heaviness of her own doubt, Violet slipped on her domino and mask and made her way to the luxurious town house in Bloomsbury. Lottie had assured her last time she would help Violet realise her own self-worth.

If ever there was a time Violet required as much, it was now.

Once she'd finally arrived, was liberated of her disguise and Lottie breezed through the double doors, Violet was beside herself with anxiety.

Lottie paused and regarded her, brows pinched with concern. 'The gentleman who took notice of you?' she asked by way of enquiry as to what had Violet looking so bereft.

Violet nodded miserably, afraid her voice might shake if she spoke.

Lottie sat on a plush maroon sofa and patted the seat next to her. 'Come, dearest. Tell me what has you so upset.'

Violet sank next to her. 'He kissed me.'

Lottie's eyes snapped with a fire Violet never thought to see in such a kind face. 'Did he take advantage?'

Violet pulled at a loose thread on a seam of her pink silk gown. 'No, it was only a kiss.' A heart-stopping, head-swimming, stomach-flipping kiss that went on for ever and yet was over far too soon.

'Was it forced?' Lottie asked.

Violet abandoned the loose thread and shook her head. 'No. I… I welcomed it.'

The rage fled from Lottie's gaze and she gave a relieved sigh. 'Then I am pleased to hear of the kiss. Especially of his restraint and respect.' Lottie's expression shifted to one of tenderness. 'Might I guess, then, as to what has you in such a state?'

Violet tensed for Lottie's assessment.

'You do not feel worthy,' Lottie said softly.

Hearing the words aloud made tears prickle anew in Violet's eyes.

Lottie put a hand to Violet's shoulder in comfort. 'Come now, you needn't worry over such things. You're a clever woman with a sharp wit and you're far too beautiful—'

'Please.' Violet gritted her teeth. 'Please don't placate me with such casual praises. If you genuinely wish for there to be honesty and trust between us, you cannot offer platitudes on my appearance.'

Lottie's dark blue gaze searched Violet's face. 'I think I see a different person than the one who stares back at you in the mirror.'

Violet shifted her focus to the interlacing vines woven into the carpet. 'I'm well aware of my deficiencies.'

'Deficiencies?' Lottie repeated as though she found the statement incredulous. 'Why do you feel this way?'

'It is evident in this body, is it not?' Violet hated the tears burning hot in her eyes and kept her gaze averted lest Lottie see them. She had already bared her soul once that day. What difference did a second make?

'I try not to eat, but even when I deprive myself of all sustenance, I never manage to slim down. And I do try to limit myself, but it's so hard.' Her voice choked off. 'What's worse is that I love food. I think of it. Far too often.'

'Of course you do when you're starving yourself.' Lottie put a hand to Violet's arm. 'Darling, you are lovely, truly. I would not say it if it wasn't so.' She pushed up to her feet and rang for a servant.

Violet squeezed her eyes shut, anticipating being escorted out at any moment.

Soon-to-be spinster remains in such a sorry state that a famous courtesan has rescinded her decision to offer instruction. And, yet again, soon-to-be spinster is an utter failure.

'Bring me a mirror,' Lottie demanded of the servant.

Violet lifted her head as the man returned moments later, carrying a large cheval-glass mirror. He set it soundly on the thick carpet, then promptly took his leave.

Lottie beckoned Violet with a wave of her hand. 'Please do come here.'

Violet grimaced at what she knew she would be expected to do, then got to her feet and stood in front of the blasted thing.

'What do you see?' Lottie asked.

Violet's reflection regarded her with a mournful gaze. 'I see myself.'

'What do you like?'

Violet considered herself in the mirror thoughtfully. She had spent so much time loathing the frumpiness of her body, she hadn't taken the time to relish any positive attributes of herself. The turquoise gown she wore made her pale blue eyes stand out. She wore blue often because of her eye colour.

'My eyes,' she answered finally. 'I like the colour.'

'You have beautiful eyes,' Lottie agreed. 'And such thick, long lashes. I would give my eyeteeth for such lashes. Look again and tell me something else.'

Violet appraised her appearance and noted the smoothness of her skin. 'My skin is very clear.'

'It's lovely. And what of your hair?'

Violet shrugged. 'It's brown.'

'Oh, it's more than brown.' Lottie stretched a hand towards Violet's curls and traced a graceful finger over the pinned locks. 'There are gold tones and even red ones there, too. Did you know that?'

Violet tilted her head towards the mirror and caught the glint of the aforementioned colours in the glass.

Imagine that.

'Now tell me what you don't like,' Lottie said.

That took no thought whatsoever. 'My body, the thickness of my brows, my upturned nose, how I look in—'

'Your upturned nose?' Lottie shook her head and stood behind Violet. 'Your nose is perfect, your brows are wonderfully shaped and add expression to your face, and your body is not at all what you think.'

Violet slid her gaze from the mirror.

'It is *en mode* at present to be ridiculously thin, yes, but it is not worth starving yourself over,' Lottie continued. 'You have a lovely figure with a slender waist and a full bosom. I am candid in my lessons, you must understand. Believe me when I tell you that men love breasts.'

Violet's eyes went wide, and Lottie laughed. The sound was sweet and gentle, not at all mocking. 'I assure you, Lady Violet, you will captivate any man who takes the time to speak with you. You happen to have a particularly nice décolletage.'

Violet regarded her figure in the mirror once more. The tops of her breasts rose round and full over the neckline of her gown. She'd always hated it, thinking it as extra flesh squishing up from her clothing.

'Has the gentleman you fancy happened to glance down

more than once?' Lottie asked. 'Even the good ones can't help themselves from taking a peek or two.'

Violet recalled how Seth's gaze had lingered on her bosom, how he'd cupped her breasts and groaned. Her cheeks burned at the realisation and Lottie laughed again.

'I knew it!' She spun Violet around and beamed at her. 'Darling, you must admit that you are far comelier than you've duped yourself into thinking all these years.'

'I suppose it isn't as bad as I had assumed,' Violet conceded.

'No,' Lottie said earnestly. 'It is far, far better. You are beautiful, Violet, and I do not mean that as a platitude. I mean it with the utmost sincerity. I have no doubt your gentleman did, too.'

A smile spread over Violet's lips. All at once the crinkles of anxiety smoothed from her mind. Seth had told her he thought her beautiful the night of her debut, that he'd wanted to kiss her.

'Thank you.' Violet beamed a smile at Lottie, grateful that the burden of humiliation and doubt had been plucked from her chest the way one might remove a stone from their shoe.

A vase of hothouse flowers stood behind Lottie. A new one, filled with pink and red tulips. 'From a friend?' Violet asked with a smile.

Lottie regarded the flowers with a sigh. 'A friend who is rather insistent, I'm afraid. One I wish I could welcome back into my life.'

'It's complicated,' Violet surmised.

Lottie gave a sad smile. 'Not all past hurts can be healed with time.'

Violet understood exactly. All the time in the world would

not change what she'd done with Lord Fordson. It certainly would not undo her actions and make her pure once more.

Lady Cotsworth's ball had been as awful as Seth had anticipated. Worse. He hadn't lasted beyond the first set. As before, it had been too hot, too crowded, too bright. He'd had no distractions to take the tension from his mind.

Now, he paced his bedchamber and ran a hand through his hair. The footfalls of his shoes were silent on the thick carpet.

At least he was alone. Bennet had been fluttering around him like a nervous hen. But then, William's former valet was a little too attentive in his duties. Too eager to please.

Ghosts edged into Seth's thoughts—Brent's bright blue eyes, afraid in that fraction of a moment before his life had ended. Brave. Selfless. Death.

A knot of emotion lodged in Seth's throat.

It should have been him, damn it.

He lifted his glass of brandy and hurled it at the fireplace in a surge of rageful energy. The glass hit the hearth and shattered into pieces as the liquid flared in the flames.

It should have been him.

He sank on to a leather chair before the broad fireplace and cradled his head in his hands, squeezing, as if he could crush the images from his thoughts.

Think of Violet. Think of that kiss.

He brought it forefront in his mind and immediately the knots in his upper back melted. Her mouth, sweet and soft, that delicious moan that spoke of passion hidden beneath her reserved exterior. It had been torture to stop. But he knew if he kept going, he wouldn't be able to control where his hands went. How he'd longed to learn the body he'd dreamt of for so long, eliciting more of those breathless little whimpers of pleasure.

A knock came at the door. An unwelcome interruption. He'd told Bennet he didn't wish to be disturbed, but clearly the old valet wouldn't be so easily put off.

Startled from his fantasies, he shifted his focus to the ornamental carving on the corner of the fireplace. It was a medallion with a corner chipped off and repainted with the same white paint as the other. He'd never noticed it until now. The house was full of these old wounds that had been polished over with paint, with stucco. Even with the fresh covering, the old wounds were still there beneath, pocked and chipped and broken.

A knock came again.

He scrubbed a hand over his face. The urge to roar at his intruder gripped him. He didn't want this disturbance to ruin the solace his aching head so sorely needed.

The knocking finally stopped. The reprieve, however, was short lived and followed by the soft click of the doorknob.

'Leave me,' he said from the cradle of his hands where he held his face.

'Seth.' The quiet, feminine voice was tender and painfully familiar.

He didn't want her to see him, not like this. 'Please, Caroline.'

The rustle of her skirts whispered across the room and carried with it the gentle scent of lilacs as she sank on to the floor in front of him.

'You left the ball early.' Her tone was absent of accusation. 'Bennet told us you were unwell.'

'I am and I'd very much like to be left alone.' He kept his

hands over his face, desperate to be rid of her. To be rid of all people. He wanted nothing more than the press of solace, without questions, without concern or probing glances.

He'd left the ball almost as soon as he'd arrived. And even those few moments had been unbearable. The woman he'd been speaking with, a marquess's daughter who had just been introduced to him and whose name he couldn't recall, had prattled on, her shrill voice like sharp-edged pins in his ears, her cloying perfume suffocating. He had been rude, no doubt.

He didn't care.

He couldn't care.

There was so little of himself left to worry over it.

'Seth, what troubles you so?' She put her hands over his and carefully lowered them. 'You haven't been the same since you've returned. We used to talk.'

He kept his gaze fixed on the floor, not wanting to respond, not bothering to look up. Not when it took so much energy to do so.

He *used to* tell her everything long ago. When life was simple. When the worst weight on his conscience had been infuriating their mother or staying out until dawn. Long before he'd spent years fighting one battle after another, watching men die in front of him, facing down death with each new fight. Waterloo. His chest went tight.

'Seth.' Caroline raised his face to look at her. 'Do you remember how we used to talk late into the night?'

He nodded, unable to speak around the ache knotting at the back of his throat. What would it be like to tell her, to share the burden of memories slowly crushing beyond the armour of his ribs and squeezing his heart, his lungs?

Could he truly tell her how every time he closed his eyes,

he saw that cannonball hit Brent? Could he tell her how social engagements with the crush of bodies and rise of a collective body heat was enough to put him back in the centre of that terrible battle on Mont-Saint-Jean?

Even thinking of saying these things aloud brought the stinging threat of tears to his eyes. He slid his gaze from hers lest she see his shame, his cowardice. He was a soldier, a man who led others into battle, not some weeping ninny.

'Is it because of the man you mentioned?' Caroline asked. 'Your soldier who...' Her words trailed off, as though she couldn't bring herself to repeat what he'd shared.

His mother had scarcely spoken to him since that incident, so appalled by the details he had so crassly thrown at her in spite. The reminder of what he'd said summoned him back to his senses.

He had not returned to London and assumed the earldom to be Caroline's confidant. No, he was here as man of the house to care for her and Lady Dalton. To be their pillar of strength. He could not let them know how terribly he crumbled beneath his polished exterior.

She didn't need to know that his skull was etched deep inside with horrors, or how he dreaded sleep and the awful terrors the night brought, or how simple memories could make his heart race, his breath pant.

He cleared his throat, breaking through the hurt.

Be a man, damn it.

'I have been in communication with Lottie,' he said finally.

Caroline frowned. 'We don't have to talk about that now.'

But they did. *He* did. 'She will see you tomorrow evening, just after midnight,' he continued. 'You'll need to wear a domino and mask, both of which have been provided.' He indicated the box tied with a black silk bow that had been delivered while they were at Lady Cotsworth's ball.

Caroline shook her head. 'Seth, we can discuss my lessons with Lottie tomorrow.'

'I meant to give it to you in the morning.' He proceeded on as if she had not spoken, in an effort to be well and done with the conversation. He lifted a shoulder in a casual shrug. 'Since you are here, it seems rather ridiculous to hold off on giving it to you.'

Caroline didn't move to take the box. She stood upright, the red silk of her fine evening gown crumpled and crinkled from where she'd knelt in front of him as she pleaded with him. Her gaze was fixed on him now, glistening with pain.

'I don't know why you won't talk to me,' she said with measured words. 'Something has been hollowing you out from the inside and it's breaking my heart to see it.'

The knot returned to Seth's throat, tighter and causing a deep ache.

Caroline gave a chagrined nod. 'I am always here if you change your mind.'

Seth kept his face impassive despite the storm of emotion raging inside of him. Caroline was the one person he had tried the hardest to never let down. Until, apparently, this moment.

She looked at the box with the black-silk ribbon and issued forth a quiet sigh. 'Thank you for allowing me to see Lottie. I know that was not an easy decision.'

'I want you to be happy.'

Caroline gave a wry smile. 'The same as I want for you, dear Brother.' She leaned forward, pressed a kiss to his cheek and departed the room, leaving the box from Lottie behind.

Seth pushed up from the chair and made his way to the window. The curtains were drawn, thick, heavy things that they were, but he had a mind for one last look at the elm tree before descending into the hell that passed for sleep these days. Perhaps visions of an angel would keep him from the devil's clutches this night.

He pushed aside the heavy green velvet and looked out to the garden below that adjoined to his. A hackney drove up to the back of the town house next door and a woman alighted from the carriage, the same woman he had seen before.

Except this time, he recognised that domino and mask. They were the very same ones sitting in the box with the black-silk ribbon that he'd received for Caroline. From Lottie.

The realisation struck him like a jolt of lightning. Lady Violet had been attending clandestine lessons with a courtesan.

Chapter Thirteen

Violet kept her head down as she navigated through the garden at the back of her home, intent on the rear door where she would be safe. Her heart galloped in her chest as her feet swished over the low-cut grass.

How did people sneak about without their hearts giving out?

She was only halfway to her destination when the worst sound cut through the silent night air: that of a door opening. And not the one she ran towards. She pulled the hood of her domino low and prayed that she might, by some miracle, blend in with the darkness and remain unseen.

That, however, was not to be the case.

'Lady Violet,' Seth's voice called quietly out to her.

If she were more adept at illicit activities, she might have been able to continue on as though she had heard nothing, then feign ignorance with an expert skill the following day. But Violet was an obedient girl. She always had been.

With the exception, of course, of that night of her debut.

And she'd paid dearly for it and would continue to do so for the rest of her life.

She snapped bolt upright at the sound of her name being called and—horror of horrors—issued forth an anxious squeak.

'I didn't mean to frighten you.' He spoke in a hushed tone, clearly trying to keep from calling attention to them.

'Oh.' She waved a hand, the gesture stiff and awkward. 'You didn't. I was just...in the garden...um...admiring the flowers?' She turned a hopeful glance in his direction.

'You should see the peonies,' he offered drily. 'They're quite lovely this time of year if you can see them through your mask.'

'I thought violets were your favourite,' she said, unable to help herself.

'Oh, indeed they are. The loveliest by far.' He tilted his head at her. 'Even when adorned all in black with her beautiful face covered.'

Beautiful.

Lottie had called her beautiful. Indeed, when Violet stood before the mirror and opened her heart to what Lottie told her, Violet had even *felt* beautiful.

The very thought of it bolstered her confidence.

She made her way over to the hedge separating their properties and gave him a coy smile. 'Is it not mysterious?'

He wasn't wearing a jacket or cravat and his shirt was untied at the neck, revealing his strong throat. Such an appearance was decidedly improper and intimate.

'Oh, very mysterious.' His gaze skimmed her face, flicked down to her bosom, visible through the parted cloak, then darted away.

Violet almost chuckled at that. Lottie had been right. Men could not help themselves. Even the good ones.

'Dare I ask what illicit activities you've been engaged in this evening?' He lifted his brow in a very earl-like manner.

Her face flamed hot and she was glad for the shadows cast over the darkened garden. She ought to make up a benign lie. Gambling would be an optimal choice.

It was not unheard of for ladies to don disguises such as the one Violet now wore and attend gaming hells. But if he probed her with questions or for answers, ones he well knew the answer to from his past experiences, she would certainly falter.

'May I guess?' he asked.

Violet swept her hand to him, palm up in invitation. 'By all means.'

'There is only one reason I can think that would have Lady Violet Lavell, notoriously missish wallflower, slinking through the night in a disguise.'

Violet lifted her chin, giving him her full attention.

He strode towards the gap in the hedge. 'You're burgling the homes along Grosvenor Street and you plan to abscond with your booty to a faraway island.' He made his way through the gap with two large, careful steps. 'Or you're attending private lessons from the very courtesan I asked you about.'

Violet wanted the ground to open up and swallow her. She regarded the firm soil underfoot and knew such a thing would be impossible. There was nothing for it but to tell the truth.

'You've caught me.' She put up her hands in surrender as he stepped closer. 'Do you think diamonds or rubies for my first day sailing in search of an island to inhabit?'

'Sapphires,' he answered without hesitation. 'With the blue of your eyes and the brilliant ocean at your back, you'll look utterly enchanting. Dare I ask if you need a second in command for this ship you intend to...commandeer? I do have considerable experience in battle.'

'Very well,' she replied breezily. 'I'd considered hiring a pirate, but I believe you'll do quite nicely.'

'I hope not to disappoint.' There was a note of sensuality hovering above his words.

Violet's skin flushed with desire and her heart doubled its beat.

He stepped closer, narrowing the distance between them and carrying with him that clean, wonderful scent of his soap and sensual tease of warm male. 'Why are you, of all women, seeking out Lottie?' he asked.

She parted her lips, uncertain what to say.

'If that is indeed where you've been.' His brows furrowed. 'Unless you have a lover...?' The question hung in the air with uncertainty.

'No,' Violet gasped. 'Of course not.'

Seth's mouth curled into an easy smile that made her recall the feel of his kiss.

'Yes, I've been seeing Lottie.' Violet glanced away with her admission, too embarrassed to watch his expression as she confessed.

'Because you can't get a husband?' Seth probed.

Violet sighed, hating how her whole body burned in what must be the greatest blush in all of London. She couldn't tell him of her plans with her gossip column, so she had no choice but to lie. 'Yes,' she breathed.

The skin around Seth's eyes tightened. 'The men of the *ton* are all fools.' He tenderly took her hand and lifted it to his lips. 'You don't need Lottie to help you win a husband, my darling Violet.'

A clash of emotions lurched through Violet. Excitement for the implication that there might be a man who was not a fool, one who was ready to claim her hand in marriage. Fear of having to be honest with him about her ruination.

Could she do it?

'What do you mean?' she asked through numb lips.

He took her hand and bent over it, delivering a tender kiss on her gloved knuckles. 'Good evening, Lady Violet.'

'What do you mean?' she asked again, her heart thudding so violently in her chest, she worried she might retch.

He straightened with a wink. 'Time will tell.'

He was impossibly handsome with his mussed hair and dark eyes, the way he watched her as though she were the only woman in all of existence. It would not be the way he would regard her if she was forced to reveal her greatest, darkest secret.

Her stomach slid down to her toes as he picked his way through the gap in the hedge and returned to his own home. She stayed beneath the elm tree for a long moment, letting her racing pulse still to a heavy, dread-filled beat.

What had she got herself into?

Seth hoped the odour of the public house wouldn't stick with him after his departure. Especially not with what he planned to do once his meeting with Nash had concluded. He couldn't possibly go reeking of old tallow smoke, sweat and ale.

Even in mid-afternoon, the interior of the public house was awash with shadows despite the weak sunshine trying to eke its way through the dirty paned windows. The seats around them were full, mostly with men who appeared defeated and tired, some wearing the vivid red jackets of soldiers who had fought for the British Army at Waterloo.

Seth fixed his attention on Nash.

The former Runner hunched over his drink as though he could curl into himself and disappear. 'After Pattinson left London, he made his way to Bath. He was recognised and promptly left before the ball at the Upper Assembly Rooms that evening.'

'Where did he go afterwards?' Seth demanded. 'Did he attempt to sell the jewels?'

Nash's gaze slid about the room, taking note of every soul who entered, every person who rose or sat. He never once moved his head, keeping his actions discreet. 'No one has seen the jewels. I'll notify you if I locate them.'

'You'll find where he went next?' Seth lifted his glass of porter and took a sip of the heavy, dark brew.

Nash nodded. 'I hear the bastard is skittish, so I can't move as swiftly as I'd prefer. I'll report back to you once I have more information.'

Nash's eyes tightened.

'What is it?' Seth asked.

'Sometimes these men emerge after Parliament recesses, when everyone departs for their country estates.'

Seth tapped his finger on the spotted glass of his porter. 'It doesn't matter how long it takes. I want him brought to justice.'

'Then it will be done.' Nash lifted his own glass and the two men drank their beer down.

Seth swallowed a second time to clear the grittiness of the dregs, thanked the man and took his leave out into the muddy streets where a hackney awaited him. He didn't have to sniff his jacket to know it held the fetid odour of stale tallow smoke.

It was indeed fortunate then that he lived directly next door to his destination: Hollingston House.

Bennet was beside himself with unmitigated elation as he helped Seth into his second outfit that day. The valet even insisted on another shave and proceeded to do so with such a skilled hand, Seth didn't feel a whisper of chafed skin afterward. The old valet might be a missish sort with a proclivity towards meticulous detail, but he did do a damn good job.

Seth looked in the mirror and nodded in approval. He looked far more respectable than he was. Even his unruly hair had been combed smooth. 'Good God, man, you are a wonder at what you do.'

Bennet puffed out his chest with pride. 'It's kind of you to say, my lord.'

'Well, it's the truth.' Seth clapped the man on the shoulder with gratitude. 'Thank you.'

With that, Seth made his way next door and requested a moment of Lord Hollingston's time. Nerves jittered through him as he wondered if he was doing the right thing. For him, yes. But for her...?

He was summoned almost immediately into the Earl's study, before he could allow himself the luxury of second-guessing his decision further.

There was a lot you could tell by the items a man surrounded himself with. Those who had paintings of every family member since the dawn of time had a tendency to look down their nose at anyone less aristocratic than they. Men who kept an array of liquors readily available, lined up in various shades of amber in cut-crystal decanters, had a penchant for alcohol.

Then there was Lord Hollingston who had simply books. A considerable number of books. The shelves covered the walls from the thickly padded carpet to the scrollwork on the ceiling above.

'Lord Dalton, forgive my delay in greeting you upon your return.' Hollingston rose from his seat behind the large desk. 'Thank you for requesting to see me.'

Seth crossed the room and shook Hollingston's hand. 'I confess I came with a purpose today.' He hadn't realised how hot his palms had become until they were encased in Hollingston's cool, dry hand.

An uncomfortable unease crept into Seth's awareness. He hadn't anticipated being so nervous.

'I assumed as much.' Hollingston's eyes crinkled with a smile. He went to a side table with one small decanter upon it, splashed a finger of liquid into a glass and handed it to Seth. 'I'm afraid all I have is brandy.'

Seth would take straight fire at this point. He accepted the glass with an appreciative nod. 'Brandy is fine, thank you.'

The Earl poured a second glass and sat in the large chair behind the desk. 'Please have a seat.'

Seth settled into proffered chair, which gave a wretched groan of ancient springs beneath his weight.

What the devil?

Seth cleared his throat to mask the creak of the springs still grumbling underneath him. 'I'm here to ask if you might consider allowing me to court your daughter.'

Hollingston furrowed his brows. 'You want to court Violet.'

'I do.' And it was true. Seth had wanted to court Violet

for the better part of his life. Only, he had known she could do better. He still knew she could do better. But he would be damned if he let her attend lessons with a courtesan because she felt she wasn't good enough.

Hedgehog leapt on to the desk at that very moment in one deft move and splayed out on the polished surface. Hollingston untied the green bonnet from the cat's head, tossed it aside with disdain and rubbed at the fur between the feline's ears. 'Why?'

'I beg your pardon?' Seth asked.

Hedgehog's vibrating purr occupied the silence between them. Hollingston continued to stroke the little beast. 'Violet is my fifth daughter and her dowry is not as substantial as a first-born debutante who is seeking an eligible earl.' He lifted his gaze from the cat to Seth.

'Money is of little concern to me,' Seth replied.

Hollingston lifted his brows and frowned, tilting his head as though considering such a response. 'My daughter has been uninterested in marriage for years. Are you aware of this?'

'Perhaps she hadn't met the right eligible Earl.' Seth had said it in a bid to sound confident, but the words came out with an arrogant edge. He was certainly the furthest thing from the right eligible Earl. How the devil was he supposed to convince her father he was?

Hollingston speared him with a glare. 'You broke her heart the night of her debut. Do not think that has been forgotten.'

Seth shifted on the chair and it gave out a squeal. He immediately stilled. 'I haven't forgotten either.' Seth considered his next words carefully. 'I have apologised for my shortcomings to Lady Violet and explained my flawed frame of mind then. I was a troubled youth.'

Hollingston snorted.

'A *very* troubled youth,' Seth amended. 'I'm not that man any more and have been trying to prove it since I returned.'

Only he was still flawed. With different demons. It would be best to put an end to this now, to simply walk out. But thoughts of Violet—her laugh, her smile, her kiss—stayed his concerns and left him rooted in the squeaky chair.

A door closed somewhere on the first floor. Hedgehog leapt from the desk and darted from the room.

Hollingston chuckled. 'We all come second to Felicity.'

'I believe Lady Violet's opinion of marriage might have altered,' Seth continued.

Hollingston leaned back into his large chair. 'Oh? Why do you say that?'

Why else would Lady Violet be attending lessons with Lottie if not to seek out a husband? Seth nearly asked the question aloud, but the questioning look on the older man's face stopped him.

Confound it. Lord Hollingston did not know his daughter was having lessons with the notorious former courtesan.

'People change,' Seth said simply.

Hollingston nodded slowly. 'If what you say is true and my Violet truly has had a change of heart, then I give you my permission to ask if she is willing to be courted by you. If she says yes—and that is a very heavy *if*—then you have my permission.'

'Thank you, Lord Hollingston.' Seth rose from the chair as it gave a rusty cry of indignation.

The Earl simply gave a little grunt. 'Don't thank me until

she agrees.' He narrowed his eyes. 'And if she does, heaven help you if you break her heart again.'

Everything in Seth winced. He would not hurt her again. No matter what it cost him.

Seth smiled at the older man and waited for the servant to show him to the drawing room. The doors opened almost immediately, and Felicity skipped in with Hedgehog bounding behind her.

She stopped short and gave him a fine curtsy. 'Lord Dalton.'

Hedgehog stared blandly up at him, already adorned in a pink-silk hat with his little grey ears poking out of the top through two slits cut into it. Good God, how did Felicity have so many?

'I say, Hedgehog's bonnet is quite fetching today.' He approached them and patted the cat on the head. 'I'm waiting for your aunt Violet. I mean to speak with her.'

'Alone?' Felicity giggled.

He winked. 'I have something very important to ask her.'

Felicity grinned and nodded. She hefted Hedgehog into her arms, carrying the creature like a doll, and made her way back towards the open double doors.

'My mother says Violet is too fat to attract a fine husband,' Felicity said. 'But I don't think she's fat. I think she's pretty and perfect just how she is. And I think you would be a fine husband for her.'

'Felicity, who are you speaking to?' Violet's voice rose over Felicity's.

The little girl jumped in surprise. 'Good luck.' She plopped Hedgehog to the ground, and together they scampered off as Lady Violet rounded the corner.

She stopped abruptly and her mouth fell open in surprise. Her hands immediately went to her hair where the dark strands were carefully pinned into place.

He bowed to her. 'Lady Violet, I'd like to speak with you alone if we may.'

'Let us go to the drawing room, and I'll ring for tea.' Contrary to her words, her smile was brittle and her face pale. As if the surprise of him being there, of the obviousness of what their conversation would be, was entirely unwelcome.

Chapter Fourteen

Violet should have expected Seth's arrival at Hollingston House. In fact, she had expected it. It was just that she had not come up with a satisfactory response to what he ostensibly intended to ask.

She took her time leading him to the drawing room as her mind scrambled for purchase and a logical explanation.

'I trust you are well,' she said politely.

His smile was tinged with confusion. 'Yes, of course, and you?'

About to be ill.

'Perfectly well, thank you.' She opened the double doors to the drawing room with its decorative plaster white walls, yellow-silk curtains and lush carpet. Usually the room gave her a sense of happiness. Now it appeared more sallow than sunny. 'Here we are,' she said brightly.

Too brightly?

'I'll ring for a servant to bring tea.' She reached for the bell pull.

Seth shook his head. 'That isn't necessary, Violet.' He wore a fine, dark jacket and white cravat with a deep-red silk waistcoat. His wild hair had been tamed into place and there wasn't a hint of a whisker on his smooth jaw.

He had taken care with his appearance before arriving.

Her hands went once more to her own hair. She'd just removed her bonnet. Surely it was a mess. Surely *she* was a mess. After a stroll through Hyde Park to help work out some of Felicity's pent-up energy, Violet was entirely mussed and not properly prepared for company.

Or a proposal, for that matter.

She pressed her hand to her chest as if she could catch and still the anxious flutter of her heartbeat.

'I've enjoyed spending time with you in the garden,' Seth said.

Something cold and unyielding gripped her. *Please, no.*

'It's been quite pleasant,' she admitted. And indeed it had been. Why could it not remain as it was? Secret and hidden.

'I'd like to spend more time with you,' he said. 'Away from the garden, where we do not have to worry about prying eyes and whispers.'

'There will always be prying eyes and whispers.' She gave a weak smile.

'I have the utmost care for your reputation, Lady Violet, and will not see you besmirched.'

Besmirched.

It was such an ugly word. It sounded as if it had a big charcoal line crossed through it.

'I see,' she said softly.

He reached for her and, even as she hated the idea of marriage, of being forced to expose her secret, she craved his touch. It was for that reason she did not move away.

His hand curled around hers and he closed the distance between them, bringing the familiar smell of him that had followed her into her dreams the night before. That icy grip of fear loosened, softening with her affection for him.

His dark, fathomless gaze searched hers. 'Lady Violet, it would be a great honour if you would allow me to court you.'

She swallowed.

She wanted to say yes. She wanted to say no. Instead, silence pressed heavily between them as her pulse ticked with a frenzied beat at her temples.

'Your father said you had no mind for marriage.' Seth's warm timbre lightened the silence. 'I gather he is not aware of your visits with Lottie.'

Oh, bother.

Violet cringed. 'I...didn't tell him.'

'I presume your mother is not aware either.' He shook his head. 'I believe I may have got the wrong impression. Or perhaps I am unfavourable to you. I assumed you were interested in marriage since you were engaging in those lessons...'

Those lessons.

Violet's face burned.

'It isn't you,' Violet said quickly. 'It's...'

'You?' Seth suggested.

'Yes,' Violet said miserably. 'I...' She went through her mind, upending every idea she could imagine in search of a proper explanation. 'I am afraid of marriage. It's why I've been seeing Lottie, to help me get over my fear.'

There. And what was best, it wasn't even a lie.

'I see.' Seth's worried gaze did not appear any more relieved. 'If that is indeed the case, would you perhaps consider allowing me to court you? I don't need an answer immediately.'

Violet pressed her lips together. The simple action reminded her of how her mouth had tingled after their kiss, how her entire body had glowed from his attention, alight with desire and pleasure.

Dangerous. Dangerous. Dangerous.

'I'll think about it,' she whispered.

He smiled at her. 'I'm very pleased to hear it.'

'Will you be at Lady Norrick's soirée tonight?' Violet asked.

'I believe my mother has confirmed our attendance.'

'I will be there,' Violet said.

'Then I look forward to it.' He studied her, as though memorising her face. A soft smile touched the corners of his lips. 'You are so very beautiful, Violet.'

His words were like honey pouring over her, golden and sweet and perfect. He lifted a hand to her face and hovered just before actually touching her jaw. She tilted her chin slightly higher, making it easier to touch his lips to hers.

But he did not. Instead, he stepped back to put a proper amount of space between them and bowed. 'I shall see you this evening, Lady Violet. Please do consider my request.'

'I will,' she said softly. 'Thank you for coming, Lord Dalton. And for your patience and understanding with my response.'

He paused as though he intended to say more, but instead offered well wishes for a good day and departed. She watched his proud, handsome figure disappear from the room and her knees went soft, barely strong enough to keep her upright.

As soon as the door clicked closed behind him, she

sagged against the wall, nearly upsetting a small table with fragile notions. The door to the drawing room opened even as her head still spun. Lord and Lady Hollingston stood in the yawning doorway, their expressions keen.

'Well?' Violet's mother came closer. 'Will you allow him to court you?'

Violet's stomach tightened. 'I told him I would think about it.'

'That you would…?' Lady Hollingston gave an exasperated sigh. 'Violet, where are your senses? This is the best offer you will receive. Most likely the only one. You are too old to attract anyone else. And certainly age will not do your figure any favours—'

'Enough, Judith.' Lord Hollingston shot his wife a hard look. 'Is it any wonder she lost her confidence after her debut when you shamed her into wearing the dress you preferred?'

'Is it any wonder she detests the idea of marriage when you offer such an example of being a husband?' Lady Hollingston snapped back.

Violet pushed off the wall and waited for their bickering to stop. Their disagreements were a common occurrence. They used to hide their lack of affection for one another, but it had become more open as the years crept onwards and the house emptied of children.

Theirs was indeed an unhappy marriage, but that had never been the cause of Violet's trepidation. If anything, it had been the reason she'd wanted to wed, to escape.

'If you feel as though you can mother her better than me, then by all means.' Lady Hollingston held her hand out in invitation towards Violet and quit the room with her back ramrod straight and her skirt whipping around her ankles.

'Should I call you Mother now?' Violet asked with a little smile.

He scoffed. 'Insult me and see where it gets you.' He winked to soften his words. 'Lord Dalton seemed to think you had taken a liking to him. That perhaps you had changed your mind about marriage. Is that true?'

'I do like Lord Dalton,' she said cautiously.

'You do know not all marriages are like the one I have with your mother.' He cast a scowl over his shoulder. 'I didn't even much care for her when we first wed. Her family was ridiculously wealthy.' He sighed. 'And my title had little behind it but a name.'

Violet said nothing, afraid of interrupting this rare confession from her father. Generally his life, his past, was something he did not speak of.

As abruptly as it had started, it stopped. He smiled at her. 'If you enjoy Lord Dalton's company and you promised to think about the matter, I hope you truly take it into careful consideration. It would be a shame to lose out on a good match due to pride.'

He pressed a kiss to her forehead and left her in the capacious room with a war of indecision raging in her mind.

Was it worth the risk?

As soon as Seth entered the soirée, Rawley was at his side, asking after Caroline.

'Even if I told you she was here, which she isn't, you wouldn't do a thing about it.' Seth frowned at his friend, fighting back the temptation to tell Rawley what Caroline had been reduced to doing because of his crippling shyness.

'I keep meaning to approach her.' Rawley swiped a hand over his parted hair. 'I even walk towards her, but every time I get close, once I see her...' Rawley shook his head. 'She's so beautiful.' He pressed his lips together like an old man. 'I believe you may be mistaken about her feelings. Surely she doesn't mean *me*.'

'She does mean you and you're driving her mad with your inability to approach her.' Seth tried to keep his tone tolerant.

Rawley was a good man. A shy one, but a good one, none the less. It was on the edge of Seth's tongue to tell the Viscount the lengths he'd forced Caroline to go to in seeking lessons from Lottie.

In the end, Seth swallowed the words down and patted his friend on the shoulder. 'Out of consideration for my sanity and the number of times I must endure your name being brought to my attention, please speak to her when next you see her.'

Rawley grinned at Seth. 'Truly?'

'Truly.' Seth grimaced. 'I don't know how much more I can stomach hearing about Lord Rawley.' He put the back of his hand to his brow in mockery of a feminine swoon.

'Now you're just being rude,' Rawley accused despite the twinkle in his eyes.

'I wish that was indeed the way of it,' Seth muttered.

A woman with dark hair in a lovely white-silk gown with blue ribbons came into Seth's peripheral vision. *Violet.* His pulse tripped.

He'd been home scarcely a fortnight and already he couldn't take the tedium of so many balls and dinner parties and soirées. On and on they came in an endless stream. The time they took to prepare for, especially with a valet like Bennet, the polite facade Seth had to plaster on to his face, the idle conversations that required too little of his brain and too much of his patience.

But then there was Violet. The *only* reason he was in attendance at all.

Truly. He had a note prepared to beg off from the soirée, complaining of an ailment he presumed would serve as a valid excuse.

Lady Hollingston saw him and practically dragged Violet in his direction. The woman gave him a sharp-toothed smile. 'Lord Dalton, what a lovely surprise.'

But it wasn't the Countess who drew his attention, not when Violet stood before him with a smile on her full lips and amusement sparkling in her eyes.

'Would you mind if I took a turn about the room with your daughter?' he asked Lady Hollingston.

'Not at all,' she replied, her demeanour overly gracious.

Seth offered his arm to Violet, who slid her hand into the crook of his elbow, bringing with her that wonderful, sweet, powdery scent of violets. She didn't speak until they were out of earshot of her mother.

'I hope you're aware of how happy you've made my mother,' Violet said.

Seth recalled how Lady Dalton had ordered Violet's debut gown in a smaller size and suddenly found he didn't much care about what pleased the Countess.

'It isn't her happiness that concerns me.' He smiled down at Violet. 'You look beautiful this evening.'

Colour touched her cheeks and she thanked him.

The soirée was decidedly less crowded than the balls he had attended to date. And thank God for it. He might be able to actually make it through an evening. Especially with Violet at his side.

'I appreciate you taking the time from Lottie's to be here with me,' he teased suggestively in a low voice meant only for her.

'You must promise to keep my secret,' she whispered.

The lilting music grew louder as they approached the musicians and then softer as they passed around them.

'I assure you,' he said. 'I shall guard all of your secrets to my dying breath. Might I ask a question, though?'

Violet's slender arm on his tensed slightly. 'Yes.'

In truth, Seth had a string of questions he had wanted to ask her, but settled on the one most pressing. 'Why are you afraid of marriage?'

She laughed, an unexpected sound tense with apparent nerves. 'It's a tedious story.'

He'd made her uncomfortable. While he hadn't intended to put her off, he didn't want to abandon the question. As an earl, his duty was to wed. He couldn't see himself marrying some insipid debutante. He wanted Violet, with life brimming over from her bright smiles and lovely blue eyes, with her sharp wit and confidence. The woman he didn't deserve.

There was something about her that settled him. All the anxiety usually roiling through him seemed to calm when she was around. He liked the relaxed ease he could enjoy while speaking with her. As though Waterloo had never happened, as if his mind wasn't terribly broken.

'I don't mind tedious stories,' he replied patiently.

'My parents.' Her fingers curled around his arm, gripping him more firmly. 'Their marriage is—'

A bang exploded from behind Seth. Quicker than gunshot he shoved Violet behind him even as the images descended upon him.

Brent standing straight and tall, his blue stare meeting

Seth's for one brief, determined moment before the cannonball slammed into the young soldier.

Blood everywhere. On Seth's uniform. In his mouth. Hot pieces of the man who had been in front of him.

Oh, God.

Bullets whizzing by him, slow and thick, as if in water, like fat bees buzzing past. Until one tore into the head of the man beside him. The collision of metal with flesh sending the soldier careening backwards...

Blue eyes entered his line of sight, watching him carefully, mouth moving slowly.

'It was a tray,' a gentle voice said as the woman's lips moved. 'A dropped tray just behind you. Come, let us go outside.'

A hand curled around his and he found himself being led through a room that was threatening to close in on him out into the cool embrace of darkness.

'Breathe.' That same voice spoke in his ear.

He sucked in a mouthful of air. It carried with it the sweetness of flowers, a damp chill of night on the edge of a rainstorm. There was no gunpowder in his nostrils. No blood in his mouth. He blinked and found he stood on the veranda with his hands braced on a stone railing.

A comforting heat pressed against his fingers. He glanced to his left hand and found a woman's lace glove resting atop it. He followed her arm to a pair of perfect breasts, then a beautiful face. A familiar face.

Violet.

Mortification fired through him. 'Forgive me.' He cleared his throat and straightened. 'I...'

I what? I'm a coward? I'm broken? I can never leave this

hell in my head? Or maybe, *You should forget me before I draw you into these depths with me?*

She gave him a gentle smile, one absent of pity, thank God. 'You needn't explain if you'd rather not.' Her hand continued to rest on his and he had no plans to move it.

In truth, he didn't care to explain it. He never wanted to speak of it again.

However, he had an obligation to. He had asked to court her because he hoped to eventually wed her. If he were to do either of those things, she should know him. Truly know him.

And that started with telling her the truth.

Chapter Fifteen

Seth drew in a deep, calming breath in anticipation of what he needed to say, what he'd been dreading to confess. 'I am not the same man I was when I left for the military.'

'I'm quite aware of that,' Violet said it sweetly and he knew she misunderstood.

'Yes, outside of all that.' Seth looked out to the garden with the small lamps burning like golden globes in the distance. Half the moon's face was hidden, obscuring the natural brilliance of its light. It looked like a night for wooing angels, not sharing demons.

The veranda behind them was empty, lit by the glow from the town-house windows. The muted sounds of laughter and music wafted from the closed double doors.

He and Violet were alone on the balcony, but for how long?

This was the ideal opportunity to tell her. Why, then, did it feel like ripping off a bandage that had become stuck to the wound?

'I spent a lot of my time away fighting in battles,' Seth said. 'But none was as bad as Waterloo.'

Violet kept her attention fixed on him, her face illuminated by the half-moon, making her smooth skin appear creamy. 'I imagine no battles are easy,' she said softly.

He gave a mirthless chuckle. 'They are not. I remember the first time I fought when I—' His mother and Caroline had reacted poorly to the details of Brent's death and he immediately staunched his words lest he cause offence.

'When you...?' Violet asked.

Seth shook his head. 'Such things are not fit for a lady's ears.'

Violet's fingers curled around his hand and it was as if she had wrapped all of him in an embrace. She was comfort and peace and acceptance.

'You needn't worry about me,' she said. 'I am not prone to sensitivity. And I think speaking of it will do you good.'

He nodded. 'My first battle—it was the first time I took a life.' He swallowed around a ball of tension. 'He was an older man with dark hair that had gone grey at the temples and wide brown eyes. I remember thinking of him afterwards, about his family. His sons and daughters, his wife. Maybe he didn't have them, but I imagined he did and he would never come home to them because of me. It was a horrific realisation, but when you are in the thick of it, when it's you or them...'

Violet's free hand rested on his forearm. 'I am glad it was not you.'

'Sometimes I wonder about how I feel about that,' Seth responded in truth.

Violet's smooth brow crinkled and she opened her mouth

to speak, but the doors to the ballroom opened. Quickly, she pulled her hands back.

The warmth she left behind cooled, but a subtle hum of her touch lingered. Through the layers of his gloves and his sleeves, he continued to detect that pleasant presence.

A gentleman passed them with a nod and slipped off into the garden where a woman's soft laugh rose up from the distance.

The veranda went silent once more and Violet regarded Seth anew. 'If you hadn't come back, your mother would have been beside herself.'

He scoffed. 'I doubt that.'

'*I* would have been disappointed,' Violet said.

A smile lifted the corner of his lip at that. 'Would you?'

'Well, you did owe me a dance.' She lifted her chin in a coquettish tilt that made him want to catch her face in his hands and kiss her soundly.

If all worked to his advantage, if the cards fell in his favour, he would have a lifetime to kiss her. Again and again and again. And so much more.

'I'm grateful for having the opportunity to finally make amends for my foolish, youthful mistake.' He cast a surreptitious glance around the empty terrace and slid his hand towards hers, desperate for her touch. 'I only wish I could have returned to you a better man than I am.'

She settled her fingers over his with a shy glance. 'What happened?'

He knew exactly what she meant. 'I didn't think anything could be worse than killing another man. Until my own men died through the years. Ones who I knew had wives and families waiting for them. I was an officer, a captain—those men were my responsibility and I took it seriously.'

Many of his soldiers did come back alive, far more than other regiments, and he was damn proud of that. He cared for his men more than he cared for himself.

'But Waterloo...' Seth gathered his strength against the tightness blazing in his chest. 'It was unlike any battle I'd fought before. It had rained the night before and I'd been with the fellow officers in attendance at the Duchess of Richmond's ball when we learned that Napoleon's army was advancing on Quatre Bras. We were told to go to our regiments. We had no idea what the battle would become. Many of us were still in our dancing slippers.' He tried to give a wry laugh, but it choked off.

'How awful.' Violet shifted closer and cast a look at the door to the ballroom. Their proximity to one another skirted the edge of propriety, but he could not bring himself to ask her to step back. Even for her own good. Not when her nearness brought such comfort.

'We fought there before moving on to Waterloo two days later. It was that battle...' He clenched his jaw. 'It didn't matter what I did to help my men, we were decimated.' He closed his eyes to stave off the visions pressing at his brain. 'The cannons tore through my soldiers. At one point...'

His throat went tight, cutting off his words. He looked out at the garden to gather his wits.

Violet's hand rested on his shoulder. But he shook his head. For the life of him, he could not summon those terrible words.

'What I saw...' He swallowed at the ache, but it did not abate. 'It stays with me.' His voice caught and he had to pause a moment before resuming. 'The battle was so crowded, we were bumping into one another, and it was hot as a furnace with the blasts of the guns and cannons. It was hell: all fire and smoke and death.'

He rubbed his free hand over his face. His palm had been made cold by the stone he'd gripped and was a blissful reprieve against his cheeks.

'Seth.' The way she whispered his name pulled at his heart in the most exquisitely painful way. As if she understood his pain and accepted him despite it.

'It's not just at night in my dreams.' He stared hard out into the garden so she would not see the pain of his confession. 'It happens during the day as well. The smallest instances will take my thoughts back to Mont-Saint-Jean. When the hearths are lit and there's the chalky odour of flint and fire, when I'm at a ball and someone bumps against me, when the heat of a room blazes from all directions, or drums are added into an orchestra. Who puts drums into an orchestra?'

'The drums were an awful addition,' Violet agreed. 'Or when a serving tray is dropped?'

'Yes.' His head sagged forward. 'This is my worst self, a part of me I don't know that can ever change. I am uncertain if I will always loathe attending social functions because of what emerges from my mind. I may be haunted for ever by memories of men who died too soon, too violently. Especially the man who died for me.'

This was the part of his confession he'd dreaded the most. He'd had it in his mind earlier that night to try to convince her to allow him to court her, not discourage her.

'I wanted you to know this in your consideration.' He looked away as that damn ache returned to his throat. 'I'm a broken man, Violet. I do not know that I can ever be made whole. I think it only fair you ought to be aware of this as you make your decision. I'll never deserve a woman like you.'

She didn't say anything for a long moment. Finally, he turned to study her face in the moonlight and found silent tears running down her cheeks. She blinked at them and swiped her cheeks with the back of her fingers.

The double doors opened and Lady Hollingston stood in the doorway, a foreboding shadow backlit by the soirée. A reminder they had lingered too long outside.

The Countess cleared her throat noisily, calling attention to how close they were standing together.

Violet drew back and cast a regretful look towards her mother. 'The garden. Tonight. I'll give you my answer then.' She swept her hands over her face, clearing away the remnants of her tears.

He inclined his head, knowing the answer he deserved and selfishly hoping against it. 'I'll watch for you.'

She offered him a quick curtsy and swiftly made her way back into the soirée, pausing once to glance at him over her shoulder.

He had not expected his words to sway her towards a swift yes, yet her lack of an answer had struck him deeper than anticipated. It would be better when they were alone, without having to be concerned with potential interruption.

Now came the worst part: the waiting.

Violet was not outside in her garden more than a moment when the rear door to Dalton Place opened. Her heart leapt into her throat and she spun towards the sound.

Seth.

He strode towards her, wearing only his shirtsleeves and breeches, no hat upon his head or gloves on his hands. His gait was sure and confident, not at all the man who had been cracking at the seams only hours ago.

He made his way to the gap in the hedges and stepped on to her property.

He offered a small bow. 'Good evening, my lady.' His voice was silky smooth in a way she found she rather liked.

'Lord Dalton.' She stepped forward in the dark and took his hands in hers, pulling him towards the shadows where they wouldn't be seen.

He followed her, looming over her, so masculine and powerful. But she knew how vulnerable he could be and it endeared him to her all the more.

'You left after I went inside,' she accused. 'I didn't see you again.'

'I don't relish social events.' He stroked her cheek with the back of his hand. 'I only attended to see you.'

After what he'd told her, she understood why he didn't enjoy social events, yet he had still gone. For her.

'I have your answer.' Had her voice trembled as she spoke? She hoped not, but was nearly certain it had. Her nerves tangled on themselves and left her practically rattling.

This was dangerous. Impulsive. No, she'd thought far too much about it for her decision to be considered impulsive.

It was, however, a great risk.

Courting more often than not led to marriage. Perhaps this time together would show her that Seth had not changed from the reckless youth after all. Perhaps she would realise she'd been a fool to lose her heart to him.

But maybe she would realise he was exactly the man she feared he had become, one who could sweep her off her feet and make her fall in love.

Definitely dangerous.

He was gazing down at her with expectation.

She had wanted to say no. It would have been safer, a guarantee that her secret would remain safe. But learning how imperfect he was had swayed her.

He had shown her his best self when he came to ask her if she would allow him to court her, with his hair immaculately tamed and wearing his finest clothes. But it was his worst self, as he'd called it, that had drawn her.

Because he was not the only one to have a worst self.

'Yes,' she whispered.

'Yes?' He repeated her answer with a modicum of uncertainty. 'You'll allow me to court you? Even...even with what you know of me?'

She nodded, pushing aside her fear for once. After all, it need not even be considered as yet. It was only courting, not marriage.

'Violet.' He cupped her face in his hands.

Their eyes locked and the connection they'd shared before immediately snapped together again. His mouth lowered to hers as she closed her eyes in expectation.

His lips were as soft as she remembered, brushing ever so tenderly before fitting against hers. Kissing him again was like the satisfied sigh at the end of a good book, or like a meal when one was starving—it was everything right exactly when it was needed most.

He tilted her head back at a deeper angle and her mouth parted. His tongue swept against hers and prickles of pleasure bloomed over her skin. She touched the tip of her tongue to his.

It was brazen to do so and perhaps spoke of experience she shouldn't possess for her to exhibit such audacious behaviour. But she could not hold herself back. Not when she wanted to taste him and his sensual, masculine spiciness. Not when she wanted her hands on his body and his on hers. Not when she had spent the rest of the evening after they met consumed with thoughts of *this*.

Shared breath panted between them as the stroke of her tongue grew bolder and his more aggressive. As if they were both ravenous for the other.

His hands shifted over her back, sliding lower as their kiss deepened until his palms cupped her bottom and pushed her against that wonderful hardness of his arousal. She gasped in pleasure, her knees so weak with longing they nearly gave out.

He nuzzled her chin with his mouth, then her neck, followed by the sensitive place behind her ear. Delicious chills teased down her skin, thrilling her in the most wonderful ways.

'Violet,' he moaned into her ear.

Her nipples tingled where they pressed into her stays. That didn't stop Seth's hand from curving a path up her body and brushing the nub with his thumb as he'd done the night before.

She whimpered with delight and ran her hands over him, unable to stop. Unwilling to stop. And hoping he'd do likewise.

Her greedy fingers trailed over his chest and the solid muscle beneath his thin shirt. Their kisses had gone beyond passion to something out of their control.

It wasn't until a clattering carriage drew to a stop behind Seth's town house that they pulled apart, gasping for breath, eyes wild with lust. A carriage door clicked open and a woman dressed in a black-silk domino and mask stepped out as Seth drew Violet deeper into the shadows.

He pressed a finger to his lips to show she ought to remain quiet as the woman raced quickly through the garden and in through the rear doorway of Dalton Place. Violet turned sharply to Seth.

He had claimed to be different and yet a woman was joining him at his home in disguise.

'Who was that?' she demanded.

He shook his head.

Violet smoothed her dress and took a calming breath to still her thoughts. They still spun after going from being kissed senseless to suspecting Seth had a lover attending him at his town house. 'You don't know who she is?'

He held out his hands in a helpless gesture and shrugged.

'Don't you dare presume I'll believe she was your mother.' Violet stiffened as an excuse silently worked over his lips.

'She wasn't my mother.' A muscle ticked at his jaw and Violet sensed the truth was near. He heaved an aggravated sigh. 'She was my sister.'

'Lady Caroline?' Violet blinked in surprise. The dark-haired beauty had remained unwed despite many suitors. And many offers of marriage, if the rumours were to be believed.

Perhaps she had vices that ran too deep for marriage. Gambling. Drink. A darker, more salacious sin?

'Did you not recognise the attire?' Seth asked, incredulous.

Violet shook her head and glanced back towards the door Lady Caroline had slipped through as if doing so might recall the image of her more clearly.

'It's the same one you wore the other night when returning home at a late hour,' Seth prompted.

Violet hadn't purchased those items. They had been given to her by—

She gasped.

Seth groaned. 'Tell no one. She insisted and wouldn't be put off. I had no choice but to agree.'

'But why?' It was Violet's turn to be incredulous. Lady Caroline had the perfect figure—slender, willowy, graceful. She was well accomplished and possessed a genuine warmth that made her instantly likeable.

Why would someone like Lady Caroline possibly need Lottie's assistance in obtaining a husband?

'Lord Rawley,' Seth said drily. 'The man is far too shy for his own good, so my sister is trying to see what she can do to encourage him to demonstrate his affections. It's ridiculous, really.'

Violet thought of Lord Rawley with his impeccable appearance. Every hair was in place and smoothed regularly to ensure it remained so. His clothes were neatly pressed and without as much as a stray thread or hint of lint. While polite and respectful, he was hardly a sought-after gentleman.

'She must be quite enamoured of him,' Violet said wonderingly.

Seth scoffed. 'You don't know the half of it.' He met her eyes and his expression softened. 'Though I feel the interruption came at just the right moment.'

Heat scalded Violet's face. She had wanted it to go further, the way it had gone the other evening. It was wrong, she knew. And sinful. And so indescribably tempting.

He stroked a hand down her face. 'You're so innocent,

Violet. Beautiful and pure. I would never forgive myself for marring your pristine reputation.'

Her stomach clenched.

Innocent. Pure. Pristine.

Fraud.

She offered a tight smile.

'May I call upon you tomorrow?' he said. 'We can go for a walk, perhaps through Hyde Park.'

Hyde Park, where the *ton* paraded themselves, on display for everyone to see. He wanted *her* to be with *him* for all to see.

Her smile relaxed into something more genuine and everything within her melted. 'Yes,' she replied. 'I would like that very much.'

'As would I.' He lifted her hand and bestowed a gentle, affectionate kiss. 'Goodnight, my Violet.'

She swallowed. 'Goodnight, Seth.'

He remained where he was as she made her way into the town house where she pressed her back to the garden door once it was closed behind her and gasped for breath. What was she doing allowing him to court her? To take her to Hyde Park? To steal kisses in the darkness and abscond with her heart?

She should never have agreed to allow him to court her, but she had given him her answer and now it was too late. There was no way this would not end badly.

Soon-to-be spinster dared place herself in the arms of war hero Earl, a gentleman far too handsome ever to be with the likes of her.

All was well and good between this mismatched couple until he asked her to wed him.

It was then, Dear Readers, that the lady confessed to having placed herself on the shelf—not because she was shy or uninterested in marriage, but because she was spoiled goods. A social pariah.

Violet exhaled a pained sigh.
What had she done?

Chapter Sixteen

Seth skimmed over the *Lady Observer* column the following morning while sipping a piping-hot cup of tea. Sunlight poured into the window and lit the blue and white room with such brilliance, it nearly hurt his eyes.

Details of Lady Norrick's soirée were described in great detail: what was worn, down to the ostrich feathers in a certain lady's turban that had accidentally jabbed her husband in the eye. Allusions as to who danced with whom, people Seth didn't know well enough to care about. Apparently, the baked custard was worthy of the saints themselves and was described in such gratuitous detail, Seth regretted leaving before having had the opportunity to sample it.

Strange that his abrupt departure was not mentioned, nor was Caroline's absence or even the amount of time he was on the veranda with Violet. Surely at least one of those occurrences would fall under the scent of a social-function gossip hound.

Come to think of it, he hadn't seen himself or Violet's

interactions mentioned at all in the gossip column. At least nothing outside of a brief mention of his return to London. It was for the best, of course. But still, it was quite odd.

'Do you actually read that?' Caroline sank gracefully into her seat across the small table from him.

A beam of sunlight streaked over the table and made the curl of steam rising from Seth's teacup glow smoky grey.

'I wanted to see what all the hullabaloo was about.' He lifted his shoulders.

'And?' Caroline reached for it.

Seth scowled. 'There's considerable detail about gowns.'

She laughed. 'Oh, but did you see Lord D.—that's Lord Devonington—danced with Lady S. in her sparkling gown—that's Lord Norrick's eldest daughter?'

'No,' he said slowly.

'She's barely come out.' Caroline gave a shocked gasp. 'He's beastly old to consider such a young thing for a wife. Last year, he set his sights on Lady Eleanor, now the Duchess of Somersville.'

'Ah, yes. Lady Violet's cousin, correct?' He vaguely recalled the red-haired young woman. He did, however, know Somersville quite well. They had gone to university together with Rawley and Kentworth. He was a good chap with an eye set on adventure like his father.

'Yes. The new Duchess was the first one to hire Lottie to help her find a husband and she landed a duke!' Caroline tapped her spoon at the top of her egg, gently breaking its shell.

'And you've set your cap at a viscount,' Seth drawled. 'I feel as though I ought to be charged less.'

'Oh, stop—you.' Caroline cast him a chastising glance

as she peeled back a sliver of delicate eggshell to reveal the quivering white beneath.

'While we're on the topic, how did your first lesson go?' he asked.

'Capitally.' Caroline dashed a few grains of salt over the egg and buttered a toast point. 'I'm quite sure I'll know exactly what to do when I next see him.'

'Thank God.' He rolled his eyes with exaggeration.

She glared at him with mock outrage and he laughed.

'I only wish to see your happiness,' he said with sincerity.

A smile replaced her false hostility. 'I'm well aware. It appears you've taken quite an interest in a certain lady yourself.' She dipped her toast in the egg so the tip dripped with golden yolk. 'Lady Violet. Cousin to the Duchess of Somersville.'

Seth felt his mouth curl up at the corners. 'She has agreed to allow me to court her. God knows I don't deserve a woman the likes of her.'

Caroline swallowed the bite of toast in her mouth and clapped her hands. 'Of course you do,' she protested. 'I'm so pleased to hear it. She would be a wonderful sister to have. It appears everything is going well for us.'

Indeed, it certainly did seem to be the way of it. How he'd become so fortunate to have Violet to see past his demons, he would never know. He settled his fingertips on the folded note beside his plate, received from Nash only an hour before describing a ruby bracelet in perfect detail that had been discovered just outside Bath. There was no question about it, the bracelet was the exact one that had belonged to Seth's grandmother and was one of the missing gems.

Seth had previously ordered Nash to purchase any of the jewels located and had funds at the ready to procure the valuable family heirloom. Once Seth had the brace-let, he would show his mother and tell her what it was he'd sought to do. After all, caring for one's family and easing their troubles was what an earl did.

Lady Dalton appeared in the room, blending into the shadows with her black mourning clothes. Her cold gaze fell to Seth. 'I hear you had quite an eventful evening last night.'

'Oh?' he asked in a bored tone.

'I'm referring to the inordinate and highly inappropriate amount of time you spent on the veranda with Lady Violet.' Lady Dalton waited by a hard-backed chair for a servant to pull it out for her. Only then did she sink into the seat with a regal air most reserved for supper parties. 'Really, Dal-ton. You should have remained in the ballroom with her. It would have been far more respectful and earls are always respectful. It's what they do.'

Seth bit the inside of his cheek to keep from rolling his eyes. After all, refraining from rolling one's eyes is also what earls did.

'Lady Violet has agreed to allow Seth to court her.' Car-oline waggled her brows at Seth while their mother's gaze was averted from her.

'Is that so?' Lady Dalton lifted her teacup to her lips and took a dainty sip.

'It is.' Seth didn't bother to stifle the indulgent puff of pride from his chest. 'She has agreed to let me escort her to Hyde Park this afternoon.'

'Indeed.' His mother replaced the teacup on the saucer with such grace, it did not so much as clink.

He awaited her praise like an overeager hunting dog. After all, finding a wife was also what an earl did. Courting her and bringing their relationship to the public notice in a very socially acceptable way was also what earls did.

'Mind you're careful,' Lady Dalton said slowly. 'Not all ladies are as they seem.'

Caroline cleared her throat and popped up from the table before Seth could question what his mother meant.

'I must be off,' Caroline said quickly. 'I've promised to help roll bandages with some of the ladies to send to Brussels to aid the wounded soldiers who are still recovering.' She came around the table and pressed a kiss to Seth's cheek. 'We are terribly grateful to have you returned home safely to us.'

Her tone was pointed and sharp and appeared to be aimed directly at Lady Dalton.

'Is there something I ought to be aware of regarding Lady Violet?' Seth asked once Caroline had departed.

Lady Dalton didn't bother to look up from the scandal sheet she was skimming. Not the *Society Journal*, he noted. One she'd carried in with her. One which clearly had more detail in it than the *Lady Observer* had detailed in its column if she already knew about his time on the veranda with Violet.

'Of course not.' Lady Dalton's reply was brusque and cool.

Which meant that there was indeed something he ought to be aware of and Seth *would* get to the bottom of it.

For all the contents of her wardrobe, Violet had absolutely nothing to wear. Poor Susan was red-cheeked and glistening with a sheen of sweat from her efforts of pulling gown after gown from the wardrobe.

The one with the pink roses was too large, the lavender

one was too small, the muslin gown's bows weren't quite right and another had stitching across the sleeves that was far too silly.

'What are you doing, Aunt Violet?' an all-too-familiar voice enquired.

Violet nearly cringed. The last thing she had time for was Felicity's antics.

'I thought my door was closed,' Violet said.

'Oh, it was.' Felicity flopped on to the edge of Violet's white-lace canopy bed and patted the empty space next to her. Hedgehog leapt up to her side like an obedient dog. Though how the cat could see where he was leaping with his large, beribboned blue hat was beyond Violet.

'Are you dressing for your first public outing with Lord Dalton?' Felicity kicked the back of her heels against the bed frame.

Clack-clack, clack-clack, clack-clack. 'You're going to marry him,' she said in a sing-song voice.

'Not necessarily,' Violet protested. 'We're simply deciding if we're compatible.'

Clack-clack, clack-clack, clack-clack.

Felicity gave a knowing smile that revealed a missing tooth. 'You'll be wed before the end of the Season.'

Her certainty knocked at Violet's heart. It was a ridiculous reaction to the claim of a little girl. What did a child know of love or marriage?

'Do stop that.' Violet indicated Felicity's feet. 'Why would you possibly say something so bold?'

Felicity hopped from the bed and approached the pile of gowns. 'Because I've seen how you look at Lord Dalton.'

'And how do I look at him?' Violet demanded, responding to Felicity's taunts despite herself.

When would she ever learn?

'It's how Father used to look at our governess.' Felicity said it so matter-of-factly that Violet was shocked into silence.

The girl continued. 'She was the one we had before all the others. She was plump, like you. We liked her. Father loved her. That's what Mother said once.'

Susan gave a sound somewhere between a grunt and a squeak.

Felicity did not acknowledge it or, hopefully, had not heard and continued. 'Mother doesn't know I overheard that conversation, but I'm sure it's why she's always off visiting with friends and why Father is as well. And they definitely don't look at each other like you and Lord Dalton do.' She pulled a blue frock from the pile. 'This one, I think.'

Violet took the gown with a note of thanks. The poor child, to have seen such a scandalous dissolution of her parents' marriage. 'I'm terribly sorry that happened,' she said.

'I miss Lady Emily.' Felicity lifted a shoulder, as if she didn't care, but it was evident from her lowered gaze she truly did.

It did not escape Violet's notice how Felicity claimed to miss her governess, but not either of her parents. The more time Violet spent with Felicity, the more she realised Seth was right about the girl. She felt abandoned and unwanted.

'Yes, definitely this one.' Felicity fingered the silky fabric of the blue gown.

Violet cast her niece a sceptical look. 'Are you suggesting that because it matches Hedgehog's bonnet?'

'It brings out your eyes,' Felicity said innocently. Then she giggled. 'And it does rather become his bonnet nicely.'

He glared at the three sets of eyes that turned to him and Violet couldn't help but laugh. 'The blue one it is, then.'

Felicity beamed with pride at having her opinion taken and Susan appeared glad to finally have a gown selected. And Violet…well, Violet was simply anxious no matter what she wore.

It would be the first time, the *only* time, she'd ever let a man escort her. Never before had she thrown herself so recklessly to chance. But then, never before had it been so tempting.

With little time to spare, Susan worked a miracle in not only getting Violet into the gown, but managing a fetching style of curls and twists for her hair as well.

Because of her contribution towards the overall ensemble, Felicity was invited to join them, as long as she remained with Susan. Felicity readily agreed. As long as she could bring Hedgehog.

Violet allowed the bartering, seeing no harm in it. That is, until the little girl pulled out a collar and long lead and attached them to Hedgehog so that he could be trotted about like dog.

It would be almost laughable if it wasn't so embarrassing. After all, they were going to be entering Hyde Park at the fashionable hour. Violet nearly reprimanded her, but when she found herself nearly prefacing the rebuke with what 'ladies didn't do', she quashed the protest.

She'd listened to a lifetime of what 'ladies didn't do'. If it made the girl happy to walk her cat, then she could walk her cat. Especially when Hedgehog lived up to the expectation of being highly fashionable.

As they had a gate on their street leading directly to Hyde Park, it seemed ostentatious to take a carriage and meet Seth there. Instead, they had agreed to meet in front of Violet's town house at exactly five o'clock.

'What luck to stumble upon such lovely ladies.'

Violet sucked in a breath at the masculine, sensual voice. It took only a small statement, but immediately her skin tingled with awareness and incredible sensitivity.

Seth.

She straightened from where she'd been standing over Hedgehog and smiled at him.

'You told her to meet you in front of our town house,' Felicity said. 'That isn't luck. It's good planning.'

'That it is.' Seth laughed.

His gaze skimmed respectfully over her and his smile widened. 'That's a lovely gown, Lady Violet.'

She curtsied. 'Thank you. Felicity selected it for me.'

'That is quite an eye for fashion you have, my lady.' He knelt in front of Felicity, heedless of his trousers. 'I trust you and Hedgehog are quite well.'

She grinned at him and nodded emphatically. 'I hope you marry Aunt Violet so you can be my uncle,' she whispered.

Violet's mouth fell open with horror.

Seth, however, simply laughed. 'I'll do my best not to ruin my chances.' He got to his feet, dusted off his knee and offered Violet his arm. 'Shall we?'

'There are only two and a half hours left of the fashionable hour.' She slipped her hand into the crook of his elbow.

'Then we shall have to make the most of them, shan't we?' Seth smiled into her heart.

The wonderful clean scent of him surrounded her, the same as it had the previous night. She'd fallen asleep with that scent clinging to her skin.

'Do you think the ribbons might be too much?' Seth asked discreetly.

Violet startled and glanced at her gown where a narrow line of ribbon ran along the seam.

'I don't mean you,' he whispered and looked pointedly at Hedgehog, who skulked forward on his lead with several ribbons trailing after him from his hat.

Violet smothered a laugh behind her hand. 'It may be a bit much,' she conceded quietly.

Seth winked at her. 'You know I have to ask something of a personal nature.'

'A personal nature?' Violet glanced behind her to ensure Susan and Felicity were out of earshot. As the maid had promised, they were. In fact, it would be easy to imagine Violet and Seth were alone were it not for the cat on a lead trotting a foot in front of them.

'Yes.' Seth regarded her and the skin around his eyes tightened somewhat. 'I want to know a little more about the *Lady Observer.*'

Violet's blood chilled. All this time she had been worried he would discover she was no longer a virgin. Never once had she suspected he might realise she was the *Lady Observer.* It hit her like a hammer and left her reeling.

Chapter Seventeen

Seth had hoped he appeared more nonchalant than he felt. Her agreement to allow his courtship had left him elated. And anxious. She made him want to be better—to be the courageous war hero society expected of him, to be stronger than the tidal wave of memories on the battlefield.

The combination of it all left him far more nervous around her than he'd ever been before. As it was, his question about the *Lady Observer* was most likely ridiculous. After all, what man actually bothered to read such drivel?

'The Lady Observer?' Violet said in a strangely choked voice. 'Do you mean the…scandal column in the *Society Journal*?'

Dear Lord, was she laughing at him?

He inwardly winced. He was as bad as Rawley at this moment.

'I do.' He tried to catch a glance of her face beneath the brim of her straw bonnet. Without success.

He did, however, immediately recognise the bonnet.

It was the same one she'd worn that day in the garden when they'd first kissed. When he'd pulled free the silk ribbon and let it slide from her hair. When he'd sampled the sweetness of her lips.

The garden had been his favourite place when he'd been a boy, a reprieve from the stuffy doldrums of the house where the rules were heavy and freedom was practically non-existent. As an adult, it was swiftly becoming a favourite place yet again, for a series of very different, very tantalising reasons.

They followed the trail of people walking into Hyde Park from Grosvenor Gate. Shade from the large walnut trees blotted out the late afternoon sun momentarily as they strode on.

'What about the *Lady Observer*?' Violet asked.

'It is your preferred gossip column, is it not?' He knew it was, of course, but hoped his aloofness might come off more masculine than his bumbling start to the topic.

Why the devil had he brought it up in the first place?

He knew why. It had been an attempt to find some ground for conversation between them. Between his nerves about finally courting Violet and the intense vulnerability he'd displayed with her the night before, he'd been afraid his mind would go blank.

'Do you feel the scandals reported within are…well… somewhat deficient?' God, he was sounding like a ninny now. The idea to bring up the topic had seemed like such a good one earlier when he'd tried to think of ways to impress her. Speaking about it aloud now made him realise how foolish a topic it truly was.

'Why would you possibly say such a thing?' There was a sharp note to her tone, as if he'd offended her.

He was botching this into a proper mess.

'Do you not think it's odd that she has not reported a thing about our interactions?' He tilted his head. 'It appears my mother reads *Ladies and Notions* and they wrote quite the article on the amount of time we were missing from the soirée when we were on the veranda last night.'

'Surely the author of every gossip column cannot see everything,' Violet offered.

'Then perhaps it is a good thing she could not see us in your garden,' he whispered.

She laughed and surreptitiously glanced about as if she was worried someone might have overheard. A flush covered her fair cheeks and her eyes sparkled.

The memory was clearly a pleasant one for her as well. Good. He'd certainly spent a considerable amount of time savouring their moments in the garden together.

Her kisses had been as hungry as his own, her body so lush and alluring under his hands.

Whatever layer of ice he'd let frost over his confidence finally cracked with her sweet laughter and the conversation resumed between them with a more natural flow. Without the subject of the *Lady Observer* coming up again. Thank God.

What was more, the walk accomplished exactly what he had wanted. As they strolled through Hyde Park, led by an odd little feline and trailed by a precocious girl and doe-eyed maid, every man and woman took notice.

Violet seemed oblivious as she reminisced over hilarious moments from their youth together. But Seth was quite aware of every eye that swept over them. And he especially noted the ones that lingered. He squared his shoulders with pride. Lady Violet Lavell was his to court, his to wed. And he wanted everyone to know.

Prior to the moment he saw Violet with her scandal sheet, he'd never considered reading one on his own. He'd done so only to see what it was she found so fascinating. Aside from making him hungry with the detail in which the food had been described, he'd found them tedious and bordering on intrusive.

Seeing how gossip swarmed around them right now, however, left him craving the need to purchase every one printed about this day. *Ladies and Notions*, the *Society Journal* and anything else he could get his hands on. He wanted to be well aware how many people had acknowledged his courtship of Violet.

When the fashionable hour drew to an unfortunate close, Seth saw Violet, as well as her entourage, home. He could only imagine what the scandal sheets might say about Hedgehog. The idea of it nearly made him laugh.

Seth let the smile of his restrained mirth linger on his lips. 'I've enjoyed myself immensely.' In truth, if he'd known what a pleasurable experience it was to court Violet, he would have done it six years ago. If he hadn't been such a cad then.

Violet slanted her eyes coyly at him. 'As have I.'

Her maid and Felicity stood off to the side as they awaited Violet.

He lingered despite needing to let her go. 'I want to see you again.'

'I'm going to see Lottie tonight.' Though she said the words softly, they plunged into his chest like a dagger.

Why would she need to continue to see Lottie if she was already being courted?

She licked her lips, nervous in a way that suddenly set him on edge. 'I need to speak with her,' Violet said. 'At least one final time.'

Seth nodded slowly.

'Will you meet me in the garden after I return home?' Violet asked with a breathlessness that piqued his arousal.

'I shall be watching for your return.' He offered her a cordial bow, then tipped his hat to her maid, Felicity and finally Hedgehog before departing to his town house next door.

Gibbons welcomed Seth home and advised him that a parcel and note had arrived from a Mr Nash. The quirk of his eyebrow as he said Nash's name implied how the stodgy butler felt about the man.

Excitement shot through Seth. The parcel was no doubt the ruby bracelet. He grinned at Gibbons and patted his shoulder. 'I've paid someone to seek out the solicitor who stole the jewellery from us,' he confided in the older man.

Gibbons opened his mouth, then closed it. 'I'm glad to hear it, my lord.'

Seth narrowed his gaze. 'But...?'

'But nothing, my lord.' The man snapped his lips shut and lifted his head, hands stubbornly tucked behind his back as though he could physically hide the words he clearly wasn't saying.

What the deuce was amiss with the household at Dalton Place?

Seth suppressed a sigh. No doubt the servant was doing what he thought best. Seth couldn't fault him for that. Instead, he left instructions with Gibbons to notify Lady Dalton that Seth wished to speak with her upon her arrival home, then went to his study.

As the butler had said, a small box and note were left on the centre of the desk.

Seth lifted the box to reveal a bracelet of fat rubies arranged like the petals of a summer rose, its centre winking with diamonds. The piece was set in a dainty gold bangle. There was no mistaking the item. Not when he'd seen it so many times in his childhood on his grandmother's wrist and had even seen it on many occasions on Lady Dalton's. It had been one of her favourites as it always reminded her of her mother when she wore it.

She would be pleased to see it returned.

Seth unfolded the note and the elation in his chest dimmed at the words.

My contacts indicate that Mr Pattinson suspects he is being followed. This will cause further delays.

Seth ran a hand through his hair in frustration. If the solicitor had become even more suspicious than he already was previously, he would be even more difficult to follow. Seth only hoped it wouldn't slow progress too much. Not when he was so eager to have the man apprehended before the Season came to an end.

Violet floated up the stairs to her bedroom. She shouldn't allow Seth to affect her so. She ought to steel her heart against his charm, cast aside the trove of shared memories and lock away her dreams.

For that was what so much of it came down to: her dreams. The ones when she thought Seth only flirted with her to tease her and couldn't help but desire him regardless.

The ones she'd thought she'd cast off after what happened with Lord Fordson.

Her stomach curdled at Fordson's name and soured the happiness of her mood with the reality of the situation she must face. Seth's question earlier about the *Lady Observer* reminded Violet she had more than one secret that left her vulnerable.

Did he suspect anything?

His question had been so abrupt, Violet had nearly choked on it. It had been a dangerous oversight to leave herself out of her own scandal sheet. Then again, she'd done nothing to warrant space in any scandal sheet for years. Until now.

Heat flushed through her at what she had done to deserve to be the opening line of the *Lady Observer*.

Soon-to-be spinster meets war hero Earl for a lovers' tryst in the garden behind a town house, where the wallflower found herself blooming with kisses that rendered her senseless...

Goodness how that would set the tongues of the *ton* wagging.

Fortunately for her, that was not the story that would be told. Still, something needed to be put out there.

She flopped herself on her bed, stared at the ceiling and let her thoughts drift.

The door to her room was flung open and the clatter of little feet raced across the floor before going suspiciously silent. Felicity flew over the top of Violet suddenly and landed on the mattress with a plop and a raucous laugh.

Violet shrieked in mock surprise. 'I'm being attacked.' She lifted a pillow and carefully pushed at Felicity with it.

The little girl wrinkled her nose and giggled, taking up

her own pillow. They battered each other with the soft weapons for a spell, until they were both out of breath with laughter and collapsed to the large mattress once more.

Through it all, Hedgehog had sat at the foot of the bed, one leg stretched out while he cleaned himself in a most vulgar fashion. No doubt his behaviour was the result of vengeance for the collar and lead on their public outing. Violet couldn't blame him.

'Why don't you want to marry Lord Dalton?' Felicity asked.

'I… It isn't that I don't wish to marry Lord Dalton, it's that…well, it's a very large step.' Violet pulled herself to sitting.

Felicity did the same and nodded solemnly. The girl had a habit of appearing far older than her seven years. Most likely that came from being the eldest of her siblings.

'Lord Dalton cares for you and I know you care for him.' Felicity pursed her lips. 'Perhaps you can think more about the idea of marriage? You'd be a wonderful mother.' She gave Violet a gap-toothed smile.

'That's kind of you to say.' Violet ruffled Felicity's silky fair hair. The girl had been extraordinarily well behaved of late. All directions were followed without argument and there hadn't been a single tantrum.

'It's true.' Her niece looked down at the white cotton coverlet and gave a little sniff.

'Are you well, Felicity?' Violet asked. 'Shall I have an infusion made for you?'

Felicity shook her head. 'It doesn't matter.'

Violet drew up short, startled by the hard edge to the little girl's tone. 'Hedgehog needs a new bonnet. The blue one looks ridiculous.'

'Felicity?' Violet said.

The cat's green gaze flicked towards the little girl as she slid towards him, scooped him up and ran from the room.

Violet called after her once more, uncertain if she ought to go after her niece or not. As it was, Violet knew she preferred solitude when she was upset. Perhaps it was best to leave her for a while. By the time Violet was finished writing the latest edition of her gossip column, Felicity would surely be more amenable to conversation.

Violet eased off the bed and glanced down the hallway, finding it absent of a little girl or even a beleaguered cat. With one final worried look at the empty hallway, Violet returned to her room and shut the door, leaving it unlocked should Felicity decide to return. Violet went to her desk and withdrew a sheet of paper and picked up her quill. She tapped it against her lip as she always did when she considered what to write.

It was how she'd got started in the business of scandal sheets. She hadn't always been able to find her voice, but she had been able to find a pen. Writing what she witnessed, who scorned who, what victories some shared and defeats others endured.

Most especially, she preferred to write about women who had gone through a rough time of it to come out gleaming on the other side. Like her cousin, Eleanor. A lady cast off so late in the Season for another. It was shameful what Lord Ledsey had done to her, though he'd certainly got his just deserts. After being stripped of his title for attempting to murder the Duke and Duchess, his hand had become infected and he'd perished from his wounds.

Writing about the Duchess's success in attracting the

attention of the Duke of Somersville the prior year had brought a note of vindication for Violet.

It was that idea she now focused on for herself. Except she could not mention Lord Fordson, of course. Or that she was indeed the author of the *Lady Observer*.

She drew in a satisfying inhale then let it slowly exhale out between her lips as she closed her eyes and envisioned herself as she would one of the subjects of her gossip column. It took only that brief moment to capture herself in her mind's eye. She held it there, dipped her quill in a pot of ink and began to write.

Happily-ever-afters can come to the most mundane of wallflowers. A certain lady once deemed too plump for marriage and all but set firmly upon the shelf has finally found a man to draw her from the background she'd spent a lifetime fading into.

Since the certain gentleman's return from his brave efforts on the Continent, he has been seen with the perhaps-not spinster. And, while their meetings have always had an air of the clandestine, they have now been seen for the first time truly together in public.

Led by an odd-looking creature in a bonnet...

She smiled as she wrote that bit.

...the perhaps-not spinster strode through Hyde Park at the peak of the fashionable hour on the proud arm of the newly minted Earl...

She paused and read what she wrote, noting she had unintentionally written *perhaps-not spinster* rather than *soon-to-be spinster.* This time, however, even the part about Hedgehog did not keep the smile on her face.

Oh, heavens. That didn't sound at all flattering.

She scratched a large X over the piece and tried again.

> *Love is not only for the conventional beauty, but also for the perhaps-not spinsters who have blended into the background of society—*

Violet set her quill down with a puff of frustration.

No matter how she put it, describing her circumstances was far from complimentary. How had she put it for others?

She slid open a drawer, removed several stacks of texts on etiquette and revealed a bundle of the *Society Journal* beneath. She flipped to her column one by and one and skimmed over the articles. Her heart slowly stopped.

What she had intended as capturing a lady's victory, especially one where a man was at fault for having led to her unhappiness in the first place, she had instead succeeded in revealing their greatest weaknesses. Her fingers came to her lips to stifle a gasp.

There had been the debutante who had fallen at her own ball, only to wed Lord Bastionbury, the Marquess every woman had fawned over. Except in describing the lady, Violet had used the words 'calamitous' and—she winced— 'lacking grace'.

Heart pounding, Violet flicked through the previous instalments of the *Lady Observer* to the *on-dits* she'd written about her own cousin, the Duchess of Somersville. Violet had been proud of that piece and felt as though Lord Ledsey had truly been proclaimed the cad he was.

And truly he did appear perfidious. But then, Violet got to the part she'd written about her cousin.

Regardless of where the blame lies, the tale has not ended happily for a lady who masks it so well she's earned the unfortunate moniker of Ice Queen.

She has watched the entire heartbreaking scene unfold before her dry eyes with a composure tightly reined, as if she were bored.

While this only perpetuates rumours of her cold nature, one cannot help but wonder at her ability to maintain such stoicism after everything she's been through in recent years.

If her heart is truly ice, as some claim, it stands to reason that it will shatter more easily when broken...

Tears stung Violet's eyes. In her attempt to put Lord Ledsey to shame, she had trumped up Eleanor's deficiencies to elicit more sympathy for her. And while perhaps it had done that, it had also made her appear, well, pathetic.

Violet gave a soft cry and the paper crumpled under her hands. All this time, how had she never realised what she was doing?

And she now intended to do the same to Lottie? The woman who had helped her, who had championed Violet's success and encouraged her to be kind to herself when most others fed words of deprecation.

Violet tried to drag in air through the burning pain in her chest. She had never meant to write hurtful things about all those ladies. She'd only meant to help them. Oh, how miserably she'd failed.

She realised now she couldn't do the same to Lottie. Which meant her lessons and the exposé—all of it—would have to come to an end. And that meant Violet had only two options remaining: the first was to become an unpaid governess to Sophie's children. If the other three were like Felicity, it might not be so bad.

She shook her head at herself, unable to believe she was actually considering being responsible for all those children as a viable option.

And perhaps that was because the second option was even more frightening: telling Seth the truth about Lord Fordson. Because it wasn't just that she was no longer a virgin. It was that she had been so swiftly won over, that she'd capitulated to his fake charm with such ease.

Unlike the ladies whom she had written about in such poor light, Violet truly was pathetic. And now she understood just how much.

Chapter Eighteen

Seth opened the double doors of the sitting room to find Lady Dalton perched rigidly at the edge of the blue velvet sofa.

His mother turned to him. 'I was told you wished to see me.' She smoothed her black skirts. 'I've already rung for tea. It should arrive momentarily.'

Seth sat down beside her and offered her the small box.

She regarded the parcel, but didn't take it. 'What is this?'

'A gift.' He grinned in anticipation.

For the first time in his life, she would be pleased with him. He passed the box to her and anxiously bounced his knee.

A hesitant smile touched her lips. 'A gift?' Her fingers hovered over the seam of the box in preparation to pull it apart.

Seth leaned closer, eager to see the surprise on her face. 'I put a considerable amount of effort into obtaining this. I believe you'll be quite surprised.'

She drew the top away, revealing the ruby bracelet nestled in a bed of white silk. The colour drained from her face as she stared down at the lost piece of jewellery. Stark tendons stood out against her slender throat from the high black collar of her mourning gown.

Seth's elation melted into confusion. 'It's your mother's bracelet.'

She turned slowly to him, her eyes aflame with emotion. 'How could you?'

'How could I?' Seth stammered. 'I went to great expense and effort to procure your mother's bracelet. I intend to have all your gems tracked down and repurchased. I thought...' He shook his head, baffled and angry. Yet again he'd managed to make a mess of things.

She crushed the lid back on the top of the box. 'Do you have any idea what you've done?'

'No.' The final thread of his patience pulled taut and broke beneath the immense pressure. 'I don't know what I've done. I haven't a clue what I've possibly done to displease you after a lifetime of always causing you so much unhappiness. I've never been perfect like William. I'll never be perfect like him.'

'Don't even speak of him,' his mother snapped. 'You have dredged up the past to lay yet more scandal at our feet. I had become reconciled to these items being lost. A worthy sacrifice to salvage our good name.'

Seth got to his feet. 'What the devil are you talking about?'

He had gone too far. As he always had. Only this time he didn't care.

His mother rose from the sofa, tears bright in her eyes. 'William was always the one who caused unrest.'

Seth startled at her words. 'I beg your pardon?'

'He needed constant praise or he became a beast of a child.' Colour rose in his mother's cheeks. 'He was in line to be the next Earl. We couldn't have him react in such a manner in public. Not an earl's heir.'

Seth stared at her incredulously. Was he hearing correctly?

'You never required the constant reassurance he did,' Lady Dalton said. 'You were such a good child. Well mannered, intelligent. Until you got older and discovered drink and ladies.' She gave a cry of displeasure and put a hand to her chest as though merely thinking of it caused a sharp pain. 'At that point, I didn't know what to do with you and was too embroiled with your brother's scandals.'

'William had scandals?' Seth pressed.

His mother exhaled a heavy sigh. 'Mr Pattinson was well aware of those scandals. He threatened to let word of them drip out one at a time if we did not comply with his wishes.'

'And what were those?'

'Mr Pattinson wished to have the jewels and be left in peace.' His mother's eyes filled with tears. 'I hadn't meant to alert anyone, truly. But when I went to collect all the jewellery...'

'It was noticed,' Seth surmised.

She offered a stiff nod. 'He was greatly displeased and fled town so quickly, he left before the final few pieces could be given to him.' She fingered the delicate emerald earbobs she wore. 'It didn't matter. News of how easily I'd been duped made its way through the *ton* like wildfire. I'm sure I looked like the greatest of fools. Only no one understood why I'd been so readily hoodwinked.' She turned away and touched the crook of her forefinger to the corner of her eye.

It was that one subtle move, evidence of his mother crying over what he had left her to face alone, that pushed him over the edge. Guilt burned a hole straight through him.

'If you don't stop him, what's to keep him from demanding more money from us in the future?' Seth asked. 'What did William possibly do that was so bad?'

'Please do not make me speak of it,' she said on a shuddering exhale.

'I must know.' Seth approached his mother and put his hands on her shoulders.

He hadn't noticed how slender she had become. The mourning gown covered almost all of her in voluminous dark skirts. Beneath the black bombazine, her arms were little more than twigs that felt thin enough to snap. Up close, he could see how the worry of the last few years had etched lines on to her regal face.

All this time, he'd assumed the weight beneath his mother's burden had been all his doing. Now he understood it had been William's. However, it was Seth who had left his mother vulnerable for a man like Pattinson to rob.

'I must know.' Seth spoke more softly as he guided her back to the plush sofa.

A servant came in as she was lowering herself to the blue velvet. Seth sat beside her and poured his mother a cup of tea, adding in the lump of sugar he knew she preferred and stirring until it was thoroughly dissolved.

Lady Dalton accepted the tea with a grateful smile, though tears still shone bright in her eyes.

'Will you tell me?' Seth asked. 'I will do everything in my power to ensure we are protected.'

'Oh, Seth.' His mother's gaze searched the surrounding air as if she could find an answer there. 'He debauched ladies.'

Seth winced. It was scandalous, of course, but nothing that might cause familial ruin.

'Unfortunately, there are many rakes in the *ton*. I'm sure such gossip can be ridden out—'

'He died from syphilis.' Lady Dalton's face hardened. 'He had been diagnosed by a physician three years prior to his death.' She sucked in a deep breath. 'Yet he continued to try to debauch ladies of the *ton*. I…' She swallowed. 'I had him committed and made excuses of him being too ill for company. I couldn't think of anything else to keep him from hurting others. And he was truly ill. He needed care I couldn't provide.'

Seth's mother stared down at the floor, the perpetual rigidity of her back bowing under the burden of such awful secrets. 'Mr Pattinson found the receipts and called them to my attention. No matter what excuse I gave, he saw through it. I don't know how he knew, but he did. All of it. He threatened me with that knowledge. We would have been totally ruined if I hadn't done what he asked.'

Seth stared at her in horror. It was a good thing he was sitting rather than standing when faced with such news. William. The brother he had always assumed to be so perfect had actively sought pleasure at the possible harm of others.

Syphilis.

'I gave up on him.' A sob erupted from his mother. 'He died in there. Alone.' She put her hands over her face and wept with a force that crushed Seth's heart.

He opened his arms and his mother, his fragile, broken mother, fell into them and cried until her tears ran dry. He patted her back, painfully aware of how the cage of her ribs jutted against the fine black fabric of her gown.

He understood then that the black attire was not mourning for the son she had lost, but for what it had cost her to do what was right.

Seth would face that now. Not only would he bring Mr Pattinson to justice, but he would ensure the scandal never emerged.

Violet was nearly in tears with resolve by the time Lottie entered the double doors of the drawing room. The woman rushed to Violet in a rustle of grey silk.

'Darling, what is it?' Lottie asked.

Violet kept her attention fixed on the interwoven vines on the rug beneath her slippers. Before she had begun her lessons with Lottie, she had thought this would be an easy thing to do: learn a bit about seduction, write about the courtesan and her wanton ways and publish an exposé that would get the *Society Journal* into every household.

She had not expected Lottie to be so considerate, so forthright and kind. Nor had Violet anticipated she would learn so much about her own heart or finally begin to truly accept herself. Certainly she had not expected Lottie to become a friend.

But there it was. Violet was in agony over what she had almost done and Lottie stood there, oblivious to the ugly truth as she sought only to console.

'I have not been honest with you.' Violet's words trembled as she spoke. 'I have lied to you about my purpose from the first.'

'Have you?' Lottie said in a gentle voice.

'I am…' Violet swallowed hard and set some steel to her

spine. She had to do this. It was only right. Violet squeezed her eyes shut. 'I am the author of the *Lady Observer*.'

Her admission was met with silence. She blinked her eyes open.

Lottie stared at her, brow furrowed. 'I see,' she answered slowly.

'I am being forced to choose between marriage or retiring to the country to look after my sister's children. They seemed like little beasts until I met the eldest.' Violet couldn't help her affectionate smile as Felicity came to her mind. 'She's actually rather pleasant, but I imagine the others are still quite...well, feral. Is it terrible to say that about one's family?'

Lottie tilted her head.

Violet clamped her teeth down to prevent herself from speaking further lest her nerves make her ramble on and on for all of eternity.

'I don't believe it's terrible if it's true.' Lottie said with a patient smile.

'It very well may be,' Violet admitted. 'I thought to avoid it all by earning money from...well...'

'Exposing the truth behind Lottie's Ladies,' Lottie offered.

Lottie's Ladies. Well now, that *did* have a nice ring to it.

Not that Violet would be using it.

The truth of what Lottie said squeezed at Violet's chest and she nodded sheepishly.

'It's not a bad idea.' Lottie touched a finger to her chin. 'I'm surprised no one has attempted as much before considering the amount of speculation as to what my lessons entail.'

'But it was a bad idea,' Violet countered. 'I deceived you. I pretended I required your assistance.'

'Did you not require it?' Lottie lifted a single dark, perfectly sculpted brow.

Violet fell quiet at once as she recalled how Lottie had brought in the cheval-glass mirror. How Violet had been forced to confront what she actually liked about herself and what it had meant to her to finally concede she was not as hideous as she had presumed all those years.

'I don't teach seduction,' Lottie said softly. 'I will not help a lady learn to kiss better, or take off her clothing in a sensual manner, or whatever lurid details the *ton* likes to say of me. My purpose is to enable women to realise their true potential, to push beyond the box society shoves them into. To know it's empowering for a woman to be confident, to like herself.'

Lottie gave a little pout. 'Sadly, I do not think that makes for a very interesting article.' Her pout blossomed into a coy smile that expressed an absence of any remorse as she made her way to a fine cherrywood table with a crystal decanter of rich red wine atop it beside the bosom of a sculptured naked woman. Lottie poured two glasses and handed the first to Violet, keeping the second for herself.

Violet cradled the heavy crystal glass in her palm. 'But you do help women find husbands.'

Lottie chuckled and shook her head. Her thick, glossy locks caught the candlelight and shone purple-blue like a raven's wing. 'I help women find themselves.' She drank from her wine glass, the action lovely and dainty. Even the flex of her slender throat as she swallowed the wine held allure.

'Women generally lack confidence in themselves.' She curled her fingers around the glass as she casually held it. 'Something men have in abundance for a reason unknown to me. It's quite an imbalance.' She sighed. 'I merely seek to right the scales of that injustice and set a woman's assuredness in herself to the same level a man possesses. Or as close as can be obtained.'

'So, you weren't trying to help me find a husband?' Violet concluded.

'I was trying to make you appreciate yourself for the woman you are.' Lottie ran her hand over the top of the maroon sofa, the movement graceful. 'Though it appears you have found a man who would make a fine husband.'

The pain returned to Violet's chest, vice-like and terrible. 'I'm going to make a mess of it all.'

Lottie's hand fell away. 'Whatever do you mean?'

'I'm ruined.' Violet set her wine glass to the marble-surfaced table and her knees gave out. She plopped on to the firm sofa.

'Did he take advantage of you?' Lottie asked, her voice hard.

'*He* didn't.' Violet folded her arms over her chest and bent over. As if she could cradle her own hurt within.

Lottie lifted her head in understanding. 'That's why you faded into the background in the first place.'

Her assessment was so accurate, it brought tears to Violet's eyes anew. 'I couldn't let anyone know.'

Lottie sank on to the sofa beside Violet and brought with her a sweet, delicate scent of gardenia. 'Please don't let your past transgressions interfere with your chance for happiness now.'

Violet shifted her gaze from her instructor and let it settle on a harp placed at the side of the room near a shuttered window. 'What are you saying?'

Lottie's warm hand folded over Violet's. 'Tell him the truth.'

Violet gasped and snapped her attention back towards Lottie.

The former courtesan's eyes softened. 'If he loves you, he'll understand.'

Violet slid her gaze to the flowers on the solid marble surface of the table. Peonies this time, so fresh, the water in the vase was probably stained green with the juice dripping from the base of their thick stalks.

'Like a certain friend you know?' Violet ventured.

This time Lottie did not bother to mask the hurt puckering at her brow. 'Yes.' She reached out and ran the tip of a manicured nail over a fragile pink petal. 'Some relationships are sadly beyond repair.' She smiled, a despondent, tired smile that shadowed the smooth area beneath her eyes. 'Do not allow yours to become irreparable. You have a chance at happiness.' She shook her head and her face brightened. As if melancholy could be so easily released. 'Take it.'

Violet sucked in a hard breath to gather in her strength.

'It won't be easy,' Lottie said. 'But it will be better than having a secret hanging over your life.' She lowered her head, pointedly watching Violet. 'If you truly love him, of course.'

If you truly love him.

The words hit Violet like a slap.

Did she love him?

She floundered with a response and finally gave an insipid nod.

Lottie got to her feet and smoothed her skirts. 'I suppose this will be the last time I shall see you, Lady Violet.'

Violet rose as well and was surprised by a clench of sorrow in her chest. As if she were bidding farewell to a good friend for a final time.

Much to her surprise, Lottie wrapped her slender arms around Violet and pulled her into a warm embrace. The way a mother might do with a child.

'Take care of yourself, Lady Violet.' Lottie pulled away

and met Violet's eye. 'Know that I am always here.' A devilish glint flashed in her eye. 'And I'll never tell your family you were here. Now or later, should you need to see me again.'

Violet's mouth fell open in preparation to ask how Lottie knew.

The courtesan simply winked and strode towards the door. 'Most of my clients do not pay in actual coin when they get my bill,' she called over her shoulder.

Violet had guarded the incoming correspondence like a hawk. A job not easily done with their butler eyeing her with suspicion. When Lottie's bill came in, Violet had sent Susan with the payment post-haste in coin. Violet hadn't paid like a peer. She should have known better.

Her thoughts shifted to Seth and apprehension curled into a tight ball in the pit of her stomach. Lottie was right. He needed to know.

Chapter Nineteen

For the second time that night, Violet waited with anticipation knotting her stomach. She wanted the hackney ride home to last a lifetime, so she could delay having to tell Seth that she was no longer a virgin.

Would he be horrified? Disappointed? Disgusted?

She clenched her eyes shut, unable to bear the anticipation of such a reaction from him. He was the only man to ever make her feel beautiful. Aside from Lord Fordson, though considering how quickly his compliments had fled once he had what he'd wanted, he no longer counted.

She clenched her hands in her lap as the carriage drew to a stop at the rear of Hollingston House. The duration of the trip had gone far too quickly. Her heart was beating like a frantic drum, her breath came too short and fast. Her thoughts spun in her mind, dancing headily.

The door snapped open and, just like that, she was out of time.

She stepped from the carriage. All too soon, the path underfoot went from firm brick to soft grass.

She walked slowly into the small garden behind her home and looked up at Dalton Place. A man's shadow appeared in a second-floor window, backlit by the golden glow of candlelight.

Seth.

He was gone as soon as he appeared, no doubt making his way down the stairs and to the back door. Violet settled a hand over her chest as if she could physically stop its frantic pounding.

She should never have put herself in this position. She should never have allowed him to court her. She should never have allowed herself to kiss him. She should never have allowed him to ease his way into her heart.

The rear door to Dalton Place clicked and his voice filled the night air, quietly calling to her.

She stepped from the shadows, and he traversed the gap between their gardens.

A smile lit his face. 'Violet.' The way he said her Christian name was so tender, so intimate, it made her insides flutter.

'Seth,' she breathed.

He rushed to her and drew her into his arms. His hand immediately found her jaw, stroking her skin and tilted her face towards his to gently bestow a kiss. His lips were warm and he tasted rich and smoky, like brandy.

It was a tantalising combination when mingled with his clean, naturally masculine scent. She could breathe him all day. Kiss him all day. All night.

No.

She pulled her head back from him. 'I have to speak with you.'

His gaze skimmed her face and lingered on her bosom before sliding back up once more. 'You look beautiful.'

'You mean my breasts do?' she accused in a chastising tone.

'You look beautiful and I also have a fine appreciation for your breasts.' He grinned.

'You're wicked.'

He drew her more tightly against him. 'My love, you don't know the half of it.' It was said with a growl, almost like a threat.

My love.

Chills danced over her skin and desire pumped through her body in hot, dizzying bursts that left her breathless.

Which was, of course, why telling the truth was so hard. It would be easy to fall into banter and kissing with Seth rather than do what she needed to do and confess.

'I'm so grateful you've allowed me to court you.' Seth's tone turned tender. He ran the back of his hand down her cheek and his dark eyes shone with affection. Solely for her.

'You're witty, intelligent, and beautiful.' He lifted his mouth in a boyish half-smile that knocked her senses askew. 'You're so innocent, my sweet flower.'

Her pulse caught at his last words.

Fraud. She was a fraud.

He lowered his head and nuzzled his nose against hers as though he intended to kiss her again. 'What did you wish to tell me?'

She wanted to tip her head back and allow him to kiss the confession from her mouth. But she couldn't. She didn't deserve him. He was the best thing in her life and she would have to give him up.

'I have a confession to make.' She leaned back from him once more.

His brows pinched together and he released her, opting to hold her hands instead of her body. 'Of course. What is it?'

'I...' Her frantic mind summoned an imaginary picture of Seth's lip curling up in disgust. What if that became reality? What if he cast her off and she lost him for ever?

Her heartbeat slammed with such force, she could scarcely think straight.

'Nothing you've done could possibly be that bad.' Seth's tone was patient and kind.

Oh, but it could be. Violet drew in a long inhale, though it did nothing to quell the raw hurt in her chest.

Of course, she could wait. Until he proposed. *If* he proposed. Why subject herself to the humiliation now if it was all for naught?

In an instant, without any additional time spent dwelling on the thought, the words were out of her mouth before she could stop them. 'I'm the author of the *Lady Observer.*'

He blinked once and his smile dimmed slightly. 'Are you serious?'

She nodded and tensed for his reaction. This was not the secret she had tried to prepare herself to tell. But now it was out and she couldn't draw it back in.

'I was going to do an exposé on Lottie,' she admitted. 'It's the true reason I went to see her.'

Shame burned her face.

Seth's wary smile pulled into a slight frown. 'You didn't intend to share the identities of her other students, did you?'

Violet should never have brought this truth up for discussion. She never should have even mentioned a confession at all. In a single moment, she had ruined everything.

She swallowed around the tension building in her throat. 'I meant to initially, but then I got to know Lottie and now that I know Lady Caroline...' Violet shook her head. 'I looked back on what I had written previously and realised how hurtful those words could be to others.' Her voice broke. 'I couldn't do the exposé. I don't even want to write the *column* ever again. Of all people, I know how deeply words can cut.' A hot tear slid down her face. 'I never meant to hurt anyone.'

Seth brushed the moisture from her cheek. 'You've never been malicious. I know you didn't mean to cause harm.'

'It's terrible.' Violet looked away, too ashamed to even face the man who meant more to her than she cared to admit. Even to herself.

'You stopped before anyone could get truly hurt.' He closed the distance between them. 'Violet, you are a good person. Better than someone like me deserves.'

She was going to protest, but he pulled her against him, wrapping the strength of his arms around her. Her eyes closed at the embrace as all her senses gave in to him, savouring him. His clean scent, the heat of their bodies together, the undercurrent of desire humming in her blood.

Slowly, tenderly, he tilted her face upwards and closed his mouth over hers.

Seth would keep things chaste between them this time. Especially when they'd been nearly caught before. The garden in the rear of their homes was hardly a place for a tryst.

But when his mouth touched hers, when the sparks of attraction flickered to life, it was far too easy to linger. An extra caress of his lips against hers, a sampling just a beat too long of her sweet, delicate scent.

The powdery perfume of violets scented the air around him, immersing him in her. In Violet.

All of her consumed him, overwhelming his memories and ghosts with the most exquisite euphoria until Mont-Saint-Jean wasn't even a whisper in his mind. He wanted to lose himself in the sensations of Violet—her softness, the sweetness, her lovely perfection. There wasn't another place in all the world he'd rather be at that moment.

She gave a little hum of enjoyment and leaned into him, opening her mouth. Seth caught her face in his hand and kissed her once more, intending to keep things between them innocent.

But then Violet teased at his mouth with the tip of her tongue. The act was brazen and far more enticing than Seth wanted to admit. In that moment, he ought to have released her, backed away and bid her goodnight.

He ought to.

But he did not.

Not when the draw of losing himself in her was so damn alluring. Not when he had wanted this for so many years.

His hand slid into the back of her coiffure to gently angle her head to better access her mouth. The glossy strands were cool silk against his fingers. All of her was that way: smooth, lovely, perfect. His lips parted and he took control of the kiss once more, stroking his tongue against hers.

She whimpered and put her hand to his chest. The touch was simple, but the feelings it wrought were entirely far too complex. Longing, of course, but also affection, respect.

He shouldn't—

She rose on her toes to further deepen their kisses and

arched her body against him. He tried to resist the temptation. For her sake. For her reputation...

He shouldn't be doing this, but damn him, he couldn't walk away.

His hands skimmed down her body, brushing aside the fine fabric of her domino and whispering over the sides of her breasts as they descended down her curves. He recalled how she'd felt in his palm, her heavy breast, the hard nub of her nipple. He had fantasised about that moment often, replaying it in his mind, imagining taking it further.

Her hands smoothed over his chest, sampling the feel of him with the barrier of linen between them.

Seth kissed his way down her chin, to the length of her graceful neck where the delicate violet perfume grew headier, spiced with the natural feminine fragrance of this woman's beautiful scent. It went straight to his head, the same as drink on an empty stomach, and left his thoughts swimming.

His lips found the sensitive place between her neck and her shoulder. She leaned her head back with a moan, yielding herself to him completely. He ran his hands back up her waist to her breasts. He cupped the weight of them in his palms and pushed them up slightly so the rounded tops of her bosom nearly spilled out.

He stared down at them, unable to stop himself from imagining how they might bounce with each thrust of his body into her. With a groan, he leaned over her, tracing the neckline of her muted grey dress with his tongue.

She held tighter to him and whispered a single word into the night.

'*Yes.*'

Before he could stop himself, he tugged at her bodice

with trembling hands. Her full breasts spilled out into the moonlight for him to admire, smooth, creamy skin and topped with rosy nipples. He bent and ran his lips over the right nipple, an intentional tease that had her writhing with anticipation before he suckled the first bud into his mouth.

She gasped and practically fell against him. He easily caught her with one hand while cradling the silkiness of a breast in the palm of another and kissed her full lips again. His manhood throbbed with desire, rock hard and straining at his fall.

She curled her right leg around his left one, drawing their pelvises close, so close, until his arousal nudged her lower stomach. The pressure from even that brief contact was nearly his undoing. He groaned and suddenly they were lowering to the ground together. His mouth found her breasts again, nuzzling, kissing, licking, sucking.

Her gasps and whimpers in response to his attentions quickly disposed of the last shreds of his morality. Suddenly, he was reminded of that rake again, the man he'd been before he left. The one with skilled fingers and a wicked tongue who knew well how to pleasure women.

But he wasn't that man any more. And it wasn't women he wanted. It was just one. Violet.

He lay over the top of her in the soft, summer grass. The dewy freshness of it rose around them and the shadows obscured them in a shelter of privacy.

'Touch me,' she whispered.

Touch me.

Dear God. He hesitated, plagued with thoughts of William who had debauched ladies. Except he'd had no intention of marrying them. Not like Seth had with Violet.

'Please.' Her tone was pleading now, desperate.

He shifted his hands between them, skimming down her skirts to run his fingers over the cleft between her legs. She cried out.

He kissed her swiftly to muffle the sound and froze. When it was apparent no one had heard, or bothered to investigate the sound, he curled his middle finger into the folds of her gown where it nudged between her legs, rubbing her sex beneath.

The heat of her yearning was evident and he knew, if it were not for the layers of fabric separating them, she would be slick with need. Her hips ground against his touch, the quickening of her breath indicative of how close she was to climax.

The mere thought of hearing her cries of release were almost more than he could bear. In fact, he *needed* to hear them. A sweet memory to cling to that evening as he drifted to sleep, enveloped in recollections of Violet.

He prudently lifted the neckline of her gown to cover her breasts once more.

She clung more tightly to him. 'Please, don't stop.'

'I won't, but nor will I ruin you.' Even as he spoke, he lifted the hem of her gown. He paused to stroke her stocking, marvelling at her neat ankle and shapely calf. His touch skimmed over the white cotton to the bare skin inside of her knees.

'I think you don't know what *ruin* means,' she gasped.

'But I do,' he murmured. Up her inner thighs he went, the skin there impossibly soft. He didn't stop the agonisingly slow trail of his fingers up her legs until he brushed the slit of her sex.

Her hips jerked and she sucked in a hard breath.

He lay on his side as he leaned over her, propped on his

elbow, intending to kiss her, to swallow up every moan and whimper she would issue.

'There?' he teased.

She nodded.

He found the bud of her sex with his thumb where it was swollen and hot with the need to release. 'And there?'

She leaned her head back. 'Oh, God, yes.'

With his free hand, he carefully held the back of her neck, drawing her face higher once more to kiss her as his fingers moved over her with an expertise he had not used in many, many years.

Chapter Twenty

Violet should not have been lying on the grass in her garden with Seth next to her. Certainly she should not have allowed him to put his hands under her skirts or touch her so intimately.

But she did not have a single regret on the matter. Not with the way her body seemed to soar above that garden, above London, above any amount of morality that had been scolded into her throughout her life.

Seth's mouth moved over hers while his hand… Heavens, she didn't know what he did with his hand, but it was exquisite. Heat prickled at her palms and feet and every muscle in her body went taut with anticipation.

Her breath came faster and her heart slammed against her ribs so frantically, it was a wonder they didn't crack.

'Yes,' Seth growled between their kisses. 'Come for me, love. Come for me, my beautiful Violet.'

Love.

My beautiful Violet.

Even if he had pulled his hand from her at that very moment, his words alone were enough to tip her over the edge where she recklessly fell into utter bliss. Her body clenched in delicious spasms that spiralled her senses beyond a place they'd ever been before.

Seth kissed her again and again, muffling the sounds of her pleasure until she had control of herself once more. Spent and languid, her head fell back on to the soft, damp grass as she gazed up at Seth and the starlit dark sky above him.

Lord Fordson had never touched her like that. He'd never made her body react in such a way.

'That was the most sensual, lovely thing I've ever seen,' Seth said quietly.

Heat singed her cheeks. 'You watched me.'

He groaned. 'The pleasure on your face, those little breathy cries.' Despite the gruff, blatant lust in his voice, he eased his hand from her and carefully smoothed her skirt into place.

A glance down at his groin confirmed he was still fully aroused. A thick column of hard male flesh strained against his breeches.

Violet bit her lip, eager to show her own attraction to him as he had so generously done to her. She pulled him closer and kissed him again, this time letting her hands roam further than she'd been daring enough to do before.

Her fingertips grazed the tip of the large bulge, but he caught her hand. 'No.' He shook his head. 'I won't take your innocence.'

She opened her mouth, ready to confess it all. To tell him about how she was already ruined, how she burned for him, how if she didn't have all of him at that exact moment, she might go truly and completely mad.

Except it was at that exact second that the rear door to Hollingston House was flung open and her mother's voice cut through the air. 'What is the meaning of this?'

Violet jerked her hand away from Seth, hoping they were shielded enough by the shadows that her mother hadn't seen... Her insides clenched with mortification and shame.

Oh, God, what *had* her mother seen?

'I fell,' Violet said quickly. 'And Seth was—'

'Seth?' Lady Hollingston snapped.

Violet winced.

Seth jumped to his feet and helped Violet to hers. Thank goodness, he'd pulled the top of her gown up earlier. Or at least as well as he could with her lying down. If she faced her mother with her breasts draped over her neckline, she might truly perish from mortification.

'Forgive me, Lady Hollingston,' Seth said. 'The fault is entirely mine.'

'Come in at once, both of you.' The Countess pulled the door open wider. 'This instant.'

Violet closed her eyes and wished to be anywhere other than where she was.

Seth offered her his arm, as if they were in a ballroom preparing for a dance rather than having just enjoyed a moonlit tryst in a place where anyone could have seen them.

Where, of all people, *her mother* had seen them.

God, this could not be any worse.

'I'll do what's right,' Seth said under his breath.

Her eyes widened. *What's right.* That meant he would marry her.

Apparently it could be worse.

Shamefaced, Violet allowed herself to be led into the kitchen where a candle lit the room in a brilliant glow.

'I fell,' Violet protested. 'Lord Dalton was simply helping me to my feet.'

Her mother frowned. 'You must have fallen several times to appear in such a state.' Her gaze slid to Seth, skimming down his body. She stopped at his midsection, then darted her eyes away as if the corner of the ceiling had suddenly become the most fascinating thing she'd ever seen. 'You are hardly properly attired. Your dishabille is not only unacceptable, but paired with your lack of a chaperon could ruin a lady.'

Violet cringed at her mother's delicate dance around Seth's very obvious arousal.

Seth shifted uncomfortably from one foot to the other. 'I believe I have forgotten my jacket. And my cravat.' He cleared his throat. 'As well as my waistcoat.'

'Yes,' Lady Hollingston agreed. 'I can see that.' She turned to him and looked somewhere over his head. 'Did you seek to debauch my daughter on the grass like some field hand?'

'I'll marry her,' Seth said firmly.

Lady Hollingston met his eyes. 'I trust you will.'

'I beg your pardon?' Violet said, finally finding her voice. 'Do I not have a say in the matter?'

Lady Hollingston spun on her. 'You lost that opportunity when you allowed him such liberties with your person. Truly, for a woman nearly on the shelf you should know better.'

Violet opened her mouth, but before she could get another word out, her mother continued in a voice that could only be described as shrill. 'You should be grateful for this happenstance, Violet. Truly, I thought no man would ever want you. Perhaps if you'd been able to keep your fingers from the dessert tray, or could try a little harder to eat less, you would not be in this situation.'

Violet stung as if she'd been slapped.

'You're a fool,' Seth said sharply.

Lady Hollingston put her hands on her hips. 'I beg your pardon?'

'I said you're a fool,' Seth repeated. 'Violet is a beautiful woman who is admirable and intelligent and everything you have never been. How such an incredible lady managed to blossom beneath such sharp words is a testament to her strength. I would caution you to have a care in how you speak to your daughter as she is soon to be my Countess.'

Lady Hollingston's mouth fell open and her cheeks coloured. She pulled open the door, stepping back to allow him to exit. 'I suggest you call upon Lord Hollingston first thing in the morning to discuss the marriage contract. You may leave, Lord Dalton.'

He cast a glance back at Violet, clearly seeking confirmation she would be all right. She nodded, though in truth she dreaded being alone with her mother after his departure. Not out of fear for her safety, but for the stinging rebuke she would no doubt receive.

Seth frowned, clearly not eager to leave. Lady Hollingston cleared her throat and he slipped out into the night.

The Countess methodically closed the door, engaged the lock and turned to Violet, arms crossing over her chest. 'It appears we will be having a wedding after all.' She paused and studied her daughter. 'Should I even ask about the domino?'

Violet shrank inside of herself and shook her head.

Lady Hollingston sighed. It was a long, exhausted sound that implied she would rather not know, that she was past the point of continuing to care, that she knew Violet would soon be someone else's problem. 'To bed with you, child.'

Grateful to have avoided coming up with an excuse to explain the domino, Violet quickly slipped from the room. It wasn't until she was alone in her bedchamber that the enormity of her situation crashed down upon her shoulders.

She would be marrying Seth. She would be Lady Dalton. And she had an enormous secret she hadn't yet shared with him because she had been too much of a coward.

Seth had woken early the following day. While he had not been plagued by nightmares of his time at Waterloo, he had not slept well. He had nearly ruined Violet.

After having been so disgusted with his brother's antics, Seth was little better himself. No, he hadn't tupped her, but they had been intimate. Very intimate.

In truth, if Lady Hollingston had not emerged when she had, would Seth have been able to resist taking Violet? She'd been ready enough, her body slick and hot and swollen. For him.

His thighs twitched at the memory, but he shoved the thoughts from his mind. Now was not the time for thinking of titillating transgressions. It was for making them right.

He waited with barely tethered patience in the drawing room for his mother and sister to join him. They came in some time after ten. He'd already penned a missive to Lord Hollingston asking for an urgent meeting first thing that morning.

His mother and sister came down within minutes of one another. They exchanged pleasantries and he allowed them a moment to take a sip of tea before speaking up. 'I shall be speaking with Lord Hollingston this morning.'

A smile spread over Caroline's face. 'Oh? About what?' She sat forward, her brows raised in expectation.

'About marrying Lady Violet.' He had thought of what he would say to his mother and sister, of course, but he hadn't considered how proud it would make him to say those words.

His mother gave a brittle smile. 'That's fine news, Seth.'

'We could have a wedding at Dalton Manor.' Caroline sat upright in her seat, her eyes shining with eagerness. 'We can use the summer roses for decoration. And there's the small parish church just in town. Oh, it will be lovely.'

Seth chuckled at her enthusiasm. 'The Season is very nearly over. I should think we will want to wed prior to then and in one of our homes here.'

'By special licence, then.' Though his mother gave an approving nod, a small line showed between her brows.

'Before either of you anticipate planning her wedding, I shall speak more with Lady Violet and inform you of my lady's desires.' Seth lifted his teacup.

'Seth,' Lady Dalton said softly.

Seth? She hadn't called him Seth in an age.

He regarded his mother and disliked the concern creasing her brow.

'Regarding Lady Violet...' She drew in a long, slow breath. 'You should know that William—'

The door opened and Gibbons entered.

They all turned to him. He offered a bow and held out his silver tray with a note upon it. 'Lord Hollingston asks that you read this post-haste.'

Seth took the missive with thanks and unfolded it.

I would see you immediately.

Seth had been anxious about his discussion with Lord Hollingston, but the single line sent tension tightening through his body. This would not be as easily done as the conversation with Lady Dalton and Caroline.

He offered an easy smile to them now, as though nothing were amiss. 'If you'll excuse me.'

Seth had it in mind to stop off with Bennet so the valet might freshen up his appearance. However, knowing the man's penchant for perfection, Seth might never leave Dalton Place and Lord Hollingston's note encouraged expediency.

After a brief pause in front of a mirror, Seth made his way next door and was promptly shown into the study where a dour-faced Lord Hollingston glowered at him from behind a large desk. He indicated the chair on the other side of the desk. 'Sit,' he commanded. 'If you please.' The latter was added in an apparent effort to be civil when his demeanour was anything but.

Seth sank on to the seat, remembering too late how loud the damn thing was. He suppressed a cringe as it squawked in protest beneath his backside.

'You've taken liberties with my daughter,' Lord Hollingston accused.

Seth sat with such stillness, the chair didn't make a sound. He kept his shoulders squared and his gaze level as he replied. 'Yes. And I intend to wed her, as I told Lady Hollingston. I wished to speak with you first thing this morning to ask for her hand in marriage.'

'That is the right thing to do, isn't it?' The anger drained from the older Earl's face. 'Do you love her?'

Love?

The chair groaned from beneath him. Seth had never loved a woman enough to know what love was.

'I care greatly for her,' he replied.

'That's luckier than most,' Hollingston grumbled. 'What did she say?'

'"She", my lord?'

Hollingston's bushy brows drew together. 'Violet. I'm assuming you've already asked her.'

Seth opened his mouth, ready to say she'd agreed, but then recalled the night before. When Lady Dalton and Seth had done most of the speaking as Violet's life was planned out for her.

Hollingston scoffed. 'I'll give you the same answer I gave you when you asked permission to court her: if she says yes, then that is my answer as well.'

'Is she available that I might speak with her?' Seth rose from the damnable seat.

'I'll see to it that she is.' Hollingston rang for a servant. 'You can wait for her in the drawing room.'

Silence fell over them as they waited on the servant to arrive. In that time, Hollingston openly appraised Seth. 'My wife informed me what you said to her before you left last night.'

Seth's mouth tightened, a hint of his rage returning anew at what the Countess had said to Violet. Seth's mother might have been indifferent to him for the better part of his life, but Violet's mother was downright cruel to her. He'd hated leaving Violet at her mercy the night before. Had it been up to him, he would have wed Violet on the spot and brought her home with him to Dalton Place.

Seth set his jaw. 'I won't apologise for it. I don't condone what she said to Violet, nor do her words hold any truth.'

The lines around Lord Hollingston's eyes crinkled deeper. 'You've grown into a man of conviction, Lord Dalton.' His mouth lifted in a half-smile. 'I find myself hoping my daughter says yes to you.'

'As do I.' Seth inclined his head graciously towards the Earl as a servant entered.

Seth followed the servant to the yellow drawing room. The lingering scents of breakfast hovered in the room, steeped tea with a sweet note of jam and a briny hint of ham.

He was directed to a matching sunny-coloured sofa, which he sat on for a moment before his nerves overcame him.

He rose to his feet, prepared to pace when the double doors opened and Lady Violet entered.

She wore a white-muslin day dress, virginal and lovely. Her hair was bound back in a knot that was less intricate than the styles he'd seen her wear. There was a quiet intimacy to it and he couldn't help but wonder if she wore her hair in such a manner at breakfast with the family where things were less formal—before house calls and social functions required a more put-together appearance.

He liked seeing her thus. It made him think of informal breakfasts with her and a quiet, happy life together, one where he could trade nightmares of the past for dreams of the future.

But first, she had to agree to marry him.

Chapter Twenty-One

Violet knew precisely why she'd been summoned to the drawing room. That suspicion was confirmed when she walked in to find Seth waiting for her.

Apprehension gripped her and the exhaustion of a night without sleep left her thoughts spinning. No doubt he was there to speak to her about what had happened, to confirm their marriage.

He came to her in two strides. 'Violet, forgive me for what transpired last night. I... I should have refrained from kissing you.'

They'd done more than kiss, of course, and his words brought back a hot tingling sensation throughout her body. His fingers had moved against her most intimate place, stroking her to a state of such exquisite pleasure.

'I enjoyed our kisses,' she replied. 'I am as much at fault.'

He reached up and gently caressed her face. 'You are always so gracious.' The corners of his mouth ticked downward. 'I should have been more in control of myself.'

Violet's stomach clenched. Would he still feel the same way once he knew the truth?

She had to tell him. Now. She drew in a breath to speak, but he rushed on. 'I realised this morning that the decision to wed was made not between you and me, but your mother and me.' He reached for Violet's hand, cradling it in his large one, and gazed deeply into her eyes so she felt as though she'd tipped headlong into the depths of his soul. 'Lady Violet, will you do me the immense honour of agreeing to marry me?'

She hesitated, unprepared to be given a choice at all in the matter. Nor was she prepared for how the question would make her emotions soar.

How wonderful it would be to say yes, to agree without caveat. Without having to confess such an awful truth.

'Seth.' She opened her mouth to speak and fear shuddered through her. She could lose him. She probably would lose him.

But he had to know.

He shook his head. 'Please don't say no just yet, Violet. Please take a moment to consider my proposal.' He folded his other hand over hers. 'I'm not asking because we were caught in a compromising position. I'm asking because I want to marry you. Because I care greatly for you. I have no desire to wed anyone but you. You're unlike any other woman of the *ton* in all the best ways.'

He cared greatly for her? He might as well have plunged a dagger into her chest. Her throat went tight with the ache inside her ribs.

She pulled her hand from his and bit her lip. 'Not all the best ways. I'm not…'

The words stuck fast in her throat and welled there, practically choking her.

'If you're not ready, we can have a long engagement.' He offered her a small smile, one that flicked up at the corners in a brief show of nerves. 'I'd thought to procure a special licence if you wished to wed before the Season ends, but if you'd prefer to wait, we can.'

She shook her head and swallowed. 'Seth, I… I'm not a virgin.'

His brow furrowed. 'I beg your pardon.'

'It was the night of my debut.' Her words caught. 'I was in that hideous dress my mother made me wear due to my failure and…' She slid her gaze away, hating to admit Seth's part in that night. 'You had just left. I assumed you thought me ugly and, well, my heart was shattered to bits. There was a gentleman who comforted me and asked if he might dance with me that evening.'

Seth watched her silently as she spoke, his face absent of any expression she could use to gauge his emotions.

'He was charming.' She sighed at her own foolish younger self. 'He said all the right things. He…'

'He what?' There was a sharpness to Seth's tone.

'He made me feel beautiful.' A warm tear trickled down Violet's cheek at the admission. 'All my life, I had been made to feel as though I was unattractive—too fat. My mother, my sisters…'

'Me,' Seth said quietly.

Violet kept her head lowered, unable to look at him as she nodded silently. 'He was the only person who ever said things that made me feel as though I was something more than a frumpy woman. I thought him in love with me, I assumed he was of a mind to marry me, but I was too afraid to ask. As though I might break a spell somehow woven over this man who was far too attractive to be drawn to someone like me. I was desperate to do anything to keep his attention.'

She sat on the sofa. 'When it was done, he left immediately. He didn't call upon me the following day or the one after that. When next we saw one another, he treated me with a cool, cordial politeness that indicated what I had been suspecting, what I'd been fearing the most.'

She swallowed in an attempt to clear the hurt from her throat, but it did little good. 'He had used me.' She fingered the edge of a ribbon on her gown. 'I knew myself to be ruined and so I allowed myself to melt into the background. If no one paid me any notice, I would never have to share my secret. I could remain quietly ruined and no one would be any the wiser.'

It was the first time she'd spoken the truth aloud. Hearing it in her own ears made her realise how absolutely pathetic it truly was. She covered her face with her hands, not wanting to see Seth, or the obnoxiously sunny yellow room. She didn't want to face any of it. Least of all herself.

The cushion shifted beside her and the familiar scent of warm male and shaving soap told her Seth was at her side.

'Violet.' He said her name softly.

She scrunched her eyes and kept her face down towards the carpet. Every part of her was scraped raw by finally exposing the truth. Her eyes were gritty from lack of sleep and barely contained tears. She wanted nothing more than to be left alone, to throw herself upon her bed and weep until her eyes ran dry.

His fingers brushed her cheek, turning her face towards

him. She kept her eyes closed, as though somehow that might prepare her for his rejection.

'Open your eyes,' he said.

She did as he asked and held her breath, fearful of what would follow.

Seth's heartbeat slammed in his chest and his thoughts reeled. Of all the reasons he'd suspected Violet had let herself fade away, being ruined was not one of them.

Violet watched him, her wide blue eyes fixed on him with a cautious trust, hesitant hope. Tears left her lashes spiked and cheeks wet.

She looked so vulnerable that he wanted to curl her into his arms to protect her for ever.

He had done that to her. By not dancing with her that night. He'd made her feel as though he thought she was so unappealing that he'd rather leave spend a single moment with her. He had pushed her into that man's arms. Whoever it might be.

Ice chilled his blood.

He knew exactly who it might be. His mother's words prior to Seth receiving the missive summoning him to Hollingston House flew back in his mind. Something regarding William and Violet.

'Who did this to you?' he demanded. 'Who took your innocence?'

She shook her head. 'It doesn't matter,' she whispered.

But it did. To Seth. If William had lain with her and now Seth was to marry her... His stomach churned. William had been diagnosed with syphilis. Seth was no physician—he didn't know how long someone might have the disease before a diagnosis could be ascertained.

'Who was it?' Seth asked again.

Violet's eyes filled with tears. 'Please, I don't wish to say.'

'I want to know,' Seth replied. 'I *need* to know.'

'It doesn't matter,' she repeated. 'He's dead now anyway. He was killed in a duel with a jealous husband.'

Ice formed into sharp-edged knots in his gut.

He's dead now anyway.

Dear God, it *was* William.

An image flashed in his mind of his brother drawing Violet into the dark shadows of the garden as Seth had done, kissing her as Seth had, sliding up her skirts...touching her.

Anger lashed at Seth. If his brother was still alive, it would only be long enough to meet over pistols at dawn. Energy swelled like a savage beast inside Seth's chest. It flared through his muscles and left them tense in preparation for battle. His senses heightened as they did before a fight, hearing everything, seeing everything, *feeling* everything.

And there was much to feel.

Betrayal. Fear. Disgust.

'Tell me his name,' Seth said in a low voice.

Violet stiffened at the ugliness of his tone. 'Please. It's too...' Her eyes welled with tears and she wiped them away. 'It's too mortifying. I've already humiliated myself enough.'

Seth frowned. She was insistent on keeping her secret.

But did she know about William? About his illness? Could it remain dormant in the body and affect the victim years later?

'Have you had any symptoms of syphilis?' he asked.

She blinked at him and her mouth fell open in outrage. 'I beg your pardon?'

Seth drew from his memory to recall soldiers who had

suffered from the disease. 'Sores on your person, a rash. Sometimes a sore throat or—'

She leapt up from the seat and backed away from him. 'How dare you?'

'Violet, I—'

'I confessed to you the secret I've been carrying inside of me for six years, the secret that ended any dreams of marriage or children or love.' A sob escaped her lips and she covered her mouth with her hand as if she could catch it and pull it back in. 'And you are concerned I might have syphilis?'

'I don't think you do,' Seth said hastily. 'I don't understand why you just won't tell me who did this to you.'

Her face coloured a vivid shade of red. 'Because it's utterly mortifying, Seth. Because I've been a fraud for six years and the one person I thought might actually accept me has made me feel worse than the man who ruined me.'

Good God. When she put it that way, it was terrible of him. What had he done?

'Violet.' He got to his feet and reached for her, but she snatched her hand away from him.

She stiffened her back. 'Good day, Lord Dalton.' Her words frosted over the sunny room, then she spun on her heel and departed the room despite his calling after her.

He pursued her to the double doors of the drawing room and paused. Should he chase her through the house? It seemed rather uncouth, but it was better than letting her get away.

Her footsteps pounded up the stairs over his head. He turned down the hall towards the staircase and met their butler, Wilson.

The older man remained stoically in Seth's path. 'May I help you, my lord?'

A door closed upstairs with considerable force and disappointment crushed Seth. Violet would not be accessible today.

Emotions swirled through him like a chaotic blizzard, pieces so powerful, so thick as they congealed together in a massive blob that they were indistinguishable together. Indiscernible and overwhelming.

Seth's shoulders sagged. 'I'd like to be shown out if you please, Wilson.'

'As you wish.' Wilson indicated with a white-gloved hand. 'This way.'

Seth was shown out of Hollingston House, but didn't bother to take the short path home. Instead, he made his way to the mews and asked Harold to bring the carriage round. He could use some time at White's, in the company of gentlemen, without all the drama of marriages and debauching brothers and ladies who had fornicated with one's brother.

Even as he climbed into the carriage, another image flashed in his head of his brother drawing up Violet's skirts, touching her creamy inner thighs. Did she make the same breathy cries of pleasure for him? Did she look up at him with that same dreamy expression?

He put his head in his hands as he did so often when plagued by memories of war and wished he could expunge the thoughts from his mind with sheer willpower alone. The carriage came to a hard stop that nearly sent him flying from his seat.

He burst from the carriage before Burton could get the door for him and leapt down without using the dainty little step. 'Have a care with those stops, Harold,' he called sharply over his shoulder.

'Sorry, m'lord.' Harold's jovial voice met Seth's back.

If Seth hadn't been so drunk the night of Violet's debut, he would not have leered at her in that dress. He would not have had to hide his lustful thoughts behind an unapologetic absence. She would not have been left at the mercy of other men with her pride bruised and her confidence crumbled.

'Dalton.' Rawley joined Seth. 'Are you well?'

Seth requested a glass with two fingers of brandy. 'I've been better.'

'I spoke with Caroline last night.' Rawley gave him a shy smile. 'Do you think she minded that I spoke of my adverse reaction to shrimp?'

Did William tug down Violet's dress? Did he fondle her full breasts? Kiss them as Seth had?

'I worried after the fact that it might have been ill mannered.' Rawley brushed his fingers inside his pocket where his watch sat. 'I've been plagued with worry over it all night.'

Did William's teeth tease over her rosy nipples? Did she cry out for him?

Rawley cleared his throat. 'I say, Dalton, you really don't seem well at all.'

Seth pinched the bridge of his nose. 'There is a courtesan—'

Rawley began vigorously shaking his head. 'I'll have none of that.'

The servant delivered the brandy to Seth and he took a deep, burning sip. Could fire cleanse hell?

He was about to find out.

'There is a courtesan who instructs ladies of the *ton* in

the art of flirtation,' Seth finished his original statement. 'Her name is Lottie. You ought to see her. Not for pleasure, but for instruction in how to talk to a woman. For God's sake, man, it could not be easier. My sister is infatuated with you. Yet at every turn, you make her think you are lacking in interest. Do yourself, and her, and me for that matter, a favour and make an appointment for instruction.'

Rawley's nose twitched. 'She instructs men?'

'I imagine she does.' Seth took another swallow.

Rawley nodded in quiet consideration. 'Thank you for your counsel.'

Seth grunted, not certain if he was pleased to be done with the vexing conversation or annoyed that he would be left at the mercilessness of his tortured thoughts. Perhaps it was a little of both.

If he had been at the ball that night to dance with Violet, William would never have had to fill in for him.

A sudden realisation slammed into him that left the brandy in his empty stomach swirling.

Even if William had taken advantage of Violet, Seth's sin was far worse than hers, for he had turned his back on her.

He was right when he said she was better than he deserved and not just because he was a broken man. He was an idiot.

It was time to show her that he had truly changed from the foolish youth who had walked away all those years ago into a man who cared about her above all else. A man who might some day be deserving of her.

Chapter Twenty-Two

Violet could cry no more. Or so she thought. Every time she considered she might truly be emptied of all tears, a single thought of how Seth had looked at her reduced her to a watering pot once more.

Syphilis.

The gall of that man! To presume she might be diseased.

Clearly he didn't believe it to be only one man who had ruined her. Might as well be all of London for how he perceived her. She wanted to laugh at the ridiculousness of it, except that the question had made her feel vile. She'd said enough terrible things to herself throughout the years she'd chastised herself for her transgressions. But never, *never*, had she felt as low as she had when he asked if she'd exhibited signs of syphilis.

A knock came from Violet's bedroom door. She cringed deeper into a vast mountain of pillows.

The rap sounded again.

'Please go away,' she muffled into a pillow.

'It isn't your mother, if that makes a difference,' Lord Hollingston said.

Violet dragged herself into a sitting position. 'It does.'

'So I may enter?'

'Yes,' she replied in a small voice.

Lord Hollingston entered the room with tentative steps, his gaze slowly descending on his surroundings. He hadn't been in her bedchamber since she was a girl just out of the nursery.

'Your mother took Felicity to the park to take some air. The girl has been melancholy.' His stare lingered on the silver-tissue gown on the dressmaker's form. 'Why the devil do you keep that?'

She didn't bother to glance in the direction of the gown. Doing so only reminded her of Seth, of the night of her debut, and caused far too great an ache in her chest. 'To remind myself I can do better.'

'Rubbish.' He stalked his way to the gown. 'I've half a mind to burn the wretched thing.'

'Please don't.'

He hissed out a breath and glared at the gown. 'Very well.' He tucked his hands behind his back. 'Tell me why you're so upset, sweet girl.'

She shook her head. 'It doesn't matter. All you need to know is that my schedule has cleared and I am now available to Sophie to be at the beck and call of her children.'

'Do you wonder if they all have cats?' her father mused with an affectionate smile.

A tentative smile spread over Violet's lips. 'Is it wrong that I rather hope they do?'

'The girl has turned out rather well.' Her father stepped closer to where Violet sat up in bed. 'Spirited as ever, of course, but she's a good child. I have no doubt you would tame the others as well. But it isn't necessary.'

'Not necessary?' Violet studied her father curiously.

He heaved a heavy sigh. 'I had thought to have you find a man you could love. Not all marriages are happy ones, I understand that.' He rolled his eyes. 'Be assured, I understand better than most,' he muttered. 'But many are. Your cousin, Eleanor, has a fortunate marriage. I'd hoped you'd find a match like that, a man to make you light up the way you used to.'

'The way I used to?' she asked.

'Before your debut. Before your mother harangued that joy out of you.' Her father indicated the pink-silk chair near the table by Violet's bed. 'May I?'

Violet nodded and sat on the edge of the bed.

'She wasn't always so difficult.' Her father sank into the dainty seat. 'Before any of your siblings were born, we had a child—a little girl. She did not live past the age of three. Your mother blamed herself. Once your eldest sister was born, your mother became obsessed with ensuring everything was perfect when it came to her children.'

Violet pressed her lips together. She hadn't known about a sister who had died, nor her mother's reaction to it. The anger in her heart softened with sympathy.

'Everyone gave way to her,' her father continued. 'Until you. You've always been a free spirit, my Violet.' His eyes crinkled with affection. 'I dare say you nearly gave her an apoplexy on more than one occasion. The more you defied her as a child, the more she tried to control you.' Lines showed on his face as he frowned. 'I should have spoken up before, prevented her from…' He spread his hands. 'From taking your light. I thought love might bring it back. I see now that is not the case. Forgive me, Violet.'

She shook her head. 'You've nothing to apologise for.'

'Your tear-stained face would suggest otherwise.' Her father pushed up from his chair. 'I'm afraid I've made quite the mess of things. But if you do not wish to marry, then I will not force you. Nor will I force you into the country. You may choose what it is you wish to do.' He hesitated. 'Do you know what that might be?'

The thought of going to the country for ever did not hold appeal, but neither did regressing to a muted life once more. Nor would she continue her efforts in writing the *Lady Observer*. Not after realising the hurt she'd most likely caused.

Marriage. To Seth. For a whisper of a moment, that had held considerable appeal. Until she recalled how terribly he'd rejected her.

What would Lottie say in this moment?

But even the woman's wise words fell silent in Violet's mind.

Violet shook her head miserably. 'No. I don't know what I would like to do.'

'You have some time.' Lord Hollingston went to her and pressed a kiss on the top of her head as he'd done when she was a girl. 'But a decision will need to be made.'

Yes, it would. And not a single one promised to make her happy.

Her father cleared his throat. 'If I may make a suggestion...'

She looked up at him.

'Lord Dalton appears to a man of conviction.' Lord Hollingston puffed his chest out as he presented his endorsement. 'And he seems to care for you a great deal.'

Violet choked down a sob. Even if Seth truly did care for her a great deal, it clearly wasn't enough.

Hollingston House's butler was rather cross with Seth. Wilson wouldn't outwardly say it, of course, but then, he didn't need to. It was evident in the flush about his face that made the wisps of snow-white hair stand out like tufts of cotton.

'My lord, I'm afraid Lady Violet is not accepting callers.' Wilson's tone had lost its sympathy.

'Go to her again,' Seth replied. 'Tell her I refuse to leave Hollingston House until I've spoken with her.'

'My lord, I've gone to her three times already—'

'A fourth time, then,' Seth countered. 'And a fifth and a sixth. However many it bloody well takes.'

Wilson bowed, most likely to cover a grimace. 'As you wish, my lord.'

This time the butler did not come down for a longer stretch of time and Seth dared to hope. Perhaps that meant Violet had changed her mind, that she would indeed come down.

His realisation at White's, and even his irritated conversation with Rawley, had sparked an understanding in him. Seth had lowered Violet's confidence that night of her debut—he'd left her at the mercy of William as surely as he'd abandoned his own family in their greatest time of need after William's death. Hell, even in handling him when he became so ill.

As he was making reparations to his own family, so, too, did he need to make them to Violet. And that included putting William from his mind to be with her.

If it wasn't too late, that is.

He stared at the closed double doors of the drawing room. Would she give him the chance?

He didn't deserve it. Even Seth knew that. But it didn't mean he couldn't hope.

After an interminable stretch of what felt like an eternity, the double doors opened. But it was not Wilson who walked through—it was Violet.

She wore a different muslin gown, this one with yellow ribbons that were as sun-coloured as the room he was in. Her hair had been neatly styled from the knot it'd been in earlier that day. She lifted her head, appearing entirely put together and nonplussed.

'You insist on seeing me.' She put her hands to her hips. 'I'm here to inform you that I wish for you to leave.'

Seth widened his stance. 'I won't go.'

'I don't want you to stay.'

Seth shook his head. 'Please give me a chance.'

'Seth.' Her voice cracked.

'Violet,' he said her name with all the regret roiling inside him.

Her face crumpled. 'Leave me be.'

He rushed to her side. There was a pink tinge to her nose and a red-rimmed, bloodshot appearance to her eyes told him what her stoic demeanour tried to mask: she had been crying.

And he'd been the cause.

'I will not leave you.' Seth reached for her.

'I trusted you.' She pushed him away. 'Leave me to pick up the pieces you left when you shattered me.'

'No.' He didn't reach for her again, not if she didn't wish him to. But he wouldn't leave, damn it. Not until they had this conversation.

She shot a hurtful glare at him. 'So you can break me again? And again? And again?'

He winced. She was right. He had spent a lifetime hurting her when all he'd ever wanted to do was be there for her, with her.

'I want to help you pick up the pieces.' He stepped closer and the ache in his chest was nearly more than he could bear. 'I want to ensure you will never be anything but whole again.'

Even if he was not.

She drew in a shuddering breath and strode towards the chair nearest the tea tray that had been laid out by a servant some time earlier.

He followed her. 'I'm an idiot.'

She lifted her head and regarded him. 'I believe we've had this conversation before.'

'And I told you I'd changed.' He gave a mirthless chuckle. 'Clearly, I have not.'

She did not contradict him. Instead, she poured them both tea with hands that trembled so badly, the delicate china rattled.

Seth sank on to the chair beside her. 'You accepted me as I am. I have not afforded you the same courtesy.'

She lowered her head, appearing to be rather taken with her teacup, and gave a little sniff.

'Violet,' he said softly. 'Forgive me.'

'Even if I forgive you, it does not change what I've done.' She set the teacup down untouched and wrapped her arms around herself.

He shook his head. 'I don't care what you've done. It was never the act in any event. I certainly cannot judge you with my tarnished past. I confess...' He grimaced. 'I confess, it was a shock to discover you had...'

'Lost my innocence?' she supplied with a bitter note.

'No.'

Damn. This was harder than he'd anticipated. He got to his feet and paced. 'I mean, yes. It's only that, well, the idea that William had taken such liberties with you, it was hard to accept.'

She furrowed her brows. 'William?'

'Yes, William. My brother.' The weight in his soul lightened with a thread of hope. 'Was the man not William?' he asked slowly.

'No,' she said softly. 'He was...' She scrunched her eyes shut. 'Lord Fordson.'

Fordson.

Seth knew something of the man. He was a year younger than himself, a foppish profligate who was far too pretty for his own good with a silver tongue that'd eased his passage under many skirts. It did not strike Seth as uncharacteristic that Fordson would stoop to debauch an earl's daughter.

'Why would you not say?' Seth asked.

'I told you why,' Violet cried. 'It was hard enough to be honest with you about the one moment I ruined my entire life. To give you details—it felt so sordid. It made me feel too exposed. Too vulnerable.'

'I'm apparently a complete fool.' He leaned his head back in frustration at himself. 'I assumed it was William since he would have been in such close proximity to you and with his penchant for debauching ladies...'

Violet cast him an incredulous stare. 'Your brother? Truly?'

'He had syphilis,' Seth explained. He didn't stop there,

he detailed the whole of it. William being placed in an insti-tution to protect women and even what happened with Mr Pattinson and the jewels. 'It is why I asked you questions about it,' he concluded. 'Please do forgive me.'

Violet nodded slowly. 'I had no idea.'

'My mother...' Seth sighed. 'She tried to tell me some-thing about William and you. I thought...' He ran his hand through his hair with irritation at himself.

'William tried to flirt with me on several occasions,' Vio-let confessed. 'But he was not the brother I wanted.'

'Wanted.' Seth lifted his brows. 'Still want?'

Violet looked down, not with anger, but with a shy demur. His heart skipped a beat. Seth took her hand in his and loos-ened her arm from its tight grip around her torso. 'I am not perfect. I have not led a perfect life. And clearly I have a penchant for speaking before I think. I don't deserve you, Violet, but I hope to God you are willing to take me any-way.'

She bit her lip. 'Are you...?'

'Proposing? Yes.' He sank to his knees before her. 'I love you, Violet. I was too daft to realise it before I very nearly lost you. But, looking back, I've always felt this way. The reason I never said goodbye to you before joining the army, the reason I never danced with you the night of your debut, was because I was a coward. I loved you and it scared me witless.' He took her hand in his. 'The only thing that fright-ens me now is the possibility of losing you.'

Tears swam in her eyes.

'Marry me, Violet.' He kissed the back of her hand. 'Please.'

She put her free hand to her mouth and gave a little sob. He hoped it was one of joy.

'You do deserve me,' she whispered. 'You see imperfection in yourself and find so much wanting. But I see you as you are, Seth. You are brave and you are strong, far more so than I think you'll ever realise.'

Seth swallowed hard. She wouldn't say these things to him if she didn't believe him. She'd never been a woman for idle talk. If she saw these things in him, he would not contradict her. But he would spend a lifetime proving her right.

'Do you mean...?' He lifted his brows, wanting her to say it.

She nodded. 'Yes. Yes, I will marry you.'

Yes.

Had ever so small a word held such visceral impact?

He leapt up and swept her into his arms. Lady Violet Lavell, soon-to-be Violet Dalton, his wife.

Even as he held her to him, even as he longed for nothing more than to kiss her and touch her, he swore to himself he would not be alone with her until they were wed. He had abused her trust and would do anything to get it back, for it was not lost on him that she had not returned his sentiments of love.

The hollowness inside his chest filled that moment with a promise—to himself and to her: to spend every day being the man she thought him to be. To be fully and completely worthy of her love.

Chapter Twenty-Three

A special licence was procured to minimise the wait for marrying and to allow them to wed in Violet's home. The morning of their wedding had arrived in the blink of an eye only days later.

Violet sat before her dressing mirror as Susan curled the last of Violet's dark locks with heating tongs in preparation for the simple coif she'd chosen for the wedding.

Violet glanced at the blank corner of her room where the silver gown used to stand in reminder of her failure. Like her father, Seth had declared his desire to burn the thing, but Violet had insisted it be set up in her new suite.

This request had been made during a walk in Hyde Park together as Seth had refused to see Violet alone until their wedding. Though he knew she was not a virgin, he would not bring himself to take her until they were wed.

A knock sounded at the door.

Susan carefully set the tongs down and gave a little squeal of delight. Violet gave her maid a curious look as Susan rushed to the door, opened it and returned with a wide box in her arms. 'For you, Lady Violet.'

Violet got up from her seat and went to the bed where Susan had laid the box.

A note was on top with careful writing.

For you to wear or keep or burn as you so desire.
I want only your happiness, now and for ever.
All my love,
Seth

All his love. He had proclaimed that love with a vehemence that had stunned her when he'd proposed to her. And despite the considerable affection she held for him, she had been too much of a coward to tell him how much she loved him.

She had been hopeful about marriage and love too many times over. First with Seth when they were younger, then Lord Fordson, then again with Seth. It had been a miscommunication, yes, but his initial reaction to her past had cut her to the quick and left her with the pathetic need to secure a guard around her heart.

Experience had taught her it was far too fragile.

Violet lifted the lid off the box and sucked in a breath. The silver gown was nestled in a cloud of tissue paper. Seth had not only given her the hope for happiness in the future, he had given her the silver gown back. The gesture was marvellously considerate.

She cast a look to Susan, who just kept grinning.

'Do you want to wear it, my lady?' Susan asked.

'Yes, I do,' Violet said softly.

The maid set to work, fastening Violet into the silver gown. The panelling at the sides to make it a size larger had been expertly inserted and was nearly imperceptible. Violet made her way to the cheval mirror by her wardrobe. The skirts rustled as she walked, whispering of the dreams she'd once had when she'd put it on order at the modiste six years ago.

Those dreams were now being realised. Finally.

She stared into the mirror and ran her hands over the fitted bodice. It was every bit as beautiful as she'd imagined it would be. She'd never had the opportunity to put it on, always being slightly too large to fasten it regardless of how much she'd starved herself.

She turned to the side, marvelling at the delicate pleating in the skirts, how the waist nipped in at the middle and the way the top hugged her breasts in an elegant but enticing manner. Seth would approve most enthusiastically of that last bit.

Seth. He had been her friend when she'd been a lonely child in London, a flirtation when she'd been on the cusp of womanhood and nothing more than a dream when her world had shattered. He'd come back into her broken life and helped her make it whole again.

'Oh, my lady,' Susan breathed. 'It's lovely.'

'It is,' Violet agreed. 'Please take it off now.'

Susan's elation faded. 'I beg your pardon?'

'This gown has represented failure for far too long.' Violet put her back to her maid. 'I prefer to begin my married life in a gown ready for new memories rather than one stained with old ones.'

'I rather like that.' Susan set to work unfastening the back of Violet's gown.

Violet looked to the dressmaker's form, now adorned in an elegant frock of pale blue silk with small puffed sleeves and a skirt that swept the floor behind her as she walked. It was simple and complemented her colouring. 'I do, too.'

Susan helped her out of the silver gown and folded it back into the modiste's box. The blue gown went on easily and floated against Violet's skin like a whisper. How would it feel as it slid from her skin and puddled on the floor? A chill of anticipation prickled over her. Soon, she would be wed and, not long after, she would be alone with Seth. In the privacy of his master suite in Dalton Place where most of Violet's belongings had already been relocated.

Susan put her hair into a series of twists with violets sprinkled throughout her dark tresses.

A soft knock came at Violet's door, and Felicity entered upon permission to do so. Her hair had been drawn into a wonderful coiffure that made her look rather grown-up and she held herself with the decorum of a lady. Well, if ladies carried fat cats in their arms, of course.

'Felicity, you look lovely,' Violet said with genuine delight.

Her shoulders lifted, clearly pleased with the compliment. 'As do you. And Hedgehog.' She scratched the cat under the chin and his vibrating purr filled the room. 'Do you recognise the silk?'

She stopped petting him long enough to point to his bonnet. It was the very same ice blue as Violet's gown. Violet's mouth fell open and Felicity grinned. 'The modiste had some scraps left over and I asked her if I might have them.'

'You made the bonnet?' Violet asked.

Felicity shrugged. 'Of course. I make all of them.'

The child's melancholy had lifted with the wedding preparations, though Violet suspected Felicity was dreading returning home, which was the source of her unhappiness.

Felicity cocked her head suddenly and raised her brows. 'I believe I hear music. Hurry or you'll be late for your own wedding.' With that, she rushed from the room, leaving the door slightly ajar in her haste.

Violet and Susan looked at one another and chuckled. 'I wonder how she can love that cat so much,' Violet mused.

'I believe...' Susan said slowly. 'She treats the cat the way she wishes she might be treated.'

Violet opened her mouth to protest the notion, but stopped. Ever since Felicity had arrived and Seth had demonstrated how best to speak to the girl, Felicity had been wonderfully behaved.

'I think you're correct,' Violet said softly.

'I believe you treat her exactly how she wants to be treated, my lady.' Susan fidgeted with a flower in Violet's hair and smiled. 'Now go downstairs where your handsome Earl awaits you.' Tears filled her maid's eyes and Violet had to turn away before she, too, began to cry.

Lord Hollingston waited for Violet by the double doors leading to the drawing room. His chest swelled with pride as she approached.

'You look lovely, Daughter,' he said.

She embraced him. 'Thank you, Father. And thank you for encouraging me to wed. I think I'm going to be very happy.'

'I truly hope so.' He kissed her cheek. 'I truly do hope so.'

He offered her his arm and led her into the drawing room where the vicar waited for them with the *Book of Common Prayer* in his hand. She scarcely noticed the man, or anyone else for that matter.

Seth waited at the end of the room with his arms folded behind his back like the soldier he'd been for so many years.

His unruly hair had been combed into submission, and he wore cream-coloured breeches with a gold and cream brocade waistcoat, finished off handsomely with his dark superfine jacket.

He watched her with affection shining in his expressive eyes and when he spoke the vows binding them together for ever, she felt the depth of his sincerity in his fathomless gaze. At last, when the ceremony was complete and his mouth brushed over the backs of her knuckles, the skin under her gloves tingled with anticipation.

In fact, *all* of her tingled with anticipation, for this man she had spent a lifetime wanting.

The time after the wedding ceremony had been spent in a blur of congratulatory toasts and well-wishes. But to Seth, nearly all his attention had remained focused on the exquisite beauty of his bride.

It had not escaped his notice how her ice-blue eyes continued to slide over to him, heating him from the inside out. How was it that even a glance from her could make his body go tense with eagerness?

After a hearty wedding breakfast had been consumed, several more toasts made and the cutting of the lovely frosted cake, finally it was time to take Violet to their home. They left Hollingston House amid a flurry of felicitations and entered the quiet hall of Dalton Place.

Seth wanted nothing more than to draw Violet up the curved staircase to his bedchamber and watch the silky gown flutter from her body. He wanted her naked and writhing with need beneath him. He wanted her to be *his*. Fully and completely. In body as well as in name.

He reined in his impatience as his Countess was introduced to the staff of her new home, though she already knew them all well from years of close familial acquaintance. Instead, he observed her, noting the genuine warmth on her face as she spoke to each member of his staff, remembering not only their names, but also those of their families and asked after them.

His blood stirred as he watched her, cherishing from afar the woman he would soon worship up close. She would be a wonderful mistress of Dalton Place, as well as Dalton Manor when they relocated to the country once Parliament let out. More than that, she would be an ideal mother. Her consideration and care with Felicity had demonstrated as much.

At last, the final servant had been properly introduced and they all began to resume their duties.

Violet turned back to Seth with a coy gaze that slammed straight into his groin. Her pretty mouth lifted at the corner. 'I saw you staring at me, my lord.'

He hummed in acquiescence—no sense in denying it—and offered her his arm.

She accepted his offer, her touch sensual as it crept slowly over the crook of his elbow. 'Dare I ask what you're thinking?'

'Dare me to show you and you've got yourself a bargain.' He lifted a brow at her.

She sucked in a breath and glanced about.

'You needn't worry,' he assured her. 'We're quite alone.'

She stepped closer, bringing with her the sweet scent of violets that adorned her dark hair. 'I'd rather be even more alone.'

He grinned. 'Who am I to deny my lovely young wife her wishes?'

He led her up the stairs to his bedchamber, closed the

door and turned the key in the lock. His heart slammed like a drum in great, heavy thuds.

She looked up at him with a coquettish smile. 'Now you'll show me what you were thinking?'

A kiss on the back of her gloved hand hadn't been enough for him earlier. He'd wanted her full lips under his, her curves pressed against him.

'With immense pleasure, my wife.' He pulled her into his arms and lowered his mouth to hers the way he'd longed to do.

She met his kiss and parted her lips so her tongue brushed his. Fire shot through him, singeing every nerve ending with the force of his blatant desire. He had held off on being alone with her after their engagement until this very moment, when he knew he would not have to hold back.

'Violet,' he groaned into her mouth. 'My beautiful Violet.'

She echoed his desire with a moan and ran her hands down his chest, plucking at the buttons of his waistcoat. He tipped her head back further and deepened the kiss as his hands met the cool silk of her gown and the lush curves beneath.

His palms skimmed over her hip, over her round rump and up to her full breasts. He wanted to hold every voluptuous part of her to him and marvel at the movement of her breasts while he took her in hard, steady thrusts.

A growl slid from somewhere in his throat. He dragged his mouth down to her neck where the sweet, powdery scent of her violet perfume fired through his senses like erotic gunpowder. His fingers fumbled with frantic need over the silk-covered buttons. The damn things were impossibly small and slipped beneath his fingertips before finally releasing from the narrow closures.

The task was rendered all the more difficult by the way Violet's hands roamed over his torso. She pushed his jacket down his shoulders, forcing him to briefly part from the buttons. Next came his waistcoat.

Damn it, how many bloody buttons were there?

He was somewhere midway down her back when her fingers curled around his shaft and his mind went utterly and completely blank.

He didn't recall undoing the rest of the buttons, but he did remember the exact moment that he eased the delicate fabric from her shoulders with a simple caress and how it fell like a sigh to the ground in a shimmering pool of fine silk.

Her fingers abandoned their exploration while he took her in.

The short corset she wore was of a heartier silk, also blue where it cradled her breasts in offering to him with the globes of firm cleavage rising high on her chest. Good God.

He cradled her breasts in his hands and buried his face in their bounty. They were likewise perfumed with that quintessential violet scent. He grazed his mouth over her smooth, warm skin while his fingers teased at the edge of the heavy silk, drawing it down to free a single pink bud of a nipple.

It popped free of the binding and his mouth closed over it, his tongue flicking until the little nub was instantly hard against the tip of his tongue. Violet cried out and cradled his head, holding him to her generous breasts.

He continued to love her nipples while his fingers found the silken cords used to tie the bodice. He unknotted the dratted thing, unlaced it and shoved it aside so she wore only her chemise.

He was practically panting with need. His hands shook as he reached for the small ribbon that held the neckline of the chemise drawn closed. Now. He would finally see her now. Love her now. Have her now.

And, oh, how he wanted her. With a lust that couldn't be slaked by a single night together. A lifetime might not be enough for him, especially with how she moaned and squirmed under his touch. She'd hidden that passion with the wallflowers for years and he would make her experience it to the fullest every day for the rest of their lives.

He took that simple ribbon and wound one end around his forefinger securely. His gaze slid to hers. The delicate muscles of her neck stood out and she watched him with what almost appeared to be shyness.

Despite the confidence she exuded, there was still self-doubt lingering on her face. Her forearms flinched where they hung awkwardly at her side, as though she longed to cross her arms over her chest and press the thin linen closer to her body so it couldn't be lifted off.

Her self-consciousness wouldn't be apparent to most, but a lifetime of knowing her made it apparent to him.

His sweet Violet. He would ensure she knew exactly how beautiful he found her, exactly how much she stoked the inferno of his desire.

Without dropping his gaze from her, he pulled gently on the ribbon wrapped around his finger and the bow at her chemise slipped free.

Chapter Twenty-Four

Violet had to will her heart to remain in her chest. As it was, she feared at any moment it might leap out through her throat or knock through her ribs.

No man had ever seen her disrobed. Not even Lord Fordson. He'd had her in a quick moment in the garden during the night of her debut.

Seth's dark gaze glittered with desire as he brushed his finger over her collarbone, stroking her skin with a feather-light touch as he loosened the neckline of her chemise. She fought to keep her hands at her sides when she longed for nothing more than to cross her arms over her chest to keep the flimsy fabric in place.

The neckline gaped around her shoulders and slipped down several inches. Seth's stare dropped lower.

It was in that incredibly vulnerable moment, the most awful thing trickled through her mind: her mother's words.

Men wanted women who were fashionably slender.

Plump women were unseemly. A body like Violet's would never be considered attractive.

She sucked in a breath and her arms flew up before the chemise could ease down another inch, clutching it to her chest.

Seth didn't chastise her for her action, or demand she pull her arms away. Instead, he tilted her face up towards him. 'I've spent more moments than I can count fantasising about what you look like.'

She shook her head and hated the tears burning in her eyes. If he had indeed fantasised about her, she did not wish to ruin it with reality.

'I imagined your breasts are firm and lovely.' He skimmed his fingers over the fallen neckline of her chemise and her skin shivered at the caress. 'Enough to overflow from my hands.'

His touch swept lower to her waist. 'I imagined your hips are full and feminine, something to hold on to while I thrust into you.'

Her breath caught at the boldness of his words.

'And as for this…' He caught her bottom with both hands and pressed her to the very obvious erection rising hard between them. 'I want to clutch it in my hands while you ride me.'

His eyes held hers. 'Remember when I told you how seeing you in that gown on your debut made me want to kiss you?'

She nodded, unable to even speak.

His hips flexed against her rhythmically as he spoke, pressing his arousal into the softness between her legs where she thundered with need.

He was breathing heavily, his chest rising and falling with the evident longing he felt. 'I lied.'

Violet blinked at the unexpected words and turned away so he couldn't see her flash of hurt.

He released her bottom and gently turned her face back towards him. 'I didn't want to kiss you. I wanted this.' His hands ran down her body. 'I wanted *you*.'

He reached up and slid a pin from her hair. A liberated curl fell over her shoulder as the violet pinned in place tumbled to the floor.

'I wanted you so badly that I didn't trust myself to dance with you.' He drew another pin from her locks, then another. 'I've never experienced lust as powerful as that. It's why I left. I worried... I worried I wouldn't be able to control that longing.'

Her hair was loose around her shoulders now with a dozen dark purple flowers dotting the floor. She gaped at him, unable to fully process what he'd just told her.

'And you...you still want me?' she whispered. 'Like that?'

He growled and pulled her to him. He kissed her hungrily, thoroughly, so the breath fled her lungs and didn't bother returning. His kisses went down her neck and his teeth nipped her earlobe. A fresh wave of tingles skittered over her skin.

'I still want you that badly,' he said against her ear. 'Even more. Even after all these years. Even after all this time. Good God, Violet.' He took her hand and carefully lowered it from where she held her chemise. '*Feel* what you do to me.'

Touching his arousal had been different earlier, when it was of her own volition, when it was not him guiding her to see her effect on him. She pressed her fingers obligingly to the blazing heat bulging against his placket. It was hot as a fever and hard as steel.

He hissed out a breath from between clenched teeth. '*You* do that to me.' He kissed down her collarbone to the expanse of her chest and lower still to where she still held her chemise with her free hand. 'Let me see you, my beautiful Violet.'

She released her hold on the final bit of clothing and let it join the silk gown on the floor. He stepped back to look at her and drew in a quiet breath. Violet clenched her hands to keep them from crossing back over her chest while his gaze rose from the blue satin slippers to the white silk stockings tied just above her knees, and up to where there was nothing but, well, her.

'Violet.' Her name was little more than a groan on his lips. He reached for her, kissing her, gliding his hands over her naked body. 'You're even lovelier than I imagined.'

It was on the edge of her mind to question his compliments, but he stroked her with too much reverence, his ardour too convincing. And even when the last shreds of doubt clung to her mind, he gripped her to him and thrust against her with a soul-deep groan that bespoke of a desire that couldn't be feigned.

He truly did find her beautiful, not only in her fine gowns, but out of them. It made her want to be closer to him, for all of him to touch all of her. She arched herself against him and pulled free his cravat, then tugged up the hem of his shirt.

The daylight coming in from the windows shone like gold on his powerful torso, highlighting the carved muscles over his chest, his shoulders and arms, and flat, banded stomach. A tantalising line of dark hair trailed from his navel into his breeches.

The pulse of desire between her legs thrummed and made her heady with the need to release as she had the night they were caught by her mother, when his caresses had played so expertly over her that she'd been swept somewhere she'd never been before. Somewhere she wanted to go again.

Her hands ran over the heat of his skin, soft despite the hard strength beneath. The dark hair sprinkling his chest rasped at her palms as she explored his nakedness. He kissed her hungrily and nudged her back towards the large bed.

The room was masculine with dark wood and luxurious deep red velvet coverlets on the thick mattress. She allowed him to lay her back, stretched out over the rich velvet. He crawled over the top of her while still wearing his breeches and continued kissing her while his fingertips worked a slow path down her body.

She parted her legs in anticipation and his caress swept at the source of her longing. She cried out as he stroked her the way he'd done that one blissful, fateful night.

'I want to hear you climax for me again, my love,' he whispered.

Except he withdrew his fingers from her and instead shifted down her body to the foot of the bed where her thighs were still parted. Quickly, she pulled her knees together, but he tutted and gently edged them open once more.

Her breath came quick with nervousness, embarrassment and…and anticipation for what he might do next. He leaned over her sex and slowly, carefully, drew his tongue over her.

She gripped the sheets, unable to think, to move, to even breathe. The swirling licks and sucks he'd once employed on her nipples, he now performed between her legs. Fire and wet heat combined into complete and total bliss.

Somehow she managed to draw enough breath to cry out again and again until her voice was hoarse. He inserted a finger carefully into her, working the digit within her body even as he continued to lick, to tease.

When her release did finally come, it was hard and fast and sent her spiralling over the edge of a control she had no intention of reining in. Even then, he continued to kiss her intimately until the sensitivity overwhelmed her and left her hips jerking with each pass of his tongue.

He straightened with a somewhat arrogant grin. Somehow in the time since their wedding ceremony and now, the smooth combing of his hair had given way to its natural proclivity and was attractively mussed. Just the way she'd always liked it.

Heavens, but he was handsome. And he was hers. Her husband, her lover.

'I want you.' Her voice had gone husky with desire. 'Please.'

The grin slipped away, replaced with something far more serious that made her core clench. His hands went to his breeches and he began to unbutton his fall.

Lust hammered through Seth's body. It pulsed in his manhood as it sprang free from his breeches and ran molten in his veins. The musky scent of Violet's arousal nearly drove him mad with need.

The cries of her climax still hummed in his ears. He wanted to hear them again, to draw out more whimpers, more moans, more pleasure.

He pushed his breeches to the ground, along with his stockings and shoes. Her eyes swept down his body and lingered over his hardened shaft as her stocking-clad knees rubbed against one another, as if she could scarcely contain her own lust.

He braced himself over her with one arm while he guided the head of his arousal against the wet heat of her sex. The tip nudged against her, burying slightly within.

'Yes.' The word was sighed out on a long exhale and her legs spread wider as she pushed her hips towards him.

He flexed forward, edging deeper inside her. She sucked in a hard breath and moaned. Seth could only fist the coverlet in his free hand and clench his teeth to keep from spending inside her right then and there.

Her dark hair spilled over her creamy, smooth skin, her lips were red from his kisses, her cheeks flushed and her eyes bright with desire.

She was exquisite.

He withdrew gently and pushed into her until he was buried to the hilt. She gasped and he immediately paused, not wanting to cause her any discomfort. It had, after all, been six years since she'd been with a man.

'Don't stop,' she whispered.

It was an order he could easily follow. He moved inside her, slow at first, then in steady strokes in and out of her body. The sheath of her sex around him was a tight grip that squeezed with each movement. Every lift of her hips, every wriggle of her bottom.

Her full breasts gave a bounce with every thrust, jiggling as he increased his speed, as the friction between their bodies built and built and built. He tensed in preparation for release, but he held himself in place for a breath to still his own climax as his fingers reclaimed the bud of her sex.

He wanted her clenching around him when he found his

release. His thumb circled over her. He needed only two passes over the sensitive nub before she threw her head back with the force of her pleasure. Her cries echoed around him, beckoning him towards his own release.

He gripped her hips and plunged hard into her as her orgasm spasmed around his shaft. He came with a roar, his seed spilling into her with each jerk of his hips that brought their pelvises pressing flush together.

He waited above her until their panting breaths slowed and then collapsed at her side. She remained on her back with her eyes closed, as though savouring the languid tranquillity of the moment. She opened her eyes and gazed up at him as a lazy smile spread over her lips.

He propped himself up on his elbow. 'I do hope this puts your worries about my attraction to you to rest.'

She rolled towards him. 'If it didn't, would you have to convince me further?'

He grinned. 'I might have to.'

'Then I fear I remain unconvinced.' She put a hand to her brow in a mock demonstration of distress.

He leaned towards her and kissed her full, pink mouth. 'You saucy minx.' He pulled her towards him. 'I love you, my beautiful Countess.'

Her coquettish expression turned shy. 'Do you truly?'

He pulled back and studied her. 'You know I do. I told you as much when I proposed to you the second time. Or does that officially count as the third time?' He considered. 'The proper second time,' he concluded.

She put a finger to her chin in contemplation. 'I believe it was the second time. Officially.'

He caressed her soft cheek. 'I shall always show you how I've always held you in such high esteem, how I value how different you are from every other lady of the *ton*, how my heart responds so viscerally when you're near. I thought you were lost to me six years ago when I left to fight for England. And now that you're my wife, I want you to know what you mean to me. Every moment of our lives.'

She drew a circle on the bedsheets with her fingertip and gave the action her whole attention. 'You've always been so handsome, so confident. It's a wonder you would ever love a woman like—'

He put a finger to her lips to still the words from falling free. 'A woman whose affection I am not sure if I'll ever be worthy of, but will still readily seek.' He grinned. 'I suppose there's still a bit of rogue in me after all.'

She peered at something on his shoulder and her brows furrowed. 'Were you injured?'

He glanced at the scar from a healed bullet graze. 'It was nothing of note.'

'I could have lost you.' She spoke softly, as though musing more to herself than speaking to him. 'You could have gone to war and never returned.'

'You could have danced with an honourable man who stole your heart and I'd never have had the opportunity to wed you,' Seth replied.

'Is it fate that kept us for one another?' Violet asked.

'If it is, I don't intend to question it.' He kissed her. 'I will, however, take full advantage of it.'

And he did. Throughout the day and well into the night. She was everything he'd ever wanted, everything he'd felt he never deserved. She was his and he would do everything in his power to ensure she always knew she was loved and well cared for.

For the first time in his life, this task felt like one he could perform with ease, for with a union as perfect as theirs, nothing could possibly go wrong.

Chapter Twenty-Five

Seth fell asleep some time in the night with Violet curled in his arms, both of them spent to the point of sheer exhaustion.

Ghosts, however, were not so easily placated. No sooner had his eyes closed and darkness pulled at him than the distant thunder of a cannon firing echoed through his mind.

Men in red uniforms ran forward around him, their bodies jerking with the slamming of bullets.

Someone shoved him—hard. The ground rose up, crashing into his side with such force it knocked the wind from his lungs.

Brent cast him a resolute stare before the cannonball crashed into him...

'You're in your bed at Dalton Place,' a soft voice said in Seth's ear. 'With your wife, Violet.'

Cool, gentle hands slid in comforting circles over his shoulder, drawing him from the dream.

He woke with a start and stared into the darkness at where Violet gazed down at him.

'It was only a dream,' she soothed.

'I know,' he replied, suddenly feeling rather ridiculous. Night terrors were something left back in the nursery.

But she didn't chastise him. Instead, she smoothed her hand over his brow, presumably brushing a bit of his unruly hair back. 'Do you have them often?'

He clenched his jaw.

'Then know that I will always be here to rouse you and soothe you.' She lay on his chest and embraced him, saying with her body what she had not yet said with words.

I love you.

He craved it with a ferocity he'd never before experienced. Those three words. The weighty impact behind them.

He wrapped his arms around her and let his senses savour all of her—the gentle violet scent still lingering in her hair, the warm silkiness of her nakedness against him, the beauty of her dark locks spilling over the white sheets. All of her washed away the horror of his dream and soothed his ragged nerves.

Whatever he had done in his life to earn such a treasure as Violet, he didn't know, but he was damn grateful for it. Sleep claimed him once more and carried him without interruption. That was, until the warmth curled around him shifted and slid away.

He opened his eyes and found a very naked, very lovely, Violet easing from the bed.

'I didn't want to wake you,' she said softly.

'I'm awake.' He reached for her. 'Come back to bed.'

'I can't sleep any longer.' She laughed.

He grinned. 'I didn't mean to sleep.'

A pretty flush blossomed in her cheeks. 'I wish I could.' Her gaze raked over his body where he lay on his side amid the tousled sheets. 'I truly do wish I could,' she said with apparent sincerity. 'But I'm afraid I promised to meet with Felicity and my mother at Gunter's for ices.'

'Nonsense, you're a newly-wed bride.' He sat up and reached for her again. 'Come back to bed, my love.'

'Felicity wanted Gunter's to celebrate. You know I can't let her down.'

Seth chuckled. 'I know. Has she continued to be well mannered?'

'Yes, thanks to your advice.' Violet went to the wash-stand, wet a cloth and rubbed it over her face and neck. 'If you hadn't shown me how to care for her, how to be sensitive to her need for attention, I don't know that she ever would be so properly behaved.' She paused in her washing. 'Would you mind, perhaps, if we invite her to the manor this summer?'

'I wouldn't mind at all,' Seth said with a smile. 'I think Hedgehog would get on nicely with the stable cat. Though sadly little Sadie has never worn a cap to speak of.'

'Well, not all felines can be so fashionable.' Violet set aside the cloth. 'Thank you, my lord.'

He wrinkled his nose. '"My lord" is so formal. I'm a second-born son regardless of my title now. Seth works nicely. Or the greatest lover there ever was.' He winked. 'That has rather a nice ring to it as well.'

'In that case, *the greatest lover there ever was*, I must ready myself to meet with Felicity and my mother, but I shall see you later this afternoon when I return.'

He pushed himself from the bed and retrieved a robe for

her. 'I'll have Harold ready the carriage for you.' He approached her with the heavy robe slung over his forearm. 'Though you are forewarned, there's a bit of a jolt to his stops. He's one of my former soldiers who lost an arm. He's getting better, though my mother would disagree.'

Violet turned her back to allow him to aid her into the robe and glanced over her shoulder at him. 'I appreciate the warning.'

'It is only fair.' He turned her around to secure the sash at her waist and gave her a tender kiss. 'I shall see you when you return.'

She walked backwards towards the door adjoining their suites and blew him a kiss before slipping into her own bedchamber. Seth summoned Gibbons to have Harold prepare the carriage while Bennet helped Seth prepare for a new day.

The valet entered the room with a twinkling smile. 'Felicitations on your union, my lord. I dare say Lady Violet is an excellent choice for you. Excellent.' He bent to retrieve Seth's cast aside jacket.

Seth relished the contented hum in his chest. 'Thank you, Bennet.'

The valet straightened with the clothing gathered in his arms and set it on the bed to tend to later. 'Shall we prepare you for the day with haste or with care, my lord?'

With haste or with care. Seth's way or Bennet's way. There was a difference of at least two hours between the two, but Seth had nothing else planned for the afternoon.

'Bennet's way,' Seth replied, and the valet's eyes lit with delight.

A fraction of a lifetime later, somewhere between the twentieth swipe of the razor and the thousandth, a rapid knock came from the door. 'Forgive me, my lord,' Gibbons said from the other side. 'This is most urgent.'

Bennet backed away and Seth sat upright, wiping the remainder of the shaving soap from his face. 'Come in.'

Gibbons rushed in immediately. The older man was in such a state, he didn't even close the door behind him. 'A Mr Nash is here to see you. My lord, he—'

'Finally.' Seth got his feet. Seth had been sending messages to the former Runner for the past week for news on Mr Pattinson's whereabouts with no response.

A dot of red on Gibbons' collar caught Seth's attention. 'Is that blood?'

'Mr Nash is quite unwell, my lord,' Gibbons said weakly.

It was then Seth noticed the butler's face had gone a peaked shade of grey. Alarm spiked through him.

'Where is he?' Seth demanded.

Gibbons wavered on his feet. 'The study.'

'Bennet, see to Gibbons.' Seth strode quickly to the open doorway.

Gibbons shook his head. 'I'd prefer you find a physician immediately, Bennet. Mr Nash has sustained grave injuries.'

Grave injuries? Seth's stride lengthened into a run as he raced down to the study. He shoved through the door and almost didn't see Nash where he lay slumped in a leather stuffed chair. A slash of bright blood showed on the yellowed shirt he wore under an old jacket.

'Nash,' Seth called.

The man's eyes flew open. 'Mr Pattinson,' the former Runner groaned. 'Back in London.' He winced through a pained breath. 'Means to stop you.'

Seth sank to his knees by the chair. 'Save your breath,

man. Let me see the extent of your wounds.' He lifted Nash's shirt and grimaced at the deep wound in the man's side.

Seth was no surgeon, of course, but he'd seen enough injured men and had even done his part to aid when he could. If the blade went between Nash's ribs, there could be irreparable damage to the lungs, or other soft organs. An injury that could prove fatal.

Seth tugged off his cravat and pressed it to the wound to staunch the bleeding. Nash hissed at the pressure against his injury.

'We've summoned a physician,' Seth said.

'Don't worry about me,' Nash gritted out. 'Protect your bloody family.'

Violet stepped out into the sunshine with Susan at her side. She was tempted to walk in the golden glow of warmth and breathe in the scent of fully bloomed flowers as she did so. That is, until she caught sight of Seth's carriage waiting for her.

It would be her first time taking the Dalton carriage, her first outing as the Countess of Dalton. Surely it wouldn't do to walk. A footman limped around the carriage and opened the door for her with a flourish.

She thanked Burton, who beamed at her in response, and stepped on to the small stair to climb into the small cabin.

A posy of violets waited on the cushioned seat and scented the air with their delicate perfume. No doubt a gift from Seth. She smiled and touched a dark purple petal as the carriage pulled away.

'It was kind of him to think of you so, my lady,' Susan said.

'Indeed it was.' Violet leaned back on the padded seat back and smiled.

Seth.

Her heart seemed to whisper his name every beat. Seth, Seth. Seth, Seth. Seth, Seth. The way he had looked at her when he loved her, his eyes locked on hers as if their souls were as perfectly joined as their bodies.

I love you.

Those words had hovered on the tip of her tongue every moment they were together. Yet of all the confessions she'd already made to him, she found it the hardest to say.

She'd got to know him so much better last night than she had during the short period of their courting. Not necessarily through their intimate moments, though those certainly had been enlightening and highly enjoyable. It was also through the scars upon his body, placed there by war and fighting and danger.

The jagged white line on his shoulder from the graze of a bullet some time ago as well as other healed injuries. Several slashes that peppered his side and dotted his chest. Nicks along his forearms and hands and the bruise that had gone yellow along the top of his thigh.

She had thought never to see him again when he left her at her debut, but she hadn't ever considered it might be due to his death. Never had it been more apparent as a possibility than it was last night when she saw the physical effects on him from years of fighting. If some of those injuries had been slightly to the right or left, or up or down, they might have ended his life. He might never have come home.

The very thought gripped her heart with a fear she could not bear. It was then she knew she had to tell him she loved him. No matter how frail her heart, no matter how vulnerable it made her, she had to proclaim the truth of it as bravely as he had.

Seth was worth the risk. He would *always* be worth the risk.

Susan's brow wrinkled, and she sat forward to better look out the window.

'Is something amiss?' Violet asked.

'It's only that we seem to be driving in rather a roundabout way to go to Gunter's,' Susan replied, her attention fixed outside. 'And this does not appear to be Berkeley Square.'

Violet glanced out the window and a chill of apprehension trickled down her spine. Susan was right. It was not Berkeley Square outside, but an expanse of cobblestones with the visible, choppy water of the Thames visible in close proximity. Were they at the wharf?

The carriage drew to a smooth stop.

Goosebumps prickled over her skin.

'I was expecting a hard stop,' Violet said softly.

Susan frowned. 'I'm afraid I don't—'

The door flew open and a man filled the narrow opening. His dark hair was combed fashionably back to reveal a handsome face lined with wrinkles around his eyes. He wore a fine black jacket and a stark white shirt and cravat. The pale green of his waistcoat, however, was smeared with red.

Violet's heart nearly stopped as she recognised the mess to be blood.

'Who are you?' she demanded.

'We haven't yet had the honour, my lady.' The man inclined his head politely while keeping his gaze fixed on Violet. 'I'm Mr Pattinson.'

She continued to stare at him, looking for anything on his face that might indicate who he was or what he was doing.

Pattinson. She rolled the name over in her mind. Why did it sound so familiar?

'Your family's solicitor.' He waggled his head. 'Former solicitor,' he amended.

Recognition dawned on her. Mr Pattinson was the man who had stolen Seth's mother's jewels.

'You have some gall,' she exclaimed. 'It takes a despicable man to swindle the jewels from a widow whose son had only recently died.'

'And it takes a despicable family to hide a man's misdeeds.' Mr Pattinson's upper lip pulled back to reveal fine, white teeth.

'I'm afraid I don't know what you're speaking of.' Violet spoke innocently even as she wondered if he referred to Seth's older brother.

'Defending him to the end, eh?' Mr Pattinson scoffed. 'Just like you wealthy nobs, thinking the rest of us are beneath you, to use for whatever you need us for and then discard us.' He reached into his jacket and withdrew a pistol. 'The time for the rich to crush those below them has come to an end.'

Susan gave a little scream and Violet put her hands up in silent plea. 'Please, you needn't use that.'

'Oh, I won't shoot you.' Mr Pattinson swung the pistol towards Susan. 'I'll shoot her.'

Fear spiked through Violet. 'Stop, please. What is it you want from me?'

The disgusted grimace on Mr Pattinson's face peeled up into a cold smile. 'Revenge.'

Chapter Twenty-Six

'What do you mean "protect my family"?' Seth demanded.

Nash's head lolled and his breath came in shallow gasps. 'Pattinson's daughter…'

'My lord, a message for you.' A servant rushed into the room, a young maid with blond hair who usually worked in the kitchens. 'Gibbons wasn't about and someone knocked at the door. I didn't wish to keep them waiting, so I opened it. When I did, I found this.'

She held out a folded piece of paper as Seth got to his feet.

He took it from her. 'Gather my family immediately. And tell Harold not to dare leave and have Lady Violet brought in. Post-haste.'

The woman hesitated at this new round of orders. Her gaze slid to Nash and widened.

'Now,' Seth commanded fiercely.

She leapt at the demand and bolted from the room. With shaking hands, he unfolded the note. The script there was bold, the two lines stark black against the white background.

I have your sister. Meet me at the abandoned brick building by the wharf and come alone.

Seth jerked his head up. Caroline. Pattinson had Caroline.

He knelt at Nash's side once more. 'What does Pattinson want with my sister?' he demanded.

Nash shifted and gave a pained wheeze. 'His daughter. Dead. Your brother...' He grimaced. 'Syphilis.'

Seth's blood went cold. The man's broken sentence was plain enough to understand. William had given Mr Pattinson's daughter syphilis and it had been the cause of her death.

Seth's chest went tight with fear. Whatever Pattinson wanted with Caroline, it was not good.

Seth would do as he asked and come alone, but he would not arrive unarmed. He pushed to his feet and went to his desk. He jerked open the drawer and pulled out his pistol. It was heavy and cold in his hand, the familiar weight of death.

Footsteps pounded out in the hallway and his mother entered the study. 'Dalton, what is the meaning of this?'

Someone followed closely behind her. Confusion rattled Seth's brain and made him look up to stare at the woman behind his mother. Caroline.

Seth regarded his sister curiously. 'Caroline?'

'Yes, I'm here,' she said breathlessly. 'What is it, Seth? You've given us all quite a fright.'

He looked down at the note. Was it a jest of some kind? It was a bloody awful one if so.

Who the devil would claim to have Caroline when he did not?

The blonde maid returned to the room at a mad dash

pace that stopped abruptly short upon her catching sight of the Dowager.

'Forgive me, my lord.' She kept a cautious gaze on Seth's mother. 'I could not find Lady Violet. It appears she'd departed some time ago.'

She paused a moment and dragged in a ragged breath, clearly winded from having rushed about with such haste.

Seth cursed to himself. If Violet was outside the town house, she could be in danger.

'That isn't all, my lord.' The maid's face fell and she put a hand to her chest.

'What is it?' Seth asked, his voice hard.

'Harold and Burton…' A sob broke from her throat. 'Harold and Burton are horribly injured.'

Seth braced himself on his desk at the news. The men who had fought at his side for years were injured. And if they had been attacked—

'What is the meaning of this?' Seth's mother demanded.

Seth looked down at the note in his hand as the terrible understanding dawned on him. 'Caroline, did you ever meet Mr Pattinson?'

Caroline blinked and shook her head. 'No.' She turned back to the maid who was openly sobbing. 'What happened to Burton and Harold?'

'A physician is on his way,' Seth said. 'Mr Nash requires assistance as well.'

Seth's mother followed his gaze and gave a choked cry.

'When the physician comes, have him see to Nash, Harold and Burton.' Seth checked the chamber of his pistol.

'Where are you going?' Seth's mother demanded.

'To the wharf.' He clenched his hand into a fist, balling up the note. 'Mr Pattinson thinks he has Caroline.'

Caroline's brow furrowed. 'Me?'

'Except there is now another dark-haired young lady in this home,' Seth said grimly.

Caroline gasped. 'Violet.'

Seth closed his eyes against the pain radiating from his very soul. 'Yes. Pattinson doesn't have you. He has Violet.' Seth tucked the pistol into the band of his breeches. 'And I'm going to get her back.'

Violet wriggled in an attempt to free her hands of their bindings. Not that she could be so easily liberated, not when the ropes were tied so tightly they sawed into her raw skin with every movement.

At least she had been told to tie up Susan and had been able to do so with looser bindings. Her maid sat in the chair Violet had been forced to strap her to. Sobs hiccupped from Susan and echoed in the large warehouse.

It was empty within, save for a stack of crates at the rear of the building. Mr Pattinson stood beside Violet, his arm locked on the crook of her elbow. She twisted her wrists.

His hand tightened on her. 'Enough struggling, or I'll shoot your maid.'

'What are you going to do with us?' She glared at him.

His pale gaze swept to the single small door leading into the warehouse. 'I'm going to kill your brother.'

Her brother?

Her confusion was fleeting when she recalled how he'd referred to being her family's solicitor. It wasn't because she was Seth's wife and now a Sinclair. It was because Mr Pattinson thought she was Caroline.

Well, she wouldn't correct him and she certainly wouldn't let him succeed in what he planned to do. She stopped moving as he'd demanded and glanced around frantically. There had to be something, anything, she could use as a weapon. The ground was filthy, a mess with piles of dirt and refuse.

And then she saw it: a rock. Just larger than the palm of her hand.

'I want no part of this.' Violet jerked her arm free from Mr Pattinson's grasp.

'You're already involved.' He snagged her arm again. As she had anticipated.

She yanked herself from his hold once more and used the momentum to topple over. She slammed hard to the ground and a puff of dust welled up around her. Quick as she could, she patted behind her for where she expected the rock to be. Grit collected on her fingertips, then she bumped something soft and wet. She wouldn't think too hard about what that could be.

Mr Pattinson uttered a gruff curse and reached down to pull her up. Violet floundered and kicked her feet on the filthy floor in an effort to free herself from his grip. More dust stirred up, but though it covered her actions of trying to locate the rock, it did little to aid in its recovery.

The solicitor grabbed her shoulders and hauled her upright. As she was dragged over the floor, she snagged something hard and rough. The rock.

She closed her fingers around it and hid it within her hand tied beneath the other, concealing it from view. Mr Pattinson gripped Violet so hard, she had to bite the inside of her cheek to keep from crying out.

'If you do that again, your maid suffers for it,' he growled. 'Do you understand?'

Violet nodded.

'No.' Susan's scream cut through the air with a suddenness that made both Violet and Mr Pattinson turn towards her.

Susan stamped her feet on the floor, sending up a cloud of filth as she rocked back and forth in her chair like a woman possessed. 'Don't you dare use me as a threat against my lady. You vile creature. We'll have you—'

The cocking of a gun sounded.

'Killed,' Susan finished saying. She gave a smug smile and settled back into the chair.

Seth appeared from behind her with a gun aimed directly at Mr Pattinson.

'If you miss me with that bullet, you'll hit your own sister,' the solicitor said.

'She's not my sister,' Seth growled. 'She's my wife.'

Mr Pattinson gaped at him. 'You aren't married.'

Violet took advantage of the man's surprise to wriggle her wrists once more. A bend, a twist, a flex. The rough rope ripped into her skin like fire.

'We were very recently wed.' Seth came closer. 'Yesterday. She's innocent in all of this, Pattinson. She's not from my family.'

The solicitor hesitated and slid a glance towards Violet who immediately stilled in her attempts to liberate her hands. She needed only to get one free. Just one.

'Did she know about your brother?' Pattinson demanded.

Seth ignored the question. 'I know about your daughter. Nash told me.'

'Nash.' Mr Pattinson spat upon the ground. 'That pathetic excuse for a man followed me all over England before I finally let him catch me.' The solicitor gave an angry hiss from between his teeth. 'Why couldn't you leave me to the jewellery? I wanted to get away from London, to start a new life. Why did you have to chase after me?'

Violet twisted her hand until her thumb joint strained against the rope. She was so close, just a smidge more and she would be free.

'You took advantage of my family while I was at war.' Seth narrowed his eyes.

'Your brother stole from my daughter.' Lines creased Mr Pattinson's brow and spittle flew from his mouth. 'First her innocence, then her life. He took everything from me. I couldn't stay in London, seething in loss and bitterness.'

He lifted his pistol and pointed it directly at Violet. 'Maybe you need to know what it feels like to lose someone you love.'

She had never looked down the barrel of a pistol before. It was a fathomless hole with seemingly no end. Ironic for something that could cut short lives with such finality. She pulled harder at her hand, until something popped and pain shot up her arm. A little whimper emerged from her throat, but it didn't matter.

She was free.

'Don't,' Seth's voice cracked. 'Take me and let her go.'

Mr Pattinson's gun cocked. 'You will know loss before you die.'

Violet tightened her grip on the rock in her good hand. Before she could swing it, Seth ran at her, shoving her to the ground. A fraction of a second later, an explosion boomed in her ears and she knew with sickening certainty that the gun had gone off.

Chapter Twenty-Seven

The thundering gunshot ricocheted around in Seth's brain, echoing off the chasms of the experiences that haunted him. Gunpowder burned in his nostrils and stung at his eyes. Ringing clanged in his ears, the high-pitched whine drowning out everything else.

Something else hung in the air. Coppery. Wet.

Blood.

His mind spun. Waterloo. No—Violet. Something at his side ached and swirled into the mix of his confusion.

He staggered and it made the pain at his side sear in agony.

'Seth.' It wasn't the baritone of a soldier, but the pitch of a woman's voice. Violet's voice.

He turned in her direction as she lifted her hand and brought it down hard on Mr Pattinson's head. His eyes went wide as blood flowed from the wound, washing over his face, over his pale eyes. Like Brent.

Brent had pale blue eyes. They'd met Seth's just before—

Everything around Seth moved impossibly slowly, the way it had when the cannonball had collided with Brent's body. Pattinson glared at Violet and drew his gun back in an obvious attempt to strike her with it.

All at once, everything clicked into place and Seth's mind fell back on instinct. He wasn't an earl—he was a soldier facing his enemy. He took aim at Pattinson's face, braced for the kick of the weapon and pulled the trigger.

The force of his gun jolted his arms, a familiar sensation he was well prepared for. Pattinson's head snapped back and he dropped to the ground. Seth stared trance-like at the body slumped on the ground atop a growing puddle of blood.

'Susan.' Violet grabbed his arm as she ran past, breaking whatever spell death wove around him.

Together, they loosened Susan's ropes and freed the maid. Once she was safe, Seth put his attention fully on Violet, noting the dust peppering her dark hair and the smattering of blood on her neck and face.

'Are you hurt?' he asked.

She shook her head slowly, her eyes wide in the way one looked when they witnessed death for the first time. 'Oh, Seth, he was planning to kill us.'

Seth's back tensed with irritation. 'I should have shot him first.'

'It doesn't matter.' She shook her head. 'I thought we were all going to die, that I'd never have a chance...' Tears filled her eyes and her lower lip trembled. 'That I'd never have the chance to tell you I loved you.'

He lifted his arm to put it around her shoulders when a

sharp pain lanced through his side. One he had been acquainted with several times in his life. He'd been shot.

He glanced down at his side to assess the damage and grimaced at the hole torn through his red waistcoat, glistening with blood.

'Seth,' Violet exclaimed. 'You've been shot.'

A light-headed sensation fogged around his brain. 'So I have.'

It was more than his waistcoat that was wet with blood. So, too, were his black breeches. His white stockings were stained crimson and droplets splashed the filthy ground around even him. He regarded it with a momentary confusion. Where had all the blood come from?

He staggered and small hands caught him, keeping him upright.

'Seth?' Violet said, her words somewhere distant and faint.

He whispered her name and then the ground rose up to meet him as he collapsed.

Violet waited outside Seth's bedchamber door, her heart lodged firmly in her throat. The physician had been with him for well over an hour.

She paced down the hall, passing the worried faces of the Dowager Lady Dalton, Lady Caroline, Gibbons and even her own parents. Hedgehog sat at Lady Caroline's side, one eye partially obscured by a ridiculous yellow bonnet. Felicity had sent him there to be of assistance in keeping everyone's spirits elevated. Thus far, they all felt as dejected as Hedgehog looked.

Nash's injuries had been stitched closed and he was recovering in one of the guest rooms. Harold and Burton had both suffered head wounds and were also recovering in guest rooms. It was now Seth they were all worried about.

The physician finally emerged from the room. His mouth was set in a grim line, but then Dr Franklin's mouth was *always* set in a grim line.

Violet ran to him. 'Will he recover?'

Doctor Franklin studied her from the bent bridge of his nose. 'He will, but he will need a considerable amount of rest.' He sighed. 'Lord Dalton has been asking after you and won't be put off.'

Violet peered into the sunlit room behind the physician. 'May I go to him?'

Doctor Franklin stepped back to allow her entry into the bedchamber. 'By all means.'

Violet strode swiftly, but quietly, into the large bedchamber. The last time she'd been inside, she lay snuggled in the red-velvet bed with Seth, their bodies damp with sweat from sport and their naked limbs tangled in soft sheets.

He sat up in bed now with only a slight grimace. 'Violet. Thank God you're safe.'

'I am, thanks to you.' She sank gently on to the mattress beside him.

'As am I, thanks to you.' He winked at her.

A bandage was visible beneath the collar of his shirt. It appeared to wrap around his shoulder and waist. She reached her hand out to his. 'Is it terribly painful?'

He lifted a brow. 'You say that assuming I've never been shot before.'

She cast him a chastising look. 'Don't jest.'

'I'm not.' He smirked. 'I've been shot twice.' His gaze wandered to his side. 'Three times,' he amended. 'Stabbed through once and sliced at too often to count. It will take more than a solicitor to bring me down.'

She bit her lip. 'Was it true? What he said about his daughter?'

Seth rubbed his fingers over the back of Violet's hand. 'I believe it is. I wish he had come to me to speak of it rather than trying to kill you. All of this could have been avoided.'

'Is there anything we can do?' Violet asked.

'We can seek out his remaining family, if he has any, and offer restitution of some kind.' Seth's eyes deepened with a sadness Violet could feel in her chest. 'We will pay for his funeral costs as well.'

Seth's hand tightened on hers. 'I'm sorry I had to kill him, but I would do it again to save you. I thought I'd lost you all those years ago when I went to war. When you looked so beautiful in that gown you thought I hated. I knew someone would marry you and I'd never have the opportunity.' He scoffed. 'Hell, I didn't deserve the opportunity being the kind of man I was then.'

'And I could have lost you several times over while you were off fighting for King and country.' Violet lay a hand on his shoulder. 'I think parts of us were missing the other.' She bit her lip. 'It sounds foolish, but before you returned home, I felt so broken. But with you here, I feel—'

'Whole,' he said.

She sucked in a breath. 'Yes. As though you're the piece of me I was missing.'

'And together we're stronger.' He gently stroked her cheek. 'I love you, Violet Dalton.'

Her throat went tight. 'And I love you, Seth Dalton.'

He grinned. 'I'd like to hear that again, if you please.'

Violet pulled in a soft breath. 'I love you, Seth Dalton.

I love you, I love you, I love you and I'm sorry I was too great a coward to say it sooner.'

She kissed him lightly on the lips and imbued in that one innocent kiss all the love she held for him.

'I'll never put you at risk again,' Seth vowed passionately. 'I will never lose you again.'

She shook her head. 'We'll never lose each other. Now get some rest.'

'Only if you stay with me.'

She crossed her arms stubbornly over her chest.

He did likewise and winced.

Violet gave an exasperated sigh. 'Very well, but only so you'll sleep.'

She lay on the bed at his uninjured side with her hand resting on his chest, reassuring herself of every beat of his heart, every inhale of his breath. He was safe. He would recover. And their life together would go on. With both of them whole.

Seth only remained in bed for three days before he was too restless to be detained any longer. Much to the disapproval of the physician—the stodgy old goat—and every woman in Dalton Place, he refused to be bedridden any longer.

Granted he wasn't moving as swiftly as he did before his injury, but he'd sustained enough wounds to know it was only temporary. It was for that reason that he insisted the house be packed up for the family to relocate to Dalton Manor for the summer.

Violet's maid, who had recovered remarkably well from the ordeal of being abducted, not only orchestrated Violet's belongings being packed efficiently, but also rushed Bennet along. If left to his own devices, the valet would surely have taken a month to pack everything away.

'Are you checking on Bennet again?' Violet asked from behind Seth where he stood in his bedchamber doorway. 'That poor man.'

'You have no idea,' Seth said drily. 'He would take two hours to shave my face if I let him. And I wish that was an exaggeration.'

'He only wants to make sure you're perfect.' Violet ran an assessing touch over his jaw and nodded. 'I don't believe it gets much closer than that.'

Seth put his arm around her and pulled her against his good side. He breathed in her delicate powdery scent and let his thoughts drift back to how that perfume was more enhanced along the sides of her neck when he'd kissed her there, when they'd spent the night loving each other.

More and more in the last few days, he found his memories wandering from recollections of violence, death and war. Instead, they were replaced with ridiculous moments of a cat named Hedgehog, tender ones with the woman he loved, and even amusing ones like when he'd fallen through the gap in the hedges between their homes.

Those were the memories he wanted in his mind. And he had a lifetime to build them with Violet.

'Your mother's jewels were all recovered with the exception of the bracelet found in Bath that you purchased.' Violet glanced up at him, as if she was worried he might not wish to discuss Mr Pattinson.

Seth nodded. 'I'm pleased they were all intact. And Mr Pattinson's remains were handled accordingly?' His chest ached with the loss of the man's life. Seth knew what he personally was willing to risk to save his sister and his wife. He could only imagine what he would do to avenge a daughter who had been wronged as egregiously as Pattinson's had.

'I handled it personally,' Violet said. 'Nash is seeking any additional living relatives, but is not hopeful.'

'He's already up and about?' Seth chuckled. 'And to think you were worried about me. The man was run clean through.'

'You tough men.' Violet rolled her eyes in playful exasperation. 'I'm told Harold and Burton are already back to work as well. Your mother claims Harold's stops are getting smoother now.'

'As long as Mother is happy…'

Violet tapped his arm in light chastisement. He chuckled and drew her against him more tightly. Soon they would be at Dalton Manor, away from balls and soirées and societal obligations—where the days would stretch out with leisure time and sunlit skies.

He looked forward to picnics and horseback rides through the property. All of them with Violet. And some day, perhaps even with their children.

'Dare I ask what that smile is for?' She tilted her head, studying him.

'I'm wondering how many children we'll have.' He pressed a kiss to her brow. 'You'll be the most wonderful mother. Felicity agrees with me. She's already requested six cousins.'

Violet's eyes went wide. 'Six?'

'We'd best get started.' Seth nudged her back against the door frame. 'The sooner the better.'

Violet bit her bottom lip and he knew she was weighing his injury against the call of desire. He knew well how he'd find her when she looked at him like that—wet and hot with need.

Someone cleared their throat behind Seth. 'Forgive me, my lord.'

Seth turned to find Gibbons intentionally averting his gaze. 'Lord Rawley is here to see you. I'm afraid he's rather insistent.'

Seth cast a regretful look at his beautiful wife and backed away. 'Yes, of course.'

'He's in the study.' Gibbons gave a light bow.

Seth thanked his butler, pressed a kiss to Violet's lips with a murmur of promise for later and made his way to the study. Rawley was not at the seat in front of the desk as Seth had expected. Instead, he was by the decanter of brandy with an empty glass in his hand.

He caught sight of Seth and quickly set it aside. 'Forgive me, I needed...' He straightened. 'I took your advice.'

Seth lifted his brows and wondered how Rawley had built up the temerity to go to Lottie's. He must truly like Caroline as much as he claimed to. Seth slowly walked to the decanter. 'Would you like a brandy?'

Rawley's cheeks went pink. 'I already had one.'

Seth smirked. 'When did you start drinking like Kentworth?'

'When I knew I had to come here.' Rawley padded the trembling fingertips of his hands together.

A smile crept over Seth's lips. Caroline had been beside herself with melancholy since Seth's decision that they remove to Dalton Manor until Parliament reconvened. She'd hoped to hear from Rawley, who had been disappointingly silent.

'Did you mean to ask me something?' Seth poured the man another brandy which Rawley took without hesitation.

In the entirety of his acquaintance with Rawley, Seth had never known the man to have more than one glass of any libation.

'I would like permission to…' The Viscount drew in a deep breath and drank a gulp of brandy. 'To write to Lady Caroline over the Parliamentary recess.'

'To write to her?' Seth tried to hide his disappointment. He'd been hoping for more. Far more.

Rawley swallowed. 'Yes. Please.'

Well, it was a start. 'You have my permission. You also may visit us at any time if you should desire to do so.'

Rawley smoothed a hand down his hair. 'That is kind of you. I confess, I have rather a full schedule at my own estate.'

'Of course.' Seth patted his friend's shoulder in an attempt to put him at ease. 'The offer stands regardless. Caroline will be most pleased to hear from you.'

Rawley ducked his head and grinned to himself. 'Thank you.'

'Lady Caroline is here, if you'd like to join us for tea,' Seth ventured.

A sudden panic seemed to seize Rawley and Seth feared for a moment he would say no. Then an expression of determination set on his face. 'Yes. I should love to. Thank you.'

Seth rang for tea before the Viscount could change his mind. It had been years since Seth had been at Dalton Manor, but even with a lifetime of visits, he suspected this might be the happiest yet.

His mother's jewellery had been restored, Caroline would have the suitor of her choice to exchange letters with and Seth would have Violet at his side. He and Rawley made their way to the drawing room and met three happy faces: Caroline, the Dowager and Violet.

Seth sat beside his wife, revelling in the wonderful scent of her and how she made every internal inch of his chest seem to glow. He had been reluctant to return home to the duties of the earldom. Giving up his life as a soldier had felt as though he'd lost a piece of himself. Now, he realised it was not an amputation, but the end of a chapter. And while he didn't know where life would take him in the future, he knew those around him would make for a happy tale indeed.

Epilogue

September 1815—Dalton Manor

It had been years since Violet had held a picnic outdoors. Far too long to be certain. The white blanket was spread out over sunlit emerald grass and a silk awning was the only break in the endless blue sky overhead. A gentle breeze caressed their cheeks, keeping them cool in the shade despite the summer's heat.

The afternoon could not have been more perfect.

Felicity had joined them at Dalton Manor for the summer and now ran about with a large red ball with Hedgehog, wearing a straw bonnet, chasing after her. She was now a well-behaved child who always did her lessons without complaint—well, almost always—and relished the freedom to run about on the large estate.

'I ate outdoors often in my time in the military, but never was it a picnic.' Seth took a reverent breath and slowly exhaled, his mouth lifting into a smile. 'This is far more pleasant than my previous experiences.'

He had been relaxed since their arrival at the estate. Nightmares still plagued him from time to time, but they were fewer as the weeks passed. When they did come back to haunt him, he reached for Violet in the night and she held him until the worst of it had passed. While her chest ached to see him suffer from his memories, it soothed that hurt to know he found comfort with her.

The Dowager set a cup of lemonade on a small table beside her chair. 'I'm glad you're done with the business of war. I like you being home.' She glanced away, as she often did when emotion got the better of her. 'I like knowing you're safe.'

Caroline cast a glance towards the manor once more. 'Do you think Harold will be back soon?'

'Waiting on another letter?' Seth teased.

She squared her shoulders, but the flush to her cheeks answered well enough for her. The correspondence between Caroline and Lord Rawley had been consistent throughout the summer.

Violet grinned at Seth, who winked in return. After all, they had a wager about when Rawley might actually ask permission to wed Caroline. Seth optimistically suggested it might be towards the beginning of the Season, while Violet presumed midway through.

'There's a carriage in the distance,' Felicity called out, abandoning her ball to instead race towards the manor.

Caroline got to her feet and made a show of dusting invisible bits of grass from her skirt. 'Well, I shouldn't let the child go alone.'

'Indeed,' the Dowager said with a secretive smirk as she got to her feet to join her daughter.

'We shall all go.' Seth rose and offered his hand to Violet, who accepted it and let him help her to her feet.

As soon as she was upright, however, the world spun about and nearly knocked her off balance. Seth's strong arms caught her. 'I'd tease you for having too much wine, but you haven't had a drop of it.'

Violet held on to him a moment longer than necessary. 'Just a bit of light-headedness.'

Felicity was already nearly at the manor and Caroline was halfway there with Seth's mother trailing behind them.

'We don't need to go to the house,' he said with apparent concern. 'We can remain here, if you prefer.' His gaze turned suspicious. 'You've had several light-headed spells lately. Is there…perhaps…something you care to tell me?'

Violet lost herself in the darkness of his gaze and felt herself yielding her hold on the secret she'd tucked against her heart for the better part of a month. 'I wanted to be certain first.'

He pulled in a soft inhale. 'And you are now?'

Violet nodded. 'It's been over two months since my courses. Sometimes issues can still arise—'

A wide grin split his face, silencing her caution. 'Not this babe.' His eyes sparkled with emotion and he put a tentative hand to her lower stomach. 'Not our child. Violet, we're going to be parents.'

She choked back a sob and nodded. 'We are.'

He lowered his head and kissed her over and over again until they were both somewhere between laughing and crying.

'The post came,' Felicity yelled in the distance.

Seth put his head to her brow. 'Perhaps the only one who might be more excited than me is Felicity. Though even then, I doubt it.'

Violet chuckled. 'I think we can all be equally elated.'

Seth folded his hand over hers and together they strode towards the house where the familiar carriage now stood. Harold waved his one arm at them in a jovial greeting as Burton limped over with a small bundle of folded missives in his hand.

Violet and Seth arrived in time to witness Caroline's joy at receiving a new letter from Lord Rawley and Felicity had her own letter from her siblings who had gone to their country estate for the summer.

'And one for you, my lady.' Burton handed her a letter.

She glanced down at the neat script and gave a cry of delight. 'It's from my cousin.' It had been an age since she'd last heard from Eleanor. In fact, not since the Duke and Duchess of Somerville had left for India where they'd unearthed the famed Heart of Fire ruby.

Violet read through the contents and spoke aloud as she did so. 'They're briefly in London before going to Egypt. How exciting! And they wish us both the same happiness they've found in marriage.'

The last part, however, she kept to herself. The bit about how Eleanor was so pleased Violet had gone to Lottie and news that Violet's farewell to the *Lady Observer* column had only helped to further Lottie's popularity with the *ton*. She even had her first male student now.

Violet glanced at Caroline's beaming face after she read that part and made a note to tell Seth later when they were alone. It appeared Rawley had indeed taken Seth's advice.

'They should like to come for a visit while they're in England,' Violet finished.

'Of course,' Seth said. 'It would be wonderful to see Somersville again. It's been far too long since we've had a chat.'

'My sister and brothers want to come, too.' Felicity hefted Hedgehog into one arm and held the letter up with the other. 'They would like to arrive next week.'

Seth shrugged. 'It's a large house. It can entertain a few more visitors.'

'Even Lord Rawley?' Caroline asked softly.

Violet stifled her gasp of happiness for her sister-in-law.

'Especially Lord Rawley.' Seth put his arm around Violet.

'I'd like to change my prediction,' Violet whispered.

'Oh, it's far too late for that,' he replied.

Caroline spun around and clutched the letter to her heart.

'Far, far too late, my love,' Seth repeated.

'I'd like to see her happy,' Violet said. 'Like us.'

'I don't know that it's possible for anyone to be as happy as us.' He turned slightly, putting his back to everyone as he pressed a quick, sweet kiss to her lips. 'And how that joy will double soon.' His fingers lightly caressed her lower stomach where their child grew in her womb.

'I love you,' Violet said with the whole of her heart.

'As I love you, my beautiful wife.' He took her hand in his and led her back to the picnic where a lovely trifle was waiting for them. And she knew in the depth of her soul that berry trifles would now always taste like sunny days on the Dalton estate with a child's laughter, giddy delight and eager anticipation for the future.

After all, life was sweeter with happy memories and they now shared those in abundance.

* * * * *